An Amish Christmas Letter

My dearest cousins,
I write this letter with a deep and growing sense of doom.
Christmas is but four weeks away, and it appears I shall
be the one to host Great Aunt Ingrid for her fortnight
holiday visit to Sugarcreek this year. No single event fills
my heart with dread as much as knowing I will be sub-
jected to her constant criticism, fault-finding and disap-
proval for two full weeks during the season when joy
should fill our hearts and homes. Do I dare I mention her
horrible fruitcakes? I know it is unchristian of me to feel
that way. I can't help it. Pray that God gives me the pa-
tience to endure this trial, or that by some miracle I find
one more couple to prod into declaring their love for
each other before Christmas Eve. . .

The AMISH CHRISTMAS LETTERS

PATRICIA DAVIDS

SARAH PRICE

JENNIFER BECKSTRAND

KENSINGTON BOOKS
www.kensingtonbooks.com

KENSINGTON BOOKS are published by

Kensington Publishing Corp.
119 West 40th Street
New York, NY 10018

Compilation copyright © 2018 by Kensington Publishing Corp.
"Marybeth's Circle Letter" © 2018 by Patricia Davids
"Love Delivered" © 2018 by Price Publishing, LLC
"Sealed with a Kiss" © 2018 by Jennifer Beckstrand

All Kensington Titles, Imprints, and Distributed Lines are available at special quantity discounts for bulk purchases for sales promotions, premiums, fund-raising, and educational or institutional use. Special book excerpts or customized printings can also be created to fit specific needs. For details, write or phone the office of the Kensington special sales manager: Kensington Publishing Corp., 119 West 40th Street, New York, NY 10018, attn: Special Sales Department, Phone: 1-800-221-2647.

Kensington Books and the K logo Reg. U.S. Pat. & TM Off.

ISBN-13: 978-1-4967-1763-4
ISBN-10: 1-4967-1763-5
First Kensington Trade Edition: October 2018
First Kensington Mass Market Edition: October 2019

ISBN-13: 978-1-4967-1764-1 (ebook)
ISBN-10: 1-4967-1764-3 (ebook)

10 9 8 7 6 5 4 3 2 1

Printed in the United States of America

Contents

Marybeth's Circle Letter

PATRICIA DAVIDS

This story is happily dedicated to Sarah Price.
Thanks for thinking of me, girl.

Chapter 1

November 24

My dearest cousins,
I write this letter with a deep and growing
sense of doom. Christmas is but four weeks
away, and it appears I shall be the one to host
Great Aunt Ingrid for her fortnight holiday visit
to Sugarcreek this year. No single event fills my
heart with dread as much as knowing I will be
subjected to her constant criticism, fault-finding
and disapproval for two full weeks during the
season when joy should fill our hearts and
homes. Do I dare mention her horrible
fruitcakes? I know it is unchristian of me to feel
that way. I can't help it. Pray that God gives me
the patience to endure this trial, or that by some
miracle I find one more couple to prod into de-
claring their love for each other before
Christmas Eve.
As you may have surmised, Cousin Wilma has
for the first time in four years facilitated more

matches than I did this year, and she must soon be declared the winner of our annual contest. It is truly humbling to know how badly I misjudged Sarah Troyer's affections for the handsome Isaac Stutzman, while Wilma correctly read that the young woman's eye was on Isaac's plain-looking and shy brother Carl. Her idea to have Carl build an array of birdhouses for Sarah's garden was a stroke of genius. I was unaware they were both bird-watchers. Who knew the sight of a blue-winged warbler could unlock a shy fellow's tongue?

I know this game of ours must seem silly to you, but our hobby does help pass the extra time that two old maids sometimes have on their hands. Before you insist that my advanced age of thirty-two is not ancient enough to be declared an old maid, let me assure you that I am content to wear the label. Both Wilma and I have accepted that God's plan for us does not include husbands, but we enjoy helping other people discover the best qualities in potential mates. I still believe in love, although it has never come my way. I reckon after having Great Aunt Ingrid stay with her for the last four Christmases, Wilma will be glad of the respite, but Ingrid really does like Wilma better than she likes me.

My brother, David, is in fine health and says he has no news to share. Does he ever? Please write soon and tell me all about your Christmas plans. Your wonderful, entertaining letters fill me with envy, for nothing much ever happens here in Sugarcreek.

Yours sincerely,
Marybeth

Marybeth Martin removed her previous letter from the mail packet and tucked her new note in with the ones her cousins had included. Circle letters kept her in touch with her distant family members and made sure everyone heard the same news. She sealed the envelope and stuck it in her bag to drop off at the post office after she met Wilma for lunch. When the packet made its way around the family and returned to Marybeth in a few weeks, it would contain all new letters from her cousins to enjoy.

She slipped on her coat and tied her black traveling bonnet over her white *kapp*, then opened the door. Pausing on the front porch of her brother's home, she took time to savor the beautiful day. Indian summer was hanging on by a thread. The trees had dropped most of their brightly colored leaves, and only the dark green of the pines and cedars kept the woods along the ridge from looking bare. The fields still held traces of the fall harvest in the bundles of cornstalks stacked together like teepees, but most of the land sat empty, waiting for the snow to cover it.

The brisk breeze that fanned her cheeks held the promise of cooler days ahead. She wasn't ready for winter. The short days and dreary weather left her feeling low and lonely. More so this year than most. It was hard to muster holiday cheer when two weeks with Aunt Ingrid loomed in her future. How could she make a match before Christmas? Should she simply admit defeat to Wilma at lunch today?

Marybeth shook off her gloomy thoughts. It wasn't like her to give up. If there was even a sliver of hope, she would find a way. Matchmaking was more than her hobby. It was her God-given gift. Surely someone she knew needed only a tiny push from her to find the love of their life.

Having renewed her determination, she started down the steps. Her brother had harnessed her mare Trixie to her two-wheeled cart as she had asked him to do at breakfast. David didn't always remember her instructions, or perhaps he preferred to ignore the ones he didn't want to carry out. Either way, she rarely counted on his cooperation, but today was a pleasant surprise. He was sharpening an ax at the grinding wheel beside the barn. She waved to him. "*Danki*, David, I'm happy you remembered."

"Beats being nagged," he snapped without looking up.

"I don't nag, I simply remind you of things you have forgotten."

She couldn't hear his muttered response. Perhaps that was for the best. As an unmarried woman, she lived on the charity of her brother and tried to make the best of it. David was fifteen years her senior and a confirmed bachelor who was becoming more set in his ways by the year. He might miss her cooking if she ever left, but nothing else. He had his own way of doing things that didn't always mesh with hers.

Climbing into her cart, Marybeth headed her mare down the lane to the narrow blacktop that ran between Sugarcreek and Berlin. Trixie trotted along at a steady pace and traffic was light. Twenty minutes later, Marybeth turned into the parking lot beside the grocery store. She needed to pick up a few things, and she was early for her date with Wilma.

Inside the store, she began filling her shopping cart with flour, brown sugar, spices and other ingredients she would need for her holiday baking. She added a large tin of cocoa. There were sure to be skating parties if it got cold enough and hot chocolate was a must. Stopping beside the shredded coconut, she decided on two bags. Cookie exchange parties required several dozen cookies of assorted types to share, and her coconut macaroons were always in demand. She added several assorted cake mixes she could whip up quickly for any spontaneous visits by out-of-town guests. Marybeth was nothing if not prepared.

"Great minds think alike."

She looked up to see her cousin Wilma pushing a shopping cart toward her. Wilma pointed to the nearly identical items in her own basket.

Marybeth chuckled. "You should have mentioned that you needed groceries. I could have picked up two of everything and dropped it by your house."

"I'm not so old that I need someone to do my shopping for me." Wilma would be fifty-five in January, but she and Marybeth were great friends despite the differences in age and in looks. Wilma was tiny and spry at five foot one with graying brown hair. Marybeth towered over her at six foot. Her white-blond hair didn't show a touch of gray, but no one would call her spry. Her brother said she tromped through life. She preferred to think of her manly stride as purposeful. The two women often visited back and forth even though they belonged to different church groups and lived more than ten miles apart.

Wilma adjusted her glasses as she peered into Marybeth's cart. "You forgot the fresh ginger. You know how Great Aunt Ingrid loves her gingersnaps."

Marybeth rolled her eyes and headed to the checkout. "My cookies won't hold a candle to yours in Ingrid's opinion, but I'm not conceding defeat just yet."

Wilma's grin widened. "Come, come, you must know you are beaten."

"Your overconfidence will be your downfall, Wilma. Don't count your chickens before they've hatched."

The checkout line hadn't moved. Marybeth looked to see what the holdup was. Josiah Weaver was paying for his groceries at the checkout counter two people ahead of her. If she wasn't mistaken, he was a widower. He had only recently returned to the Sugarcreek area, but she had known him when they were children. She studied him carefully as he counted out his loose change to cover his bill.

His flat-topped black Amish hat didn't hide the fact that he needed a haircut, and his winter coat hung loosely on his tall frame. She knew he'd suffered a broken leg and other injuries when a car hit his buggy six months ago. The accident had followed painfully close on the heels of his wife's passing, and Marybeth's bishop had spoken of Josiah's trials at a recent church service, asking the congregation to assist him with his medical bills. She, along with other church members, had donated generously to his fund.

She rose on tiptoe to watch the cashier sack Josiah's purchases: a jar of peanut butter, grape jelly, celery and six boxes of macaroni and cheese. No wonder he was thin if the meager foodstuff he was buying was his usual fare.

A girl about four years old clung to his leg like a silent shadow, keeping her face hidden against him. When she did look up, her eyes darted around fearfully. The dark green winter coat the child wore barely covered her wrists. The hem hung loose on one side. The *kapp* covering her brown hair was a dull gray instead of white. It needed to be bleached and starched. It was clear Josiah wasn't coping well as both mother and father.

It took Marybeth all of ten seconds to decide she was looking at her next matrimonial prospect. The child needed a mother. Josiah Weaver needed a wife. Marybeth tapped a finger against her lips. Which of the unmarried women in the area would be a good match for him?

"What are you staring at?" Wilma asked, leaning to look around Marybeth.

"Hush." Marybeth turned and pretended to study the candy bar display beside her. "I don't want him to know I'm interested, and I saw him first, Wilma Martin. He's mine."

Wilma clapped a hand over her mouth as she chuckled. "He won't do you any good. Christmas is only a month away. I'll grant you are a skilled matchmaker, but even you aren't that good. You should concede defeat and prepare to welcome Great Aunt Ingrid for her visit."

"I haven't given up. Our little contest goes until Christmas Eve. Besides, you have done such an excellent job of hosting Ingrid these past four years that I wouldn't dare think of trying to take your place."

"Do you even remember how our contest got started?" Wilma asked. She was covertly studying Josiah, too.

"Of course, I do. You and I were both wondering which of us Ingrid would decide to grace with her presence ten years ago. I noticed Jenny Yoder making eyes at Herman Beiler, who was making eyes at Constance Miller. You said he would ask Constance to marry him before the end of the summer. I said he would ask Jenny Yoder, and if he didn't, I would volunteer to invite Ingrid to my home."

"That's right. How did you get him to notice Jenny? She was such a quiet mouse of a girl."

"By doing my research. I learned Herman had a weakness for flashy horses and strawberry rhubarb pie. Constance was a pretty girl but not much of a cook. My father had just purchased a fine-looking, high-stepping Standardbred that he hoped to resell for a higher price to one of the local boys. I got him to agree that Jenny could drive the animal for the summer. I explained that having all the young men see the horse in action would have a dozen fellows or more competing to purchase him. I told Jenny she was to take a strawberry rhubarb pie as her covered dish at every youth gathering."

"So, the boy noticed the horse."

"Then he noticed the girl driving, and then he noticed she brought his favorite treat to every singing and picnic. When she offered to let him drive the horse, he was smitten."

"Did he buy the horse from your *daed*?"

"He did and for a hefty sum. My father was very pleased."

"Who will you match Josiah with?" Wilma whispered in her ear.

Marybeth went over the potential candidates in her mind. "Anna May Miller is close to Josiah in age. She is twenty-three. I think Josiah is twenty-seven or twenty-eight."

She knew he was younger than she was because he had grown up in the area and had been several years behind her in school. He took his daughter's hand and walked out with his bag of groceries. She noticed he walked with a limp.

"How are you going to find out if he is interested in someone already?"

That was a problem. How did she ask a man who was practically a stranger if she could provide him with a potential wife before Christmas? She saw him stop at his buggy. She didn't have time to waste with social niceties. "I'm simply going to ask him. I'll meet you at the café."

Marybeth moved her cart out of the checkout line and parked it beside the newspaper display. She hurried and caught up with him as he lifted his daughter into his buggy. "May I have a word with you, Josiah?"

Chapter 2

Marybeth swallowed the lump of apprehension in her throat and composed her features into a friendly smile. A puzzled expression crossed his face but quickly faded. "Marybeth Martin, right? You are David's sister."

"I'm surprised you remember me." She wasn't. There wasn't another woman her height in the entire county. He was tall enough that she didn't have to look down on him as she did most men. It was a welcome change. Up close it was easy to see the strain his injury and illness had placed on him. There were dark circles under his eyes; his cheeks were lean and sunken behind his short beard.

"What can I do for you?"

She cleared her throat, for she was about to stretch the truth. She had several women in mind for him, but they didn't know that. "This must seem strange and perhaps very forward, but I am acting as the go-between for a young woman. I am here to discover if you are in a relationship or if you would be open to meeting her."

His eyebrows shot up. Marybeth anticipated his surprise. It was unheard of for a woman to send a go-between to gauge a man's interest in dating her. It was the would-be suitor's responsibility to find a male relative of the woman and have him discover if she was willing to go out on a date.

Josiah turned away, unsnapped his horse's tether, and picked up the weight used to keep the horse from wandering away. "I am not interested in dating your friend or anyone else, but if you know someone who can work as a nanny for the next three weeks, I will gladly meet her."

Marybeth smiled at his daughter. The child hid her face behind his arm, but not before Marybeth saw the fear in her eyes. Her heart went out to the child. "I'm sure you can find someone to fill that post without difficulty."

He put the weight in the buggy. "You would think so, but I need someone to start on Monday. I'll be working the second shift over at the RV factory. That means someone must stay with Simone at my home until nearly midnight, and no one wants to do that."

"Can't she spend the night with a friend or relative?"

"*Nee,* please, Daed, I want to stay at home," Simone whispered with a catch in her voice. She was on the verge of tears.

"It's all right. You can stay home." He patted her arm before turning back to Marybeth. "She had a rough time while I was in the hospital. I want her to stay where she feels comfortable. Can you think of anyone for the job?"

His compassion for his child's welfare touched Marybeth deeply. "I can't think of anyone offhand, but if I do, I will send her your way."

"*Danki.*" He nodded, but she could see he didn't feel much hope. "Tell your friend I'm flattered by her interest and mean no disrespect by my refusal."

"I will."

He climbed in his buggy and drove away. Marybeth

was still standing on the sidewalk staring after him when Wilma pushed her loaded cart up beside her. "What did he say? Tell me. Tell me this instant."

Marybeth chewed on the corner of her lower lip. She couldn't shake the feeling that he was hiding the depth of his desperation. His air of sadness was almost palpable. "He's not interested in dating, but he should be. The child almost breaks my heart. Did you see how frightened she was of everyone and everything? Karen King might be just the woman for him. She has a very kind heart."

"I thought you said he isn't interested in dating."

"He's not. He's looking for a *kinder heeda* to take care of his little girl for three weeks."

"Why only three weeks?"

Marybeth fisted her hands on her hips as she gazed at his buggy until he turned the corner. "I don't know. There's a lot about him I don't know. This isn't going to be easy, but I can't give up. I must find a way to help him."

"Forget it. Let's get some lunch. I paid for your groceries by the way."

"*Danki,* but I don't think I can forget about the man."

Wilma's eyebrows rose a fraction. "Really?"

"He desperately needs someone to take care of him and his daughter, and not just for a few weeks."

"If you feel that strongly about the man, then you should take the nanny job."

"What?" Marybeth looked to see if Wilma was joking. She wasn't.

Wilma laid a hand on Marybeth's arm. "My dear, what better way to discover the type of man he is and the kind of woman he needs than to see him and his child daily? What's stopping you? You have three weeks you can spare to aid them, don't you?"

Marybeth realized her cousin was right. She did have

the time to help him. In the short term and in the long term. She slowly smiled. "Wilma, you are a genius."

Wilma laughed and started walking toward the café. "*Nee,* but I'm a *wunderbar goot* matchmaker. Don't forget I said that when Christmas Eve rolls around."

Josiah sat across the kitchen table from his daughter and watched her stir circles in the macaroni and cheese in her bowl. Very little found its way to her mouth. She worried him deeply. Every day she seemed to fold inside herself a little more. He was afraid one day she would be lost to him.

"What's wrong, Simone?" He knew exactly what her answer would be, but he asked the question anyway.

"Nothing," she whispered.

Always the same answer if she even bothered to give one. "I thought you liked macaroni and cheese? Am I wrong?"

Silence.

He should be used to it by now, but he couldn't reconcile the engaging chatterbox she had been at three years old with the mute child she had become within a year. Losing her mother and then having him hospitalized less than four months later had changed his daughter drastically.

He stirred the unappetizing pasta in watery yellow sauce around on his plate. "Your *mamm* was a much better cook than I am."

Simone glanced up at him and then stared at her plate again.

"I look forward to the day when you can take over the cooking. That will be fun for you, won't it?"

She shrugged.

He couldn't think of anything else to say. Every meal

since his release from the hospital had been pretty much the same. He tried talking to his daughter and she said as little as possible in return.

He gave up on eating, rose and scraped his plate into the trash before placing it in the sink. When he turned around Simone was behind him. He took the plate from her. "Go get ready for bed. Make sure you brush your teeth. Let me know when you're ready and I'll come tuck you in."

She walked with lagging steps down the hall. At the door to her room she looked back at him for a long time and then silently went inside.

After washing the dishes and placing them in the rack to dry, he stepped outside. The sun had set, but clouds in the western sky were still ablaze with red and gold colors. He walked to the swing at the end of the porch.

Emma's swing.

His wife had insisted on having one although he thought it was too fancy for an Amish home. A plain wooden bench or chair provided an adequate spot to rest or remove muddy shoes before going into the house. A porch swing invited a person to linger and while away time best spent on other projects. He had brought the swing with him from their last home along with the other furniture, knowing she would never use it again. Even so, he couldn't leave it behind.

He sat down and rubbed his aching thigh. The bone had knit with the help of a steel plate, but it ached when he was tired. He closed his eyes and gave a little push, letting the motion bring back the memory of swinging beside Emma and listening to her recount her day or regale him with stories of Simone's antics. He missed her so much.

"I beg pardon for interrupting your evening, Josiah."

He opened his eyes. Marybeth Martin came striding

through the front yard gate and up to the steps. Annoyed at the interruption, he scowled at her. "I thought I made myself clear earlier. I have no desire to walk out with your friend."

She smiled, not the least bit intimidated by his scowl. "I believe you also said you needed a nanny."

He sat bolt upright. "You know someone who will take the job?"

"I do." She smiled brightly. "Me."

"You?" He leaned back in the swing. He hadn't expected that.

She folded her hands primly in front of her and cocked her head ever so slightly. "Is that so surprising?"

"I guess not." David Martin was a successful farmer. There was no reason for his sister to go to work unless she wanted to.

A smile twitched at the corner of her lips. She quickly subdued it. "Please control your enthusiasm."

She was right. He should be overjoyed, but something about this didn't seem quite right. Was she here out of pity? "You understand this is only for three weeks?"

"I do."

"You understand you will have to stay here until almost midnight, Monday through Friday?"

She bowed her head once. "I do."

"And you understand that my daughter has some special needs. She doesn't like change."

She met his gaze without flinching. "I understand. I will take great care not to upset her."

"About the question of pay."

She waved her hand dismissively. "I don't require payment of any sort. I will take the job on one condition."

He knew it couldn't be this easy. "What kind of condition?"

"I am perfectly willing to care for your daughter and manage the household chores for three weeks without pay if you will agree to go out with the woman of my choosing."

He folded his arms over his chest. "I am not interested in courting anyone. How much plainer can I be?"

"Your feelings are quite clear. I am not suggesting that you court this woman. I'm asking you to spend one evening in her company with an open mind."

"Who is she?"

"I'd rather not say."

"Why not?"

"I don't want you to form an unwarranted prejudice against her because of my forward behavior."

"Was this her idea?"

"Absolutely not. The woman has no idea that I'm here. Just so we know where we each stand, you are desperate. I am taking advantage of that fact. I am also providing a needed service free of charge."

"I wouldn't say it was entirely free of charge."

"You have me there. A single evening spent with a pleasant companion is a bitter pill to swallow, I'm sure."

When he didn't answer she continued. "If you find someone to take the job before Monday, feel free to hire them. If you find you have changed your mind about courting someone, I will withdraw my condition and still stay the three weeks."

"When does this outing you insist on having to take place?"

"I haven't had a chance to work out that detail. I wasn't sure you would agree and actually, you haven't."

He rose to his feet and walked behind the swing to lean on the porch railing and look out at his poor excuse of a farm. If he didn't find someone, he would have no choice but to stay home with Simone and lose the only job he had been able to get.

His mortgage was already falling behind because he'd been unable to work. To make his payments, he had sold all his livestock except for one buggy horse. The church had taken care of most of his medical bills, but he had paid what he could. There was nothing left. If he didn't start bringing in some money, he would lose the farm. Simone needed a home and security. He needed to give her that. Otherwise she might never come out of the shell she had withdrawn inside.

How was turning her over to a woman she barely knew going to help her? He sighed heavily and faced Marybeth.

She took a quick step forward and held out her hand. "Do we have a bargain?"

Chapter 3

"It seems I have no choice. One outing and that's it," Josiah stressed. "Your friend will be disappointed if she expects anything else."

A joyful smile brightened Marybeth's face. "You won't be sorry."

He was sorry already. Reluctantly, he took her hand.

Her grasp was as firm as any man's, but her skin was surprisingly soft. He glanced down at her slender, delicate fingers. She had very feminine hands.

Feminine wasn't a word he would have used to describe David's sister. He was used to thinking of her as a plain, no-nonsense *madel* who spoke her mind as she saw fit. He'd never given her more than a passing glance. Up close he could see her pale eyes were a beautiful clear blue, not cold, but warm, like the blue light of a gas flame. They seemed to draw him in with the promise of comfort.

Surprised by his fanciful notion, he dropped her hand and took a step back. "The RV company sends a driver to pick up their Amish employees and bring us home again. They will pick me up at two-thirty in the afternoon."

"That will be fine." She clasped her hands together tightly. Her voice held an odd breathless quality. She took two steps back and licked her lips, making them glisten rosy pink in the twilight. They were full and soft looking, something else at odds with her manly attitude.

He focused on the floor instead of her mouth. What was wrong with him?

She took another step back. "I will . . . I will see you on Monday. Please tell your daughter I look forward to getting to know her better."

He laughed bitterly. "I wish you success with that."

She spun on her heel and fled.

Josiah Weaver was a very attractive man. Why hadn't she noticed that before now? Marybeth rubbed her tingling palm against the side of her dress. She couldn't remember the last time a simple handshake had rattled her so.

She couldn't remember one because there hadn't been one. Ever.

She needed to focus or her actions today would be in vain.

That he was attractive was a good thing really. Finding someone willing to date an attractive man was easier than finding someone to go out with an ugly one. Although the Amish stressed that physical beauty was not important, she knew a young girl's heart fluttered faster when a good-looking boy paid attention to her.

She was not a young girl whose heart skipped a beat because an attractive man held her hand. She was much too practical for such a silly notion. This odd reaction was merely excitement at the chance to unseat Wilma and avoid Aunt Ingrid. Satisfied that she had an explanation, Marybeth drew a deep, calming breath.

She slowed her pace as she went over Josiah's assets as a potential mate for some blessed woman. Yes, he was a fine-looking man, perhaps a bit too thin for her liking, but well enough in other aspects. He owned a farm that wasn't large but big enough to support a family if it was managed well. His buggy horse was a fine animal, proving he had an eye for horse flesh. Most importantly, he was determined to get back to work, and that proved he wasn't a slothful fellow.

Which woman was she going to match him with?

She went through her possible candidates. Karen King was at the top of the list. Anna May Miller was a close second. Dorcas Yoder was only twenty-one, but her outgoing personality and deep faith made her a contender. As the oldest of ten siblings, she wouldn't have any trouble taking care of a four-year-old. Marybeth knew she would have to decide which one quickly. She didn't have time to make a mistake. Josiah wouldn't give her a second chance. This was going to be tricky. She would have to be certain the woman she picked was perfect for him.

So engrossed was she in thoughts of Josiah Weaver that she almost passed the turnoff to her brother's farm. Walking to the Weaver farm in the afternoon would be easy, but hiking home alone at night wasn't ideal. Once the weather turned colder, she would take the buggy. She didn't like driving after dark, but she would if she had to.

When she opened the kitchen door and walked inside, she saw her brother seated at the table waiting for her. He raised one eyebrow. "Where have you been?"

"I went to see Josiah Weaver about a job."

"Job? What kind of job?"

"He needs a nanny for his little girl. I applied for the post."

"You want to be a nanny? What do you know about taking care of *kinder*?"

She rolled her eyes. "They can't be that difficult to take care of. Besides, the girl is four years old. It's not like she's a baby."

"When does this job start?"

"Monday. I'm to watch her while he works at the RV factory on the second shift. I'll be gone from early afternoon until late at night."

"Late at night? What about my supper?"

David thought of his stomach first. She wasn't surprised. "I will have something in the oven for you every night."

He made a grunting noise. "I don't like the idea. What if I forbid this?"

Marybeth turned around to stare at him. "Why would you forbid it? I'm helping a neighbor in need. It is the Christian thing to do. Shall I tell the bishop you won't allow me to give aid to one of our own congregation?"

"I didn't say that."

"*Nee*, you would not say such a thing," she scoffed.

"Have it your way. You always do. There are times I wish someone had been brave enough to marry you."

She gaped at him. "Brave enough? What does that mean?"

"You've always been prideful and full of your own importance. You always have to be right. What man wants to wed a woman like that?"

"What a mean thing to say, David."

"Tell me it's not the truth."

"I can't help it that I'm usually right. What would you have me do? Pretend to be foolish and witless?"

"You might catch a man if you did."

She blinked back tears. Crying had never gained her anything. "David, you wound me."

"I don't expect you to change. But when you do get your way, resist the urge to rub a fellow's face in it. I'm going out."

"But it's suppertime."

"I'll get something in town." He stormed out the door.

Such behavior was so unlike her brother that she was tempted to run after him, but she didn't. He was a grown man. If he wanted to eat at the café, who was she to stop him? He was upset with her, but he would get over it when he saw she wasn't going to neglect him. He would have his supper ready and waiting every evening.

After fixing herself a small chicken salad with grapes and walnuts, she took a cup of leftover chicken and went down to the barn with a battery-powered lantern in her hand. She slid open the door and an explosion of small, furry kittens came piling out of the first stall to mill around her, meowing their greetings. "Hello, my babies. Let me see if everyone is here." She began counting. "I see three black ones, I see two fuzzy marmalade faces, two gray tabbies, but where is my calico? Callie, here, kitty, kitty."

She shuffled through the churning felines determined to get under her feet and entered the stall. Callie was curled up beneath her mother's chin. Lola licked her baby's head, rose to her feet, and stretched before walking over to twine herself around Marybeth's legs. Settling to the ground, Marybeth soon had a lap full of fat fur balls begging for her attention. Lola put her paws on Marybeth's chest and butted her head against her chin. Marybeth laughed. "You just love me because I smell like chicken."

Marybeth began to share her treat with all the kittens

and Lola. The meat disappeared quickly. Once it was gone, the kittens turned the evening into playtime. They chased each other and pounced on one another in fierce mock battles. Lola remained on Marybeth's lap, purring loudly.

"You won't believe how rude David was tonight. Well, you might believe it because he's not a great fan of cats. He said no man had been brave enough to wed me. Brave enough, indeed. It wasn't like I chased suitors off with a pitchfork. If they weren't as intelligent as I am, if they didn't enjoy conversations about something other than cows and corn, why would I want to waste my time with them?"

A low moo came from the brown and white dairy cow in the next stall.

"No offense, Pricilla," Marybeth called out. "You are an exceptional cow, worthy of conversation. One need only look at your beautiful new calf to see that."

The impatient bleating of a goat came from a stall farther down. Marybeth laughed as she plucked a kitten from her apron and put it aside. "Cleo, you are a most exceptional doe who provides us with delicious milk and cheese. I meant no disrespect to my friends. I'm coming to feed and milk you as soon as I free myself of kittens."

Marybeth rose to her feet, still holding the mother cat in her arms. She stroked Lola's soft fur and listened to her loud purr. "Being single isn't a curse when I have such wonderful friends. You think I was right, don't you, Lola? I wanted an equal for a partner and I never settled for less."

If she was lonely sometimes, it was better than being tied to a man she couldn't respect. The right man had never come along for her, but she could pick out the couples that did belong together from across the room.

A kernel of excitement began unfolding inside her. On Monday she would have a chance to learn a great deal more about Josiah Weaver and decide who would make him a fine wife.

Josiah paced the length of his porch and back on Monday afternoon, waiting impatiently for Marybeth to arrive. He had tried explaining to Simone that a very nice lady was going to stay with her while he went to work. He was sure she understood, but she gave no outward sign of it except to return to her room. He didn't know what else to do or say. He had to work and she had to understand that.

He saw the company van turning into the driveway and there was still no nanny. Would the driver wait? It would be a poor way to start a new job by making everyone else late. He heard running footsteps behind him and turned around. Marybeth, her cheeks rosy red from the cool air or exertion, came hurrying through the garden gate at the back of the house.

"Good afternoon. I realized it was shorter to cut across the fields since I was walking."

"The van is almost here."

"I'm not late. You said two-thirty."

"I expected you would come a little early to meet my daughter, hear my instructions, and ask any questions."

"Instructions? Your child isn't an infant." She waved aside his concern as if it was nothing. "I'm sure we will manage just fine."

This was a bad beginning. "If Simone becomes ill or is injured, how will you reach me?"

"I don't expect either of those things to happen. God willing, she will be sleeping quietly in her bed when you return tonight."

He struggled to contain his rising annoyance. "I didn't expect my wife to hemorrhage to death from a miscarriage. I didn't expect a pickup truck to plow into the side of my buggy. I didn't expect the woman who had agreed to watch Simone to have surgery for appendicitis. Bad things happen. You have to be prepared for them."

She opened her mouth and then clamped it shut. She studied his face a long moment and then nodded slightly. "I'm sorry. I understand your concerns and I apologize for treating them lightly. How do I contact you in an emergency?"

The van pulled up beside the house and stopped. Josiah handed Marybeth a piece of paper. "This is the number for my company's office. They will get ahold of me. You know where our phone shack is?"

"I saw it on my way over yesterday."

He pointed to a red barn across the field to the east. "Aaron McClellan is my nearest *Englisch* neighbor. He will drive you to the hospital if the need should arise."

She took the note from his hand. "*Danki*, but I've already had my appendix out."

He didn't smile at her poor attempt at humor. "If anything goes wrong—"

She laid a hand on his arm. "Nothing will go wrong, but if it does I will take what steps need to be taken and then contact you. Your daughter's well-being will be my first concern."

"I guess that's it." He couldn't make his feet move. He glanced at the door, but Simone hadn't come out to say goodbye.

Marybeth tipped her head toward the van. "You'd better get going."

"It's hard." He couldn't believe he'd admitted it out loud.

"I can see that. Have faith, Josiah Weaver. God is our strength when we are weak."

He couldn't bring himself to agree. He left her standing on the porch and got in the van without another word, but he turned around in his seat to watch her as the driver sped down the lane.

How soon would the call come, and how bad would it be?

Chapter 4

The poor man. It was clear Josiah hadn't fully recovered from losing his wife so tragically or from his accident. No wonder he was worried about his child. Marybeth tucked his note in her pocket. He would soon see he had nothing to worry about with her in charge.

She opened the door and walked into his home. The kitchen was tidy but sparsely furnished with a round, wooden table and two chairs. The cupboards were a mellow natural pine that contrasted nicely with the dark countertops. The floor was covered with a tan patterned linoleum that was worn through to the backing in front of the sink. As much as she wanted to explore his home, she was here to take care of his child.

"Hello? Simone, it's Marybeth Martin. We met at the grocery store—do you remember?"

The silence was deafening. She frowned slightly as she walked into the living room. The blue sofa that sat in front of the window had seen better days. An overstuffed chair upholstered in the same fabric and showing the same amount of wear occupied one corner of the room. A reading lamp and a small table sat beside it.

One wall held a large bookshelf that was nearly filled with books. She walked over to the chair. A novel with a red bookmark lay on the table. The title was one she had read and enjoyed.

It seemed that Josiah was a reader. That was very good to know. She would examine the titles in the bookshelves later and give the woman she chose a list to guarantee the couple had something in common to talk about.

She called again for Simone but got no answer. She walked down a short hallway with several doors and discovered a bathroom that needed the shower tile scrubbed. The next door led to a bedroom that clearly belonged to Josiah. Very neat and tidy.

That left only one door. She knocked on it. Still no answer.

She opened the door and saw Simone sitting on the bed with the covers pulled up to her chin. She wasn't wearing her *kapp*. Her hair was loose, tangled and greasy looking.

"Hello, I'm Marybeth. Your father didn't tell me that you were unwell." A pinch of apprehension stirred her annoyance with Josiah. In all his talk of bad things happening, he might've mentioned that his child was sick.

She crossed the room and sat down on the side of the bed. She laid a hand on Simone's forehead, but the child was cool. "You don't have a fever. Can you tell me what's wrong?"

Simone pulled the covers over her head. "Go away."

"I see you're not up to having a conversation with me. Does your throat hurt? Does your tummy hurt? Does your head hurt?"

Marybeth wasn't used to being deliberately ignored by anyone but David. She tugged the quilt down, exposing Simone's face. "Are you being rude on purpose?"

The only response was a slight narrowing of Simone's eyes. She had annoyed the child. It was something, although not what she was hoping for. Simone yanked the quilt away from Marybeth and pulled it over her head again.

"Okay." Marybeth wasn't one to stay where she wasn't wanted. Was this excessive shyness, or was there something else going on? "I will be in the bathroom cleaning the tile if you need me. Supper will be at five-thirty."

Even shy children had to eat.

Marybeth spent the rest of the afternoon doing some light cleaning and dusting and searching the home for clues to Josiah's personality while still respecting his privacy. Simone did not put in an appearance. Marybeth took the opportunity to investigate the basement. She couldn't believe her eyes when she took a lantern down the steep steps. There were floor-to-ceiling shelves, work tables, and a washtub, but there were only six jars of canned produce on the shelves. Six jars! At last count, Marybeth had over three hundred jars in her basement. She doubted that their bishop knew how poor Josiah and Simone actually were. Otherwise the women of the community would have filled these shelves with at least six months' worth of foodstuffs. She would certainly be bringing canned fruits and vegetables with her from now on.

Outside, she found a farm in name only. There were no chickens, turkeys or geese. The henhouse was empty, as was the barn except for a single horse that whinnied a greeting when she entered the building. She walked down to speak to the pretty mare with a white blaze down her face. "I can see that you are lonely. No other horses to keep you company. No cow or goat for milk, not even a pig or a dog."

A black-and-white cat jumped up on the open Dutch

door but turned tail and vanished before Marybeth could call to it. She followed outside, but the cat was nowhere in sight. A survey around the barn showed a corral with a few loose boards but otherwise in decent repair. She looked out over the lay of the land and decided the place had plenty of potential if Josiah could get a crop planted in the spring. His garden plot had grown up in weeds during the time he'd been in the hospital and hadn't been cleared for next year's planting. Any new wife certainly had her work cut out for her.

Back in the house Marybeth found evidence that Simone had been out of her room. There was an open jar of peanut butter and a smear of grape jelly on the counter. The store-bought bread wrapper was undone. Marybeth closed the twist tie. "I was right. Even shy children have to eat."

She spent the rest of the evening making a list of the books in Josiah's library. Surprisingly, many of them were titles she enjoyed. Twice she tried to coax Simone out of her room to no avail. Finally, Marybeth sat down with one of her favorite adventure stories and watched the clock. At nine she went in to check on Simone and found the child asleep. Even in slumber the little girl wore a worried frown. Marybeth stroked her hair. "Don't worry. I will find someone to take care of you and your father," she whispered.

On the way out of the child's room, she plucked the grimy *kapp* and worn green coat from their pegs on the wall. After being washed, bleached, and starched, the *kapp* was once again white. She ironed it smooth, then let out the cuffs on Simone's coat. She repaired the hem, then returned the items to Simone's room, closing the door quietly behind her.

Much later, Marybeth was nearly done with the last chapter of a novel when the lights of a car flashed across the window. The clock showed five minutes until midnight. It was late, but she had wasted an entire day without finding out much about Josiah or Simone except that they needed a lot of help. She was determined to spend a little time visiting with Josiah before going home. She was certain he would want to know how his daughter had spent the day.

The door opened and he came in, limping badly. She started toward him. "Are you hurt?"

He shook his head. Weariness had deepened the lines on his face and the circles under his eyes. He gingerly lowered himself onto a kitchen chair. "My leg aches a little, that's all. How is Simone?"

"Exactly the same as when you left. I don't believe she was happy to have me here."

"Don't feel bad. She isn't happy to have me here either. Fred, the van driver, has agreed to take you home. It's on his way. Will you be back tomorrow?"

"Of course."

"*Danki,* then I bid you good night." He leaned forward, crossed his arms on the table, and laid his head on them. He looked worn down with pain and fatigue.

Marybeth longed to comfort him, but she didn't know how. She had no recourse but to leave. As she closed the door behind her, she decided that tomorrow would be different. Much different.

> *Dear Wilma,*
> *It is after midnight as I pen this quick note, but I know you are dying to hear how my first day as a nanny unfolded. Truthfully, it was an abject failure. I learned nothing except that Josiah and I enjoy reading many of the same books. Simone refused to come out of her room*

*except when I was out of the house. So secretive
is she that I am tempted to call her Little Mouse.
I don't know if it is shyness or something else
that makes her want to stay shut away from the
world, but I intend to reach her somehow. It
breaks my heart to imagine how alone she must
feel and how painful her actions must be for her
father. They need so much help. I pray the Lord
will inspire me to select just the right woman for
them.*

*On a different note, I was stunned to see
David had waited up to make sure I got home
safely. I was flabbergasted but very touched. I
assured him it wasn't necessary. He, of course,
said he was only up to take some bicarbonate of
soda for his indigestion, caused by the
overcooked dinner I left for him in the oven. It
always amazes me how men can say one thing
and mean another. I must stop now. My eyelids
are as heavy as horseshoes. I will mail this tomorrow and write more later.*

*Your loving cousin,
Marybeth*

The next morning, Josiah limped to the kitchen stove
and put a pot of coffee on to boil. He grabbed three aspirin from the cabinet beside the sink and washed them
down with a quick drink. He sat at the kitchen table and
rubbed his left thigh while the coffee perked. It was late
and he had overslept. The list of chores and repairs he
wanted to tackle around the place would have to wait
for another day. Again. He wondered if his strength
would ever return.

Rising with a weary sigh, he went down the hall to check on Simone. She was under the covers. "Rise and shine. Breakfast in ten minutes."

She peeked her head out from under the covers, her eyes wide. "You came home."

"Of course I came home. I will go to my job again today, and tonight I will come home. You will see me in the morning just like today."

"Will she come again?"

"Marybeth? *Ja,* she will stay with you. Do you like her?"

"Not really."

He was surprised to get that much of an answer. "Not really? What did she do that you didn't like?"

"She cleaned the bathroom." Simone went back under the covers.

"What's wrong with that?"

"Nothing."

It wasn't a glowing report of Marybeth's abilities as a nanny, but it could've been worse. He left Simone's room and stopped by the bathroom. It had been cleaned. It had escaped his notice before, but he barely had his eyes open even now. He wandered through the rest of the house, wondering what else the woman had found to tidy up.

Back in the kitchen he made pancakes for two and sat at the table. Simone joined him a few minutes later. He bowed his head to say a silent blessing and ask the Lord to take special care of his child. When he looked up, he saw his daughter's head was bowed and her hands were folded. At least she was talking to God if not to him. He cleared his throat and she looked up. "What are you and Marybeth going to do today?"

She shrugged.

"Christmas isn't far away. Maybe Marybeth can help you make some greeting cards to send to our friends. That would be fun, wouldn't it?"

She didn't comment.

He gave up trying to find the spark that would engage her, and finished the meal in silence. She laid down her fork and rose from the table. She headed toward her bedroom, but he stopped her. "Simone, take the plates and utensils to the sink."

She gave him a disgusted look but did as she was told and cleared the table. She was only four and he couldn't give her a lot of chores, but as her father, he needed to make sure she did the ones he gave her. He wanted to chide her for her show of attitude, but he was afraid to destroy the fragile truce they had been sharing.

Two o'clock rolled around before his aching leg was ready. He downed two more aspirin with some cold coffee and waited for Marybeth to arrive. When he caught sight of her striding up the lane with two large baskets over her arms, some of the gloom left his day. He went to the door to meet her.

"I wasn't sure you were brave enough to return." He held it open so she could come in. "What's in the baskets?"

"You'll see." Her soft smile lifted his spirits and left him wondering how she managed to do it so effortlessly. She wasn't like any woman he'd met before. He couldn't decide if that was a good thing or not.

Chapter 5

Josiah breathed in a whiff of lavender as Marybeth walked past him and he smiled. Amish women didn't wear perfume, so it had to be something in her shampoo. The scent was fresh and light, at odds with her sturdy demeanor, and yet it suited her.

She put her baskets on the counter, untied her black bonnet, took off her coat and hung them on a peg on the kitchen wall. "It didn't take courage to come here. I've been looking forward to it from the moment my eyes opened this morning."

She wore a plum-colored dress with a matching apron that accented the red bloom in her cheeks brought on by her walk in the cold air.

"It's chilly today. I'm surprised you didn't drive here."

"I don't mind the chill and I do love hiking through the countryside. Today was a perfect day to do just that. How is Simone?"

The shadow of gloom returned. "The same. Did she speak to you at all yesterday?"

He was surprised at the understanding and sympathy in Marybeth's eyes. "Only to tell me to go away. I know that she came out of the room once because I saw she had made herself a peanut butter and jelly sandwich when I was outside. Has she been like this . . . for long?"

"You mean since her mother died?"

"You prefer plain speaking. *Goot*. So do I. That is exactly what I meant. Was it her mother's death that made her retreat from the company of others, or has she always been a shy child?"

"Simone was the opposite of shy. It was hard to get her to stop talking long enough to eat. She was grief stricken when her mother passed away, but it wasn't until I was hospitalized that she stopped talking to everyone."

He closed the door and stared at the doorknob as if it could tell him how to unlock his child. "Some people say she will grow out of it. Others say she's only doing it to gain attention. Still others have suggested I'm spoiling her by allowing this to go on."

"That just goes to prove there are a lot of foolish people in the world, even among the Amish." She grinned at him and he smiled back, his mood growing brighter with every minute spent in her company.

"As her nanny, do you have any words of wisdom on the subject?"

"None. I believe actions speak louder than words." She pointed over his shoulder. "I see your van coming. Do you have any instructions for me?"

"Only what I said yesterday."

"I have the phone number you gave me memorized."

"Then have a pleasant afternoon and evening." He started for the door.

"Wait a moment." She went to her coat, withdrew something from a pocket, and held out a narrow brown jar with a cork stopper. "This is a liniment I make. My brother, David, has a shoulder that pains him sometimes.

Rub it on your leg two or three times this evening. It will help."

He took it, bemused by her generosity. "Will it make me smell like a sick horse?"

She laughed. "If it does, the pain relief will be well worth it."

"*Danki*."

"You're welcome. Please tell Fred I was grateful for the ride home last night and I will pay him for his trouble if he will continue the arrangement."

"I'll tell him." Josiah left the house and climbed in the van with six other Amish men. As the driver started down the lane, Josiah looked back. Marybeth was standing on the porch. She raised a hand to wave and he waved back. For the first time in a long time, he wasn't worried about leaving Simone.

Marybeth lifted the lid of one of her baskets and peeked inside. Satisfied at the condition of her cargo, she went down the hall to Simone's room. She knocked once and got no answer. Opening the door, she looked in and saw a lump under the bed covers. She put the basket on the floor and opened the lid. "I've brought a friend to visit you today. Her name is Callie."

Stepping back, Marybeth closed the door. She waited outside until she heard a faint meow.

She listened a little longer to the increasing calls of the kitten. When she heard the thud of small bare feet hitting the bedroom floor, she knew her plan was off to a good start.

"One way to get a little mouse out of a room is to put in a cat," she whispered. Chuckling, she went back to the kitchen and began unpacking her second basket. She set out a loaf of her homemade bread, a package of cold cuts, and marshmallow cream for making church spread along with two dozen homemade chocolate chip cookies.

She carried the basket downstairs to the cellar and added eight jars of canned produce to the shelf. By the time her three weeks was up, Josiah and Simone would have a sizable collection of nonperishable food.

Once she figured out what vegetables and fruits Josiah enjoyed, she would make certain to provide an ample quantity of those. The idea of supplying him with things he liked brought a warm glow to her heart. His life had been filled with sorrow and pain in the past two years. She wanted to do what she could to lighten his burdens.

Back upstairs, she went about scrubbing the kitchen floor and waiting for Simone to come out of her room. After an hour, Marybeth's curiosity got the better of her. She went to knock on the door. She wasn't expecting an answer, so she opened the door and leaned in. She saw the same lump under the covers, but a smaller lump was moving around near the foot of the bed.

"I will be having my supper at five-thirty. You are welcome to join me. After the dishes are done, we will have a time of quiet reading and then you will take a bath at seven-thirty and you will be back in this bed by eight."

"*Nee.*"

Marybeth walked over and pulled the covers down. "It speaks! Which of my activities are you rejecting?"

"I don't want a bath."

Marybeth started for the door. "If you wish to continue stinking like a skunk, who am I to object? However, I insist that you stay in your room, so I won't have to put up with your stench in the rest of the house."

"I don't stink."

The kitten found her way out and slipped off the end of the bed, meowing loudly.

Marybeth stooped to pick her up. "Callie says that you do. Maybe not as bad as a skunk, but too bad for her to stay under the covers with you."

"She didn't say that."

"Do you speak cat?"

"*Nee.*"

Marybeth held the kitten up to her face and made a few mewing noises, which the kitten replied to promptly. Marybeth looked over the ginger, white, and black bundle of fur to Simone's guarded expression. "Callie says her mother gives her a bath all the time and it makes her feel *wunderbar*. Why don't I run a bath for you now? That way you can spend the rest of the day feeling refreshed, and perhaps Callie will decide she wants to play with you after all."

While the child didn't agree, at least she didn't outright refuse. Marybeth carried the kitten to the kitchen and produced two bowls from her basket: one of cat food and one for water. With the kitten occupied, Marybeth found the towels and shampoo and began filling the tub. When the water was deep enough, she turned off the faucet. Simone appeared beside her.

Pleased that there wasn't going to be a battle, Marybeth grinned. "Do you need my help to wash your hair?"

Simone shook her head. She certainly was an independent child.

Marybeth left her alone and when she came back to check on her ten minutes later, Simone was wrapped in her bathrobe with a towel draped over her head. A glance at the ring left around the bathtub told her Josiah had been losing the bathing battle for some time, or else Simone had been rolling in the dirt in the garden.

"Come into the kitchen where it is warmer and we will get your hair dry."

Marybeth had a chair pulled up next to the stove. She held a wide-tooth comb in her hand. Simone snatched it away from Marybeth and began trying to comb her hair herself with limited success due to all the tangles. Marybeth took the comb away from her. "Let me help."

Simone dropped her gaze and closed her eyes. Her little shoulders were tense and hunched. She clearly expected it to hurt. Marybeth leaned over to look the child in the face. "Do you have some detangler?"

Her question was met with a puzzled expression before Simone closed her eyes again.

Deciding that meant no, Marybeth began searching through the kitchen cupboards. They were frightfully bare, but she found the few ingredients that she needed, apple cider vinegar and olive oil. After mixing the vinegar and olive oil with water from the rain barrel outside, she placed the ingredients in a small spray bottle and shook it vigorously.

She began misting Simone's hair. "We'll leave this on for a few minutes."

Simone wrinkled her nose. "It stinks."

Marybeth laughed. "It does smell bad, but once we get your tangles out, we can rinse your hair again and get rid of the vinegar aroma. I add lavender oil to mine at home. It smells much better."

While they waited, Callie came to sniff at Simone's toes and bat at the edge of her robe. "I see that Callie is ready to play with you. I have just the thing."

Marybeth went back to her basket and pulled out a small rod with a length of yarn and a feather tied to one end. She handed the stick to Simone. The child stared at it with a puzzled expression on her face. Marybeth planted her hands on her hips. "Don't tell me you have never seen a catfish pole?"

Simone shook her head. Marybeth chuckled and took it from her. "This is how you go cat fishing."

She dangled the feather in front of Callie and got the kitten to chase it around Simone's chair. Marybeth handed the stick to Simone. "You try it."

While the child played with the kitten and occasionally smiled, Marybeth set about combing the tangles out of her long hair. When she had it straight and smooth, she pulled Simone's chair to the kitchen sink and rinsed the smell of vinegar away. After that, she positioned the child close to the stove and let the heat begin drying it as she ran her fingers through it.

"Doesn't your father comb your hair for you?"

"He makes it hurt."

"I will have to show him how to do it so it doesn't hurt. There are lots of things to know about taking care of long hair."

"Like what?"

"Well, never brush your hair when it is wet because it breaks more easily. Always use a wide-tooth comb like this on wet hair. Start at the bottom and work out the tangles there instead of trying to pull your comb all the way from your head to the end. That will only make the tangles worse at the bottom. If you braid your hair at night before you go to bed, it won't be tangled in the morning and it will be much easier to manage. Do you know how to braid your hair?"

Simone shook her head, sending the damp strands dancing.

"I will show you how later."

Marybeth laid her comb aside and began to assemble sandwiches of peanut butter and marshmallow cream the Amish called church spread on slices of her home-made bread.

Simone continued to play with the kitten. "How do you know this stuff?"

Surprised by the question, Marybeth tried not to let on. She kept her voice as normal as possible. "My mother told me these things."

Simone bowed her head and looked away. "My mother is dead."

Marybeth stopped working. She wanted to gather the sad little girl in her arms, but she knew it was too soon for that. "I'm sorry, Simone. I know how much it hurts. My mother is in heaven, too."

Simone looked up. "She is? Do you cry when you think of her?"

"Sometimes. Not as often now because I know she is happy with God in heaven and she would not like to see me crying or unhappy."

"I cry sometimes."

"That's natural when we lose someone we love and nothing to be ashamed of. Your *daed* may remarry someday and his new wife will love and cherish you as your mother did." Marybeth swallowed the catch in her throat, turned back to the counter, and cut the sandwiches lengthwise. "Do you want a whole one or a half?"

"Half. Is there milk?"

Marybeth checked the fridge. "I don't see any. Water will have to do."

They ate their sandwiches and cookies in silence by the stove with the kitten playing under their chairs. When Marybeth decided Simone's hair was dry enough, she plaited it into a single braid at the back of Simone's head and brought the strands around to show Simone how to finish it herself. Marybeth tied the end with a strand of cord she found in a kitchen drawer. "There. All done."

Simone hopped off her chair, scooped up Callie, and hurried down the hall to her room.

"I guess that means our conversation is over." Marybeth smiled to herself. All it had taken was a kitten to get the little mouse out of her room. She withdrew some mending from her basket, moved a kerosene lamp to where it would give her more light, and set to work.

At ten o'clock, she checked on Simone and found her fast asleep with the kitten dozing on the pillow next to her. Marybeth tenderly brushed her hand over Simone's head. "I think you made a friend," she whispered.

After taking Callie outside, Marybeth fed her again and put her back in the basket, where she soon settled down to sleep. Without anything else to do, Marybeth chose a book from Josiah's bookshelves and tried to read while she waited eagerly for him to come home.

Chapter 6

Josiah entered the quiet house and immediately noticed the lingering smell of vinegar in the air. The second thing he noticed was a plate of chocolate chip cookies on the kitchen table. He snagged one and bit into it. It was delicious. If this was any indication, Marybeth was a good cook.

He was surprised that she wasn't waiting for him. He called her name softly, not wanting to wake Simone, but got no answer. He walked into the living room and saw why. She was asleep in his chair. A book lay open on her lap.

She wasn't as imposing when she was asleep. In fact, she was adorable. Her *kapp* was crooked. Her lips were curved in a faint smile as if she were dreaming about something sweet. He hated to wake her, but Fred was waiting outside, eager to get home after a long day at work.

"Marybeth. Marybeth," he called a little louder.

She snuggled a little deeper in the chair. "What, dear?"

That took him aback. Who was her dear, and was he the reason for her sweet smile? "Time to go home."

Her eyes fluttered open and focused on him. She sat bolt upright. "I'm sorry. I must've fallen asleep. I didn't hear you come in."

"Fred is waiting to take you home."

She rubbed her face with both hands. "It will only take me a minute to get ready. How is your leg?"

"It's not great, but your liniment helped."

"*Goot,* I'm glad."

"How was Simone?"

"Better. We actually had a conversation." She rose to her feet.

She was standing so close he could have easily reached out and brushed an errant strand of hair off her cheek. He pushed his hands into the pockets of his jacket. "That's great. I'd love to hear all about it, but we shouldn't keep Fred waiting."

He did want to hear about her day. He wanted to tell her about his, too, about the new machine he had learned to operate and about his coworkers, who were turning out to be friends.

She moved past him into the kitchen and began gathering up her things. "I mustn't hold up Fred. It would be a long walk if he left without me."

"He wouldn't do that. We'll talk about Simone tomorrow."

She looked as reluctant to leave as he was to let her go. "I'll come a little earlier."

"That's a fine idea. I'll see you then."

She picked up her baskets and he heard a faint meow. "Do you have a cat in there?"

Her bright smile filled him with warmth. "I do. Callie, one of my kittens, came to visit Simone. Ask her about it. I think she will tell you."

He followed her out onto the porch and watched her open the passenger side door and get in. As Fred drove away, Josiah waved. He had no idea if she waved back, but he wanted to believe that she did.

Josiah felt a hand on his shoulder shaking him. He pried open his eyes and lifted his head off the pillow. Simone stood beside his bed. "Daed, have you seen my kitten?"

His head dropped to the pillow. "You don't have a kitten, Simone. You're dreaming. Go back to bed."

"I do. She's black and white and yellow. Her name is Callie."

The name triggered a faint memory. It took a moment for his foggy brain to find it. "Marybeth had her in her basket. She took her home."

"Then I'll never see her again."

The anguish in his child's voice brought him wide-awake. He rose on one elbow. "*Liebschen,* I'm sure Marybeth will bring the kitten back to visit if you ask her."

"Do you really think so?"

"I'm positive." He looked toward the window. It was dark outside. He tried to read his alarm clock but couldn't make his eyes focus. "Simone, what time is it?"

"I don't know."

"I think you need to go back to bed."

"Okay. Are you sure Marybeth is coming again?"

"I'm sure."

She left the room and he tried to drop off to sleep again, but he couldn't. That was the longest conversation he had had with his daughter since he'd returned from the hospital. A feeling of hope and thankfulness swelled inside him. He rolled to his back and gazed at the ceiling.

"Please, Lord, don't let Simone retreat from me again.

And thank you for sending Marybeth our way. I don't care for her scheme to fix me up with her friend, but hearing Simone speak to me will make it all worthwhile."

He did eventually go back to sleep and when his alarm went off, he got out of bed, eager to see if he had dreamed his conversation with Simone. She was already up at the kitchen table. She had a bowl of dry cereal in front of her and he cringed when he remembered he should've brought milk home. "Morning."

"Good morning."

She looked different. Her hair was neatly braided instead of being a bird's nest. "How was your day with Marybeth yesterday?"

"It was *goot*. She brought a kitten to play with me."

"I'm glad to hear that. Did she make you take a bath and wash your hair?"

"Yep, I don't stink now."

He wondered how Marybeth had managed such a remarkable feat when he'd met nothing but resistance from his daughter for the past four weeks.

"She's going to teach you how to comb my hair without making it hurt." Simone took her bowl to the sink and went back to her room.

"I'm beginning to think there are a great many things Marybeth can teach me."

He put on a pot of coffee. After a cup of the strong black brew, he donned his hat and coat and went out to feed and groom his horse. The animal needed to be exercised, and there was a growing list of chores and repairs waiting for his attention.

After lunch, Simone didn't return to her room. Instead, she knelt on the sofa and stared out the window. He couldn't believe the difference in his daughter. Two days ago he couldn't get her to come out of her room and now she was eagerly waiting for her new nanny to arrive. He had to admit he was eager to see Marybeth again, too. If only to thank her for the miracle she had worked on Simone.

"I see her."

He strolled to the window, hiding his excitement. His jaw dropped when he caught sight of her. "That is not a kitten."

Simone looked at him. "Why is Marybeth bringing us a cow?"

He shrugged. "Your guess is as good as mine. Maybe it's a Christmas cow. Why don't you go ask her?"

Simone scowled at him. "I can't play with a cow. I want to play with Callie."

"Let's hear Marybeth's explanation."

"Nee." Simone shook her head and folded her arms, a mutinous expression on her face.

He glanced out the window again. "It looks like Marybeth's cow has a baby calf."

"She does?" Simone scrambled back to her knees to look out the window.

It was Josiah's turn to frown. What was Marybeth up to? He could barely afford to feed his child, let alone a cow and a calf if Marybeth was gifting them to him. He hated being the object of charity. It was prideful, he knew that, but he had been forced to accept more charity than he could ever repay since his wife's death.

He walked outside to wait by the front gate. Simone soon joined him. Marybeth stopped and set her basket on the ground as she smiled brightly. "I'm sure you have noticed that I brought a cow with me today. Rest assured, Josiah, I do not intend to leave her here with you. My brother decided he must go and visit our uncle for two weeks. He tells me this at breakfast and left immediately afterward. I have no one to look after Priscilla and her new son, so I brought them along. All they require is hay and water. I will reimburse you for their feed. Even with the calf getting his share, Priscilla must be milked twice a day."

"Is she our Christmas cow?" Simone asked.

"*Nee,* she is not a gift. I must take the cow and calf home with me."

He stroked his beard with one hand. "I don't think they will fit in Fred's van."

Marybeth giggled. "Wouldn't he be surprised if we tried? I know—we can put the calf in and roll down the window so Priscilla can see him. Then she will simply follow her baby home."

He smiled at the thought of a cow galloping behind Fred's van, bellowing for her baby. "I think it would be better if you left Priscilla with us until your brother returns."

"I was hoping you would say that, but I don't want to impose. I can come and milk her in the mornings."

Simone had her hand out, trying to coax the baby closer. He had his head pressed to his mother's flank, unsure of his new surroundings.

Josiah shook his head. "I know how to feed and milk a cow. There is no need for you to make two trips a day to my house."

"Are you sure? You would be doing me a great favor. I will bring over the grain she needs so you won't have that expense."

"What's the baby's name?" Simone asked.

Josiah caught Marybeth's gaze over the top of Simone's head. "It is nothing compared to the favor you have done me."

She smiled and nodded in acknowledgment. "God is good."

She looked at Simone. "The baby doesn't have a name yet. I was wondering if you would like to help me think of one for him?"

"Bully," Josiah said. "He's a bull calf after all."

"That's a horrible name." Marybeth winked at him. "I was thinking of Leopold."

"Too formal," Josiah said. "T-bone or maybe Chuck Roast. You could call him Chucky for short."

Marybeth's mouth dropped open. She quickly snapped it shut. "You're terrible. Simone, help me out. What do you want to call him?"

The calf was investigating his new friend. He sniffed her hand and then butted it playfully.

Simone giggled. "Happy. His name should be Happy."

Josiah shared a speaking glance with Marybeth and laid a hand on his daughter's head. "Happy is a perfect name."

Marybeth could have basked in the warmth of Josiah's gaze all day, but that was nothing except foolishness on her part. The object was to find the perfect woman for him to marry, not to send her old maid's heart into a tizzy. He was a charming and attractive man. She wasn't going to have trouble finding someone to go out with him.

She now knew that Josiah was a generous man, willing to share what little he had with a neighbor in need. She knew he had a witty sense of humor and that he gave credit where credit was due. She also knew his daughter's happiness meant a great deal to him. And that, she decided, was the way to his heart for any woman interested in becoming his wife. Simone's acceptance of a new woman in the family would be every bit as important as Josiah's feelings for her.

He took Priscilla's lead rope from Marybeth. His hand brushed against hers in the process, sending a jolt of awareness through her. Marybeth quickly rubbed away the sensation. "Happy will enjoy having room to romp."

He led the cow away with her calf trotting close by her side.

Simone was trying to peek under the lid of Marybeth's basket. Marybeth jumped to stop her. "Don't open it out here."

"Did you bring Callie today?"

Marybeth picked up the basket and started walking up the porch steps. "I didn't."

"Daed said if I ask you to bring her back that you would."

"Your father is right. I will bring her to visit once in a while."

"I guess I can wait to see her again. She needs to be with her mother, doesn't she?"

"She does." Marybeth and Simone walked inside the house. Marybeth closed the door and set her burden on the counter. "I thought I would take turns letting you meet all eight of my cat Lola's litter."

Marybeth opened the lid and drew out a black kitten with four white stockings. "This one I call Boots. He can be a little rough, so be careful that he doesn't scratch you."

Simone smiled as she took the kitten from Marybeth. "I'll be careful. Come on, Boots. I have a toy in my room that you will like to chase."

She started for her room but stopped and looked over her shoulder. "*Danki,* Marybeth."

"You are very welcome. I'm going to check on Priscilla. I won't be gone long."

Marybeth left the house and headed for the barn. Finally, she was going to spend some time alone with Josiah. She had to decide who among the single women she knew would make a good wife for him. He was the only person who could answer that question. If she could get him to open up about himself.

Chapter 7

Marybeth entered the barn and allowed her eyes to adjust to the dim light. She could hear Josiah talking to Priscilla and followed the sound of his voice to a roomy box stall near the rear of the building. He was forking hay over the wall to the cow. Happy got in the way and ended up wearing a pile of hay on his back. He ran around bucking and kicking like a wildcat had him. Marybeth burst out laughing at his antics.

"I thank you again for allowing them to stay." She walked up next to Josiah.

He stopped work and reached over the low wall to brush the hay off the calf when he stopped beside his mother. "I'm glad to repay you in some small measure for your care of my daughter. I am amazed at how she has opened up."

"The credit must go to Callie."

"And not to the woman who thought to bring the kitten in the first place?"

"My humble nature prevents me from taking credit."

He turned around and rested his elbows on the wall

behind him. "I haven't seen much of your humble nature."

Was he chastising her? She couldn't be sure but decided to go with the instinct that said he was teasing. "That's because I keep it hidden behind the bossy façade I have perfected."

"Why would a woman like you need to hide behind a façade of any kind?"

"People have certain expectations for oddities like me."

"I don't see you as an oddity, but give me an example."

She hadn't intended to talk about herself, but she could hardly pepper him with questions without answering a few herself. "If a woman is tall and plain she must be manly in her demeanor and robust in her dealings with others."

"While a woman who is petite and pretty is expected to be agreeable, but not smart."

"Exactly!" Marybeth was glad he understood.

"Makes people sound shallow, doesn't it? I thought we Amish were better than that."

"People are pretty much the same everywhere."

"I admit to holding some of those preconceptions even though I have been the victim of them myself."

She tipped her head slightly. "What judgments have people made about you that aren't true?"

"That a widower with a small child needs a wife as soon as possible."

She looked down as heat spread across her face. Her motive for taking this job had been selfish and self-serving and reflected poorly on her. It wasn't a contest to him. It was his life and his daughter's life she was playing with. How upset would he be if he knew the real reason she'd forced him into agreeing to her bargain?

"I have been guilty of making assumptions along those lines before," she admitted.

"I thought as much."

"You may not want to remarry, but what about Simone? She will need a mother in her life." Marybeth truly believed that.

"She will have Esther Kauffman to fill that role once she recovers from her surgery. Esther will be a live-in nanny until I move to the first shift and Simone starts school. After that, I won't need someone to look after her. We'll manage on our own."

A widow in her early fifties, Esther was an upstanding member of the faith who would be able to give Simone the guidance and practical teaching the child needed. "Esther is a fine woman."

"I think so, too."

Marybeth looked up. He wanted her to call off their bargain. But what had started out as a benefit to her was going to be an enormous benefit to him and to his daughter if he gave the idea of remarrying half a chance. "If you think by telling me this I'll dismiss our bargain, you are mistaken. We shook on it. I will hold you to it."

"Even if you know it will be a miserable, wasted evening for me?"

"You will certainly be miserable if you take that attitude along with you."

"Who is this friend? Do I know her?"

"I'd rather not say."

He threw his hands wide. "What does your friend hope to gain from a single evening?"

"I can't speak for her, but if it were me, I'd hope to learn more about Josiah Weaver. I'd hope to enjoy talking about the books we've read and maybe discovering other common interests. I'd like to think that when the evening was over I could say that I had made a friend."

"If friendship is her aim, that's fine. If she has romantic hopes, they will be dashed."

"I will pass on your sentiments."

"*Danki.* Shall we go back to the house? Simone tells me you plan to teach me how to comb her hair without making it hurt."

"I have some suggestions to offer, that's all." She walked beside him to the barn door.

He stopped with his hand on the latch and looked at her sharply. "Why did you bring the cow here today? I can afford milk for my daughter. I'm not that poor."

He would be insulted if he thought she had done it out of pity. "I brought Priscilla here for the very reasons I told you about."

"Your brother left without any warning. Does he do that often?"

"Never before."

"Then why now?"

She drew a deep breath, knowing only the truth would satisfy him. "My brother is upset with me for taking this job. He thinks I should put his needs before yours and Simone's. He left because he knew it would make things more difficult for me. You are doing me a favor by keeping Priscilla and Happy, but I could have asked someone else to look after them. I won't lie to you. I did notice how empty your cupboards are. I thought fresh milk and cream would be a welcome addition to your meals. I'm sorry if you are offended. I was thinking of Simone."

"I believe you have Simone's best interests at heart."

"I do. And yours as well," she insisted.

"Of that I'm not so certain. It's getting late. I'm afraid your hair-combing lesson will have to wait for another day."

Josiah wanted to believe Marybeth had his best interests at heart, but it didn't seem likely. He had no idea why it was important for him to go out with her friend. It didn't make sense. What did the friend or Marybeth stand to gain from a single date? And why wasn't he allowed to know who her friend was? The longer he thought about it, the less sense it made. Marybeth didn't strike him as a devious woman, but something wasn't right.

Over the next two days things remained much the same. Marybeth came with a large basket over her arm that contained a new kitten for Simone to play with each day and some treat for the both of them—cookies; one day a cake; another day a batch of brownies. Was she trying to fatten him up?

On Friday, he followed Marybeth into the house. Simone sat on the kitchen floor playing with the kitten of the day by teasing it with the end of her hair braid. He stooped to his daughter's level. "I have just enough time for a hair-brushing lesson before I get ready for work. You told me she would teach me."

"Don't go to work today. Stay home with me."

"I can't." He stood and thrust his hands in his pockets.

"Simone, are you ready to have your hair brushed?" Marybeth asked.

"I guess." She pulled the length of cord from the end of her braid and left it on the floor for the kitten to attack. She sat on a kitchen chair while Marybeth undid her braid. Simone put her hands in her hair and mussed it up.

Marybeth opened her basket and pulled out a hairbrush shaped like a paddle. "This is one of the best types of brushes for getting tangles out of long hair. Normally you hold a bush horizontally, but to detangle hair, hold it vertically with the rows of bristles lined up like a rake's head. Start at the bottom of a strand of hair, holding on to it to keep from pulling on her scalp and work your way up. Don't try to pull the brush all the way down until you're sure you have it tangle free."

She handed the brush to him. "Try it?"

He followed her instruction, amazed at how well it worked. He leaned around to look Simone in the face. "How was that?"

"It didn't hurt at all. Please don't leave today. I want you to stay with me."

"We have been over this a hundred times. I have to go to work. Marybeth and her kitten Misty will stay and keep you company. You can go out and visit Happy. You will have a nice evening and you will see me first thing tomorrow morning just like today. Okay?"

She got down from her chair and ran out of the room. He heard her bedroom door slam. He prayed the progress she had made wouldn't be undone.

"She will be fine with me," Marybeth assured him.

"I know. I just hate to see her so unhappy."

He handed the brush back to Marybeth. "Thank you for the lesson. You were not the least bit bossy in your instructions."

"*Danki*. If she keeps her hair braided at night you'll have a lot fewer knots to work out."

"Can you teach me how to put her hair up under her *kapp*? I remember watching my wife tie and fold her hair, but I didn't pay close attention."

"I can show you how when it's a little longer. For now just pin the braid in a loop on the back of her head and put her *kapp* over it."

"Sounds easy enough. I should get ready to leave. Fred will be here soon."

"I noticed you haven't been taking your supper with you. Does the plant have a cafeteria for the employees?"

"They have a snack machine."

"I doubt you can get a decent meal from a snack machine. I'll fix you something while you get ready and you can take it with you."

"I hired you to take care of Simone, not to take care of me. I get by."

"Nonsense. Making supper for you is no hardship."

"I said I can manage to feed myself."

"How do you expect to regain your strength without decent food? I'll make it and you'll eat it if I have to pay Fred to see that you do." It wasn't much of a threat since she was trying to stifle a smile.

"Careful, your bossy side is showing."

"As is your foolish pride. We must both strive to improve ourselves. Now go get ready. Those pants are filthy. I'll wash them for you tonight. And before you object, I have to do laundry for Simone, so I might as well add in a few things of yours."

"Something tells me this is a battle I won't win."

She folded her hands demurely and smiled. "I knew there was a smart man somewhere under that beard."

After Josiah left, Marybeth went to Simone's room and knocked on her door. "May Misty and I come in?"

"I guess," was her muffled reply.

Marybeth opened the door. Simone was sitting on the floor in the corner. Marybeth joined her. "Do you know that it makes your *daed* feel bad when you behave like this?"

Simone took the kitty from Marybeth and held it close to her face. "It makes me feel bad when he goes away."

"He knows that, but he has to work. He has to buy food for you and clothing for you. He has to buy hay for the horse and for Happy. You wouldn't want Happy to go hungry, would you?"

"What will happen to Happy when Daed doesn't come back?"

"Your father will be home again tonight. You don't need to worry about that."

"Mama didn't come home. Then Daed didn't come home for a long time. I thought he was gone forever, too."

"Oh, I see." She opened her arms and Simone crawled into her lap and put her arms around Marybeth's neck. Marybeth held her close, her heart aching for the child and the fear she lived with.

"Only God can see the future. Only He knows what each day will bring. I can't promise you that your father will always be with you. No one can. I do promise that your Heavenly Father is always with you. He loves you. He wants you to be happy. He doesn't want you to worry about bad things that may never happen. You know that your *daed* loves you, don't you?"

Simone nodded.

"Your Heavenly Father loves you even more. He only asks one thing from us in return. He asks us to have faith in his goodness. Do you know what faith is, Simone?"

"Nee."

"It means that we believe God will take care of us. He will forgive our sins and he will welcome us into heaven when it is our turn to be called home. He doesn't want us to live in fear. He doesn't want you to be afraid. If we live in fear, it means we don't trust him. It's hard to have faith sometimes. He understands that. That's why we pray. We pray that he will strengthen our faith and allow us to live without fear."

Simone leaned back to look at Marybeth. "Do you pray?"

Marybeth smiled at her. "I do."

"Are you ever afraid?"

"Sometimes, but I also know that God is right beside me, and that gives me courage to face what I'm afraid of."

"I'm afraid of spiders."

Marybeth put her nose against Simone's. "Me too. Don't tell anyone that."

"I won't. The next time I see a spider, I will pray for courage."

"That's right. Pray for courage and grab a shoe."

"Daed says spiders are one of God's most wonderful creatures."

"I'm sure that's true, but so are shoemakers. The next time your father has to go to work, what are you going to do?"

"What should I do?"

"Hiding in your room doesn't make you less afraid, does it?"

"I guess not."

"Then why don't you pray for the courage to kiss him goodbye and wave to him when he leaves. I know that will make your *daed* and your Father in heaven both very happy."

"Can we go see Happy again?"

"Okay. We might as well milk Priscilla while we are there."

Simone scrambled up and dashed for the front door. Marybeth wasn't sure the child understood all that she was trying to share with her, but she prayed she had given Simone a way to combat the fear that haunted her. And to comfort the father who ached from her rejections.

Chapter 8

Dear Cousin Wilma,
*   It is nearly midnight on Friday and Josiah
will be home soon, but I wanted to take a
moment to let you know how my plan has worked
over this first week. David has decided to make
things difficult by leaving to visit Uncle Otto for
two weeks. That means I must do his chores and
mine before I leave in the afternoons. I have
brought Priscilla with me, and Josiah is
graciously allowing her to stay. Simone has been
won over by my kittens. The little mouse now
comes out of her room frequently. It warms my
heart to see the joy on Josiah's face when she
speaks to him. She has named Priscilla's new
calf Happy. I could not have imagined a child
would worm her way into my heart so quickly.
She is very lonely and frightened that she will be
left alone if something should happen to her father. I pray that having a stepmother who loves
her will erase those fears.*
*   Unlike his daughter, Josiah remains*

*something of a mystery. I am troubled by the fact
that I so blithely decided to interfere in his life
with this contest. I can only pray that my intervention brings him happiness and love and not
more heartbreak. I fear he will not approve of
the reason for my actions if it should ever come
to light. I do care about his opinion of me,
though I have known him for only a few days.*

*I see the lights of Fred's van coming up the
lane. Fred is the company driver who picks up
and returns some of the Amish workers to their
homes. He gives me a ride home every night so
that I don't have to walk. He is a very kind man.
I will write a longer letter to you on Saturday.
Sadly, I still have not decided which woman I
think will do for Josiah. I know I'm running out
of time, but I haven't given up hope.*

Sincerely,
Your loving cousin Marybeth

Marybeth folded her letter and tucked it in her bag. She
had her coat on and her basket with Misty safely inside
over her arm when Josiah walked in. She was pleased to
notice he wasn't limping as much as he had been that first
night. "Welcome home. Simone is sleeping. We had a fine
evening together. I taught her how to milk the cow, but she
needs more practice. Perhaps she can help you tomorrow
morning. How was your shift at work?"

"I was taught how to rivet. I, too, need more practice,
but I think I can get the hang of it."

"I'm sure you can. I will see you on Monday."

"Will you bring us another Christmas cow?"

She chuckled at his teasing. "I don't plan to bring
more livestock. There is fresh milk and cream in the refrigerator."

"The milk will go nicely with the brownies that are left. I haven't thanked you for those."

"There is no need."

Marybeth knew she should leave, but she couldn't seem to make her feet head toward the door. He looked better tonight. Not so worn-out or in pain. She wanted to hear about riveting and about his work. She didn't have an interest in RVs, but she was interested in what Josiah wanted to share. She could see he was reluctant to let her leave and that made her happy. No one had ever made her feel that they wanted to share her company. She savored the moment.

But it couldn't last. She made a move for the door at the same time he did and his hand closed over hers as she grasped the doorknob. His touch was like a charge of energy that seemed to flow straight to her midsection. She smiled foolishly and withdrew her hand. He opened the door.

"Until Monday, Marybeth Martin. May the Lord bless and keep you." His voice grew husky as he gazed into her eyes.

"Until Monday." She rushed out the door because more than anything, she wanted to stay.

"I don't see her." Simone was kneeling on the sofa Monday afternoon, looking more worried by the minute.

"She will be here. Stop worrying." Josiah sat repairing the sole of his leather shoe with an awl and dark cord. The repair wouldn't last through the winter. Unless he wanted to work in his stocking feet, he was going to have to invest in some new shoes. It wasn't an expense he wanted at Christmas.

"What if she has forgotten she was supposed to come today?"

"I don't think Marybeth forgets anything she is supposed to do. Unlike some little girls I know. Is your room picked up?"

From her place on the sofa she turned to look at him. "Almost."

"Do you think Marybeth will say it is almost good enough?"

"Probably not." She got down off the sofa and walked with lagging steps to her room.

He chuckled. A week ago he couldn't get her out of her room and now she was reluctant to go back there in case she missed seeing Marybeth. "What a difference you have wrought, Marybeth Martin."

He made a knot in the cord and then tried on his handiwork. It would do. He forced himself not to go look out the window. When she arrived, she arrived. He wasn't as eager to see her as his child was.

The moment that thought formed, he knew he was lying to himself. He was eager to see Marybeth again. She was like Christmas every day.

He finished packing his supper for later and went out to sit on the swing. The sky was overcast and the cold wind out of the north carried with it the smell of snow. It wouldn't surprise him to find the ground white before morning.

"Good afternoon, Josiah."

He smiled at the sound of her voice and looked up. She stood at the front gate with a black-and-white goat beside her and a large basket over one arm. He gave a push to start the swing. "I can't wait to hear this story. Why do you have a goat with you?"

"I'm not sure you will believe this."

"I'm gullible. Let's hear it."

"You make it sound like I concoct stories all the time."

"Don't you?"

"Not today. This is Cleo. Cleo is very fond of Priscilla and Priscilla's new baby. I had no idea how fond she was of her stablemates. She hasn't touched her food since Priscilla left last week."

Unnoticed by Marybeth, the goat was munching on the burgundy leaves of the Weigela shrub that grew beside the gate. He smothered a laugh. "The poor thing."

She looked relieved. "I knew you would understand. I had to bring her over to stay with Priscilla or she would starve herself to death."

"I will milk your cow, but I draw the line at milking a goat."

Marybeth's brows drew together in a frown. "Do you have something against goats?"

"Merely an unhappy goat milking incident when I was a child."

"I can sympathize. I was bitten by a dog when I was three and I've always been frightened of large dogs since that time."

"Which might explain why you like cats. Do you have another kitten in your basket? Can I see?" He got up and started toward her.

She looked everywhere but at him. "*Nee,* I've no kitten. Just a few things to work on for Christmas."

He stopped in front of her. "You are a deceitful, conniving woman, Marybeth."

A blush flooded her face. "I meant no harm. How did you find out?"

"I went to the cellar to get my awl and some cord."

She shot him a puzzled look. "The cellar?"

He pointed to her basket. "Are you sneaking in pints of canned carrots, peas, peaches or meat today?"

Comprehension dawned on her face. "Oh, the cellar."

"*Ja,* the cellar. I noticed at least two dozen new jars of produce on the shelves that weren't there last week."

He was surprised by the look of relief that flashed across her face, but she quickly recovered her composure. "You don't need to take offense. It's not charity. My brother and I can't possibly eat all that I have put up this year. I saw no harm in bringing some here since I'm responsible for feeding Simone."

"I'm not offended. I'm grateful for your kindness and generosity. I hope this is the last of your deceitful ways."

She bit her lower lip, looking as guilty as Simone when he caught her stashing her dirty clothes under the bed instead of taking them out to the washing machine. Before he could ask her why, Simone came running out of the house.

"Marybeth, you came. I thought you forgot us. You brought a goat." She reached through the fence to pet the animal's shiny black and white coat.

Marybeth's features softened into a sweet expression. "Simone, honey, I could never forget you. I have brought you a new friend to play with. This is Cleo and she has been missing Priscilla and Happy something terrible. Let's go reunite them. I know that your father must get ready for work, so we won't bother him. Goodbye, Josiah."

Josiah had the oddest feeling that she was trying to avoid his company. Why?

Simone stood still for a long moment; then she came to stand in front of him. "Bye, Daed. Have a fun time at work."

She bolted toward the barn, leaving him speechless.

* * *

Marybeth couldn't relax until Josiah was gone. She had nearly given herself away when he'd accused her of being deceitful and conniving. Canned goods were the last thing on her mind when she'd heard those words. If he only knew how deceitful she truly was, he wouldn't want her near his daughter.

Should she tell him the truth? But what purpose would it serve? He would only refuse to go out with the woman who might be his soulmate. After they went out, Marybeth decided she would confess her selfish reason for setting them up.

With Simone's help, she fed and milked Priscilla and Cleo before it got dark. The days were getting so short now there was barely any daylight left after Josiah went to work. When Simone and Marybeth left the barn, the first few snowflakes were drifting down.

"It's snowing," Simone declared with delight.

"So I see. Snow makes it feel like it's almost Christmas." Marybeth stuck out her tongue to catch one. Simone did the same. Soon they were both laughing and running about with their tongues out. The game didn't last long. It was too cold to stay outside, but it was a memory Marybeth would treasure.

In the house, she set about making cheeses from both the cow's milk and from the goat's milk. She normally sold her homemade cheeses at the farmers' market on Saturdays, but she would leave some for Josiah to enjoy. The rest of the milk she would take home with her to make yogurt or kefir, a fermented type of milk similar to yogurt but with a sharper flavor. As Marybeth worked in the kitchen, she showed Simone how to cook and make cheese, too. Simone's endless questions kept Marybeth on her toes. She decided to ask a few questions of her own.

"Simone, has your father ever talked about getting married again?"

"*Nee,* why?"

"No reason. You wouldn't mind having a new mother, would you?"

"I want my same mother." Simone's lip quivered as her eyes filled with tears.

Marybeth gathered her into a hug. "Don't cry. I know you love your *mamm.* No one can take her place, but don't you think your father is lonely living by himself?"

"I'm here. So is Priscilla and Happy."

Marybeth drew back to smile at the child. "That's right. What was I thinking?"

"Will you be here for Christmas?"

She let the child change the subject. "Your father won't go to work that day, so there's no need for me to come."

"But I want you here. What about Priscilla and Happy? They want to see you on Christmas Day."

"I suppose I can come for a visit."

"Goot." Simone smiled brightly and hugged Marybeth.

She was amazed at how much the child had come out of her shell in only a week. Would that change if another new woman came into Josiah's life?

Marybeth prayed it wouldn't because she had arrived at a decision. She knew who Josiah's new wife was going to be.

Chapter 9

"What do you think Marybeth will bring us today?" Simone was at her usual place on the sofa again, staring out the window late Friday morning.

"Maybe she will bring us a partridge in a pear tree." Busy repairing a section of his horse's harness, Josiah didn't bother looking. It was too early for Marybeth to arrive.

"What's a partridge?"

"A plump bird that tastes good when you cook it."

"I don't think she'll bring that."

"Maybe she'll bring two turtledoves or three French hens."

"I hope she brings all her kittens. She has eight of them."

"*Nee,* its eight maids a milking, not eight kittens meowing." He cut a section of harness in two and added the repair between the ends.

"Why would we need eight maids to milk one cow?"

"Don't forget, we have a goat, too."

"I wonder if she has a puppy. I like puppies."

"You'll be disappointed there. Marybeth is afraid of dogs."

"Why?"

"Because a dog once bit her."

"I see a buggy coming, Daed."

That caught his attention. He looked out the window but didn't recognize the horse. "I wonder who that could be?"

He finished stitching the last section of harness and rose to go outside and greet their visitor. Simone started to run out ahead of him, but he stopped her. "Hey, it's cold outside. Put a coat on."

She raced to her room and returned with her green coat. As he helped her into it, Josiah noticed Marybeth had been busy altering it. "She is industrious—I'll say that for her."

"Is it Marybeth?" Simone demanded, bouncing up and down.

"Hold still. I can't get the buttons done. I don't know who it is."

When he got his excited daughter bundled up, he grabbed his own coat and stepped outside with her. The buggy came to a stop by the front gate. The flashy black Standardbred tossed his head and stomped the ground. Puffs of mist rose in the air when he snorted. The sun glinted off the windshield and Josiah couldn't see who was driving. The buggy door opened. Marybeth leaned out with a cheerful wave. "Good morning."

Simone ran to her. "I knew it was you. What did you bring us?"

"What makes you think I brought anything?"

Simone's face changed from happy to downcast. "I wanted to see another kitten."

Josiah helped Marybeth to step down. "I fear you have created a kitten-loving monster."

"I can't blame her. Nothing is quite as cute as a litter of kittens playing together." She opened the back door and pulled out a basket. The sound of meowing issued from it, followed by the cackling of chickens.

She handed the basket to Simone. "Take it inside please and make sure the outside door is shut before you open it."

"Which kitten did you bring?"

"Taffy."

"Don't cry, Taffy, I'm going to play with you," Simone whispered to the basket before she hurried inside with her burden.

Marybeth pulled out a long, wooden crate and handed it to Josiah. He laughed. "I was right. I said it was three French hens."

"Actually, I have five Rhode Island Reds."

"Close enough. Please don't spin a yarn about how they stopped laying because they miss Cleo. I'm grateful for the chickens. Their eggs will come in handy. I'm tired of cold cereal and coffee for breakfast, anyway. Are you bringing us a pig tomorrow? Or just a ham?"

She cocked her head to the side. "You are in a good mood this morning."

"Why shouldn't I be? You are single-handedly re-stocking my farm."

She looked relieved. "I thought you would be offended by my charity."

He smiled at her. "It's pretty hard to be offended by someone who is proving to be such a good friend, as well as a *wunderbar kinder heeda.* I hope you brought some chicken feed because I don't have any."

"I did. There's a sack on the front seat."

"It's going to take me an hour or so to fix the chicken coop. Then we can turn them out in it."

"I repaired the wire fencing yesterday and put straw in the nest boxes so the place is all ready for them."

"You think of everything." Why was a woman like Marybeth still unwed? After just two weeks, his house was spotless, his clothes and those of his daughter had been mended, and the garden had been cleared. There was food in his kitchen from cookies to homemade cheeses, fresh-baked loaves of bread, and canned beef. A man couldn't ask for a more hardworking, generous, or sympathetic wife.

As soon as the thought occurred to him, it wouldn't leave him alone. She was a treasure. Why was she unwed? Either men in Sugarcreek were blind, or she had a reason for remaining single that she hadn't shared. He was determined to get to the bottom of it.

"I'll take the crate if you can manage the feed." He gestured toward the henhouse with his head. "I wanted to tell you that the goat cheese you left me last night was some of the best I've ever had."

"That's very kind of you to say." She went round to the front of the buggy and hefted the large grain sack to her shoulder, then walked beside him toward the henhouse.

He pondered how to broach the subject of her unmarried status. She'd once told him she preferred plain speaking, so he forged ahead. "You have many talents, Marybeth Martin. How is it that you have never married?"

"No one ever asked me."

"I find that hard to believe." There had to be more to the story than that?

"My brother, David, said no one was brave enough."

He was beginning not to think much of her brother. "That was unkind."

"The truth is sometimes unkind. No one wanted me."

She said it lightly, but he sensed the hurt beneath her words. Her smile was forced. "I'm content to be single. I shall be one of those white-haired ladies with dozens of cats to keep me company instead of children and grandchildren."

"That sounds lonely." He opened the henhouse door. She carried the sack of grain inside. He opened the lid of a wooden box fixed to the wall.

She dumped the grain inside. "We all have to walk the path God lays out for us. Your path has not been an easy one."

"I used to wonder why I was being punished."

"And now?"

"Now I'm beginning to accept the fact that I cannot understand God's plan for me, but I also believe He is with me always to help me carry my burdens."

"For many people faith is just words poured out in church meetings and prayers until something happens that rocks their beliefs. Only then can they find the true meaning of faith or they lose it altogether."

"I will have to add wisdom to your list of accomplishments."

She blushed. "Only God has true wisdom. I merely pretend to be wise."

It was what a humble Amish person should say. Marybeth might seem outspoken and bossy, but she had a true humble heart. "We will have to put some water in here for them and check in frequently, for it is sure to freeze overnight."

"My brother uses a small, solar-powered heating element to keep our poultry's water from freezing over."

"I'll have to check into purchasing one."

He opened the crate and let the hens out. They fluttered

around in apparent panic but soon calmed down and began pecking at the ground. "Let's let them get settled. I want to see what Simone is up to."

Marybeth chuckled. "I can guarantee you that whatever she is doing includes a kitten."

"I hope you plan to leave one of your kittens with us after your time is up. She'll be inconsolable if you don't."

"I've been trying to decide which one. I think it will have to be Callie."

"Isn't she your favorite?"

She slanted a look his way. "What gave you that idea?"

"Just a hunch."

"You're right, she is, but she will also make the best pet and mouser."

He walked to the house beside her, amazed at how comfortable he was in her presence after knowing her for only two weeks. He was finding a lot to like about Marybeth Martin.

When Saturday rolled around, Marybeth thought she had enough work to keep her busy at home and to keep her from thinking about Simone and Josiah, but she was wrong. Thoughts of the pair intruded throughout the day. It felt like she had deserted them. The time she'd spent with Josiah and Simone was the closest she had ever come to being part of a family. She cared deeply about both of them and missed them intensely.

She tried writing a letter to Wilma but tore it up after her third attempt. Her evening spent at home alone was long and drawn out. She finally brought all the kittens in to keep her company and to enjoy their antics, but they didn't warm the cold, empty spot in her heart. She was very much afraid nothing ever would.

Sunday dawned clear but cold. It was church Sunday and the prayer meeting was set to be held at Carl Barkman's farm. Since the service was held every other Sunday, each family in the congregation took their turn hosting church only once a year. It was a weighty undertaking that required several days of cleaning and preparations that involved the extended family and neighbors.

Marybeth dressed in her best navy-blue dress and white apron, then pinned her freshly washed and starched *kapp* over her hair. The drive took her thirty minutes. At the farm she handed over her horse and buggy to the young men in charge of parking the buggies and taking care of the horses. She looked around for Josiah but didn't see him. With a basket of pies and brownies over her arm, she walked up to the farmhouse and entered. As in most Amish homes, the walls of the lower level could be moved aside to make one large meeting space. Rows of backless wooden benches were lined up waiting for the congregation to take its place, with men and boys seated on one side of the center aisle while the women sat on the other side.

Marybeth carried her food into the kitchen, where a number of women were already preparing the meal that would be served after the three-hour-long service. As she entered, she was greeted by many of her friends. She saw Dorcas Yoder slicing the pies and went over to join her. "That pumpkin looks yummy, doesn't it?" she commented.

"I'm hoping there will be some left when it's our turn to eat." The men ate first. The unmarried women ate last.

Marybeth started cutting a peach pie and serving it onto plates. "Dorcas, I have something to ask you. Feel free to say no if you don't like the idea."

The young woman with bright red hair and freckles looked up. "What is it?"

"I have taken a temporary job as a nanny for Josiah Weaver's daughter. His little girl is four years old."

"That is a fun age. They question everything. Why, why, why?"

"You are so right. Between taking care of my own home and Josiah's, I'm falling behind in my preparations for Christmas. I was wondering if you could give me a hand. You always make the most beautiful Christmas cards and I don't have a creative bone in my body. Little Simone wants to make cards for her friends and family. I wonder if you could find time to join us and help her make some." She waited with bated breath for the young woman's reply.

"Of course. I'd be delighted. When should I come over?"

Relief put a broad smile on Marybeth's face. "Tuesday afternoon about two o'clock would work. I don't want to take you away from your own Christmas preparations or your beau." She didn't know if Dorcas was seeing anyone or not. Many Amish youth kept their relationships a secret until only a few weeks before a wedding.

Dorcas blushed. "I don't have a beau. You don't have to worry about that, and I'm done making my own cards so your timing is perfect."

"I'm very grateful and I know that Josiah will be grateful, too. He and his little girl have had so much sadness in their lives that I'd really like to see this Christmas season be a happy one for them. Do you know them?" Had she inspired enough sympathy?

"I heard that his wife died and then he was injured a short time later in a car and buggy crash, but that's all I know about the family."

"His leg was crushed. It has taken him months to regain the full use of it, but he is determined to improve. He hasn't been a member of this congregation for long, so I'm not surprised you haven't met him. Josiah is a wonderful father and a hard worker. A woman could do far worse than to settle down with him. And his daughter will tug at your heartstrings. If ever a child needed a mother, she does. She had stopped talking until I started taking care of her. She's desperately frightened of being left alone in the world."

"The poor child."

The sympathy in Dorcas's eyes was just what Marybeth was hoping for. Winning over Simone's heart was just as important as winning over Josiah's.

"I knew you'd understand. You're so *goot* with children." Now that she had planted the seed, Marybeth was content to stand back and let it germinate. On Tuesday she would be able to judge their reaction to each other and Simone's reaction to her potential new mother.

Marybeth drew a ragged sigh. If she could watch without breaking down in tears.

Chapter 10

Josiah couldn't put his finger on what was wrong, but Marybeth was acting differently. He noticed it Monday when she arrived only minutes before he was due to leave, unlike the week before when she had arrived several hours early every day. She practically bolted out the door on Monday evening when he got home. Today, she had come early again, but she was constantly looking out the window as if she were expecting someone.

"Marybeth, what's going on?"

She spun around. "Nothing."

"You sound just like Simone when there's something she doesn't want me to know. Why do you keep looking out the window?"

"The snow is so pretty. I can't stop looking at it."

Six inches of new snow during the night had turned the countryside into a sparkling winter wonderland. "It is beautiful, but you have something else on your mind."

"I invited someone over to help Simone and I make Christmas cards. She seems to be running late."

"Did you think I would be upset that you are having a friend over?"

"Not really."

"Who's coming?"

"Dorcas Yoder." She bit her lip. What was she worried about?

"The name doesn't ring a bell."

"She's a friend of mine. I don't think you've met her. She's a very sweet and charming woman. I'm hoping that she and Simone get along."

"Why wouldn't they?"

"No reason."

"Forgive me for saying this, but you seem on edge today."

"Do I?" She turned and began scrubbing the counter that she had just washed. "There's so much to get done before Christmas that I don't know where to start."

"I'll be happy to help. What do you need done?"

"Cookie baking mostly. There will be a cookie exchange on Saturday at the Barkman farm. I have to bring four large pails of assorted cookies."

"I'm not much of a hand at baking, but I will try."

"*Nee*, I'm worried about nothing. Whatever baking I don't get done on Thursday, I'll get done on Friday."

He caught movement outside. "I think your friend has arrived."

She turned around with evident relief. "Yes, that is her."

She threw a shawl around her shoulders, went out, and ushered Dorcas into the house. "I'm so glad you could make it."

Dorcas took off her bonnet and coat. "It's a good thing we planned it for today. The newspaper is calling for heavy snow for the next two days."

She smiled at Josiah, not the least bit self-conscious. She was a pretty girl with freckles and red hair. "Hello, I'm Dorcas Yoder. My father is Alfred Yoder. He works with you at the RV factory."

He knew exactly the man she was talking about. "Alfred's been a great help to me. He's a funny fellow."

"That's *Dat*, always joking."

"Doesn't one of your brothers work there, too?"

"Merle does. He's the quiet one of the family. I understand you have a daughter?"

"I do. Let me go get her."

"She's been looking forward to this," he heard Marybeth say.

Simone was under the covers in bed. He knocked on the top of the highest lump like it was the door. "Is Simone at home?"

"*Nee.*"

"Someone has come to help you make Christmas cards."

"I know. Marybeth told me."

He pulled the covers down off her face. "Then I think you should be polite and go say hello."

"I only want to make cards with Marybeth. I'm her friend."

"Marybeth can have more than one friend. And so can you. I have friends. It doesn't change the way I feel about Marybeth or about you."

"Are you going to get married again?"

Where had that come from? "That's a funny question."

"Marybeth said you might get married again."

He sat down on the bed beside her. "If the right person comes along and I fall in love with her the way I fell in love with your mother, I might marry again."

"But she won't be my mother, will she?"

"*Nee,* your mother is in heaven. If I should marry again, the lady will be your stepmother. That means while she isn't your true mother, she is a woman who will love you as if you are her very own and who will do all the things with you that your true mother would do if she could. You can love a stepmother as much as you loved your real mother."

"What if I want Marybeth to be my stepmother? I love her and she loves me. She could stay here always and then Priscilla and Happy and Cleo would never have to leave."

"I know that Marybeth loves you. And I know that you love her. But she doesn't love me the way a wife must love her husband. So she can't be your stepmother, but she can always be your dearest friend."

"Is she your dearest friend?"

"I guess she is." He wanted her to be more than a friend, but he couldn't be sure his feelings were returned. He only knew he wanted Marybeth in his life. Simone needed her. But unless he was certain, he wouldn't do anything to jeopardize what they already had together.

"I don't think we should mention this conversation to Marybeth. She wants you to come and meet her friend so you can do something fun together."

"But I don't know her friend."

"And you never will get to know her unless you are brave enough to go out and say hello." He pulled the covers back over her head. "Besides, it's very hard to make Christmas cards in the dark." He flipped the covers down again. "Are you ready to be brave?"

"In a minute." She closed her eyes and folded her hands. A minute later she nodded and climbed out of bed.

He held her hand as they went out into the kitchen,

where Marybeth and Dorcas already had the table covered with bright scraps of paper, ribbons, scissors, old Christmas cards, glue, and glitter.

Simone looked at him. "Are you going to help us?"

He nodded. "Until I have to leave for work."

The card-making party turned out to be a huge success. Josiah and Dorcas got along as if they had known each other for years. Each tried to outdo the other by making the most elaborate and impractical cards. Simone sat between them, enjoying herself and adding her special touches to their creations.

Marybeth sat across from them. She smiled and nodded. She glued ribbons together and added glitter where it was needed, all the while feeling more miserable and out of place than she had ever felt in her life. She was glad when Josiah left for work and when Dorcas admitted that it was time she was leaving, too. When Simone went out to feed the chickens and gather the eggs, Marybeth sat down at the table, put her head on her arms, and burst into tears.

No one had ever wanted her. No one ever would. Not even the man she was falling in love with. Dorcas Yoder was perfect for him. Marybeth Martin was not. She knew how to pick the perfect match for others. Why wasn't there one for her?

After a few minutes she sat up and wiped her face with both hands. Tears gained her nothing. They never had. All crying did was give her a headache. She got up and washed her face. By the time Simone came back with the eggs, Marybeth had her ragged emotions under control. She would have to spend time with Simone for another week, but she would avoid spending time alone with Josiah. She might blurt out her feelings in a moment of weakness and make a complete fool of herself.

She was putting away the eggs when the door opened and Josiah came in with a group of Amish men and women. He was grinning from ear to ear. "Get your coat and gloves. I'll get Simone dressed."

"What are you doing? Who are these people?"

"You aren't the only one who has friends. These are some of the people I work with and we are going caroling. There are two sleighs outside. Hurry up."

"Caroling? I thought you had to work."

A short, stout Amish fellow with a gray beard said, "This is a company-sponsored outing. Tonight we are being paid to spread the good news of our Lord's birth to all who hear our voices."

Josiah snatched her coat and bonnet off their pegs and held them out. "It's almost Christmas, Marybeth. It's time to spread Christmas joy to the world. Pun intended," he said as the others groaned. "Don't tell me you can't sing, because I have heard you and you have a wonderful voice."

Simone heard the commotion and came into the kitchen. "Daed, you're home already."

He lifted her in his arms. "I am, and we are going caroling."

She clapped her hands and bounced up and down. "Yay!"

"Dress warm and bring some quilts. It will get cold."

Marybeth shook her head. "You go on without me. I'm not up to it tonight."

Simone's smile turned to a frown. "But I want you to come with me."

"Ja," Josiah said, "we want you to come. We aren't leaving without you."

Everyone began urging her to change her mind and she finally gave in. During the following whirlwind of activity as everyone got settled into the sleighs, Marybeth found herself seated in the back of a sleigh with Josiah and another young couple. Simone was sandwiched between them. She caught Josiah staring at her with a look of gentle happiness on his face. She smiled shyly at him.

She wanted this. One night of pretending to be a happy family. The memory of tonight would be all she had to cherish after Dorcas took her place.

The horses stomped with impatience, their breath rising in clouds of white mist. Hot bricks were passed around until everyone had warm feet and then they were off.

The fields they passed lay like pristine blankets of white fleece. The stars overhead and a low sickle moon looked like she could reach up and touch them. The gauzy ribbon of the Milky Way stretched like a heavenly banner across the inky blackness above her. Light from the lanterns on the sides of the sleighs cast semicircles of brightness a few feet out on the snow.

The cold stung Marybeth's cheeks and made her wish she had grabbed a scarf to wrap around her face. At least Simone had one. Her eyes twinkled between the red wool of the scarf and the black brim of her bonnet. They were all Marybeth could see of her face. The jingle of harness bells and the muffled *clip-clop* of the horses' feet on the snow-packed roadway were the only sounds. Marybeth began to relax and enjoy the night. The glow of the lanterns on the other sleigh guided them forward to their destination.

In two hours' time, they visited eight homes, where they piled out of the sleighs and stood in a semicircle as they sang. Simone was off key and she didn't know all the words, but her enthusiasm made up for her lack of talent. At each house they visited they were treated to baked goods and hot drinks before they climbed back in the sleighs and drove on.

When they headed home at last, Josiah leaned close to her. Beneath the quilt that covered them, he found her gloved hand and entwined his fingers with hers. "Aren't you glad you came?"

"I am." It had been the most magical night of her life. But it had to end.

It was a night that Josiah would never forget. As they returned home, he saw the way his life could unfold with Marybeth in it. The depth of his feelings for her frightened him. He'd only known her a few short weeks, but it felt as if he had known her for a lifetime. He had loved and lost once. Did he dare to love again? He gave her fingers a squeeze and then let go of her hand. He wanted to be certain of her feelings before he revealed his growing love. He cherished her friendship and didn't want to do anything that would jeopardize it.

They delivered Marybeth to her home. Simone had fallen asleep leaning on Josiah. He moved her gently and laid her down on the seat. He got out to walk Marybeth to her front door. She turned to him with a forced smile on her face that didn't reach her eyes.

He stepped closer. "What's wrong? Tell me."

"My time with Simone will be over soon. It's time to complete our bargain."

"You still want me to go out with your friend?"

"I've picked a night. The two of you will have a chance to get to know each other better at the cookie exchange this Saturday."

A woman who cared deeply for a man wouldn't be

eager to set him up with someone else. His hopes began to fade. "What if I don't enjoy the company of your friend? What then?"

"You will. I've seen the chemistry you have together."

He didn't understand what she was talking about. "How is that possible? Who is she?"

"I'll tell you on Saturday."

"Marybeth, I thought . . . I felt that we had something special between us."

She wouldn't look at him. "We do. It's Simone."

"You love my daughter, don't you?"

She looked at him then. "It's impossible not to love her."

"Is that it? Is that all?"

"I care for you, Josiah. You know that."

But she didn't love him. She didn't have to say it. He turned and walked away.

Chapter 11

The weather turned bitter the night after the caroling party. A blizzard roared in, prompting school to cancel classes and businesses to close. Marybeth got word from her *Englisch* neighbor that Josiah's work would be closed until the following Monday. She wouldn't get to spend her final days with Simone. Esther Kauffman, Josiah's full-time nanny, would be back to work on Monday, as well.

Marybeth spent the days in a fog. She baked cookies and breads for the coming holidays, but there was no joy in it. Even the kittens didn't entertain her for more than a few minutes. She had fallen in love with Josiah and she had no idea how to fall out of love. At the back of her mind a small voice said he cared for her, too, but she was afraid to listen to it. Afraid she wasn't the kind of woman a man could love. Even if he was brave.

The storm broke Friday morning, leaving the world blanketed in sparkling snow. The sun came out and before long ice crystals hung from the roofs and the branches of the trees. She knew the cookie exchange would go ahead. Cars and trucks were no match for the snow drifts, but buggies and sleighs could go right through them or over them.

David returned on Saturday morning. She was actually glad to see him. She would send him to Josiah's house to collect Priscilla, Happy, and Cleo on Monday.

With four large pails of cookies, she headed for the Barkman farm a little after two o'clock. She was hoping to have some time alone with Dorcas before Josiah arrived. This time her prayer was granted. Dorcas arrived just as Marybeth drove in.

The two women carried their goodies to the large room in the basement, where tables had been set up and an impressive variety of cookies, pastries, and confections awaited the rest of the guests. Marybeth gathered her courage and tapped Dorcas on the shoulder. "May I speak with you for a few moments?"

"Of course. How are Josiah and Simone? She is the most adorable child."

"Josiah is the one I wish to talk about. You know that I dabble in matchmaking."

Dorcas giggled. "You call it dabbling, but there are at least a dozen people I know who owe their matches to your intervention."

"You asked me once to keep you in mind if I had someone I thought would interest you."

Dorcas grew serious. "Have you been looking for someone for me?"

"I have, and he will be here this evening."

"Who? Don't keep me in suspense. Wait, are you talking about Josiah Weaver?"

Marybeth nodded, keeping a tight rein on her emotions. "He is open to the idea of spending the evening with you. I assume that you feel the same way. The two of you got along marvelously at our card-making party."

Dorcas walked over and sat down on a nearby folding chair. "I wish I had had a little more warning. Josiah Weaver? I never would have suspected that he had an interest in me."

Marybeth came and sat beside her. "I think you two make a great couple. Actually, you three. Simone comes as part of the package."

"A ready-made family. That's a sobering thought."

"I hope the two of you have an enjoyable evening. In fact, I know you will." Marybeth couldn't keep her voice level any longer. She got up and left the room. On her way upstairs, she ran into Josiah coming down.

Her heart sped up like a wild colt racing across the pasture. She fought down the urge to throw herself into his arms and beg for his love. She had never thought of herself as a pathetic person, but it seemed that she could easily become one.

"Dorcas Yoder is waiting to see you downstairs." She tried to sound happy for him.

He wasn't smiling. "Finally I learn the name of your friend. I will do my part. But my feelings haven't changed." He brushed past her on his way down the stairs. She raced up and out into the cold night air.

Josiah reined in his anger when he saw Dorcas. She wasn't to blame. She was interested in finding a husband. He wasn't interested in finding a wife.

"Good evening." He nodded to her. "Would you like some punch?"

"I would. Thank you, Josiah. How is Simone?"

"She's fine. She's upstairs playing games with some of the other children."

He went to the table and filled two glasses with punch. A group of young people were getting a singing started at the other end of the room. He looked for a quiet place to visit with Dorcas and finally found it on the main level of the house in Mrs. Barkman's sewing room.

He and Dorcas sipped their drinks in silence for a few moments. Finally, she said, "Well, this is awkward."

"I'm going to honest with you, Dorcas. I'm not looking to marry again. I don't want to hurt your feelings. You're a nice woman. You're warm and witty, but you aren't for me."

She giggled. "You don't know how happy I am to hear that."

He frowned slightly. "You are?"

"I'm very happy to know you don't have your heart set on me. You're a fine fellow, but I don't see why Marybeth thought we would suit."

"I got the impression you insisted on this meeting."

"Me?" She clapped a hand to her chest, her eyes wide with surprise. "I did no such thing."

"Then I misunderstood Marybeth. You asked her to be your go-between, didn't you?"

"Never. I'm not so bold as that."

"Then I'm completely confused."

"So am I. I had the distinct impression that Marybeth was in love with you."

"What? When?"

"At our card-making party. She never took her eyes off you. Every time you laughed at something I said it was as if she was swallowing ground glass."

"Are you sure?"

"Believe me, I know what it is like to watch the man I love flirt with someone else. No matter how hard a woman pretends it doesn't matter, the truth is in her eyes."

Could it be true? Could Marybeth be in love with him? "Then why this charade?"

"I'm afraid she is the only one who can answer that."

"I reckon it's time for some plain speaking. *Danki,* Dorcas. Whoever *he* is, he's a fool."

She smiled sadly. "Don't I know it."

Josiah left the sewing room and went to find Marybeth. He searched the house from top to bottom and finally spotted her sitting on a bench outside in the garden. He pushed open the rear door and stepped outside.

He could hear the young people downstairs singing Christmas carols. The three-quarter moon made the snow-covered landscape as bright as day. The branches of the cedar trees around the garden perimeter were laden with a thick coating of snow that sparkled as brightly as the stars overhead. It was the perfect setting, and he had the perfect woman in front of him.

She jumped to her feet when she caught sight of him.

He stopped inches away from her. She couldn't retreat because of the bench behind her, but her eyes were searching for a way out.

He took a deep breath. "I have fallen in love with you, Marybeth Martin. I can't believe I'm saying those words. I never thought I would love again, but you have brought so much joy to me."

She tried to inch away from him. "You can't love me. You don't know what you're saying."

Placing a finger under her chin, he lifted her face until she met his gaze. "Why can't I be in love with you?"

"I deceived you. I'm conniving and deceitful."

"In what way? Only the truth now, Marybeth," he warned.

"My cousin Wilma and I have this contest every year. We fancy ourselves to be matchmakers. The one who makes the most matches before Christmas Eve is the winner. The loser has to entertain our aunt Ingrid for two weeks at Christmas. She is my aunt, and I love her, but she is a terrible person. She hates me. I was about to lose for the first time in four years. I was desperate. I saw you in the grocery store and I have never seen anyone more in need of a wife and a mother than you and Simone. I took the job as your nanny so I could learn all about you and pick the perfect woman for you. I found her. Dorcas Yoder and you are the perfect couple."

"While you might be a wonderful nanny, I think you are a terrible matchmaker. Dorcas and I have nothing in common, and we are both in love with someone else. I am in love with you. No matter what your reason was for taking the job, you proved to be a wonderful nanny. Simone adores you. And so do I."

"You don't understand. I'm too tall."

"Wrong again. You are the perfect height for me to kiss your nose." He demonstrated how easy it was. "That reason doesn't fly. Give me another one."

"I'm homely and plain."

He cupped her face with his hands. "Not to me. I see a woman with blue fire and infinite kindness in her eyes. She has skin as smooth as silk and luscious lips, beautiful enticing lips that beg me to kiss them. I'm going to kiss you, Marybeth."

"Do you really want to?"

He groaned as he pulled her into his embrace. "You have no idea how much I want to." He slanted his mouth over hers and kissed her tenderly. She held herself stiff as a post.

Puzzled by her lack of response, he pulled away.

She licked her lips. "That was nice," she said sweetly.

Nice wasn't what he was going for. "It works better if you kiss me back, Marybeth."

She brushed her thumb across his lips. "I was wondering about that. Can we try it again?"

"Definitely." He pulled her closer, holding his passion in check. He didn't need to worry. She tipped her head slightly and pressed her mouth to his and he forgot about everything except the honeyed sweetness of her mouth.

The soft white world around Marybeth faded away as a lightness filled her being. Only the warm, lush feel of Josiah's lips anchored her to the earth. She pressed closer to him, loving the feel of his arms holding her, the way his beard rasped against her skin. He tasted of chocolate mint cookies and strawberry punch. She heard a small moan from him and she pulled away. "Did I do it wrong?"

He leaned his forehead against hers. "*Nee*, my love," he said breathlessly. "You kiss very, very well."

She gazed into his eyes. "So do you."

"Now do you believe that I love you?"

She smiled as she raised her arms to circle his neck. "I'm afraid I'm going to need more convincing. And more kissing practice."

He lifted her off her feet and swung her around. "I think you had better marry me first."

"Can it be soon?"

"It can't be soon enough." He lowered her feet to the ground. "Do you love me, Marybeth?"

"What a silly question. I fell in love with you the first night you came home from your new job. You were worn-out and in pain, but despite that, you thought of my needs and arranged for Fred to take me home."

"I needed you to come back. I'm very glad you did." He kissed her nose again. "You're getting chilled. We should go in."

"I'm warm enough right where I am. I didn't know love could be like this. It's all excitement and tenderness at the same time. God has smiled on me. I am so, so thankful that he brought you and Simone into my life."

He smiled softly and stroked her cheek. "I can't wait to tell her this when we get home tonight."

She suddenly brightened. "You just asked me to marry you."

He chuckled. "I did. And I think you said yes."

"*Ja*, I did. I will marry you. Do you know what this means?"

"I'm about to become a very happy man and Simone is about to become a very happy little girl. She likes you a lot, but she really wants to keep Priscilla, Happy, and Cleo."

Marybeth took him by the hand and pulled him toward the house. "This is one more match made before Christmas Eve. This means I win the contest and the Harpy of Holmes County is going to stay with Wilma again this year. I can't wait to tell her. God is *goot*."

December 20
My dearest cousins,
I pen this note with overwhelming joy in my heart. I'm sure you will share my happiness and amazement when I tell you of my good fortune.
You must be thinking that I have managed to best Wilma at our little game, but alas, I did not. When I presented my case for having made another match before Christmas Eve, Wilma gleefully reminded me that it was her suggestion in the first place to have the unsuspecting woman become the nanny for Josiah Weaver's young daughter, Simone. Wilma maintains that she instantly saw the spark that would ultimately unite the happy couple. I had to concede. It was her idea.

Why then, you may ask, am I filled with joy to have the Harpy of Holmes County, Great Aunt Ingrid, stay with me for two full weeks this Christmas season? Because she will get the opportunity to meet the love of my life, my soon-to-be-husband, Josiah Weaver, and my adorable soon-to-be stepdaughter, four-year-old Simone.

You read those words correctly. Josiah and I plan to wed the first Thursday in February. Your wedding invitations will arrive after the first of the year.

I can't express in words how happy I am. God has seen fit to bless me with the most wonderful man on earth. To put it simply, Josiah makes my heart sing. Nothing that Great Aunt Ingrid can do or say will lessen my joy. I dare her to try.

Lastly, and perhaps the most amazing of all, David also has news to share. He returned from his two-week visit with Uncle Otto with a new dog named Daisey. I'm glad he will have the companionship of a lovely rat terrier after I marry. Daisey doesn't mind the cats, but Lola and her kittens will make the move to Josiah's farm with me. Simone insists on it.

I can't wait to see you at my wedding and tell you the whole wonderful story. Katie Mae and Carolyn, I hope you will honor me by acting as my side sitters along with Wilma on my special day. I eagerly await your answers.

I wish you a blessed and happy Christmas. The enclosed Christmas cards were made by Simone with only a little help from me.

As always, your loving cousin,
Marybeth

Epilogue

Simone climbed to the top of the rail fence and sat watching the roadway. Two cars went by but didn't turn in. A horse and buggy was approaching when she heard a familiar meowing and looked down to see Callie had followed her. "Bad, Callie. You shouldn't be down here by the road. The cars can be dangerous."

Simone jumped down from the fence and startled the kitten, who darted out into the road. She froze in front of the oncoming horse, arching her back and hissing. Simone dashed after her.

The driver tried to stop the horse and it reared in protest. Simone scrambled out of the way with the kitten in her hands, but she slipped and fell. The horse came down, its front feet missing her by inches. Callie jumped out of Simone's arms and hightailed it for the house.

"Little girl, are you injured?" An elderly Amish woman got out of the buggy and helped Simone to her feet.

Simone brushed the snow from her new coat. "I'm fine."

"What are you doing running out in front of my horse? You could have been hurt."

"I was waiting to see the Harpy of Holmes County. She's the meanest woman my new stepmom has ever met and she's coming to stay today. But Callie took it into her head to run out into the road and I tried to catch her."

"The Harpy of Holmes County? My gracious, she sounds like a terrible person. Who is your new stepmom?"

"She's not actually my stepmom until after the wedding, but I like to call her that. Her name is Marybeth Martin until she marries my *daed*. Then she will be Marybeth Weaver."

"So you are going to be Marybeth's daughter. I am very pleased to meet you. My name is Ingrid. I'm your stepmother's great aunt. I am dying to hear more about this Harpy of Holmes County."

"She must be awful mean because Marybeth isn't scared of anything except her."

"And Marybeth told you this?"

Simone stared at her shoes. "Well, I kind of overheard her talking to Daed when I was supposed to be sleeping."

"Ah, that explains it." Ingrid bent to whisper in Simone's ear. "Can you keep a secret?"

Simone nodded. "I like secrets."

"Don't tell Marybeth this, but she is my favorite niece. She always stands up for herself. The rest of my relatives don't." Ingrid straightened and smiled at Simone. "Do you like fruitcake?"

"I don't know."

"I have some with me and I think you are going to love it. I have one for Marybeth, too. Let's go say hello to her."

Love Delivered

SARAH PRICE

Dear Cousins,

Danke for your letters. With the holidays just around the corner, it is right gut to hear from you.

Nothing much has changed here in Shipshewana. Daed hasn't gotten any better and still needs my help every day and night. Thankfully, our bishop and his wife arranged for some women to come on Wednesdays and sit with Daed. It's a blessing to have that day to run errands or visit with friends.

Otherwise, my days are spent with Daed, tending to his needs and trying to manage the farm. Our herd of cows has dwindled down and I know that I'll have to fix some of the fencing in spring. Since his stroke, I just haven't had time to do much.

Sorry that there isn't much more news from our little part of Indiana. Days seem very rote and, well, not much happens in Shipshewana anymore. At least not for me. Maybe the new year will bring some exciting changes, although I can hardly imagine how that would be possible.

Yours in Christ,
Katie Mae

Chapter 1

Katie Mae heard the sound of the approaching buggy long before she saw it pull down the short lane of her father's farm. She'd have to write her own letter to Marybeth and her other cousins later. It was nice that her mother's relatives kept in touch, especially with the holiday nearing.

Setting the letter from her cousin Marybeth onto the counter, Katie Mae shook her head. *Matchmaking*, she thought. Surely there were better things for people to do than to try to match up the unmarried folk! She was sure glad that no one in Shipshewana tried to matchmake.

Wiping her hands on her black apron, she hurried to the window in time to see the familiar black buggy of Bishop Brenneman stopping next to the dairy barn. The empty dairy barn. Sighing, Katie Mae looked at her father, who sat in his wheelchair, his head tilted to the side as he stared at the wall.

"Oh, Daed!" She grabbed a clean kitchen towel and walked over to him. Kneeling down, she dabbed at his chin. "That can't be comfortable now, can it? Let me fetch you that neck pillow Cousin Marybeth sent you."

He mumbled something that Katie Mae couldn't understand. Probably a complaint. He was full of them these days, it seemed. So Katie Mae ignored him and walked over to the recliner in the section of the kitchen near the picture window. They used that area for socializing, or, rather, *used* to use it for that purpose. Now, with her mother gone to heaven and her father bound to the wheelchair, no one came visiting anymore.

Which made the unexpected arrival of the bishop even more perplexing.

She reached into the newspaper rack and grabbed the black squishy, donut-shaped pillow. Dear Marybeth, so kind and good-hearted. Just the other week, she had received Marybeth's latest letter, updating her about what was happening in Sugarcreek, Ohio. And she had sent it with this clever pillow for Katie Mae's father.

It was *the* perfect gift. And just before Christmas.

She fastened the pillow around his neck so that his head wouldn't droop to the side. Ever since the stroke, he just hadn't been able to do much of anything.

Perhaps *that* was why the bishop had come calling.

Katie Mae smiled at her father and reached out to touch his hand. She tried to do that often, knowing it was important to stay connected with her father. "I'll be right back," she said. "Seems we have a visitor today."

By the time she reached the kitchen door, the bishop was already standing there, waiting for her to open it. Had he knocked? She hadn't heard him if he had.

"Bishop Brenneman!" she said with a broad smile. "What a pleasant surprise! Come in out of the cold!" Stepping aside, she made way for him to enter the room. "It almost feels like January instead of early December!"

The bishop removed his hat and held it before him as he glanced around the kitchen. Katie Mae said a little

prayer of gratitude that she'd been able to actually clean
the kitchen that morning. Normally she didn't have time.
Between taking care of her father and the remaining
livestock they had, she didn't usually have much time
for anything at all. But Daed had slept more than usual
that morning and Katie Mae took advantage of the break
in her schedule to not just tidy up the kitchen but deep
clean it.

It smelled like citrus.

"Abram," the bishop said, nodding his head in the direction of her father.

Neither Katie Mae nor the bishop expected him to respond.

He didn't.

For a few seconds, the bishop stood in the doorway,
hat in hand, staring at her. He was tall, unusual for an
Amish man. His face was weathered from years of
working in the fields. His long white beard hung over
his chest, the wiry ends just barely touching the third
hook-eye on his coat. Unlike a lot of the younger men,
the bishop had never conformed to using buttons on his
clothing.

"Might I fetch you some coffee?" she asked, feeling
nervous under his stern but thoughtful stare. Before he
had a chance to respond, Katie Mae bustled over to the
stove so that she could pour some coffee into a mug.
"It's still warm from earlier. But it's not the first pot of
the day." She gave a lighthearted laugh. "Don't want
you thinking I'd be serving you old coffee from this
morning!"

"Katie Mae—"

"Now you sit right down and let me set out some
fresh bread, too. I opened a new jar of peach jam this
morning and—mmm—it was just delicious. We were
blessed to have such a bountiful crop of peaches this

year. I just wish I had canned more so I could make peach pies all winter." She placed a plate of sliced bread onto the table before gliding over to the refrigerator. "Don't you? There's just something about a peach pie. And apple pie, too, I guess." She looked up, leaning against the now open refrigerator door as she thought. "But I don't know about canning apples. I never heard of such a—"

"Katie Mae," the bishop interrupted. "Please."

She glanced at him as she carried the peach jam from the refrigerator to the table. He looked exasperated, even exhausted. "I'm sorry," she said softly. "I was babbling again, wasn't I?"

To his credit, the bishop ignored her question. "Sit down, Katie Mae. I need to talk with you."

"Oh help," she muttered. "Have I done something wrong?" Try as she might, she couldn't think of one reason why the bishop would need to talk to her. She always attended worship service and was the first person to volunteer to help during the fellowship meal, something she thought the other young, unmarried women in Liberty Creek should think about doing more often. Maybe then they'd find themselves a husband! No one wanted to marry a lazy Amish woman, that was for sure and certain!

But just as she thought that, she sobered. *She* wasn't lazy and *she* always volunteered to help. And yet *she* had never married. Of course, she couldn't blame *that* on any other reason than her unfortunate family circumstance.

"Of course not, Katie Mae." The bishop almost smiled, but it was an expression that rarely crossed his face. In fact, Katie Mae could only remember two times that the bishop had actually smiled: when his granddaughter Elizabeth married Jacob Smucker and when old Whitey

King told him an off-colored joke about horses carrying tales. Other than that, the bishop maintained a stern outlook on life and made certain that his expression reflected that.

"So what prompted your visit, then?"

He took a sip of her coffee and took his time setting the mug back onto the table. She felt as if he were biding his time rather than just taking his time. What on earth, she wondered, is behind this visit?

"I'm afraid the time has come to talk to you about your options."

And there it was. The truth behind the bishop's visit. It wasn't to say hello or see how her father fared. No. It was to discuss options and, even though Katie Mae wasn't certain what *that* meant, she knew it didn't bode well for her.

"Options?" she managed to squeak out. "What do you mean 'my options,' Bishop?"

His shoulders sagged as he sighed. Clearly, whatever he had to say to her was not easy. "Katie Mae, I've known you since you were born," he started. "You haven't had it easy, I know. But this . . ." He gestured around the dark kitchen. "This cannot continue."

Katie Mae froze.

"It's just not right, having a young woman living alone—"

"I'm not alone."

"—taking care of her invalid *daed*—"

"He had a stroke, Bishop. He'll get better."

"—and barely making ends meet on a farm that needs too much work for one young woman to handle."

She jutted her chin into the air and narrowed her eyes. "I'm doing just fine, Bishop. I haven't asked Amish Aid for any help since Daed went to the hospital."

"That's true, Katie Mae. And you're to be commended for that." The bishop reached out and touched the handle of the coffee mug. "But you haven't been contributing to it either."

She gasped.

"Nor have you been keeping up with the maintenance of this place. Why, that stable looks like it's seen better days, child. And your fence line's in need of repair. In fact, I had to stop on the road and shore up a break in the fence along the road."

She cringed. She had meant to fix that yesterday but had completely forgotten.

"And I near 'bout broke my buggy's axle coming down your lane." He leaned forward, his dark eyes piercing hers. "You have a rut bigger than an oak tree near the mailbox."

That, too, was something she had meant to address.

"It's time, Katie Mae. Time for you to make some firm decisions." He leveled his gaze at her. "Before those decisions are made for you."

Her eyes wandered around the kitchen. She had been so proud of herself for having cleaned everything and thought that was what the bishop would see. Instead, he had noticed everything that she hadn't finished, not the one thing she had. She took a deep breath and sighed. "This is my home, Bishop. You know that."

He nodded. "I do, Katie Mae. You've got a lot of history here. Not all of it good, however."

She couldn't argue with him about that.

"But land is scarce and you're sitting on a property that, if properly maintained, could support an entire family." He paused. "A family that needs the land."

That was when she felt the constriction in her throat and knew she was going to cry. "You want me to sell the farm?" She looked over her shoulder at her father. How could she possibly sell her father's farm? Not only had she been born and raised in this house, so had her father and his father before him! This house and property had been in the Kauffman family for generations.

And then she realized that it would end with her anyway. She was the last of the Kauffmans. Her father had no other children to pass the farm to.

"Mayhaps not sell it," the bishop said slowly. "I was thinking more along the lines of renting it."

"To?"

"A small family in need of land." He tapped his fingers against the tabletop. "Of course, you'd have to move with your father into the *dawdihaus*."

"Why couldn't *they* move into the *dawdihaus*?"

"Because Nathanial Miller has four children, Katie Mae. You can't expect him to live in a two-bedroom *dawdihaus*."

Suddenly, Katie Mae stiffened. Had she actually heard the bishop correctly? He wanted her to rent the farm and the farm house to Nathanial Miller? Was he out of his mind?

Nathanial leaned his head against the wall, taking just a moment to shut his eyes while there was peace and quiet. A rarity that he considered a gift from both God and his children.

Thomas had taken the three younger ones to the pond to go ice skating. Well, more like ice sliding since the children didn't have skates. Little Becky had agreed to go, but only after Thomas promised to hold her hand. Luke and Joseph hadn't needed any prodding, however. No sooner had Thomas mentioned the words *ice skating* than his two brothers had run from the house to race across the field to see if the pond was frozen.

Nathanial had cleaned up after supper: another night of boiled hot dogs and macaroni and cheese that he made from the box, not from scratch. He had begun using paper plates so that he could just throw away everything. But he hadn't quite gotten to the point of using plastic forks and knives. A man had to draw the line somewhere, he figured.

If only Becky were old enough to help out in the kitchen!

Now, Nathanial sat on the porch, wrapped in a heavy coat. His eyes were shut as he listened to the gentle songs of the birds in the trees, singing to each other before the sun set in the sky and they disappeared for the night.

It was cold out, but Nathanial didn't mind it. In fact, he was used to the cold air. It was summer's heat that he couldn't stand. With a nice warm coat (and lots of layers), anybody could keep warm. But during the summer, Nathanial just hated the heavy humidity that made him perspire.

The sound of a buggy pulling down his driveway made Nathanial open his eyes and sit up straight. He couldn't remember the last time he'd had a visitor. Mayhaps August, a year after Martha's death. One of her sisters had stopped over to see how Nathanial was doing. But she hadn't stayed long. Her hired driver had waited in the car, so the visit had been a short one. But she had left a basket full of ripe, juicy tomatoes that had made Nathanial's mouth water.

Without Martha, no one had had time to plant a garden that past spring. All of their produce, or, rather, what little produce they had, needed to be purchased from local food stands or the grocery market.

Which reminded Nathanial that he needed to restock the empty shelves in his pantry.

"Hello there, Nathanial!"

Nathanial raised his hand as Bishop Brenneman emerged from the buggy. He didn't bother to stand up or see if the bishop needed help with tying his horse to the metal ring hanging from the corner of the barn. Instead, he waited and watched from the comfort of the ladder-back chair in which he was seated.

Finally, after what seemed to be an eternity, the bishop made his way down the trodden grass toward the house. His heavy black boots clomped on the porch steps and he assumed the chair next to Nathanial.

"Fine evening," Nathanial said at last. "Don't you think?"

"A bit chilly, to be perfectly frank. I'm surprised to see you sitting outside." The bishop glanced around the yard. "Where are the *kinner*?"

"Checking on the pond. You know how they love skating." He sat up and put his hands on his knees. "So what brings you out this way, Bishop?" Nathanial asked at last. "I presume it ain't just a social call."

For a moment, Nathanial thought that the bishop might smile. "Now why does everyone say that when I arrive at their doors unannounced?" the bishop asked lightly.

"Couldn't tell you. Reckon it depends on whose doorstep you're showing up at."

The bishop's mouth twitched, but, as usual, he didn't break his austere façade. "Now, Nathanial, I've come to talk to you about something very important."

"Oh *ja*?" Nathanial sat up straight. It sounded serious, but he couldn't imagine what was so important that the bishop had traveled to his farm on a chilly Tuesday evening. "And what might that be?"

"Your situation."

His curiosity immediately changed to concern, causing Nathanial to frown. Not *this* again, he thought. "My situation? I wasn't aware that I *had* a situation, Bishop."

"Oh, come on, Nathanial. We both know that things haven't been so good around here since Martha's passing." The bishop leaned forward, his elbows on his knees, and peered at Nathanial. "It's been well over a year and, frankly, it's time for you to move on."

Nathanial clenched his teeth, knowing that the muscles tensed in his jawline. He knew why men cried when they were selected to become a bishop or preacher or even the deacon. Besides the belief that choosing the book with the tiny sliver of paper meant that *God* chose the man for the position, the job came with a lot of responsibility. Caring for a church district, guiding the people to follow God, and seeing people through the seasons of life were just a small part of it. But Nathanial had never known that dictating the length of time to mourn was one of the church leaders' jobs.

"Well now, Bishop, I reckon I'll move on when I feel the time is right," he said slowly, not wanting to lose his temper. Not with the bishop.

The bishop took a deep breath and then cleared his throat. "Nathanial, the bank came to speak to me."

At this news, Nathanial caught his breath. The bank? *Now* he understood why the bishop was there. Inwardly, he felt as if someone had knocked the wind out of him.

"Now I know you asked me to cosign that loan for the mortgage on this place when you first bought it, but I never once thought that you'd neglect to pay your bill." The bishop's brow furrowed and he stared directly at Nathanial in an uncomfortable sort of way. "They're threatening to foreclose, Nathanial, if you can't pay what's due."

Abruptly, Nathanial stood up and walked the length of the porch. When he reached the railing, he leaned against it and stared out at the fields. Just two months ago, he had cut the last of the corn stalks, shocking them in the field so they could dry and he could make fodder to last the winter. But he hadn't made the fodder until just before Thanksgiving last week. Late, of course.

He had planned to spread some manure last Saturday in order to fertilize for next year's crops, but Becky had come down with a cold so he hadn't had time to do it yet.

When had everything gotten so out of control? He had always been meticulous when it came to running his farm.

And, of course, the one thing he had always been bad at was paying the bills. That had been Martha's job. After she died, the envelopes had piled up on her desk, a never-ending sea of white.

At first, he had been too grief-stricken to bother; then he had been too overwhelmed. He hadn't even known where to start. Finally, he just simply gave up and let the pile grow until it covered the entire desktop.

Maybe that hadn't been such a good idea after all, he thought.

"Reckon I should just go meet with them," Nathanial said, his back still to the bishop. "Just pay whatever's due."

"Well, seems that's just the problem, Nathanial. The bank knows what's in your accounts and there just isn't enough."

Nathanial spun around. "What?"

"Why, you owe over twelve months of mortgage, taxes, and there've been fines for non-payment. And you didn't work all your fields, Nathanial. Even I know that. And your corn crop. You waited too long to cut it and sell it. You just didn't earn enough money to pay your outstanding balance." The bishop stood up and took a few steps toward Nathanial. "That's why they came to me. They want me to pay the difference, which even if I could do it, would still leave you with no money for next year."

No money. Hadn't that been the story of his life? The eighth child of twelve, Nathanial hadn't been born to a wealthy farming family. When he married Martha, his father hadn't been able to give him any land. For the first few years, Martha and he had lived in a small apartment over a neighbor's stable. That hadn't been so bad, even after Thomas was born. But when Luke arrived and Martha became pregnant again, the apartment was clearly too small.

He had thought the small farm outside of Shipshewana was manna from heaven, especially when the bishop agreed to cosign for him. And while the crops had been lucrative, at least in the beginning, starting a new farm meant a lot of extra expenses that Nathanial hadn't counted on.

And then Martha had died.

He hadn't bargained for that, either.

Sighing, Nathanial rubbed his face, his fingers pressing against his tired eyes. "What am I supposed to do?" he asked, more to himself than to the bishop. But when the bishop cleared his throat once again, Nathanial realized that *this* was the point of the entire visit. Clearly the bishop had an answer.

"I've given this some thought," the bishop said. "And I have a solution for you, one that helps you as well as someone else in need."

Nathanial was all ears.

"First, you sell the farm."

Nathanial's mouth dropped open. "What?"

"Now hear me out, Nat."

But Nathanial heard nothing else. "Sell the farm?

Give up everything that I've worked so hard for? Why, that's just downright foolishness! All I need is another season, maybe two, and I'll finally be ahead." He brushed past the bishop and stomped the length of the porch. "Nee, selling the farm is just not an option."

"Nathanial, if you don't sell the farm, they are going to take it." The bishop gave him a stern but serious look. "And if they take the farm, you will have nothing."

He almost laughed. "And if I sell the farm, what will I have?"

"Money."

"Money without a home to live or land to farm means nothing." Nathanial scowled. "I have four *kinner* to raise, Bishop. And I can't raise them if I don't have those two things: a home and a farm." He shook his head. "Why, farming's all I know."

"And that leads me to my second point." This time, the bishop's expression softened. "I know a farm to let. You rent the farm, live in the *haus*, and work the land. The only difference is that you don't own it."

Rent a farm? For a moment, Nathanial's mind tried to process this idea. It wasn't often that an Amish farmer rented out his land or house. And yet, it *was* a practical solution. By selling his own farm, he'd have a small nest egg in the bank from what little equity he had in the property. And he wouldn't have as many bills.

The big question was why would an Amish farmer want to rent out his farm? Was it too small? Was the land depleted of nutrients? Was the farmer too old? And, if so, what would happen when he passed away? Would Nathanial find himself homeless once again?

"Where, exactly, would this farm be?" Nathanial asked slowly.

"Why, right here in Shipshewana," the bishop said.

"And who does it belong to?"

For a short moment, the bishop paused. Nathanial waited for the answer, wondering why the bishop had hesitated. And then the bishop spoke and Nathanial knew exactly why.

"Abraham Kauffman," the bishop said. "Your neighbor."

Chapter 2

On Wednesdays, the women from their church district took turns coming to the farm for a few hours so that Katie Mae could drive the buggy to Shipshewana. She liked to visit the Red Barn and pick up some tea from that cute little store on the second floor. And, of course, she loved to peruse the books at J. Farvers Christian Book Store. Picking out a new devotional or seeing what Christian novels were on sale was the highlight of her week. And she always stopped at E & S to replenish any of the bulk goods she needed.

Traveling to Shipshewana on Wednesdays was the *only* break from caring for her father that Katie Mae ever got.

When Bishop Brenneman had first suggested that the women in their church district take turns tending to Abraham on Wednesdays, Katie Mae had made a fuss. She could do it by herself, and she certainly didn't want to be a burden to anyone in the community. After all, they had their own families to care for, too.

But the bishop insisted.

Just as he had insisted on this new arrangement.

The previous night, Katie Mae hadn't slept one wink. Not. One. The thought of Nathanial Miller sleeping in the bedroom that used to be *her* parents' made Katie Mae queasy and angry at the same time. And her own bedroom. Surely one of his children would sleep in her bed. That, too, did not sit well with her.

Now, as she drove the horse and buggy to town, Katie Mae did what she could to avoid passing the Miller farm. Or, rather, what apparently *used* to be the Miller farm.

Why were Nathanial's problems becoming *her* problems, she wondered as she turned left, instead of right, so that she could avoid his place.

Of course, she had known better than to complain to the bishop. But that didn't stop her from thinking the same horrible thoughts as always—that Nathanial Miller was nothing more than an old, boorish galumph. And, to make matters worse, he was just downright rude.

His wife, Martha, had been one of the women who volunteered to sit at the house on Wednesdays. Of course, she had been there less than a handful of times before the accident. And while Katie Mae had found Martha to be delightful company, she had not felt the same about her husband.

Each time Martha had come, Nathanial had dropped her off. They only had one horse and buggy, and both of them appeared to be in poor condition. The buggy was always dirty and the horse was too skinny, and the last few times Nathanial dropped off Martha, it was missing a shoe. And if there was one thing Katie Mae could not tolerate, it was people who didn't take proper care of their animals.

The first time she saw the horse, she thought it was lame. But Nathanial just shot a harsh look at her when she pointed it out. The second time she saw the horse, it was still off and that was when Katie Mae saw that it had thrown a shoe, a shoe that Nathanial hadn't replaced!

This time, it was Katie Mae who cast a dark look his way.

She hadn't seen Martha for two weeks before she returned again. To Katie Mae's horror, the horse still limped and the shoe still hadn't been fixed. And that was when she had words with Nathanial Miller about how poorly he was taking care of his horse.

That was the last time Martha Miller had come to sit with Katie Mae's father.

From behind her, a car honked its horn and Katie Mae started, torn from her thoughts. Automatically, she tensed up as the car revved its engine and passed her. Whoever sat in the passenger seat opened the window and threw a plastic bottle at the horse. Katie Mae could still hear them laughing as they rolled up the window and sped away.

She had almost reached the center of Shipshewana, just a mile from Route 5, but Katie Mae decided to take a short detour. Her nerves were frayed and she needed a minute to calm down. She guided the horse to pull down old US 20, the next road on the right, and she turned into the first driveway. It wasn't a farmhouse but a small Englische house that had been converted into an Amish home. With the electrical wires removed and a small shed put onto the back for the horse, it was just perfect for a non-farming Amish family.

And that was where her friend Linda lived with her husband and three children.

Katie Mae put a halter over the horse's bridle and tied him to the hitching rail before she hurried toward the front door.

She knocked twice before opening the door and poking her head into the kitchen. A wave of warmth hit her, the air scented with freshly baked bread. "Linda? You home?"

A voice called from the cellar and Katie Mae walked inside the house, pausing to remove her black sneakers (for Linda was fastidious that no one trek dirt onto her floors), and hurried over to the basement door.

"You down there, Linda?"

A muffled voice responded.

"You need any help then?"

But there was no need for Linda to answer. She emerged at the bottom of the stairs and began to ascend, a big box of canned goods in her arms.

"Well, hello there, Katie Mae! It's right *gut* to see you out and about! Must be Wednesday, ja?" Linda gave her a friendly smile. "Let me just set this down and we can visit a spell."

Katie Mae watched as Linda carried the box to the kitchen counter and set it down on the Formica top. Unlike most farmhouses, Linda's house had a small kitchen with not a lot of storage space, so most of her canned goods had to be stored in the basement. It was only a three-bedroom ranch house, so her husband, John David, had converted the attic into two more bedrooms. During the summer it was too hot for the children to sleep up there so they often slept in the basement or, if the weather permitted, outside in tents. But during the winter months, the house suited them just fine.

"There! Now we can visit a spell," Linda said cheerfully as she wiped her hands on her apron and sat down at the kitchen table. "Everything okay with your *daed*?"

Katie Mae nodded. "Oh ja, he's right as rain."

Linda raised an eyebrow and gave her one of her knowing looks.

"Well, as right as his rain gets, I reckon," Katie Mae added.

"You poor girl," Linda said. "I often forget what a burden you bear, Katie Mae. I need to come over and help you some more with your *daed*."

Katie Mae held up her hands, palms toward Linda. *"Nee, nee!* That's not why I stopped in. Daed and I are doing just fine."

Another look.

Katie Mae hung her head and sighed. "Or as fine as our fine gets, I reckon."

Linda gave her a serious look. "What's going on, Katie Mae?"

Quickly, Katie Mae updated her about the bishop's visit yesterday. When she told Linda about how the bishop wanted her to move into the *dawdihaus* so that Nathanial Miller—of all people!—could move into the main house, she stopped talking and waited for her friend's reaction.

But there was none.

"Aren't you going to say something, Linda?" Katie Mae prodded.

"About?"

Katie Mae tossed her hands into the air. "That ridiculous proposal! I mean, he can't really be serious?"

Linda stuck out her lower lip and made a quizzical face. "Why ever not? I happen to think that's a right *gut* idea. Seems logical that two families in need help each other out."

Exasperated, Katie Mae slumped in her chair. "I can't believe you support this idea. Why, I thought for sure and certain you'd be telling me to say no."

"No."

Katie Mae rolled her eyes. "That's not what I mean and you know it."

"What's so bad about Nathanial Miller anyway?" Linda asked. "Seems to me that he's a hard worker, and I know he was a devoted husband to Martha. Why, he's been mourning longer than any other man I know with so many small *kinner*."

To say that she was shocked was an understatement. Katie Mae simply couldn't believe what she was hearing. "I told you about that time he came over and his horse was lame, *ja?* And how four weeks later, that same horse was still lame. What kind of man does that to his horse?"

Linda laughed. "Practically every man I know if they only have one horse and need to go somewhere!"

But Katie Mae wasn't about to change her mind. She crossed her arms over her chest. "That's animal abuse."

"Oh, please!" Linda waved her hand dismissively.

"Why, just consider the fact that Martha was killed in a buggy accident," Katie Mae added. "That horse didn't make it through an intersection quick enough and, well, I think we both know why. Nathanial Miller just as well as killed his own *fraa* by not taking care of his horse!"

At this comment, Linda gasped. "Katie Mae Kauffman! That's about the most unkind thing I have ever heard you say."

"It's true. And while I might be saying it, you know that plenty of other folks are thinking it."

From Linda's expression, it was clear that she was less than impressed with Katie Mae's opinion on the matter. "Now you listen to me, Katie Mae. That man's *fraa* died over a year ago and whatever you think about the accident, it was just that: an accident. You need to clear your head of such thoughts and pray for forgiveness! Why, with our church having just held council and communion, I'm surprised at you."

The harshness of Linda's words struck Katie Mae and, for a moment, she regretted not only having spoken her mind but having come to visit her friend at all. She had stopped by for support, not a scolding.

"Well, I best get going then," Katie Mae said, standing up and hurrying to the door. "Gotta run my errands."

Linda stared after her. "You think about what I said, Katie Mae. A little humility on your part might take you a lot further than that haughtiness you're carrying on your shoulders."

Pretending that she hadn't heard her, Katie Mae ran down the steps and crossed the front yard. As quick as she could, she untied her horse and climbed into the buggy.

Haughtiness, my big toe, she thought as she pulled on the reins, clicking her tongue to guide the horse backward. *She just doesn't know that man the way I do.*

Nathanial knew he needed to take advantage of the *kinner* being in school to get away from the farm and run a few errands.

The truth was, now that the idea of selling the farm was planted in his mind, he didn't want to be there anymore. There were too many memories, both good and bad. If he had to leave, he wanted to take the Band-Aid approach: just tear it off. The pain might be more intense at first, but it would stop hurting much faster.

But to move to the Kauffmans' farm?

He shuddered at the thought. Why, that Kauffman girl was just downright undisciplined! Speaking so openly and telling him that he wasn't being a good steward of God's earth? Just because his horse had thrown a shoe? Who did she think she was?

He felt his blood pressure begin to rise as he remembered the last time he had taken Martha to help Katie Mae with her father. It had taken all of his restraint to keep from responding when Katie Mae lashed out at him about his horse being lame.

As if he didn't *know* the horse was lame!

But what did a sassy, spoiled girl like Katie Mae know about a man in financial straits? Even though her father was ailing and unable to manage the farm, he had enough money stored up so that she didn't need to worry about losing the roof over her head or putting food in her belly.

Despite being in the buggy alone, Nathanial growled. How could the bishop think that renting the farmhouse from Abraham Kauffman was even remotely a good idea? Especially with that girl staying on, living in the *dawdihaus*!

Oh, Nathanial knew that it was a terrible idea, but only because of *her*. However, putting Katie Mae aside, it *was* a good solution. And if Katie Mae could help him with the *kinner*, well, that solved just one more problem.

Of course, the bishop hadn't said anything about Katie Mae helping with his children. Nathanial was figuring that he'd be able to cajole her into doing it. Wasn't that what women wanted? To tend to children?

He stopped outside of the store and slid open the door to the buggy. Carefully, he got out and quickly tied up the horse to the hitching rail.

Of all the chores he had to do, shopping was the one he dreaded the most. People always seemed to stop and want to talk. But Nathanial didn't have time to talk. That was saved for every other Sunday after worship.

He tilted his hat a bit so that it covered his eyes as he entered the store.

"Why, Nathanial Miller!"

Upon hearing his name, Nathanial cringed.

"Haven't seen hide nor hair of you in almost a month!"

He had no choice but to glance up and force a smile

for the elderly woman at the cash register. "How you been, Edina?"

"Why, I've been just fine, *danke*! But what about you?" She plastered a fake scowl on her face as she pressed her hands against her hips. "You shopping at some other store, or are your *kinner* eating grain and hay like your herd of cows?"

This was the reason he hated shopping. What sort of ridiculous question was that anyway? "Just been busy, Edina." He reached for one of the narrow carts and pulled it toward him. "But I can assure you that no one's starving on my farm."

My farm. Those words rang in his ears. How much longer would it be *his* farm anyway? He hurried away from Edina as fast as he could without looking as if he were eager to escape her wagging tongue. As he headed down one aisle, he stopped to look over some of the fresh produce.

And that was when someone ran into his cart, causing it to run over his foot.

"Hey now! You watch where you're going!" he snapped as he turned to face the perpetrator.

For a moment, they just stared at each other.

Katie Mae looked thinner than he remembered, her dark eyes staring at him from behind dark circles. And her cheekbones practically jutted out of her face. The pale pink dress she wore drained her of color, and the ribbons on her stiff prayer *kapp* were wrinkled.

Frankly, she looked a mess.

"I . . . I'm sorry, Nathanial," Katie Mae managed to say. "I didn't see you there."

He studied her, wondering if the bishop had already told her the plan. He hadn't thought to ask that question of Bishop Brenneman, so Nathanial wasn't certain if he should say anything to Katie Mae.

But he remembered what the bishop had told him about her. That her father was suffering and she was barely holding everything together. Despite his distaste for the woman, if his future hinged on her father's farm, he figured that he'd better forgive, forget, and forge ahead.

"Aw, that's okay, Katie Mae. You just startled me."

Her eyes widened, as if she were surprised by his response.

"Bishop stopped by yesterday," he heard himself say.

"*Ja,* he stopped by my place, too."

Aha, Nathanial thought. So the bishop *had* approached her. "Reckon he done told you the same thing he told me."

She pursed her lips and stared at him, a thoughtful look in her eyes. "*Ja,* he told me how you're in a bad way."

"And I know—" Abruptly, he stopped talking. What had she just said? "Now hold on there, Katie Mae. I'm not in a bad way. I can take care of my family right fine."

"Your farm, you mean," she corrected sharply. "But not your family, I hear."

"Now you listen to—"

She interrupted him. "*Nee,* you listen to me. I'm doing you a favor letting you rent the farm. I can't imagine a grown man on the brink of being homeless." She scowled and clucked her tongue disapprovingly. "That's just shameful, Nathanial Miller."

"Shameful?" His eyes widened. Had she really just said that to him? "Seems to me that you're the one needing some help, Katie Mae Kauffman. Why, the bishop said the barn's ready to fall down with the next breath of winter wind coming across that field!"

She gasped.

"And your fencing has more holes in it than a cheese grater! It's a wonder your remaining herd hasn't wandered into the road and gotten killed!"

He watched as Katie Mae's mouth twisted, her lips pressed together, and the muscles twitched in her cheeks. She looked like she wanted to blurt out something, to respond to his harsh words.

But, to his surprise, she remained silent.

His gaze wandered over her shoulder and he noticed that an older woman stood at the end of the aisle, observing the heated exchange between the two of them. From that distance, he couldn't quite make out who the woman was, but from the way she stood there, her mouth opened in a big O, he knew that she had overheard much of the conversation.

Nathanial took a deep breath and tried to calm down. It wouldn't do him any good to irritate Katie Mae into rescinding her offer. Maybe she was right. Just a little. He *did* need her help.

"I'm sorry, Katie Mae," he mumbled.

"Excuse me?" She leaned closer to him. "I don't think I heard you proper, Nathanial Miller. Did you just apologize to me?"

He clenched his teeth. Why did she have to be so difficult all the time? "I said I'm sorry. Don't make me say it again."

From the pleased look on her face, he figured he wouldn't be challenged on that one.

Lowering his voice, he said, "I reckon we both need each other right about now and while we might not like it, that's just the way God planned it. Might as well be neighborly about it, *ja?*"

Katie Mae pursed her lips and gave him a good once-over with her eyes. Oh, he knew that she didn't care for him and, frankly, the feeling was reciprocated. She was a mouthy little gal and Nathanial had never liked opinionated women.

"*Ja,* I reckon you're right," she replied at last, the sound of concession in her voice. "I can't tend the farm if I have to care for my *daed.*"

"Mayhaps I could stop by on Saturday to discuss the particulars with Abraham," he said.

She gave him a strange look, but merely nodded her head.

"All right then." He glanced at his empty cart. "So it's settled."

"I guess so."

But she didn't move.

"I need to pass you, Katie Mae," he said, a scowl returning to his face.

"And I need to pass *you,*" she snapped back.

Sighing, Nathanial took a step to the left and tugged at the cart so that she could move past him. When she disappeared into the next aisle, he shook his head and continued on his way, ignoring the amused face of the woman who had been watching. As he approached her, he nodded his head, shocked to realize that it was none other than Dorothy Brenneman, the wife of the bishop.

Inwardly, Nathanial groaned. The bishop would be hearing all about the altercation between Nathanial and Katie Mae, for sure and certain.

Chapter 3

On Saturday morning, Katie Mae sat on the porch, enjoying the midday sun. Her father sat beside her, a heavy quilt covering his lap, even though it wasn't too cold, despite the fact that it was early December. She always tried to ensure that her father had at least an hour of fresh air every day. Even when it was cold out, with a hat, scarf, and heavy quilt, her father remained warm enough. The fresh air always gave him rosy cheeks and a sparkle in his aging eyes.

Katie Mae was crocheting a baby blanket for one of the young women who lived nearby. She was expecting her baby before Christmas and Katie Mae wanted to have the blanket ready in advance. Her fingers moved in a swift rhythm as she twisted the crochet hook and pulled the yarn through little loops. All the while she talked with her father.

"So Nathanial Miller's coming by to visit today," she said casually. "Do you remember when the bishop came over the other day?" She hesitated, as if expecting her father to answer. "Bishop thinks that we should rent the farm to Nathanial."

Another pause.

No response.

She looked up at her father and smiled. "Not that it would be forever, of course. Just until you get well, Daed."

Her father just stared at her, a blank and vacant expression on his face.

Sometimes she wondered if he heard her. And if he did hear her, did he understand her? For over eighteen months, Katie Mae had been caring for her father at home. And during that time, she always talked to him as if they were in the middle of a conversation. She knew that it made some people uncomfortable. Even when Katie Mae managed to take her father to worship service, many people avoided Abraham. They just didn't know how to act around him.

But sometimes she couldn't go to worship. It was too hard to get her father into a buggy. So she could only attend when it was within walking distance on days that the weather suited.

She missed going to worship on a regular basis. She loved singing the hymns and listening to the preachers. Most of all, she loved the fellowship time. Whenever she was able to attend, Katie Mae was quick to volunteer her help setting up the tables, serving the food, and washing the plates. She loved talking to the other women and hearing the latest gossip about which young woman was walking out with which young man.

Long ago, Katie Mae had given up any idea of courting with a young man. First her mother had been so ill with the cancer. For several years, from the time she turned fifteen until she turned nineteen, Katie Mae had helped her father with her mother's care. And then, just one year after she passed away, her father suffered his stroke. Now Katie Mae was almost twenty-two and most of the young men she would have considered courting were already married.

Unless she settled for a widower, Katie Mae knew she'd wind up an old *maedal*. And, to be perfectly honest, she didn't mind that one bit. The last thing she wanted was to marry someone who had loved another woman before her.

"So the bishop thinks we should rent the farm to Nathanial," she repeated to her father. "While I have to admit, Daed, that I'm not too fond of Nathanial, it sure would be nice to have the farm fixed up and crops growing again, don't you think?" She waited a few seconds before continuing. "The only problem is he has all those *kinner* and I can't stomach the idea of them running all over the place and making a bunch of noise."

Katie Mae took a deep breath and sighed.

"I sure do like the quiet here," she said softly. "Don't you, Daed?"

No sooner had she said those words than she heard the sound of a buggy pulling down the lane.

"Oh help," she muttered as she set down her crocheting. "I reckon that's Nathanial already."

She waited until he had parked the buggy and tied up the horse. Katie Mae stood on the edge of the porch and watched, a heaviness filling her as she saw the passenger door slide open and four children pile out. Three boys and one girl. They stood by the buggy and stared at her, their eyes big and frightened. What on earth had Nathanial told them about her?

Nathanial walked over to the porch, but he didn't ascend the two steps. "Good day, Abraham," he said to her father. "Katie Mae."

"Go on and look around then," she said sharply. "Reckon you don't need me to give you a tour."

"Well, I'm fine, *danke* for asking," Nathanial quipped.

Oh, she had no time for such pleasantries. Just seeing his buggy in their driveway made her feel angry all over again.

She scooped up her yarn and walked over to her father's wheelchair. "I'll be inside," she said sharply. "Too cool out here for Daed."

Nathanial raised an eyebrow as he watched her back the wheelchair to the entrance and, with expert precision, open the door, hold it with her foot, and pull the chair inside.

She shut the door behind herself and stood there, her lips pressed together and her heart racing. *How could this be happening?* she wondered. Everything in her life had gone from bad to worse to even worse than that! Katie Mae didn't want to question God's plan for her, but she sure could use a little break in her long string of sorrowful events.

After settling her father in the kitchen, Katie Mae put a kettle of water onto the stove. She wanted to have a nice warm cup of peppermint tea to help calm her nerves.

" 'Cuse me," a little voice said from behind her.

Katie Mae started and spun around, her hand pressing against the base of her throat. "Oh! My, you scared me!" She made a face at the little girl. "You shouldn't be sneaking up on people like that."

"I need the ba*ff*-room please."

Katie Mae frowned. The little girl was five years old, maybe six. But she spoke with a little lisp that made her sound a lot younger. "You mean the *bath*-room," Katie Mae said, enunciating the word. "It's over there." She pointed to a door near the staircase. "And make certain you wash your hands before you come out."

Irritated, she turned toward the stove, tapping her foot as she waited for the steam to rise from the kettle.

She certainly hoped that Nathanial wasn't expecting *her* to watch his *kinner* while he looked around the farm. She had much more important things to do, like caring for her father.

Nathanial took a long, deep breath as his eyes adjusted to the dark in the dairy barn. While it was mostly empty, for the Kauffmans only kept a small herd of cows, it was dark, damp, and disgusting. The windows were dirty and broken. Cobwebs clung to the walls and hung from the ceiling. And the stench! Hadn't anyone cleaned the unused stall line? Old, dried-up and decaying manure lay where it had fallen and, from the looks of it, that had been quite some time ago.

There was more manure, fresher, near one stall line, and Nathanial suspected that was the area that Katie Mae used to milk her father's cows twice a day.

He wandered toward the back of the dairy barn and saw that the cooling unit looked fairly new. That surprised him. Her father must have gotten it shortly before he'd had his stroke. At least one thing appeared to be in good shape.

"Hey, Daed!"

Nathanial looked up as his son Thomas ran into the barn, his two younger brothers behind him.

"This place is twice as large as our farm, and guess what?"

Nathanial pursed his lips, not wanting to know the answer to his son's question. Surely it would be just one more reminder that he had failed to keep his own farm and had to lease one from the Kauffmans in order to survive.

"There's a big ole pond with a stream feeding it in the back of the rear pasture!"

"You don't say," Nathanial managed to reply. "Might be some good fishing there in the spring."

Of course, Nathanial hoped he wouldn't still be there in the spring. If he could save a little money, maybe he could find a new farm in Colorado or Tennessee. He had a few distant cousins who had moved to new Amish communities in those locations. And, despite being far away, land was less expensive there than in Indiana.

All Nathanial needed was to buy some time to get his life—and finances—back in order.

Suddenly, he realized that only three children stood before him. "Where's your *schweister*?" Nathanial asked.

"Don't rightly know," Luke replied with a small shrug.

"Well, I reckon we best go find her." Nathanial placed his hand on Luke's shoulder. "She didn't go with you to the pond, did she now?"

"*Nee,* Daed. Haven't seen hide nor hair of her since we done arrived."

For a split second, Nathanial felt a wave of panic. He tried to hide it from the boys as he looked around, searching for a glimpse of a little girl in a navy-blue dress. But there was no sign of her. Anywhere.

"Mayhaps she went inside," Thomas said. "She was doing her pee-pee dance when we got here."

Nathanial frowned at his son but began to move in the direction of the house. He felt the presence of his three sons behind him. The boys seemed more curious than concerned about their sister's whereabouts. Nathanial, however, could only pray that she had wandered into the house.

As soon as he opened the porch door, his prayers were answered. He could hear Becky's small voice with her little lisp telling stories to whoever might (or might not!) be listening. He breathed a sigh of relief as he entered the kitchen.

His eyes adjusted to the darkness inside and immediately, he stopped walking. He felt one of his boys bump into him from behind.

"Sorry, Daed," Luke mumbled. It was always Luke, trailing so close behind. If he wasn't morphing into Nathanial's shadow, he was morphing into Thomas's.

"*Wie gehts*?" Nathaniel asked as he tried to assess the situation in the kitchen.

Katie Mae stood with her back against the counter and a cup of tea in her hands. The expression on her face would have made Nathanial laugh if it had been anyone else but her. Instead, he remained serious as he realized that the look of complete vexation was caused by the fact that his daughter, Becky, was holding on to Katie Mae's dress and swaying from side to side as she chitter-chattered away.

". . . And my *dae-th saths* we be moving here and I'm gettin' my own *beth*-room and maybe you could make me cookies for *af*-ter school and read me *'th*ories at night like my *mamm* us*th* to do and . . ."

Yes, that was definitely a look of irritation on Katie Mae's face. Apparently *she* didn't find Becky's nonstop one-way dialogue as amusing as Nathanial usually did.

He crossed the room in three easy strides and scooped his daughter into his arm. As Becky squealed in delight, wrapping her arms around his neck, Nathanial glanced at Katie Mae.

"*That* is not part of the arrangement," she said in a low voice and with a stern look on her face.

Genuinely perplexed at her comment, Nathanial questioned her. "What isn't?"

Katie Mae pointed with her finger at Becky and wiggled it. "I like my peace and quiet, Nathanial Miller. I may have to move to the *dawdihaus,* but I will not sacrifice my privacy."

Nathanial wanted to respond, to tell her that she sounded like a cranky old spinster who disliked small children. To him, Becky was adorable with her cherubic cheeks and big brown eyes. Clearly Katie Mae did not think so.

"Fine," he said through clenched teeth.

"And don't be thinking I'll be watching your *kinner* if you need to go somewhere."

He pressed his lips together. "I'd never dream of asking you," he said, realizing that it was the truth. He wouldn't want his children subjected to her crankiness, that was for sure and certain.

"Gut!"

She said that one word with such gusto that Nathanial wondered if Katie Mae were merely trying to establish boundaries or if she truly was just a cantankerous old maid in a young woman's body. If she was really so grouchy and insistent on being in control, it was no wonder that she had never married!

"When will you be moving your things in?"

Nathanial blinked, her words yanking him away from his thoughts. He set Becky down on the ground and gestured for Thomas to take the young ones outside. *Better to limit their exposure to Katie Mae,* he thought.

After the door shut behind them, Nathanial returned his attention to Katie Mae. "Reckon I could bring the cows over by the weekend. Will need to clean out that dairy barn first, though. And fix some of that fencing."

A muscle in her cheek twitched.

"How long will you need to move into the *dawdihaus*?"

"Not long. Mostly moving just clothing and kitchen

stuff." She paused as if thinking. "And the things being stored in the basement. Suppose I could just leave them there. Won't need much until spring."

That was fine by Nathanial because he knew that he'd be long gone by that time.

"All right then," Nathanial said, squaring his shoulders. "I'll be over during the week to start fixing up some things and, once I move over the cows, I can bring over the household items. Mayhaps by Monday next we'll all move over. Want to be settled in before Christmas."

Again, that muscle in her face twitched. He wondered what *that* meant.

"If you need any help moving heavier things—"

"*Nee,* but *danke*," Katie Mae snapped. "I can handle it all myself." She glanced over at her father. "Right, Daed?"

Nathanial followed her gaze to where Abraham sat in his chair. He had almost forgotten that Katie Mae's father was even in the room. In that moment when he heard Katie Mae talk to her father, pausing just long enough as if he might respond, Nathanial saw her in a different light. What a burden for a young woman to shoulder! Surely she was no more than twenty years old and left with so much responsibility? How had she managed to keep it all together as well as she had and for so long?

His burdens had begun at thirty-two. At least he had the happy memories of those years with Martha.

"*Ja,* well, if you change your mind, you only have to ask," he offered as he moved toward the door. "Have a pleasant rest of the day, Katie Mae." He glanced at her father. "You, too, Abraham." And with that, he slipped out the door, leaving the young woman alone to deal with her sorrowful situation as he needed to address his own.

Chapter 4

The kitchen of the *dawdihaus* was almost a third of the size that she was used to. It made the idea of cooking less exciting, that was for certain. Katie Mae had barely been able to fit all of her pots and pans in the cabinets. And her only pantry barely held any of her canned goods. She had to store the rest in boxes on the back porch, which was, frankly, too small for much more than that anyway.

Their kitchen table had been too large for the *dawdihaus* so she had left it next door for that horrible Nathanial to use. She just hoped his children didn't scratch it up, because it had been her grandmother's and Katie Mae didn't want it ruined. Right now, she only had a small folding table for serving her father his evening meal.

Katie Mae sighed and glanced at the little gathering area. While she didn't want to fool herself into thinking that she'd ever have need for a larger space to entertain guests, she knew that she couldn't even if she wanted to. There was only room for the recliner, the rocker, and a small end table.

That was it.

There was one more small room on the first floor, located to the side of the kitchen. The staircase ran down alongside it and there was a partition that could be opened or closed to turn the room into a bedroom. That was where Katie Mae had set up the hospital bed for her father. She would reside on the second floor in the larger of the two bedrooms, although even that was half the size of the room she used to have. The only good thing about the smaller house was that it was easier to keep warm and much less drafty than the larger, main house.

Still, she felt confined by the tight quarters.

"Oh help," she muttered.

From outside, she could hear the now-too-familiar noise of a hammer banging at something or another. Scowling, Katie Mae walked over to the window and peered outside.

Ever since Monday, Nathanial had been a constant presence in the barn. He kept banging away. At what, she had no idea. The only good thing about him being at the farm was that he had taken on the responsibility of milking her father's cows. But she was getting tired of the constant pounding.

"Daed, if that's bothering you, just let me know." She turned around and looked toward the hospital bed. He was sleeping, completely not bothered by the noise.

Sighing, Katie Mae moved over to the folding table and sat down, eager to make her list of items that she needed from the store. She had run out of yarn for the baby blanket so that was definitely on the list. And she'd spilt a bag of flour so she would need to make a quick stop at the natural food store. Again. And she also needed more rennet to make some cheese. She jotted it down on the piece of paper so that she wouldn't forget.

Someone knocked at the door and Katie Mae glanced up at the clock. Was it that time already?

"You in here, Katie Mae?"

"*Ja*, in the kitchen." She looked at the door and greeted Mary Esh with a smile. "I don't know where the morning has gone! Can't believe it's ten o'clock already!"

The young woman walked into the house and removed her black shawl. "Getting awful chilly out there. You have your heater ready?"

"*Ach!*" She snapped her fingers. "I almost forgot that I need more propane!" Quickly she scribbled that down on her list. "*Danke*, Mary. I don't mind the cold so much, but"—she glanced at her father—"Daed can't handle it."

Mary walked over and stole a quick peek at Abraham. "Why, he's sleeping like a newborn baby!" She returned to where Katie Mae was sitting. "And it looks like you're just settled right in here."

Katie Mae glanced around and made a little noise from the side of her mouth. "*Ja*, reckon we are. I think Daed likes his new bed."

"Where did you find it?"

"The bishop's nephew had it and brought it over on Monday evening. I like the railings on the side so I don't have to fret about Daed rolling off the bed. And the head can be raised, which is much nicer for him than those old lumpy pillows I was using."

The truth was that Katie Mae didn't want to admit that her father seemed to be sleeping more and she wasn't certain if that was a good thing. He couldn't really communicate with her except for a few grunts and groans from time to time. Even though Katie Mae thought that mayhaps he was trying to tell her something, she suspected he might not be saying anything at all.

But she had noticed that he seemed to respond better to sitting in his wheelchair by the windows. They were larger than the ones in the kitchen of the main house and they overlooked the fields. Her father appeared to enjoy staring out the window, especially when he could watch Nathanial working on the outbuildings.

So maybe things *were* getting better.

"Well, I know it's not my place to say," Mary started slowly, "but I think that this is a right *gut* arrangement. You were taking on too much, Katie Mae, if I do say so myself."

Katie Mae wished she *wouldn't* say so herself.

But Mary continued. "You're just one young woman. You can't handle the farm and your father. It's just too much."

Katie Mae bit her tongue. The last thing she wanted to hear was *that*.

"Well now, you best get going then," Mary said, and set down her black purse on the table. "Thought I'd read a spell. I enjoy reading to your *daed* and I brought my new devotional with me." She held up a book and Katie Mae squinted to read the cover. "Got it at the Red Barn," Mary added.

Katie Mae wondered if she might have time to stop by to pick up her *own* copy of that book.

"*Danke*, Mary," Katie Mae said before hurrying over to her father. She leaned down and peered into his face. "Daed, Mary Esh is here and she'll be here to help you while I go run some errands." She waited for a few seconds as if she expected him to respond. Only then did she stand up and walk toward the door. "Best go harness the horse then." She gave Mary one last smile before hurrying out the door.

* * *

Nathanial heard the sound of a horse leaving its stall. He peered around the side of the hay room and saw Katie Mae leading the horse outside. It already had its harness on.

He had forgotten that today was Wednesday, the day someone from the church came to sit with Abraham. Most likely, Katie Mae was hitching up the horse in order to drive into town.

He hurried to join up with her in the driveway.

"Heading to town then, are you now?"

She peered over the horse's flank and gave him an odd look as if to say, *What does it look like I'm doing?*

Nathanial gave her a sheepish smile. "Right." He stepped forward to help her attach the traces to the trace hooks. "I could use a few things from Yoders' Hardware. Think you might be passing near it?"

Katie Mae stopped working and squinted her eyes. "It's right on Van Buren. Of course I'm passing near it."

"If I gave you some money, might you stop there for me?"

She sighed and tugged the trace to make it reach the hook. "What do you need?"

Nathanial stood back and watched as Katie Mae grabbed the reins and tossed them through the open window. She moved fast, hitching that horse to the buggy. He was impressed with how capable she was with the animal. "Let's see. I need a new box of nails so I can fix the broken boards in the horse stalls—"

"Is that it?"

He ignored her interruption. "And I noticed the handle of your pitchfork is broken. I need a new one of those."

"Anything else?"

He could tell that she was growing impatient by the way she tapped the toe of her shoe on the gravel. "Rat poison, a new broom, four metal eyehooks, four water buckets, and one tin can to store the horses' grain. The plastic one you have is cracked. Grain's pouring out and the rats are having a field day."

Katie Mae tossed her hands in the air. "I can't remember all of that!"

Was she really going to be that difficult? Nathanial had so much to do in order to fix up the barn and dairy before he could move his livestock to the farm. The last thing he needed was to be pulled from his work to run errands. "It's not that much to pick up."

"Well, it sure seems like it is!"

He frowned. Something about her short temper irritated him. Here he was trying to make improvements to her father's farm and she was giving him a hard time? She should have been appreciative of his efforts, especially since he wasn't just providing the labor but the materials, too. The defiant expression on her face didn't help matters much. That was when he decided that he needed to teach her a lesson.

"Then I'll just ride along with you," he said, forcing himself to sound cheerful and upbeat as if it was the most pleasant notion in the world, when in reality riding with Katie Mae would be just as torturous for him as it would be for her. But knowing that she would suffer in his presence took some of the sting out of the ointment.

In fact, when her mouth opened and her eyes widened, Nathanial realized that he might have just hit upon something. Perhaps fighting fire with fire was not the way to get under her skin. Kindness and good cheer might be the route to go.

He gave her a broad smile and gestured for her to get into the buggy. "Go on and get in then, Katie Mae. I'll even let you drive."

She looked stunned and, for once, she was completely speechless. Nathanial almost chuckled at the expression on her face. Instead, he held the horse's head and waited, patiently, for her to get into the black buggy.

To his surprise, she did.

After she settled in, Nathanial climbed into the buggy beside her. The tight space in the front of the vehicle made his arm touch hers. She tried to move farther away from him as she took the reins and slapped them on the horse's back, urging it to set out. The buggy lurched forward, the metal wheels grinding the gravel beneath them. When it swayed as she turned it onto the main road, Katie Mae bumped against him and quickly righted herself.

He smiled and stared straight ahead, making certain that no cars were approaching that might spook the horse. "Careful now," he said, pointing to a speeding car.

"I know how to drive a horse!" she snapped, but he noticed that she slowed down, urging the horse over to the side of the road just a little.

Nathanial took advantage of her focus on driving to look at her, *really* look at her as if for the first time.

He hadn't realized how young she was. Probably twenty. Maybe twenty-two. And she had been saddled with so much responsibility. For a moment, he felt sorry for her.

Nathanial wondered why her parents hadn't had more children. He had never thought to ask anyone, not that it was any of his business. But it was unusual for a farmer to have only one child. Surely there had been a medical issue. It dawned on him that, like him, Katie Mae's life had just been upended, too. First her mother had died, then her father had had the stroke, and now she'd had to move into the *dawdihaus*. Perhaps her tendency toward irritability was a learned behavior, a way to protect herself from more emotional injury.

"*Danke*, Katie Mae." The words slipped out before he knew what he was saying.

"For what?" Her voice sounded hostile rather than truly inquisitive.

"For everything, I reckon."

From the corner of his eye, he caught a glimpse of her looking at him. It was almost as if she were sizing him up to see whether or not he was being sincere. *Had he caught her off guard?* he wondered.

But just as quickly, that curious expression vanished from her face. "Hmmph." She refocused her attention on the road, and they traveled the rest of the way in silence.

Chapter 5

Katie Mae stood in the aisle at Yoders' Hardware store, by the tools section. With her arms crossed over her chest, she sighed for the third time in as many minutes. What on earth was he looking for now? she wondered. He had a shopping cart full of items, none of which he had mentioned needing when he'd originally asked her to pick up a few things. She made a mental note that, should he ever again ask her to pick up a few things, her answer should always be a loud, resounding *"Ja!"*

Because his *few* things had multiplied into a few *too many* things!

"This is never going to fit into the buggy," she complained.

"I heard you say that the first time."

If it were humanly possible, there would be steam coming out of her ears.

"Nathanial, honestly." She pressed her lips together and fumed. "I only have a limited amount of time. Mary Esh needs to get home in time for her *kinner*. They return from school by two-thirty."

Nathanial didn't even look remotely concerned. "Trust me, we'll be home in plenty of time."

When he said that, Katie Mae froze. *Home?* Had he just called her father's farm home? He hadn't even moved in yet and he was calling it that?

A man walked around the corner and practically bumped right into Nathanial. "Excuse me there." The man looked up, peering at Nathanial from behind thick, oval glasses. His tired brown eyes brightened at once. "Why, Nathanial Miller!" He smiled, exposing his yellow teeth, two of which were missing. With his wiry, gray beard and weathered face, he looked far older than Katie Mae imagined he was.

Nathanial greeted him with a firm handshake and a friendly smile. "John Raber! It's right *gut* to see you!"

The man returned the greeting as he glanced from Nathanial to Katie Mae. There was a curious expression on his face as he waited for an introduction.

For a moment, Nathanial seemed to shuffle his feet as if uncertain how to introduce her. "Uh, John, this is Katie Mae Kauffman," he said, enunciating her last name as if to assure his elderly friend that she was unrelated to him. "Katie Mae, this is John Raber. He's an old friend of my family."

She smiled at the man, but it was forced. She had never seen this man before and she didn't particularly want to get to know him. Not when she had errands to run and Nathanial was taking far too long with his hardware store stop. She stood by Nathanial, impatiently waiting as he caught up with this "old friend" of his family.

"I'll be moving the *kinner* to the Kauffmans' farm," she heard Nathanial say. "Renting the main house and working the fields."

She sighed and began tapping her toe against the floor.

"You don't say?" John replied.

"Her *daed*'s had a stroke. Can't work the farm no more."

Katie Mae cringed. Was that what Nathanial thought? That he was there because her father had had a stroke? Hmmph! She wondered that Nathanial didn't tell the truth, how he was losing his farm!

She stopped listening to the rest of their conversation, which had turned to crops and farming. Her eyes wandered around the store. She had so much to do and hadn't counted on this unplanned trip to the hardware store. Nor had she counted on this spontaneous reunion between Nathanial and John Raber! Irritated, she sighed and shifted her weight from one foot to the other. Why, they were almost as bad as two old women meeting up in the fabric store and sharing stories about who was making quilts for whom!

But then John made a comment that caught her attention.

"I still can't thank you enough, Nathanial, for your help when my son took ill. After all your own troubles, why! To think you came out to help him harvest his crops." John Raber gave a click of his tongue. "You saved my son's farm from ruin. Without that crop, he'd have been in deep financial trouble."

Katie Mae straightened her back and looked pointedly at Nathanial. From the sounds of it, Nathanial had helped out John's son *after* Martha had died. Did that mean that Nathanial helped John's son while still mourning the loss of his wife? Or had Nathanial helped John Raber's son during this past harvest? Regardless, if Nathanial had dropped everything to help John Raber's son, did that mean that he had neglected his own crops? Katie Mae had heard a whisper about him missing the market window to sell his corn at the ideal time. Had he ignored his own crops in order to help another man with his? If so, was *that* the reason why he was losing his farm? While he continued talking with his friend, she studied Nathanial. It dawned on her that she knew very little about him. She couldn't help but wonder what sort of man would lose everything he had in order to help someone else. Shouldn't he have taken care of his own family's needs before worrying about someone else's?

Suddenly, a verse from Galatians popped into her head: *Carry each other's burdens, and in this way you fulfill the law of Christ.*

She caught her breath, her eyes filled with a new admiration for Nathanial Miller. She was more than certain that she had found the reason for the Miller family's financial hardship. From what little she *did* know about Nathanial, he was a hard worker. But now she suspected that he had put others' needs before his own.

Truly Nathanial was a righteous man and lived Jesus's commandment *love thy neighbor,* something that she had been neglectful in following.

For a moment, Katie Mae felt ashamed. After all, he was suffering as much as she was. Surely he was unhappy to be losing his farm and uprooting his children. That wasn't something any man wanted to face. And yet, Nathanial seemed to accept his situation as God's will. Perhaps she had misread him and, despite not particularly caring for him or the situation, mayhaps she needed to show Nathaniel a little more compassion.

Nathanial noticed that Katie Mae was unusually quiet, and at first he chalked it up to her displeasure at the delay. But somewhere in the hardware store, just around the time when he had been talking with John Raber, she had stopped sighing and making noises of exasperation. Her demeanor changed and she actually seemed more compliant and patient. For whatever reason, Katie Mae remained calmly silent. For once.

After paying for the items in his cart, Nathanial carried them to the buggy. To his surprise, Katie Mae helped. Without being asked, she reached for the box of items while he carried the heavier tools.

"You got that?" he asked, half expecting her to lash out at him for suggesting she wasn't strong enough.

Instead, she merely nodded and said, *"Ja."*

What on earth? If his arms weren't laden with the tools, he would have scratched his head. Where had the feisty Katie Mae Kauffman gone?

Once again, they rode in silence, this time with Nathanial driving the horse and buggy down the road toward the Red Barn.

Katie Mae pointed to it and though he already knew where it was, Nathanial merely nodded as he turned into the parking lot.

"I'll just be a minute," she said as she climbed out of the buggy. And then, as if on second thought, she paused. "That's not true. It will take me about fifteen minutes." Katie Mae pursed her lips. "Can't rush the bookstore."

Nathanial almost chuckled at the expression on her face. "No worries, Katie Mae. I'll go over to the auction *haus*, see what's coming up over there."

For the next few minutes, Nathanial wandered around the auction house, reading the different notices posted outside the door. During December, they didn't have too many live animal auctions. In fact, their last animal auction had been the day after Thanksgiving.

But Nathanial hadn't attended. He had no money to spend.

He noticed there was a holiday bazaar coming up. It was being held later than usual in December, probably because Thanksgiving had been late in November. He wondered if he should go to pick up small gifts for the children. While he didn't have a lot of money, he needed to get the children *something* for Christmas.

Sighing, he thrust his hands into his pockets and headed back toward the Red Barn. He was surprised to see Katie Mae already walking through the double doors.

"Finished so fast, then?"

She gave him a small smile and nodded. *What's gotten into her?* he wondered. Where was her spicy tongue?

He waited until she was settled into the buggy before he untied the horse. When he climbed in, he noticed that she was already leafing through a book.

"What's that, if I might ask?" He half expected her to bite his head off. But he was pleasantly surprised when she merely closed the book and showed him the cover. "You like to read, I reckon?"

This time, she nodded her head enthusiastically. "Oh *ja!* I love reading. Devotionals are my favorite. Mary Esh brought this one with her today to read to Daed. I thought I'd buy it so that I can read it to him, too. I think he likes listening to people read to him."

Nathanial contemplated not just what she had said, but what she hadn't said. Clearly she had not given up hope that her father would recover from the stroke. And she was committed to caring for him. Those were admirable qualities in anyone, especially a young woman.

Maybe, he thought, *I've misread Katie Mae.*

He directed the horse down a side road, hoping to avoid the main thoroughfare. The road was tucked into a desolate area along a backroad, which meant that few tourists ever went there. Along the dusty lane that cut through a small housing development, a small dog ran alongside their buggy, barking. The horse started to spook, but Nathanial's steady hands calmed it.

"Wonder whose dog that is," he mumbled.

It was irresponsible for someone to have let out the dog, especially if it was one that chased buggies.

"Good thing they don't live closer to town, where all those tourists go," Katie Mae said softly.

Unlike some of the other nearby towns, Shipshewana attracted lots of tourists because of its theater and shopping centers. Most of the businesses were run by the Englische, though they employed many of the Amish. That was all well and good, but there were an awful lot of cars on the roads. And not all of the Englische tourists drove the speed limit.

He felt a pit form in his stomach.

No, Nathanial was not a fan of the Englische with their impatient ways and fast-moving cars, especially since his wife's accident.

When a car approached, Nathanial slowed the horse.

"What's wrong?" Katie Mae asked.

He shook his head. He didn't want to talk about Martha and the accident. That was something best left in the past. It wasn't that he loved Martha any less. No, that wasn't it at all. But it had been over a year, and maybe the bishop was right. Maybe he *did* need to move on.

Besides, he feared that talking about his memories might upset Katie Mae's unusually good mood. He was rather enjoying this quieter, softer side of the usually sassy girl.

So, instead of saying anything, Nathanial glanced at her and forced a smile.

"Been a long time since I rode in a buggy with an-other person," he said. "Kinda nice, don't you think?"

Her expression changed from concern to surprise. He saw it in her eyes.

Swallowing, he took a chance and asked, "Mayhaps you might read to me a spell from that new devotional?" When she paused, he added, "Just for conversation, that's all."

"Well then," she said slowly. "I reckon that would be fine."

And she opened her book, picking a passage to read, her voice filling the buggy and triggering something warm inside of Nathanial.

Chapter 6

On Saturday, Katie Mae did everything she could to hide in her house. Her new, much smaller house. But she could hear all of the noise of Nathaniel's move in the driveway—horses and buggies, cows, people, even trucks. Some of the local Mennonites had offered to help Nathanial move. And the children. There must have been a dozen children outside, laughing and running around.

Katie Mae wanted to simply disappear.

"Oh, Daed," she cried as she sank down in the chair beside his bed. "Have I made a mistake?" She reached out and touched his hand, holding it for a few long seconds. His eyes moved and he looked at her, but he wasn't able to speak. "Maybe I should've tried working the farm for one more year. Maybe I should've asked for more help from the community for your rehabilitation." She felt a wave of tears coming and she wiped at them with her fingers. "It's going to be so noisy here for you now."

No sooner had she said that than she heard a knock at the door. Oh, she hoped Nathanial wasn't going to ask her to watch those children of his. She set her mouth in a firm line as she stood up and crossed the floor to answer the door.

To her surprise, it was the bishop.

"*Gut morgan,* Katie Mae," he said, glancing over his shoulder at her father. "I'm surprised that you're not helping with Nathanial's move."

Katie Mae's expression softened. To be perfectly frank, no one had asked her. But if they had, she would have said no. Plain and simple. She couldn't stomach the thought of helping complete strangers move into what had, until just a few days ago, been her home. However, she knew that she couldn't say this to the bishop.

"Daed's resting a spell," she said instead. "It's too cold for him outside, anyway."

Bishop Brenneman nodded. "I agree. But we could certainly bring him to the big kitchen, where all the women are preparing dinner for noon. I'm sure they'd welcome your help and your *daed*'s company." He gestured toward the hospital bed, where her father was resting in an upright position. "I can assist you with your *daed*, Katie Mae. Might do him some good to get out and be around other folk a spell, anyway."

Inwardly, Katie Mae groaned. *She* knew what was best for her father, not the bishop. But she also knew that she could not argue with the bishop. What she had presumed was a friendly visit had turned out to be a visit to chastise her. *And that would not do,* she thought.

"I'd welcome that," she heard herself say, although she didn't really feel that way. The thought of being among all of those women in what used to be *her* kitchen? Why, she wouldn't know where Nathanial wanted things to be put or, if the women had already unpacked, where they were stored. And that big, beautiful farm table that she'd had

to leave behind? Oh, just the thought of seeing a meal
set upon it that wasn't for *her* and her father! It near
broke her heart.

Ten minutes later, with her father settled in his wheelchair and positioned near the window so that he could
watch all of the activity outside, Katie Mae found herself
standing among eight women who were unpacking boxes
of kitchenware.

"Why, Katie Mae!" an older woman exclaimed
when she walked into the kitchen from outside, her arms
laden with a big box. "How *gut* to see you!" Rosemary
set the box on the edge of the table and pushed it toward
the center, causing Katie Mae to cringe and hope that there
weren't any staples sticking out that might scratch the surface. "And how kind of you to help the Millers," she
added in a lowered voice. "I always say that *gut* things
happen to *gut* people, and that Nathanial Miller is one of
the best men out there!"

Katie Mae opened her eyes, taken aback by Rosemary's comment. "Oh *ja?*"

Rosemary gave her a sideways glance, her pale
eyes studying Katie Mae from behind her wire-rimmed
glasses. "Surely you know how he helped me after
Daniel passed away. Why, Nathanial cut cords of wood
for me to keep warm that first winter and he stopped by
every Thursday morning to make sure I was doing just
fine. He even fixed my fencing when the horse broke
loose." She clucked her tongue and shook her head. "A
fine man and so deserving of your kindness when he's in
need." The older woman reached out and touched Katie
Mae's arm. "God will reward you one day, trust me."

Stunned, Katie Mae stood there, in the middle of
what used to be her own kitchen, and stared out the window in the direction of the barn. The men were busy
loading hay and grain, cleaning out the dairy barn and

stable, and organizing the new tool room that Nathanial wanted set up. She couldn't see him, not really, for he was one among many. But she knew that he was out there.

What she didn't know was *who* Nathanial Miller was. So many people had such kind things to say about him, and yet Katie Mae's experience was just the opposite. Was there a possibility that she had gotten him all wrong?

"Now isn't that the sweetest?"

Katie Mae snapped out of her thoughts as Linda walked over to her. They hadn't seen each other since Katie Mae had stopped by to visit and left in a huff.

"What's so sweet?" Katie Mae asked.

Linda watched something over Katie Mae's shoulder. "Just look at that sweet child and your *daed*," she said.

Daed? Katie Mae turned to look at her father and, sure enough, there was little Becky sitting upon his lap. She had a big, chunky book in her hand and was showing Abraham the pictures. "Oh!" Katie Mae started to walk in that direction but felt Linda's hand on her arm.

"Now, now, Katie Mae," Linda said in a soft, comforting voice. "The little one isn't doing your *daed* any harm. Why, from the look on your *daed's* face, he seems right pleased."

Stunned, Katie Mae watched as Becky flipped through her book, pointing out the different animals on the various pages, asking him questions and waiting, as if anticipating his response. Becky seemed oblivious to the fact that Abraham couldn't answer. She merely chattered on as if he had.

"Oh my!" Katie Mae pressed her hand against her chest. There was something in her father's eyes, a new sparkle, and a hint of a smile on his lips. Was he actually responding to the little girl? "I don't believe it!" she whispered to Linda.

"Believe it, Katie Mae." Linda patted her arm. "God has a plan, you see. Sometimes we're just too blind to understand it until it stares us full-on."

Katie Mae exhaled as if she had been holding her breath, if not for minutes, perhaps for months. "Now what do I do?" she asked.

Linda motioned toward a box on the table. "How about helping me unpack this box of cookware? We can set up the cabinets near the stove together."

Suddenly, Katie Mae didn't mind helping unpack the Millers' boxes and rearranging the kitchen. Maybe Rosemary and Linda were right. *Having the Millers on the farm wasn't such a bad thing after all,* she thought.

When Nathanial walked with the rest of the men into the kitchen, he was shocked to see Katie Mae among the other women helping prepare the meal. Immediately he thought back to the day he'd visited the farm after the bishop had suggested the arrangement. The kitchen had been less crowded and certainly much cleaner. Even more poignant in his memory was how stoic Katie Mae had looked, with her straight shoulders and determination not to give in to emotion.

Now, however, she appeared like a fish out of water. He couldn't remember the last time he had seen her at the worship fellowship. She normally hurried home to relieve whoever was tending to her father. And that was on the infrequent occasions she made it to worship at all. She couldn't leave her father unless someone volunteered to sit in her place.

It dawned on Nathanial that Katie Mae was still a young woman who was living the life of an old *maedal*.

With her father's condition, she couldn't attend singings or youth gatherings. She certainly had no opportunities to meet other young people, never mind court any Amish man. It was a sad state of affairs for the young woman. And now she looked completely lost in what used to be her own kitchen as the bishop's wife, Dorothy, oversaw all of the preparations.

Seeing the bewildered look upon Katie Mae's face, Nathanial almost felt sorry for her.

It was Linda who noticed him. Nathanial saw her nudge Katie Mae and motion in his direction.

Suddenly her expression changed.

While she made no attempt to approach him, she gave him a warm smile.

He decided to walk over to her. It was the least he could do, since she was helping to organize his kitchen.

"I'm surprised to see you here," he said in a low voice. "It must be difficult—"

To his surprise, she interrupted him. "Look, Nathanial." She pointed toward her father. "Look what your *dochder* is doing! She's reading to Daed."

He followed the direction in which she pointed and, indeed, saw that Becky was seated upon Abraham's lap, a pile of books on the table next to the wheelchair.

At first, he wasn't certain how to respond. Becky had never really known either of her grandfathers. And ever since Martha passed away, Nathanial certainly hadn't had time to read to her. By the time evening came around, Nathanial was tired. Being both mother and father was exhausting.

He felt a momentary wave of guilt. Becky was only in her first year at school, so she couldn't read yet. And she sure did love books.

It shouldn't have surprised him that she was "reading" to Abraham.

But what did surprise him was that Abraham looked at if he were actually listening *and* enjoying it.

"Well, how about that!" Nathanial whispered. He looked at Katie Mae, noticing that her eyes were sparkling as bright as Abraham's. "I reckon that makes all of this a bit easier then, *ja?*"

Katie Mae gave a small smile and leaned forward as if she had a grave secret to tell him. "I don't think I like where Dorothy put your spices and dry goods," she whispered. "I can't find anything and she sure is taking charge."

Nathanial laughed. *There* was the sassy girl he had known. Only this time, her sass wasn't directed at him. He whispered back, "They say birds of a feather flock together. Makes sense that she's a bit bossy, considering the man she's married to."

Her hand covered her mouth as if stifling another laugh.

"But I sure do appreciate all that you women are doing," he said in a louder voice, redirecting his attention to the other women, lest they begin to think he was sweet on Katie Mae. Wouldn't do to have the church folks wagging their tongues, he told himself.

But as he turned away from Katie Mae to go talk to Dorothy and the other women, he realized that, for the first time in a year, he'd found laughter in the presence of a woman. The fact that it had been with Katie Mae Kauffman was equally surprising.

Chapter 7

With the exception of living in a much smaller house than before, Katie Mae could have forgotten that the Miller family was even there.

The first few days after Nathanial and his children moved into the farm seemed almost surreal, mostly because Katie Mae rarely, if ever, saw them. The young boys arose early to help their father with the morning milking and then, after Nathanial presumably fed them breakfast, the farm quieted down when the children went to school. In the evenings when they returned, there were more chores before preparation for supper, prayers, and then bedtime.

They were quiet enough—that was for sure and certain. Her fear that her father would be disturbed by their ruckus, especially those three young boys, was clearly unfounded. Either that or Nathanial had told them to be extra quiet. Regardless, Katie Mae was happy that the Miller family did not intrude on her privacy.

And then Wednesday came along.

Katie Mae awoke to a dark gray sky. It was drizzling out and from the looks of it, there was also freezing rain.

The wind blew it sideways so that, at times, it sounded like tiny pebbles were thrown against the window panes. She was grateful that she didn't have to go outside at all that day, that was for sure and certain.

She had just managed to get her father out of bed, dressed, and seated in his wheelchair when she heard Nathanial's buggy leaving the farm. She suspected that he was driving the children to school. She didn't blame him. No one wanted to walk anywhere on such a miserable day.

"Daed, I need to run upstairs for a minute. You stay put, *ja*? And then I'll make you some hot chocolate. Warm you up on the insides."

She noticed that his eyes followed her as she started to leave the room. He was aware, of that there was no doubt. What she couldn't understand was why he was unable to speak or move his extremities. If only he showed some signs of wanting to try, she could speak to the bishop about the community funding his physical therapy. But without that effort, Katie Mae knew better than to waste the resources of Amish Aid.

She hurried upstairs and quickly made her bed. With the day being so dismal, she knew that it was best to get her chores out of the way as soon as possible so that she could sit downstairs and crochet. She still needed to finish that baby blanket. That was the one thing about winter she loved: crocheting. As the blankets grew in size, they covered her lap and legs, warming her even when the weather was so cold. She always felt that a gift of a crocheted blanket was a gift of love for that very reason.

With her room tidy, Katie Mae shut the door behind herself and hurried back downstairs.

To her surprise, she heard a voice.

A small voice.

Katie Mae stopped walking on the third to last step and

looked around the banister toward the kitchen area. Sure enough, her father was no longer alone. Little Becky Miller, who was still in her sleeping gown, sat upon Abraham's lap! She was snuggled against him, her back against his chest and her little legs swinging as she showed him pictures from a book in her hands.

"And then thi-*th* little bunny *th*-aid that he wa-*th* thirsty—"

"What in the world?" Katie Mae couldn't help but interrupt the girl. "Becky, why aren't you at school?"

"I'm *th*-ick." She pressed her hand against her own forehead and made an overly dramatic face as if she were swooning.

Katie Mae walked over to her. "Well, if you are indeed sick—not *th*-ick—you shouldn't be sitting on my *daed*'s lap." The last thing her father needed was to catch a cold from Becky.

Frowning, Katie Mae reached out to take Becky from her father, but something stopped her from lifting the child. Becky made a strange noise and then began to giggle. She tried to lift Becky again, but she didn't budge. This time, Katie Mae stared not at the child but at her father.

His facial expression had changed from relaxed to determined. Katie Mae looked down at Becky's waist and saw that her father was actually holding the little girl, his arm tight around her waist. Stunned, Katie Mae looked back at her father. Was he actually trying to keep Becky on his lap? Was he truly communicating that he didn't want the child to be removed?

For a moment, Katie Mae could not speak. She was too shocked by what she had just witnessed.

"Dawdi Abraham wan-*th* me to *th*-ay here," Becky said in a determined tone. "He wan-*th* to hear the res-*th* of my *th*-ory."

Stunned by her father's reaction, Katie Mae took a step backward. "By all means," she whispered. "Finish your story." Her eyes never left Abraham and Becky as the little girl continued telling him about the little bunny who went to the pond to get water but found it was frozen and decided to go ice skating instead.

As Katie Mae watched, her father's eyes began to shine and the corner of his mouth lifted, just ever so slightly.

He was responding! Her father was actually making an attempt to communicate with Becky. He loved her silly little story and was responding!

Clasping her hands together, Katie Mae held them to her chest and watched. Her heart pounded and she felt a mixture of joy and relief. Surely this was a gift from God, a sign that things were going to get better.

When Becky finished the story about the bunny, Katie Mae couldn't help but pull up a chair and sit down. "Tell us another story, Becky," she asked. "Tell us more about the little bunny who likes to ice skate."

Where on earth had that child scampered off to?

Nathanial took a deep breath, forcing himself to remain calm as he searched the upstairs of the house, looking for Becky. Her rumpled bed covers indicated that she *had* been sleeping, just as he had told her to do. Clearly, however, she had begun to feel better and gotten up while he was outside doing chores.

The fact that her shoes were gone from the foot of the bed, where he had placed them the previous evening, indicated that she had ventured outside.

Frustrated, Nathanial hurried back downstairs and flung open the door that led to the porch. He knew she wasn't with the dairy cows, for he had been there when he decided to check on her. Perhaps Becky had run into the stable to look at the horses? An image of her crawling into the stall with one of those large Standardbreds made him run toward the small stable next to the dairy building.

"Becky?" he called out. When no one answered, he peered over the stall doors and sighed in relief that she wasn't there.

He turned around and scratched at the back of his neck. Where could she have gone?

His eyes scanned the fields. Surely Becky hadn't gone to the pond. *That* would have been potentially disastrous, especially since it was a bit warmer today and the surface would not be frozen. But he had noticed that her coat had been hanging up in the entrance room, and he knew that his daughter would never venture outside without her coat, especially not that far from the house.

He began to walk back to the house, determined to check every room again. But as he crossed the barnyard, he looked up, his gaze falling on the *grossdawdihaus*. That was when he saw Katie Mae standing at the kitchen window, laughing at something . . . or perhaps someone . . . who sat upon the counter next to her.

Nathanial frowned. Through the lowest window pane, he could see his daughter's little head bobbing up and down. *No, no, no,* he thought. Not the Kauffmans! He cringed at the thought that Becky might have ventured over there. On their first day at the new farm, Nathanial had warned the children to steer clear of the *dawdihaus* and Katie Mae.

The last thing he wanted was to get on Katie Mae's bad side, as if she actually *had* a good side. And now Becky had ventured over there on a Wednesday? Katie Mae would certainly have a word or two to say about *that!*

But he was relieved that, at least, Becky was safe. A small price to pay for a tongue-lashing from his landlord's daughter, he supposed.

Standing at the *grossdawdihaus* door, he knocked once and then, after taking a deep, cleansing breath, he opened it. He was hardly surprised to hear Becky's voice as she chattered away to Katie Mae.

"Becky!" He wiped his feet on the doormat before entering the kitchen. "Child, I've been looking all over for you!"

He glanced at Katie Mae, waiting for a rebuke. He knew how she felt about watching his children. She had made that clear on the first day he had brought them to the farm to see their new home.

"I'm terribly sorry, Katie Mae," he said, hoping his preemptive apology might soften her reprimand. "I didn't know she'd run off like that."

And then, to Nathanial's surprise, Katie Mae shook her head, a smile playing on her lips. A smile that lit up her face and made her eyes sparkle. "No worries, Nathanial. Why, little Becky was just telling my *daed* all about a little bunny." She turned her head and gave her father a broad grin. "You liked that story, didn't you, Daed?"

Nathanial glanced at her father and, for the briefest of seconds, he thought he saw Abraham's mouth twitch, almost as if he, too, were smiling.

"Becky, you really should go back to bed," Nathanial said in a soft voice, leveling his eyes on his daughter. "I told you to stay there and I meant it."

But Katie Mae wrapped her arms around the little girl and pulled her off the counter, setting her upon her hip. "*Nee,* Nathanial. She shouldn't be home alone like that. Not if she's feeling poorly."

Stunned, Nathanial watched as Katie Mae walked

back over to Abraham and set the little girl on his lap. "I think Daed wants to hear more about this bunny. Only this time without sticky hands to muss his clean shirt."

Nathanial stood there, his mouth hanging open. Had the weather been warmer, he'd have worried about catching flies. But it was too cold for flies and, once again, Katie Mae was being too nice to be . . . well . . . Katie Mae! He stood there, watching as Katie Mae pulled up a chair and sat before her father, leaning forward as she listened to Becky chattering away about the bunny.

For the second time, he saw something akin to joy in Katie Mae's face and, to his further surprise, he realized that, when her eyes weren't narrowed and her brow furrowed from scowling or fretting, Katie Mae Kauffman was truly a pretty young woman.

Oblivious to his thoughts, Katie Mae motioned toward the door. "Go on now. Finish your chores, Nathanial, and don't worry about Becky," she said, her lips still curved into a pleasant smile. "I'll watch her a spell and make certain she naps if she starts looking tuckered out."

And then Katie Mae returned her attention to Becky and Abraham.

Without a word, Nathanial let his feet guide him back outside. He was too stupefied by Katie Mae's reaction to argue with her. Was it possible that there was more to this woman than he had first thought? He could hardly believe that it was possible, but he was willing to give her a second chance to show him her true colors.

Chapter 8

On Friday, Katie Mae stood in the kitchen, chewing on her fingernail as she stared at the cookbook. She wanted to make a nice supper for her *daed*, but she knew that it would take her most of the afternoon if she was going to do it right. But what was the point in cooking so much food for just two people?

Katie Mae glanced at the clock on the wall. It was almost one o'clock. She wondered how Becky's first day back at school had been. She hated to admit it, but after two days of watching Becky while she stayed home, Katie Mae realized that she missed the happy chatter of the little girl. On Thursday morning, Becky had stayed home from school again and, upon waking up, she had wandered to the *grossdawdihaus*, crawling up on Abraham's lap.

For hours, Becky had entertained both him and Katie Mae with her funny stories. Half the time, Katie Mae wasn't certain that she even understood what Becky was saying because of her adorable little lisp. But she understood something much more important: Her father's eyes sparkled whenever Becky came around.

And that meant the world to Katie Mae.

Now that Becky was back in school, the *grossdawdihaus* seemed far too quiet and Abraham sat at the window, staring at the empty fields with shallow eyes.

"Daed," Katie Mae said at last, walking over to where her father sat. "What do you think if I were to invite the Millers to have supper with us tonight?" She leaned over and peered into his face. "Would you like that, then? Or would it be too much noise for you?"

He mumbled something that she couldn't understand, but the way his eyes shone, Katie Mae knew what his answer was.

"All right then," she said as she stood up. "Reckon I'll go see if Nathanial thinks that's a good idea. But if those boys are too noisy, I'll send them all home with covered plates, okay?"

She grabbed her black shawl from the hook near the door and, after tossing it over her shoulders, she hurried outside.

It was a nice day, despite the chill in the air. Katie Mae hurried across the lawn toward the dairy barn. She hadn't been to the outer buildings since Nathanial moved to the farm so when she stepped inside, she almost stopped short. Was she in the right place?

"Oh my," she whispered to herself.

The dairy aisle where the cows were milked in the mornings and evenings was perfectly cleaned. There were no signs of manure or hay on the cement walkways. The windows had been cleaned and let in the afternoon sun, and all of the pitchfork and muck buckets hung neatly on the wall near the rear of the building. Why, she had never seen the barn look so orderly!

"Well, hello there!"

Katie Mae started at the sound of Nathanial's voice as he emerged from the room where the milk was kept in large, steel drums, cooled by the power of a diesel engine. He wiped his hands on a cloth towel as he approached her.

"To what do I owe this pleasant surprise, Katie Mae?" He smiled as he spoke and that, coupled with his greeting, threw Katie Mae for a loop.

For a moment, she had forgotten why she was there. She glanced around the barn. "I'm surprised at how much you've changed everything."

He raised an eyebrow. "I hope you approve." He hesitated. "I find that order makes it easier to work."

Katie Mae gave a slight nod of her head. "Ja, I agree. Daed used to keep the barn a bit more"—she searched for the right word—"tidy, I reckon. But I just couldn't do it all," she admitted.

"I'm surprised at how much you did, Katie Mae. Why, those fences were in right *gut* shape and you kept the milk containment system in *wunderbaar* condition. And I know how you like your *haus*. Spick-and-span, ja?"

Katie Mae laughed. "I reckon I do. A place for everything and everything in its place. That's what my *mamm* always told me."

"A wise woman."

A moment of silence fell over them and Katie Mae found herself studying Nathanial, unaware that he was doing the same. He was a large man, true, but he kept himself in good shape. His beard was neatly trimmed and his clothes were always clean. Katie Mae wondered who washed his clothing and thought that, mayhaps, she might offer to help him once a week with laundry.

"So."

She blinked. "Ja?"

Nathanial gestured toward the barn. "I reckon you didn't come out here to inspect the dairy barn."

Katie Mae felt the heat rush to her cheeks and she

tapped her forehead as if to indicate that she was absent-minded. "Silly me. I did come here for a reason."

He leaned against the wall, tossing the towel over his shoulder, and studied her with an amused expression that only made Katie Mae blush even more.

"I wanted to make a nice supper this evening and, well, I thought that mayhaps you and the *kinner* might like to join us."

Nathanial looked surprised by her offer and raised his eyebrows. "You're inviting us to fellowship?"

Something about the way he said that made Katie Mae feel bad. Was it so surprising after all? Had she been that terrible to him? Swallowing her pride, she nodded. "I am, ja. Daed sure did enjoy little Becky's visits the last two days and, well, frankly it was nice to have some company."

He pressed his lips together and Katie Mae thought he was suppressing a smile. "Even if I'm included?"

At that comment, Katie Mae made a clucking sound and frowned at him. "Nathanial Miller, it's either a yes or no. I don't need to be teased any further."

A laugh escaped his throat and he smiled. "Ja, Katie Mae, I'm sure the *kinner* would love a nice home-cooked meal tonight." He leaned forward and whispered, "And I reckon I sure would, too."

Katie Mae narrowed her eyes. "Even if it's cooked by me?"

"Especially if it's cooked by you."

She backed away, staring at him. Was he actually flirting with her? Her heart began to beat and she took another step toward the door. Was it possible that the idea of such a thing did not displease her? For a quick second, she tried to assess her own feelings and she realized that, no, she was not offended if Nathanial was flirting. In fact, from the way her blood raced through

Sarah Price

her veins and her cheeks heated once again, she thought the idea was actually rather pleasant.

She had never been courted. Never been flirted with. And, despite her first impressions of Nathanial Miller, she had learned much more about him. Perhaps he was not the terrible, horrible person she had thought he was after all. And what harm did a little flirting do?

"Well then," she managed to say, averting her eyes in the hopes that he could not read her thoughts. "I'll expect you and the *kinner* at five o'clock."

Nathanial watched her, a curious expression on his face. "That sounds right *gut*, Katie Mae Kauffman. *Danke* for your kindness."

Oh, she couldn't stand there under his steady gaze for one more second. And yet, her feet didn't want to move away. What was it about Nathanial that suddenly made her feel nervous and fluttery, as if ten thousand butterflies were in her stomach?

Forcing herself to turn around, Katie Mae dipped her head and hurried out of the barn. Once outside, she paused and leaned against the side of the building, gulping for air. *Was it possible,* she thought, *that she might actually be attracted to that man?* The idea frightened her. What if Nathanial didn't return her feelings? What if he thought no more of her than he did a milk cow? She shook her head, telling herself that she needed to stop thinking such thoughts. The arrangement at the farm was just that: a business arrangement. Two people helping each other and nothing more.

Perhaps she had spent too much time alone, tending to her father. Maybe it was time for her to step out and attend some of the youth gatherings after all. But even as she tried to convince herself of that, she knew she wouldn't. Her responsibilities at home were far too great, and she had no interest in courting just any young man. It would take someone very special to capture her affections.

Nathanial watched as she walked out of the barn, her shawl wrapped tight around her shoulders to ward off the cold air. Had Katie Mae Kauffman just invited him and his *kinner* to supper? In a hundred years, he never would've thought that would happen. And he never thought that he would agree so readily. Why, he hadn't even given it much thought, had he?

Something felt warm inside of him. Just like the feeling when he had taken her to town the previous week. Perhaps it was the way Katie Mae had asked, her eyes downcast, shuffling her feet back and forth. Had she been nervous asking him? And, if so, why?

There had been something about her smile, too, when he had agreed to have supper with her and her father. Almost as if she had been surprised by his answer. Perhaps she had expected him to say no or to make up some excuse so he wouldn't have to spend time with her and Abraham. Or maybe she wanted him to just send over Becky. It amazed him how his daughter had won both Abraham and Katie Mae's hearts.

But in truth, Nathanial didn't *mind* being around Katie Mae. Not really. They had gotten off to a bad start, that was for sure and certain, but she did take right *gut* care of her father and that spoke well of her character. And he remembered her laughing when he joked about the bishop's wife.

He had liked the sound of her laughter.

For the rest of the morning, Nathanial had a lighter spring to his step as he went about his chores. And when the children came running down the dusty lane toward the house, Nathanial stood outside, his hands on his hips, and grinned while he watched them. They were laughing and chasing each other, more like little puppies than children. And he loved that vivaciousness about them.

"Reckon you all had a *gut* day, ja?"

Becky tripped and started to fall, but Thomas caught her.

"It's Friday," Luke said, a big grin on his face. "That means the weekend and no school!"

Nathanial tried to hide his amusement at his younger son's enthusiasm. "*Ach*, Luke," he said in as stern a voice as he could muster. "Schooling's important."

"But so are weekends!"

Nathanial had to turn around so that Luke didn't see him smile. Oh, he remembered far too well how *he* had felt about school when he was younger. So it was hard to fault Luke for preferring the weekends over school days.

"What're we doing this weekend anyway, Daed?" Thomas asked as he walked in step with Nathanial.

"I'll be needing your help spreading some manure in the fields," Nathanial started. "Looks like they haven't been fertilized in a while. And we've worship on Sunday."

Joseph gave a loud sigh, which Nathanial chose to ignore.

"Oh, and I almost forgot. Katie Mae invited us to supper this evening."

Becky clapped her hands, but Luke groaned.

"She's a mean woman," Joseph said. "I don't want to go have supper with her. I bet she can't even cook."

Nathanial wanted to reprimand his son, but he had always felt that it was better to use such moments to teach his children, not punish them. "Now, Joseph, you shouldn't jump to such quick conclusions about people. Every person has goodness in them."

"Some of them have badness, too, Daed." Luke kicked at a rock in the road. "And she's downright mean."

"Now, now, that ain't so. Why, she was kind enough to invite us over. And she looked after Becky when she was sick." He paused. "I didn't even have to ask her. That's something good, ja?"

Joseph sighed. "I guess so. But it sure isn't a lot to go on."

Nathanial laughed and ruffled his son's dirty blond hair. "And yet it's a start. So let's give Katie Mae a chance. Remember, her life has been as disrupted as ours. Not one of you were happy about moving, were you now?"

Becky raised her hand as if she were still in school. "I was, Daed! 'Cause I wa-*th* getting my own *beth*-room!"

He reached down and picked her up, swinging her around so that she could sit on his shoulders. "That's sure true, Becky! You were excited. But the rest of us weren't. Now we realize that it's not so bad here."

"There's a pond for skating!" Thomas pointed out.

"And the barn's bigger," Luke stated.

"There's no kittens," Becky added, a sad tone in her voice.

"Betcha in spring there'll be kittens," Thomas said.

"I want an orange kitten."

Nathanial laughed. "I reckon you'd be happy with *any* colored kitten, Becky." He glanced at the boys. "Now, let's get our afternoon chores finished so we can get cleaned up before we head over to the *dawdihaus*. And remember, tonight, let's all be on our best behavior. It's awful nice of Katie Mae to cook a good meal for us, don't you think?"

The five of them continued down the dusty lane toward the main house, Becky on her father's shoulders and the boys lagging behind. For Nathanial, it was the first moment that he truly felt happy in a long time. He had hated to give up his farm, but, given the circumstances, he, too, thought that sometimes God's plan felt hurtful just before the truth emerged that something better was in store. And for the first time in a long time, he was beginning to believe that was true.

Chapter 9

Katie Mae stood near the stove, her hands on her hips as she studied the table. Why, it was just too small to accommodate three adults and four children! She had dragged the folding table upstairs from the basement, but even with the pretty orange tablecloth it looked like it was thrown together haphazardly. And the folding chairs were all different. She wished she had a long bench, just like she had left in the kitchen of the main house.

But at least she had her mother's wedding china.

Katie Mae smiled.

"Daed, you see how pretty Mamm's china looks?"

She hurried over to her father and pushed his wheelchair toward the table so that he could see it.

A noise escaped his lips and Katie Mae leaned over. "What was that, Daed?"

But she heard nothing more from her father. Instead, there was a loud ruckus coming from the small mudroom just off the kitchen. The door was flung open and the two younger boys, Luke and Joseph, stumbled inside, one of them tumbling to the floor.

"Oh help!" Katie Mae abandoned her father and ran over to the mudroom. "Are you boys all right?" She reached down and helped Luke to his feet, pausing to dust off nonexistent dirt from his trousers. "What did you trip over?"

Luke straightened his back and stood still.

Joseph cowered behind him.

"Boys, answer Katie Mae's question," came the loud voice of Nathanial as he stepped through the doorway.

"We were running," Luke admitted in a soft voice.

"We're sorry, Katie Mae."

She frowned and glanced at Nathanial. Were they afraid of her? She stood up straight and took a deep breath. "As long as you both are fine, there's no harm done anyway." She turned to greet Nathanial. "Quite prompt, I see."

He glanced over her head at the clock. "Five o'clock on the button."

"Indeed." She stepped aside so that he could enter. "Unfortunately, I'm not quite as prompt."

Nathanial walked into the kitchen and greeted Abraham. "Then that just gives us more time to visit, ja? Good evening, Abraham."

But Abraham's eyes were on Becky who, upon seeing the older man, hurried to him so that she could crawl on his lap. "Dawdi Abraham! I brought a new book to read to you!" she said as she nestled into his arm, putting her dirty bare feet onto the arm of his wheelchair. "Look!" She held up the book and waved it in front of Abraham's face.

For a moment, Katie Mae caught her breath for she saw a hint of a smile form on her father's lips. No. It was more than a hint. Why, the corner of his mouth definitely lifted. And his eyes! They widened and sparkled as Becky began to read him the story—or, rather, made up her own words to the story as she pretended to read.

"Well, I'll be!" Katie Mae whispered to Nathanial as she walked up beside him. "I thought it the other day, but now I am genuinely certain that Daed's really responding to her!"

Nathanial scratched at his beard. "Mayhaps he'd do well if he went to physical therapy, Katie Mae."

She watched her father's face as he listened intently to the little girl. "He never wanted to go in the past, but people can change, don't you think?"

For a long moment, Nathanial remained silent. She had almost forgotten that she had asked the question until she heard him clear his throat. She turned to look at him, wondering if something was wrong. Instead, he leveled his gaze at her and nodded.

"Ja, Katie Mae, I do think people can change." He moistened his lips and glanced first at her father and then back to her. "But mayhaps sometimes they're just misunderstood from the very beginning. Mayhaps it's us who change in how we view them."

After he stopped talking, he continued to study her face, just long enough that she felt her cheeks grow warm once again under his scrutiny. This time, he did not smile or smirk. Instead, his expression remained stoic and serious. But there was a kindness beneath it and she felt as if he were sending her a silent message.

"You speak a strong truth," Katie Mae managed to say in a soft voice, averting her eyes so that he wouldn't read her thoughts.

To distract herself, she gestured toward the sitting area on the far side of the kitchen and then hurried to check on the supper. It wasn't anything fancy, just a mixture of foods since she didn't know what everyone liked. She had made meat loaf with a thick tomato gravy baked on the top, as well as some fried chicken. And, of course, she had mashed potatoes because everyone loved those, right? She stood back and assessed the different platters that were lined up along the counter, waiting to be dished and served. The dishes that didn't need to be heated, such as the coleslaw and chowchow, as well as her personal favorite, pickled beets, were already on the table. And, of course, she had baked a fresh loaf of bread that was already sliced and placed at the head of the table, where it belonged.

Every family needed a fresh loaf of bread at supper.

Only Katie Mae hadn't made fresh bread recently because her father couldn't chew it and, with only her to enjoy it, the loaf would soon go stale.

She could hardly wait to slather pumpkin butter onto the bread and sink her teeth into it. Pumpkin butter. Her favorite thing about the autumn.

"Well, I reckon we can all sit down at the table," she said, after pulling the chicken and meat loaf out of the oven. She set them both on the stove and waved her hand over the top. They were hot so a little time cooling off wouldn't hurt. "Daed sits at the one end," she said, and started to walk toward the wheelchair, but Nathanial was already there, pushing it toward the vacant spot at the foot of the table, where there was more room to accommodate him.

"*Danke*, Nathanial," she said softly. Aside from Wednesdays, when was the last time anyone had helped her with her father?

"What about me?" Becky cried out.

"Oh, I think you best sit next to my *daed*," Katie Mae said, pointing to the chair to her father's left. "And you boys can sit along the other side." She hurried to the table and sat down next to Becky, which left the head of the table as the only empty spot for Nathanial.

For a moment, he appeared uncomfortable. Usually that spot was for the head of the household. But Abraham's wheelchair just didn't fit.

"Oh, Nathanial," Katie Mae scolded gently. "Don't act so fussy and just sit."

She thought she heard Joseph snicker.

Once again, Nathanial cleared his throat and, reluctantly, withdrew the chair. He sat down and scanned the table.

Katie Mae stared back, expectantly.

"Oh." He pursed his lips and shut his eyes before he bowed his head, indicating the before-meal silent prayer.

Satisfied, Katie Mae tried to hide her smile as every head bowed before she, too, lowered hers.

Only when Nathanial raised his head did the others follow his example.

"Well then, let me bring over the plates!" Katie Mae jumped to her feet and began bustling about the small kitchen, bringing over plate after plate of food. She placed most of them near Nathanial so that he could begin serving. When she finished bringing over the plates, Katie Mae hurried down to help put some food on her father's plate: a little bit of meat loaf, some mashed potatoes, and a hearty scoop of applesauce.

She scooped a little bit of food onto a spoon and served it to her father. But to her surprise, he slowly raised his hand and pushed hers away.

"Daed!"

She wasn't certain which she was more surprised at: that he had raised his hand, or that he had pushed hers away? But before she could ask, she felt him reach for the spoon. Stunned, Katie Mae released it and watched as he tried to feed himself. It took him a while, but he managed to do just that.

"Well!" She stood back and stared at her father, feeling the sting of tears in the corner of her eyes. "Aren't you full of surprises tonight?"

By the time he had said the evening prayer and hustled the children off to bed, it was almost nine o'clock. But Nathanial wasn't tired.

Something about the way Katie Mae had behaved that evening, the way she had taken charge of the kitchen and made certain that everything was just so, stuck with him. In a way, she reminded him of his Martha. But Martha had been softer and quieter about certain things. In that regard, Katie Mae was just the opposite.

Except when he made her blush.

Nathanial stepped outside, breathing in the cold air and watching his breath form a cloud when he exhaled.

He liked to make her blush. Catching her off guard and saying things that made her cheeks turn pink was turning into a fun pastime. And yet, he knew that he needed to be careful. She was a young woman and wouldn't be interested in the likes of him, what with a ready-made family and all. Or would she?

Still, he felt a certain level of protectiveness about Katie Mae. And her father.

"Nathanial? Is that you?"

He glanced toward the corner of the house near the walkway that led up to Katie Mae's door. "Ja, it's me." He chuckled. "Who'd you think it was?"

As soon as he said that, he immediately felt bad. What if she had been expecting a young man to come calling on her? Would she think his question rude? As if he didn't think anyone would court her? "I mean—"

She walked around the corner, her shawl held tight to her chest. "I know what you meant," she said lightly, clearly not offended by his comment. "I was hoping you might be out here."

"It's awfully cold, Katie Mae. Should we go inside?"

But she shook her head. "I wanted to ask you a question, Nathanial."

For a moment, he wondered if she might be thinking of something along the lines of what he had been thinking earlier. His heart began to race and he felt his palms grow sweaty. "And what's that, Katie Mae?"

"You've been working around here for what? Two weeks now, ja?"

He swallowed and nodded.

"I know you barely know me, but I was wondering something."

"Ja? That's funny. I was wondering something, too."

Katie Mae glossed over his statement. She stepped closer to the porch and looked up at him. In the faint glow from the kerosene lantern, her skin appeared darker and flawless, not one blemish or freckle marring it. He thought that she looked particularly pretty and wondered what she would say if he asked to court her.

But he didn't have time to ask.

She took a deep breath and exhaled. "Do you think that you might speak to the bishop?"

Nothing could have shocked him more. Wasn't *that* a little fast? He had just begun to entertain the thought, the seed being planted, but the roots not yet formed. And here Katie Mae was boldly proposing that he speak to the bishop?

He swallowed, but realized that his mouth had gone dry. "You want me to speak to the bishop?"

In the darkness, he could see her nod her head. "Ja, about my *daed*."

"Oh." Despite his previous thoughts, he realized that he hadn't considered she might mean Abraham.

"You see, Daed's changed since your family moved here. And I noticed that he's trying. He never tried before, not like he has recently. And I wonder if the life that your family has brought to the farm, especially since you moved in last week, hasn't made him want to rejoin life instead of just sitting in that wheelchair. Mayhaps the bishop might see fit to speak to the congregation about sending Daed to physical therapy at last."

As she spoke, Nathanial realized that he felt disappointment. Here he had been considering asking her to let him court her and she was talking about her father. And yet, he couldn't help but admire the respect she had just shown him. After all, there was nothing stopping Katie Mae from talking to the bishop. Instead, she had asked him.

Still, he hoped she didn't sense his disappointment.

"I reckon I could do that, Katie Mae," he responded at last.

Pulling the shawl tighter around her chest, she took a step backward. "I sure would appreciate it, Nathanial. *Danke.*"

For an awkward moment, they stood there, staring at each other in the faint light from the kerosene lantern.

"Oh," she said as if an afterthought. "You had said you were wondering something, too." She paused as if waiting for him to speak.

It took him a moment to respond. It just didn't seem like the right time to blurt out his question. Not after she had just asked him about her father. No, he'd wait and see if she continued to show any interest in him, or if he had merely misread her kindness.

So, instead, he changed the direction of his thoughts. "I was wondering if you'd go to the children's school pageant next Friday. I'm sure Becky would love it and I could help you bring your *daed*."

In the faint glow of the light, he saw her smile. "Why, Na-thanial! I think that would be just *wunderbaar*!"

He felt his heart flutter.

"Daed would sure love that, I'm certain."

And just like that, his heart stilled.

He watched as she turned and hurried back to the door of the *dawdihaus*. He had misread her after all. And that realization added to the disappointment he had felt just moments earlier.

Chapter 10

Early on Sunday morning, Katie Mae had arisen and gotten dressed in her navy-blue Sunday dress, complete with her white cape and apron. Even though she rarely went to worship service anymore, she always dressed appropriately on Sundays. She made a fresh pot of coffee and set the breakfast table so that, when she got her father dressed, she could just push his wheelchair to the table and serve him.

"*Gut martiye!*" She sang out as she knocked on her father's door. "Rise and shine, Daed!" She opened the door and immediately stopped short. Her mouth opened as she stared at the sight of her father, already sitting up in the bed as if he had been waiting for her. "Daed? What're you doing?" She hurried to his side and reached over to touch his forehead. "How long have you been sitting there? You could've fallen," she fussed.

And then, to her further surprise, he pushed her hand away from him. He gestured toward the door and, when Katie Mae looked, she realized that he was pointing at his Sunday clothes.

"Oh, Daed," she said, a sorrowful tone to her voice.

"I can't take you to church, you know that. It's too hard to get you into the buggy."

But Abraham gestured again, demanding despite his silence.

With a reluctant sigh, Katie Mae gave in and retrieved his Sunday suit. "All right then," she said slowly. "If you'd like to dress nice for our day, then so be it."

Thirty minutes later, she managed to finish dressing her father and had just rolled his wheelchair into the kitchen when she heard a knock at the door. Her eyes flew to the clock and, sure enough, it was twenty minutes before worship normally started.

"Who on earth could that be?" she mumbled as she hurried over to the door.

Nathanial.

He stood in the doorway, his black hat in his hands. "*Gut martiye*," he said in a soft voice, his eyes meeting hers and lingering for just one long moment before he glanced over her head at Abraham. "And to you, too, Abraham."

Katie Mae thought she heard her father make a noise in response. She frowned and turned to look at him. "Well, I'll be," she whispered. "Such craziness today, Nathanial. You just wouldn't believe."

"Oh, I reckon I would."

His response made her look at him and she couldn't help but wonder what he meant by that.

As if reading her mind, Nathanial gave her a sheepish look. "I've come to fetch you and your *daed* for worship service."

"Excuse me?"

Nathanial nodded. "*Ja,* it's high time you got yourself out and about, Katie Mae. I know you've been skipping worship because of your *daed*, but if you want the community to help with his physical therapy, don't you think it would be wise to have him show an effort and attend worship?"

She hadn't thought of it that way, but Nathanial certainly made a good point.

"Well then," she said, and put her hands on her hips as she turned to face her father. "Guess you will be going to worship today after all, Daed."

During the worship service, Nathanial repeatedly found his eyes drawn across the room to where the women sat. It was as if he couldn't stop himself from seeking out Katie Mae. She sat among the unmarried women in her navy-blue dress, white cape and apron, and black head covering. But she looked out of place among the others.

While she wasn't the oldest unmarried woman there, for they sat in chronological age, she was certainly the most mature. Not one of the other women could hold a candle to Katie Mae in that regard. He noticed Jenny Ecker seated beside Katie Mae. She worked in the garden store and, whenever Nathanial went there and asked questions, she knew about as much on the subject of gardening as Nathanial knew about quilting! And there was Mary Kapp, who giggled far too much for Nathanial to take seriously. Finally, he noticed Caroline Becker, who was about as exciting as a rusty old nail!

No, Katie Mae should not be seated among those other silly women.

The worship service was almost over, the bishop saying the final prayer while both the men and women stood, their faces toward the wall as they listened to his words. Nathanial, however, glanced at the backs of the unmarried men who sat behind him. They, too, seemed too tall and thin, willowy wisps of men with bowl haircuts

that their mothers had given them. He couldn't imagine
any of them milking almost sixty cows each day *and* tending to a farm. Why, there was Elmer Kapp, Mary's older
brother, who was just as giddy as she was. Tommy
Hostetler stood behind Elmer and he was staring up at
the ceiling, probably counting the heads of nails holding
up the sheetrock. He was a dull young man to say the
least. And Willard Mast, who worked at the grocery
store. Were those the men whom Katie Mae had to
choose from if she wanted to court? If so, it was no
wonder that she wasn't walking out with anyone!

Simultaneously, everyone genuflected and Nathanial
dropped his knee just in time so that no one realized he
hadn't been paying attention.

With the service over, Nathanial helped the other
men organize the room for the noon meal. Using narrow, wooden trestles, Nathanial helped John David
Mast, Willard's father, fit the legs from the benches into
the trestle tops, converting them into tables for fellowship
while the younger men helped organize other benches for
seating. Nathanial glanced up once and saw that Katie
Mae was helping the other women as they set the tables
for the first seating. Becky trailed behind her and, apparently, Katie Mae had put her to work.

Seeing his daughter helping to put plates onto the tables made him smile. Surely his daughter was enjoying
this new living arrangement more than anyone else in
his family.

"Nathanial."

He turned around and found himself face-to-face
with the bishop.

"I've been thinking about you. How are things working out at the Kauffmans' place?" the bishop asked, a
curious expression on his face.

Nathanial stepped away from the table so that the

women could set it. He noticed that Katie Mae glanced at him and, seeing him standing next to the bishop, she widened her eyes.

"*Gut*, Bishop. Right *gut*."

The older man smiled. "Why am I not surprised?"

Nathanial narrowed his eyes, wondering what that was supposed to mean.

The bishop continued talking. "I knew that you were the right man to help spruce up that farm. No man in our church district has a stronger work ethic, that's for sure and certain."

Ah. Nathanial lowered his eyes. "No more so than other men, I'm sure."

"Now, I know we're not supposed to do business on Sundays," the bishop said in a low voice, "but talking business can't be a sin. I wanted you to know that the bank man saw me yesterday and said he's got a buyer for your farm."

Suddenly, Nathanial felt as if the room were spinning. Any thoughts about Katie Mae or her father disappeared. The only thing he could focus on were those words: a buyer for your farm. Why, once that farm sold, he'd be at the mercy of Katie Mae! She could toss him out if she felt so inclined.

Swallowing, Nathanial tried to push away any such thoughts. "Do you know who?"

"A young couple from a neighboring district. Good family. Just married two years ago." The bishop reached out and put his hand on Nathanial's shoulder. "I'm sure that selling the farm isn't easy, but it is the best thing, Nathanial. You've helped the Kauffmans by renting their farmhouse and now you've helped this young couple."

Somehow that didn't quite make Nathanial feel better. At least not at the present moment.

"God has a plan," the bishop added, as if reading Nathanial's mind. "We just don't always see it when things don't go the way *we* planned."

That was for sure and certain, he thought.

Nathanial nodded his head and glanced around the room, more to collect his thoughts than for any other reason. However, he caught sight of Katie Mae once again and she was still setting the other table, her eyes watching him.

Nathanial cleared his throat. "*Ja,* that's true, Bishop. And speaking of plans, Katie Mae asked me to speak to you about her own plans."

The bishop raised one of his white wiry eyebrows. "Oh?"

"About Abraham."

The bishop pursed his lips, obviously curious about what Nathanial had to say. "Go on."

"Seems he's been doing a bit better."

The bishop glanced around the room until he found Abraham, already seated at the men's table. "Is that so?"

"He's been responding, smiling a bit, and he even tried to use his own spoon the other night."

This caught the bishop's attention. "His own spoon?"

Once again, Nathanial nodded. "He pushed away Katie Mae's hand when she was feeding him and took the spoon in his own. It took a while, but he managed to get it to his mouth." He paused. "He wore most of the applesauce, but that was quite a feat for him."

"Indeed!" The bishop appeared genuinely surprised. "What right *gut* news!"

"Anyway, she was wondering about sending him for physical therapy and—"

The bishop inhaled and held up his hand. "Say no more. She's wondering about Amish Aid, ain't so?"

"*Ja,* that's it."

The bishop took a moment before he responded. He seemed to be contemplating his response, his eyebrows furrowed and his mouth taut. Nathanial couldn't help but wonder what, if anything, there was to think about. Amish communities took care of their own people when they had a health crisis. That's why every family paid into the Amish Aid fund, rather than buying that *Englische* health insurance.

Raising his hand to his beard, the bishop stroked it in a pensive manner. "That sure does present a little problem, Nathanial."

Now it was Nathanial's turn to be surprised. "How so?"

"Well, you see, Katie Mae hasn't been paying into Amish Aid. Not for a year or more." Before Nathanial could respond, the bishop held up his hands. "Now, I'm not saying no. But I have to look at the funds we have and how much need there is among the rest of the community. Mayhaps we might be able to contribute something, but she might have to pay for the bulk of it. You know that Susie Kapp fell and broke her hip. She needs a replacement. Jacob Mast is in hospital. And John David's wife has that breast cancer. Seems everyone's needing help this time of year."

Katie Mae hadn't been contributing to Amish Aid? For a long moment, Nathanial wasn't certain how to respond. Every family contributed, even if just a few dollars. Surely things must have been downright terrible for the Kauffmans if *that* had been neglected. Even he had paid, despite having ignored his other bills.

"Well, I sure do appreciate anything you can do, Bishop." It was the only thing Nathanial could think to say. He was still stunned by what he had just learned.

After he parted company with the bishop, he noticed that Katie Mae was staring at him, a hopeful expression on her face. He tried to give her a reassuring smile, but found he was hard-pressed to find one to give. Surely she would ask him later. What exactly would he say to her?

Chapter 11

On Wednesday, Katie Mae was ready when Linda showed up to watch her father so that she could go to town. She had her list in hand and could hardly wait to get out of the house.

"You seem about as energetic as a new colt in the spring," Linda said as she removed her black coat and hung it on a peg.

Katie Mae frowned. Was she that obvious? Perhaps she needed to slow down a bit. "I'm sorry. I've been cooped up for a week. I'm eager to get out a spell."

Linda looked as if she were hiding a smile. "Cooped up? Why, I saw you at worship, I seem to recall. In fact, you helped me wash the dishes. Didn't seem so cooped up then."

"Well . . . I . . ." Katie Mae stammered. She didn't want to admit to Linda that she was hoping Nathanial was readying the buggy to take her to town. He'd done so for two weeks in a row now and, despite her outer appearance of indifference, she was rather looking forward to being in his company again. *That* was something she wouldn't admit, not even to Linda!

Just as importantly, Katie Mae was eager to find out if the bishop had gotten back to Nathanial about her father.

On the ride home from the worship service, she hadn't dared to ask. Not in front of the children or her father. And she hadn't seen Nathanial later that evening. Becky had wandered over, having taken it upon herself to visit Abraham every day after supper. Clearly the little girl had found a captivated (indeed, captive) audience for her reading. And Abraham truly enjoyed her company.

Why! On Monday evening, Becky had helped Abraham hold her book so that she could point to the different pictures as she read the story. Katie Mae had fought tears as she watched the two of them. Later that same evening, Nathanial had come to fetch Becky for bed, and Katie Mae finally had the chance to ask about his conversation with the bishop. Nathanial's response that the bishop was going to look into it did nothing to quell her eagerness to get her father into physical therapy. He was doing so well! Katie Mae knew—just knew!—that he was ready.

When she glanced up, she was surprised to see that Linda was staring at her. Was she still anticipating a response? "It's just that I have a lot to do in town," Katie Mae said at last.

"Oh?"

Clearly Linda wasn't about to let her off the hook so easily.

"*Ja,* I do. I need to stop at the store for some dry goods. I promised little Becky I'd make some chocolate chip cookie bars for the school pageant." She hadn't wanted to admit that, but Katie Mae figured Linda would know soon enough since two of her own children were in it.

"Really?"

Katie Mae clenched her teeth, biting back the *mind your own business* that she wanted to blurt out. "It seems like a festive thing to do," she managed to say calmly. "Daed's taken a liking to Becky. Why, he even used his own spoon the other night when . . ." Her voice trailed off. She didn't want to admit that it had been when she cooked for the Millers. "Well, he just did, that's all."

Linda leaned against the counter and glanced toward where Abraham was seated in his wheelchair. Katie Mae followed her gaze. As usual, her father was near the window, his eyes scanning the fields and barnyard. Just by watching him, Katie Mae could tell that Nathanial was doing something outside, for her father's face lit up whenever he saw someone working within his line of vision.

"I thought I heard something about that," Linda admitted. "What *wunderbaar gut* news, Katie Mae! You must be overjoyed."

The fact that Linda had heard about it must have meant that word had spread about Abraham's progress and her request! Surely the bishop must have talked to people. She knew that Nathanial had run errands the previous day. Certainly he had gone to visit the bishop! Katie Mae could hardly wait to find out what the bishop had said.

Oh, she would have considered asking the bishop herself, but she felt too ashamed after his comment that she hadn't been paying into the Amish Aid fund. Besides, she knew that the bishop liked Nathanial Miller—hadn't he gone out of his way to help Nathanial find a solution to his financial problems? The bishop would never say no to *him*.

"Overjoyed is putting it lightly." Katie Mae gave Linda a big smile. "Just think, if he gets better, he could actually start working his own farm again. He'd be so happy."

Linda, however, didn't share her delight. Katie Mae could tell from the way her smile disappeared. "Is that what you're thinking about then? Your *daed* recovering to work the farm?" A dark cloud appeared to pass over her face. "I'd think that would be a long time coming, Katie Mae. And given his age and what he's been through, wouldn't you be happy with him just being able to communicate again? To maybe walk a bit? Enjoy life?"

She felt the color flood her cheeks. That hadn't been what she'd meant, but she knew how it must have sounded to Linda.

"Besides, your farm is starting to look so much better. Why, that Nathanial Miller is one of the hardest workers in our *g'may*! Have you noticed how every fence is fixed? How clean the yard is?" Linda gave Katie Mae a stern look. "Would you really want your *daed* working that hard?"

"*Nee,* but—"

Linda shook her head and interrupted her. "Katie Mae, we've been friends a long time and I know you are headstrong and independent. But mayhaps it's time you realize that you need to turn things over to God and let his plan unveil itself. Sometimes I think you fight his plan and it sure does cause you an awful lot of disappointments."

Katie Mae pressed her lips together and took a deep breath. She hadn't expected to be dressed down by Linda, of all people! And that truly hadn't been what she meant. She wasn't so foolish that she envisioned her father plowing fields or harvesting corn. But she knew that he loved farming. Even if he could sit behind the horses while someone else drove them, he'd be happier than anything! But Linda had misunderstood what she had meant.

"I best get going," Katie Mae said in a terse voice. "*Danke* for watching Daed."

She started for the small mudroom and heard Linda call out, "It's awfully cold out, so make certain you bundle up."

Irritated that Linda was acting so motherly, Katie Mae purposely took her shawl and not her coat. *There,* she thought angrily. *That will show you who's the boss of me!*

Nathanial had greeted Linda when she walked down the lane and immediately had harnessed the horse and hitched it to the buggy. He waited patiently for Katie Mae to emerge from the house so that he could take her to town. In fact, he had been anticipating this time ever since the bishop had stopped by the previous afternoon.

But when he saw Katie Mae storm out of the house, wearing only her black wool shawl, he knew something was wrong.

"You're going to be cold in that," he said as he opened the buggy door for her. "Where's your heavy coat?"

She glared at him.

Oh ja, he thought. *Something's wrong indeed.*

He helped her into the buggy and unhitched the horse from the post before climbing inside. Sure enough, she was already shivering. "You sure you don't want to go get your coat?"

"I'm fine."

While she didn't look fine—her lips were trembling—Nathanial wasn't about to argue with an angry Katie Mae

Kauffman. "Alrighty then," he said, and backed up the horse. "Where to, Katie Mae?"

She reached for something under the shawl and withdrew her purse. He drove the horse down the driveway as she dug through it, looking for something.

"Oh help!" she muttered.

"What's wrong?"

"I forgot my list."

"Shall I turn back then?"

But she shook her head. "*Nee.* I'll remember what I can."

"You sure?"

"Oh *ja!* I'm sure!"

The way she said that, with such fierce determination and a scowl on her face, almost made him chuckle. But he knew that would be the wrong reaction. After all, she was most certainly bothered by something and *that* was nothing to laugh about.

"If you don't mind me asking," he started in a slow, calm voice, "you seem a bit frazzled. Something happen?"

From the corner of his eye, he saw her glance at him, a contemplative expression on her face as if she were considering confiding in him. There was a long hesitation before she must have decided to keep it to herself.

"Nothing, I suppose."

Nathanial held the reins with one hand and reached up to scratch at the side of his beard. "Nothing, eh? Well, if that nothing becomes something, I'm here should you need someone to talk to."

He felt, rather than saw, her turn toward him. He didn't risk trying to look at her. Instead, he kept his eyes focused on the road. For a moment, he thought she might snap at him, tell him to mind his own business.

But she didn't.

"*Danke*, Nathanial," she said in a soft voice. "I appreciate that."

Once again, Nathanial couldn't help but wonder about Katie Mae Kauffman. She sure had softened up toward him and he had to admit that this new side of her was rather charming. Still, he wasn't about to ask her about courting him. Not yet. It was too soon, and he was uncertain whether or not she was actually beginning to care for him. If she rejected him, he'd feel most awkward being around her in the future and, having just gotten settled onto the Kauffman farm, he wasn't ready for such a refusal.

He had almost asked her the other night after that wonderful Friday night supper. Perhaps he was motivated by nostalgia for a regular family life or more joyful suppers like that, with his children enjoying real home-cooked food and a woman hovering over the boys, making certain they ate enough and used their manners. Or maybe it was the fact that she had asked him about his day and what his plans were for the weekend. Oh! It had been right good to feel like a family, even if they weren't.

When she had come out to join him on the porch, braving the cold with her shawl wrapped around her and asking him to speak to the bishop, he had thought she must have been reading his mind.

But that moment of delighted surprise quickly dissipated. She hadn't wanted him to speak to the bishop about their getting married; no, she wanted him to speak to the bishop about her father.

"I noticed you were gone yesterday," Katie Mae said, breaking the silence that lingered in the buggy. "You didn't happen to see the bishop, did you now?"

He had known the question was coming. And he wasn't certain how, exactly, to answer. For a long moment, he contemplated his response. He wanted to tell her that, indeed, he had gone to see the bishop. Together, they had gone to the bank and finalized the details about selling his farm. He would have a nice, tidy sum of money to put in the bank after he paid off his debt.

He felt the urge to share that information with her. With *someone*.

But that wasn't what she wanted to know. He hadn't even told her there was a buyer.

No. What Katie Mae wanted to know was whether or not the community would help her pay for Abraham's physical therapy.

"Is something wrong?"

When she spoke, he started. He had been so lost in his thoughts that he hadn't realized so much time had passed since she'd asked him about whether or not he had seen the bishop.

"I'm sorry," he said quickly. "*Ja,* I did see the bishop yesterday."

It felt as if her eyes were boring a hole in him.

"And?"

He stopped the horse at the light that led into town. "Where am I taking you anyway?" he asked.

She pointed toward the left. "Yoders' Meat and Cheese," she replied. "About the bishop, Nathanial?"

"Ah, *ja.* Well, it's like this, Katie Mae . . ." When he paused, he heard her catch her breath. He glanced at her and saw a shadow of fear cover her face. She looked so vulnerable. Once again, he realized how this new side of Katie Mae Kauffman was tugging at his heart. "Abraham's physical therapy will be paid for by the community."

She gasped and clutched her hands together, pulling them into her chest in a gesture of childish delight. "Oh, Nathanial!" A laugh escaped her throat. "You scared me for a moment!" Playfully, she swatted at his arm. "I thought you were going to say that the bishop said no!" She looked relieved and sank back into the buggy seat. "What *wunderbaar gut* news, Nathanial! And just before Christmas! Why, next year, you wait and see how my *daed* gets better!"

He smiled at her exuberance. "I think you're right, Katie Mae. Next year he's going to be a whole new man."

For the rest of the journey, Katie Mae's dark cloud lifted and she chattered happily. Nathanial listened to her talk about the cookies she was making for the school pageant and how Becky had practiced singing her song for her father the night before. The difference in her demeanor made him realize that he had missed the casual banter of a happy woman, more than he had thought possible. And being in her gleeful presence made him feel happier than he'd felt in a long, long time.

Chapter 12

On Friday, Katie Mae arose extra early to get ready for the big day. It was the Friday before Christmas and that meant that it was time for the annual school pageant. After dressing herself, she hurried downstairs and put on the coffeepot. She had promised to make the Miller children pancakes for breakfast and to help Becky with her hair.

For some reason, she felt extra excited. When was the last time she'd made breakfast for anyone other than her father? And he could only eat oatmeal or scrambled eggs.

The table was set and the pancakes ready when she heard the sound of footsteps outside of her door. To her surprise, it wasn't the children but Nathanial who walked through the door.

"Oh!" She glanced around him. "Where are the *kinner*?"

"Well, *gut martiye* to you, too."

She blushed. "I'm sorry. *Gut martiye*, Nathanial."

He laughed and Katie Mae found herself smiling.

What was it about Nathanial that had changed? Gone was the stern, grumpy man she remembered from the previous year when he had dropped off Martha to watch her father. Lately, he had seemed more relaxed and good natured, willing to laugh a little.

And she liked it.

"They'll be along momentarily."

Katie Mae hurried over to the counter and poured him a mug of freshly brewed coffee.

When she handed it to him, he was staring at her with a quizzical expression.

"What?" she asked.

He shook his head. "Nothing."

"No, tell me."

She watched as he raised the mug to his lips and took a sip. For a long second, he shut his eyes as if savoring the hot liquid. "Mmm. Why is it that coffee always tastes better when someone else makes it?"

Katie Mae laughed. It was true. She loved having coffee during fellowship after worship. It just tasted better. "I know exactly what you mean," she said. "Maybe it's because *you* didn't have to make it."

"Good point." He set the mug onto the counter.

"So why were you looking at me with that strange expression?"

He groaned. "You don't forget anything, do you?"

"Not usually."

Leaning against the counter, he crossed his feet at the ankles. "Well, if you must know," he said in a very thoughtful way, "I realized that you are always rushing around. No matter what you do, you hurry. Did you know that?"

His observation took her aback. Was it true? "I guess I never thought about it that way."

The conversation was abruptly interrupted by the

thunderous noise of four sets of feet pounding up the stairs to her door.

"Katie Mae!"

Through the door, Nathanial's children burst into the room, each one looking freshly scrubbed and wearing their Sunday best. Becky ran over to her and hugged her legs.

"Look at me!" She turned around. "I did my hair myself."

Katie Mae frowned. The little girl's hair was half underneath her prayer cap and that, too, was askew on her head.

"I see that!" She leaned down and straightened Becky's cap. "And a fine job you did."

Becky beamed.

"Now, do you all remember your songs? And Luke. Thomas. Have you remembered your Scripture to recite?" she asked.

In unison, they nodded.

"Very good!" She noticed that the boys were eyeballing the stack of pancakes already on the table. "Well, best get to eating your breakfast. Make certain to eat *slowly*." She emphasized the word *slowly* and looked pointedly at Becky. "No need to dirty your clothes with syrup."

Everyone sat down and Katie Mae started toward her father so that she could push his wheelchair to the table. But Nathanial beat her to Abraham.

"I'll bring him over, Katie Mae," Nathanial said. "You sit and relax a bit. After all this hard work making breakfast—"

"It wasn't hard work!" she protested. "It was nice to cook a big breakfast. Can't remember the last time I did."

But she did as he told her and took her place at the end of the table.

To her surprise, Nathanial wheeled her father to the far end of the table, next to Becky. She started to say something, but Becky was already reaching for the napkin that Katie Mae always tucked under Abraham's chin.

Nathanial took his seat at the head of the table, to the right of where Katie Mae sat. For a moment, Katie Mae was startled. Had he forgotten that *she* always sat next to her father? And that her father normally sat at the head of the table?

He must have noticed her frown. Leaning over, he whispered, "Becky insisted that she sit next to Dawdi Abraham."

That wasn't the first time she had heard one of the Miller children reference her father as "Dawdi," a term usually reserved for a grandfather. But it was the first time that Nathanial had said it.

One glance at her father and she saw that he was beaming, clearly pleased with the distinction.

Nathanial bowed his head and everyone else followed his example. When the silent blessing was over and the children began reaching for their pancakes, Katie Mae found that she was struck with how perfect everything felt. She had never imagined that something as simple as a breakfast could feel, oh, just so right!

Watching Katie Mae as she sat at the school desk, Nathanial had made up his mind. He knew what must be done. The smile on her face, the glow on her cheeks . . . Why, he knew that she deserved only the best and he had a suspicion that he could give it to her. But he had to talk to the bishop first.

The pageant ended and all four of his children ran to her, seeking her approval on their performances. He stood behind her, listening as she praised their singing and the recitation that both Luke and Thomas had given. With each kind word, his children seemed to grow three feet in stature.

Yes, Nathanial thought, *he had to do this.*

"Daed? And what did you think?"

Nathanial broke free from his thoughts and looked down at David. "Why, you did a right *gut* job, David." He scanned their faces. "All of you."

The boys glowed at his praise. Becky, however, had grabbed Katie Mae's hand and was dragging her toward the table full of sweets.

Now was his chance.

Nathanial put his hand on Thomas's shoulder. "You stay with Abraham. I'll be right back."

Thomas nodded and, as if given a major responsibility, positioned himself beside the older man's wheelchair, clearly intent on protecting Abraham from getting accidentally knocked by someone in the crowded schoolhouse.

Making his way through the crowd, Nathanial sought out the bishop. He stood with several other men, talking about the pageant and praising the teacher for having delivered a wonderful show for the parents and grandparents. Nathanial waited until the bishop looked up and caught his eye.

"Might I have a word with you, Bishop?" he asked. "In private?"

The bishop excused himself and followed Nathanial to the back corner of the schoolhouse. "Something amiss, Nathanial?"

He shook his head. "*Nee,* everything is right *gut*. But I do have a question for you." Before continuing, Nathanial glanced over the heads of the other people, making certain that Katie Mae was still preoccupied. Sure enough, she was standing at the table of cookies and brownies and sweet homemade candies, while Becky tried one of the sugar cookies. A tall, willowy woman with ginger red hair was talking with Katie Mae, but Nathanial didn't recognize her.

"Is something troubling you, Nathanial?" the bishop asked, bringing Nathanial's attention back to their conversation.

Nathanial shifted his weight and met the bishop's gaze. "*Ja,* something is troubling me, Bishop."

He paused, uncertain how to proceed. He'd never made such a request before. Perhaps he should have spoken to Katie Mae first. But the bishop was there now and Nathanial had to trust his instincts.

"Well, it's like this," Nathanial began. "When I stopped by on Tuesday to settle the details about the farm, you told me again that Amish Aid wouldn't be able to help Abraham Kauffman. Not right now, anyway."

The bishop pressed his lips together. "I told you that we have other—and more serious—folks in need, Nathanial. While I sure do feel for Abraham, his life is not in danger. There's only so much aid to go around."

"I understand that, Bishop." Nathanial licked his lips, feeling more nervous than he should. Ever since he had told Katie Mae that Abraham would be taken care of by the community, Nathanial had known what he wanted to do. But seeing her interaction with the children had made him more determined than ever to finalize it.

"And without her having paid into Amish Aid," the bishop said slowly, "well, that didn't help her case, Nathanial."

"And I understand that, too."

"So what seems to be the problem?"

Nathanial frowned. "Well, there's no problem. Not

really. But I've been thinking and praying, Bishop, about an idea that I have. An idea to help Abraham Kauffman. You can see for yourself how much better he's doing. Why! He was tapping his knee a bit when the *kinner* were all singing that last hymn!"

At this, the bishop sighed. "I saw that, Nathanial. I expect it makes my decision even harder to accept. And it wasn't easy for me, either."

Holding up his hand, Nathanial stopped the bishop from continuing. "I've decided to pay for Abraham's treatment."

His statement clearly startled the bishop. The older man's eyes widened and he appeared taken aback. "You?"

Nathanial nodded. "*Ja,* me."

"But you've only just sold your farm and made a little money. That money was to help you start over, Nathanial." He narrowed his eyes. "Do you know how expensive physical therapy will be for Abraham? It's not like one or two doctor visits. He could need a year, maybe two of therapy. Are you sure? Taking on that commitment could wipe you out."

Nathanial knew that. He had thought long and hard about it after his visit with the bishop on Tuesday. When he had told Katie Mae that the community would take care of Abraham, he had already made up his mind. But now, he knew that it would be best if she didn't realize the money came from him. Instead, he'd give the money to Amish Aid to cover Abraham's treatment.

If there ever was going to be a future between him and Katie Mae, he didn't want her feeling beholden to him for having paid for her father's medical bills.

His eyes traveled back to where Katie Mae was now speaking to the bishop's wife, Dorothy. She was laughing and had her hand on Becky's shoulder.

"Oh, I'm sure all right," Nathanial said, his heart feeling lighter. "So you can let her know that Amish Aid will take care of everything, then. And I'll be paying for those bills."

The bishop studied him for a long moment and then gave a little shrug. "As you wish, Nathanial. The next chance I get, I'll do just that."

Chapter 13

On Saturday, Katie Mae had agreed to watch Becky while Nathanial and the boys went to a special auction in Shipshewana. She knew it was unusual for the auction house to have a Saturday auction so close to Christmas and she wasn't too convinced that there would be much for Nathanial to buy. Besides, she couldn't help wondering what, on earth, he could possibly need!

It didn't matter, though. Becky had become a fixture in the *dawdihaus*. And knowing that Abraham enjoyed the little girl's company so much, Katie Mae certainly didn't mind.

"Can you make more cookies?" Becky asked after she finished coloring a picture at the table. She held up the paper for Abraham to see. "You like it?"

He smiled at her and mumbled a muffled *"Ja."*

"*Gut!* It's for you then!" She slid off the chair and carried it to him. Then she turned to Katie Mae. "Those sugar cookies that were at the school pageant were right *gut*. You know how to make them?"

Katie Mae smiled, proud of Becky for having worked so hard to lose her lisp. "Well, I don't think I know the recipe that Myrna used, but I do know how to make sugar cookies."

Becky grinned. "And make a lot so that I don't have to share too many with my *bruders*."

Her comment made Katie Mae want to smile, but she held it back. "Now, Becky, that's not very kind. You know that sharing is a godly thing to do."

Becky gave her a look as if questioning her statement. "That's why I want you to make a lot. So I *can* share!"

Abraham made a noise and Katie Mae wondered if he was laughing. It dawned on her that one of the reasons her father reacted so strongly to Becky was that the little girl reminded him of her. As she began pulling out a mixing bowl and cookie sheet, Katie Mae realized that Becky definitely had a similar personality to hers. Perhaps that was one of the reasons that she, too, found herself so enamored with the child.

"Oh help!" She put her hands on her hips. "I don't know if I have enough butter."

Becky straightened her back. "We have butter. Daed made some while we were at school this week."

The thought of Nathanial making fresh butter almost made Katie Mae laugh. "Your *daed* makes butter?"

"*Ja!* He makes it and sells it in town."

Clever, Katie Mae thought. Just one more surprising thing that she was learning about Nathanial Miller. She couldn't help but wonder why such an entrepreneurial and hardworking man could have lost his farm.

"Well, if he's got fresh butter, mayhaps you could run over to fetch me some?"

Becky paused and cocked her head at Katie Mae. "Might I stop in to see the cows first?"

Katie Mae put her hand on her hip. "Only if you wear your jacket! It's cold out there."

"Not *that* cold.*"

"No coat, no cookies."

Becky's tune immediately changed. "Deal!" With a jovial bounce to her step, Becky ran over to the mud-room, collected her too-large black coat, and slid her arms into the sleeves. Within seconds, she was outside, the storm door slamming shut behind her.

"And shut the door!" Katie Mae called out, but too late. Becky was already headed toward the barn.

Shaking her head, Katie Mae walked over and shut the wooden door so that no cold air seeped through. Even though she had swapped out the screens for glass inserts, the cold seemed to find a way through it.

Almost twenty minutes later, Becky hadn't returned yet. Katie Mae glanced at the clock. Where on earth was Becky? In the past, whenever Becky went to check on the cows, she took only a few minutes. Could she possibly have fallen when she was trying to get the butter from the refrigerator? Concerned, Katie Mae looked at her father and wondered if she should leave him alone to go check on the little girl.

"Daed? I need to run next door for a minute," she said. "You stay there, *ja?*"

His eyes moved and focused on her. He mumbled something and tried to lift his hand.

"I don't understand, Daed." She hurried over to him. "What is it?"

"Puh."

"I'll be right back. You stay put."

"Pu-uh."

"That's right. Put. You stay put."

She hurried out of the kitchen and, without grabbing her coat, ran down the walkway toward the porch of the main house. The door was shut but unlocked. Katie Mae opened it and called out for Becky.

Silence.

"Becky? You in here?" she called out again.

No answer.

She walked into the kitchen. It was empty.

Frowning, Katie Mae retreated outside and looked toward the dairy barn. She certainly hoped that Becky hadn't gotten hurt in the barn. A wave of panic rushed through her and, without another thought, she raced across the yard toward the dairy barn.

"Becky! Where are you?"

Inside the dairy, the cows stood at their stations chewing hay. It was warmer inside than outside from their body heat, but a chill went through her body anyway. Panicking, Katie Mae ran through the dairy and the stable, checking the feed room, stalls, and any nook or cranny she could find. There was no sign of Becky. Where could Becky have disappeared to?

Katie Mae knew that she had to find the little girl. What would Nathanial think if he came home and found his daughter was missing? What would he think of her then?

She wandered back to the barnyard and called Becky's name. She turned around, calling out over and over again. As she faced the house, her eyes fell upon the window of the *dawdihaus*. Her father was sitting there and, to her surprise, his hand was pressed against the window pane, a finger tapping the glass.

That was the moment she realized. *Puh*, her father had said. But he hadn't been trying to say *put*. He had been trying to say *pond*. He must have been trying to tell her that Becky had run toward the pond.

With her heart feeling as if it were in her throat, Katie Mae ran as fast as she could in the direction of the pond in the side paddock where the cows usually grazed.

"Won't Becky be surprised with the little bookshelf we got?" Thomas sang out as Nathanial drove the buggy down the road toward the Kauffmans' farm.

"Now you remember that it's something special for Christmas," Nathanial reminded his son. "No spoiling the surprise."

While he normally gave the children only small gifts for Christmas, when he'd seen the little bookshelf at the auction, he had known it was the perfect gift for Becky. Besides, with her growing collection of books, she needed a place to keep them.

"I won't tell, Daed."

Nathanial leaned over and nudged his eldest son's arm. "And you won't tell about our other little secret?"

Thomas beamed as he shook his head.

As Nathanial directed the horse to turn into the driveway, he noticed someone on the front lawn. Huddled in a heap. "What in the world?" He slowed down the horse and buggy, trying to make sense of what he saw. "Is that—?"

"Katie Mae!" Luke cried out.

"What's she doing on the ground like that?"

Nathanial stopped the horse and threw open the door. Whatever was going on, he knew it wasn't good news. Quickly, he jumped down from the buggy and ran to her. "What's wrong?"

She lifted her head and Nathanial saw that she was soaking wet. His eyes traveled from her face to her arms, and that was when he saw Becky.

Gasping, he dropped to his knees and took his daughter into his arms. "What happened? Why are you out here?"

"She's not breathing!"

It took a moment for Nathanial to process what Katie Mae had just said. Becky? Not breathing? He put his hands to Becky's cheeks and felt how cold they were. Ice cold. That's when it dawned on him that she, too, was wet. The only good news was that she was, indeed, breathing.

"Let's get her inside." He didn't wait for Katie Mae to respond before he scooped Becky up and ran toward the house.

He couldn't imagine what had happened, but right now his main concern was warming up his daughter. He'd learn the details later. But from the look of anguish on Katie Mae's face, Nathanial suspected that his daughter was in trouble.

Once inside the house, Nathanial wrapped Becky in a blanket and held her close to his chest. "Wake up, Becky." He shook her a little and then rubbed her arms through the blanket. "Come on, little one."

Katie Mae stood in the doorway, her dress clinging to her and her face pale as winter snow. "She went for butter," Katie Mae whispered. "But she never came back."

Nathanial rocked back and forth, holding Becky tight. "She's freezing," he mumbled.

"She fell through the ice."

Immediately, Nathanial looked up. "What?"

"She must have gone to the pond and stood on the edge. It gave way about three feet out and . . ." Katie Mae sobbed, covering her mouth with her hand as the tears fell from her eyes. "I'm so sorry, Nathanial."

He frowned. Sorry? For what? Saving his daughter? "She just needs to warm up. Make her some tea."

For the next few minutes, Nathanial held Becky, continuing to rub her arms and legs. His eyes drifted to Katie Mae, watching as she bustled about the kitchen, heating up water and preparing a mug with a tea bag. She kept herself busy, although she continued glancing over her shoulder as if to make certain Nathanial and Becky were still there. When she finally brought over the tea, kneeling by the chair, the look of concern on Katie Mae's face touched him.

"*Danke,* Katie Mae," he said as he took the mug. He held it to Becky's face, letting the steam brush her skin. Sure enough, she mumbled and moved her head.

"So. Cold."

A loud sob escaped Katie Mae's lips and she turned away, covering her face with her hands.

Nathanial repositioned Becky and encouraged her to sip the hot tea. Obediently, she did, her strength slowly coming back.

"Why's Katie Mae crying?" she asked in a soft voice.

"She was scared, I reckon." Nathanial leveled his gaze at Becky. "Do you remember what happened?"

"I . . ." The little girl frowned as if trying to remember. "I saw the cows and then I went to the . . ." She stopped, bit her lower lip, and stared at her father with remorseful eyes. "I went to the pond, Daed."

"*Ja,* you did. And do you remember what I told you?"

Her eyes still wide and frightened, Becky gave a slight nod.

"And you disobeyed me."

"I'm sorry, Daed."

He frowned. "You could've died. Why, if Katie Mae hadn't found you . . ." He pressed his lips together. "Well, I don't want to think about what would've happened." He hugged Becky to his chest and tightened his arms around her. *Thank God for Katie Mae,* he thought.

Releasing Becky, he pulled the blanket around her

chest. "Now, you need to apologize to Katie Mae and then let's get you into dry clothes. You'll finish your tea and sit by the heater. No sense catching your death from the cold."

Becky slid off his lap and, with the blanket clutched around her, she stood before Katie Mae.

Before Becky could apologize, Katie Mae reached out and grabbed the little girl, pulling her into a warm, deep hug. "Oh, Becky! You scared me so!" Katie Mae sobbed. "What would I do without you? What would Dawdi Abraham do?" She clutched the girl and cried harder. "Don't ever do that again. Promise me."

"I promise," came the soft voice.

"Oh, girl!" Katie Mae pulled back and stared into Becky's face. "Don't you know how much I love you?"

Nathanial watched as his daughter nodded, his own heart beating rapidly as he watched the scene unfold. The intensity of Katie Mae's loving rebuke sent a warm burst of energy throughout his body. She'd *saved* Becky. She *cried* over Becky. Most importantly, she *loved* Becky.

He hadn't realized how important it was to not just love others but to be loved by others. And, as he watched Katie Mae fussing over Becky and taking the little girl upstairs to change her dress, forgetting that she, too, needed to change into dry clothes, Nathanial realized that it was time for all of his family to be loved again.

And not just by anyone.

By Katie Mae.

Chapter 14

On Sunday, Katie Mae woke up even more tired than when she went to sleep the night before. In fact, she wasn't even certain if she *had* slept. The previous evening, she hadn't been able to eat a morsel of food at supper; her nerves were still too frayed by Becky's fall through the ice at the pond.

Oh, Nathanial could have told her a dozen more times that he didn't blame her, but Katie Mae knew that he *had* to blame her. After all, *she* blamed herself. How could she have been so careless? While she could blame it on the fact that she'd never had any siblings, neither younger nor older, she knew the truth was that she just hadn't been thinking.

All night, she had tossed and turned, her mind reeling at the what-ifs. What if she hadn't found Becky? What if her *daed* hadn't seen Becky go to the pond? What if Becky had drowned? And, while all of those what-ifs were moot because they hadn't happened, there was one more pressing question that was very much in the realm of possibility: What if Nathanial never forgave her?

That thought had troubled her so much that she couldn't stop herself from fretting.

Just when everything had been looking so positive!

Her *daed* was making progress. Nathanial had proven himself to be a good, kind man. And the bishop had agreed for Amish Aid to pay for her father's physical therapy. Why, the new year had looked so bright and promising!

But Katie Mae knew that she had just ruined everything. By letting Becky out of her sight for just a few minutes, she had proven herself to be irresponsible and incapable of taking care of Nathanial's children. What man would ever want such a woman for a wife?

After Katie Mae had cleaned the dishes from their noon meal, she sat at the table, nursing a lukewarm cup of coffee. She sighed and stared at nothing. She didn't see the wall or the calendar that hung beneath the round clock. She didn't see the knickknacks that she had placed on a shelf just two weeks earlier when she had unpacked her box of things. Instead, she only saw a bleak future that did not include Nathaniel and his children.

And that upset her.

Was it possible that, in just a few weeks, she had grown *too* fond of the Miller family? She knew that she was more than fond of Becky. Indeed, she loved that little girl and not just because she made Abraham want to get better. She had even grown fond of the three boys, though she rarely saw them. Not like Becky, anyway.

It was Nathanial who puzzled her. Ever since that Wednesday, the very first one, when he had taken her to Shipshewana and took forever in Yoders' Hardware store, she had begun to see a different side of him. There was an important lesson to be learned from her relationship with Nathanial. Sometimes the *first* impression was not the *correct* impression.

If Nathanial never forgave her for being so irresponsible with Becky, Katie Mae didn't know what she would do. Surely he would move away and, besides not being there to tend to the farm, he would take the children away, too. *That* loss troubled Katie Mae enormously.

But she knew that she would miss Nathanial, too.

The way he teased her sometimes. The way he took her to town on Wednesdays. The way he helped care for her father—and without being asked! And, of course, the way he sometimes looked at her when he thought she wasn't paying attention. His eyes lit up, and there was something distant and soulful in his expression. As if he, too, were considering the possibilities.

Surely he'd never have that look in his eyes again, not after Becky was almost lost to him.

To them.

Sighing, Katie Mae lifted the coffee mug to her lips. There was nothing she could do about it now. As her mother had always told her, things happened for a reason. Perhaps this was God's way of hinting that Nathanial was not the right man for her. Perhaps this was God's reminder that her role was not to be someone's wife, but to continue being someone's daughter.

She looked up, curious that her father still sat by the window. By this time, he normally was already taking a nap. But he was wide-eyed and staring at something. Curious, Katie Mae stood up and walked over to stand behind him.

"What's going on out there, Daed?" she asked, not expecting an answer. Her gaze followed his, and she saw that Nathanial was busy hitching the harnessed horse to the buggy. Vaguely, she remembered him telling her that he had distant relatives in Middlebury. Certainly that was where he was taking the children for supper. Perhaps they were even staying overnight so that they could visit for Christmas Eve on Monday. Because she hadn't spoken to him that day, she had no way of knowing.

Oh, it was going to be a long night and even longer day tomorrow. She could hardly bear the thought of what Christmas Day would bring. She and her father had no plans. Most people had families to celebrate with—children and grandchildren, cousins and siblings.

Not the Kauffmans. It was just her and Abraham.

She had wanted to invite Nathanial but hadn't done so. Now she was too afraid to ask him.

Katie Mae let her hand rest on her father's shoulder. She gave him a gentle squeeze. "Let's get you to bed for your nap, Daed. And then you can keep me company later when I'm making soup for supper."

Quietly, she pushed his wheelchair toward the back of the great room where her father slept so that she could help him into his hospital bed. Focusing on her father gave her something to do and helped to take her mind off the whirlwind of thoughts that haunted her mind.

After Nathanial bundled up the children and put them into the buggy, he unhitched the horse and climbed into the front seat. It was cold in the buggy, but the children had blankets wrapped around them to keep them warm.

He glanced in the back, his eyes falling onto Becky to make certain she wasn't looking peaked. She was bright eyed and rosy cheeked, none the worse for her fall through the ice the previous day.

"Ready, then?"

Four little heads nodded and Nathanial turned around, focusing his attention on driving the horse.

The previous night, he had barely slept at all. Besides realizing how dangerously close he had come to losing Becky, he had also realized how grateful he was for Katie Mae's attentiveness. Why, if she hadn't been so aware of Becky's disappearance, the little girl could've done more than fallen through the ice! She could have slipped beneath it and drowned.

Nathanial shuddered at the thought. What if they hadn't found her? What if she had drowned and no one knew it? The thought was too much to bear and he pushed it far from his mind.

Becky had not drowned and Katie Mae had rescued her. That had been God's plan.

And all night long, Nathanial had wondered why.

In the morning, he knew. God's plans were not always easy to decipher. But, after milking the cows and returning to the house to make a pot of coffee, he was convinced that God was sharing his plan.

And that was when Nathanial decided to pay a little Sunday afternoon visit to the bishop.

"The bishop?" Luke cried out from the back of the buggy. "But it's not a worship Sunday!"

Nathanial tried to hide his smile. "The bishop is part of our community, Luke. We can visit him, don't you think?"

Luke sighed. "I guess."

"It'll just be a short visit," he said.

Less than fifteen minutes later, Dorothy greeted them with a broad smile when she opened the door. "Why Nathanial Miller! Come in, come in! It's too cold to stand out there."

Nathanial herded his children through the door before he stepped inside.

"What brings you here? Such a pleasant surprise!" She looked at each child before her eyes settled on Becky. "Let me guess. You must have heard that I baked cookies yesterday for Christmas Eve supper tomorrow!"

Becky gave her a sideways glance. "Are they sugar cookies?" she asked inquisitively.

Dorothy's mouth opened just a little as if surprised by Becky's question. "How did you know?"

Becky narrowed her eyes, giving her a suspicious look. "Are they like the sugar cookies from the school pageant?"

At this question, Dorothy frowned. It took her a minute to realize what Becky was actually asking. "Oh, you mean the ones that Myrna brought? Why, no. They aren't the exact same ones, Becky, but isn't a sugar cookie a sugar cookie?"

Becky didn't look convinced.

"Dorothy, is the bishop here?" Nathanial asked. "I've something I need to talk to him about."

The older woman straightened up. "Why *ja,* of course. He's in the sitting room. You go on back there and let me get a sugar cookie or two for the *kinner.*"

Nathanial removed his hat and, hesitantly, walked down the narrow hallway toward the room Dorothy had indicated. He paused in the doorway and saw that the bishop was reading his Bible underneath the gas lantern. The bright light was blinding, and the release of gas made a loud, hissing noise.

He hated to interrupt the bishop, but he did need to speak to him. So he cleared his throat and waited for the bishop to look up.

"Nathanial!" He shut the Bible and motioned to the chair beside him. "What a nice surprise. I can't remember the last time you visited on a Sunday afternoon."

Nathanial took the proffered seat.

"Where are the *kinner*?"

"Dorothy's giving them sugar cookies."

The bishop nodded. "Ah! It *is* that time of year, isn't it? Can't have Christmas without sugar cookies."

Nathanial smiled.

A momentary silence filled the room, broken only by the noise of the lantern.

Leaning forward, the bishop studied Nathanial's face. "I suspect you aren't here just for the sugar cookies."

At this comment, Nathanial laughed. "*Nee,* I'm not."

"So what brings you visiting, Nathanial?"

Oh! Nathanial couldn't help but twist his hands together. He wasn't any good at this! "Well, you see, I need to speak to you about a situation." He paused as if to give the bishop a chance to say something, but the bishop remained quiet, patiently waiting for Nathanial to speak his mind. "It's about Katie Mae Kauffman and the situation at the farm."

The bishop let his mouth open, surprised. "But I thought things were going well, Nathanial. That you wanted to pay for Abraham's medical bills! Have you changed your mind?"

Quickly, Nathanial held up his hand. "*Nee.* I mean, *ja!* I mean . . ." He dropped his hand and let his shoulders sag. "Oh, I reckon I don't know exactly what I mean, bishop. It's just that there's so much responsibility and—"

The bishop must have sensed his confusion. He interrupted Nathanial and said, in a soft voice, "Sometimes it helps when you start at the beginning, Nathanial."

The beginning. Yes, he thought. That was a good place to begin.

"Well, you see, when I first met Katie Mae, I was bringing Martha over to sit with Abraham and, frankly, Katie Mae and I didn't quite see eye to eye on things," he began. As he continued talking, letting the story slowly unfold, Nathanial was relieved that the bishop didn't interrupt him again. Instead, he merely listened, occasionally nodding his head.

By the time he came to the end, the objective of his visit, Nathanial saw the curious expression on the bishop's face change to something else: joy.

And, once again, Nathanial knew that, no matter how uncomfortable his meeting with the bishop, that, too, had been a part of God's plan.

Chapter 15

"**M**erry Christmas, Katie Mae!"

She looked up from where she sat at the table, writing another letter to Marybeth and her cousin Carolyn. Marybeth was getting married, and the two of them were to be her side sitters! She looked forward to sharing her cousin's joy. She had just sat down to begin writing when she heard the door to her house open. To her surprise, the bishop and his wife stood in the doorway of her kitchen.

"Bishop! Dorothy!" Katie Mae set down her pen before getting up and hurrying over to shake their hands. "Merry Christmas!"

"Merry Christmas, Katie Mae!" Dorothy handed her a plastic bin with some cookies in it. "I wanted to share some Christmas cookies with you."

"*Danke*!"

"I understand that you have some little ones around here who favor sugar cookies." Dorothy laughed. "Why, just the other night, at our *haus*, Becky ate three before I told her she couldn't have any more!"

Katie Mae wanted to ask why the Millers had been at

their house, but she stopped short. That wasn't any of her business, for sure and certain.

"I didn't want to ruin her supper, you see," Dorothy added.

Katie Mae smiled as she took the plastic container. Uncertain what to say, she glanced from Dorothy to the bishop. She didn't want to ask why they had stopped by, but she was certainly curious.

As if reading her mind, the bishop answered her un-spoken question. "We're on our way to my *schweister*'s *haus* in Middlebury and thought we'd stop by for a quick minute." The bishop looked over Katie Mae's shoulder and searched the room until his eyes fell upon her father. "Abraham! Merry Christmas!" He turned toward Katie Mae. "I'm sure Nathanial told you about your *daed*'s physical therapy."

Ah, she thought. So that's why the bishop stopped by. "He did, *ja*." Katie Mae smiled. "And *danke*, Bishop. It means a lot that Amish Aid will help my *daed*."

The bishop waved his hand at her. "Don't be thanking me. You thank that kind and generous man next door."

Nathanial? Katie Mae frowned. Why would she need to thank Nathanial? It was the bishop who had approved payment for her father's care. Of course, she *had* asked Nathanial to speak to the bishop on her behalf, but she had already thanked him for doing that. "Well, I did thank him for speaking to you—"

But the bishop wasn't listening. Instead, he continued talking about Nathanial. "Why, when he approached me and offered to pay for your *daed*'s physical therapy, I knew that Dorothy had been right about the two of you."

What on earth was he talking about? Nathanial paying her father's medical bills? And what did Dorothy have to do with anything? "I'm sorry," Katie Mae said, giving her head a slight shake as if clearing away cobwebs in her brain. "I don't think I understand."

The bishop paused. "You know that when he first asked me about getting physical therapy for your *daed*, I told him that Amish Aid couldn't help Abraham right yet. Our fund is depleted right about now, Katie Mae. Otherwise we would certainly have helped."

This was news indeed!

"And then, after the pageant, he asked to speak with me and told me that he would pay Abraham's bills." The bishop tilted his head and studied her expression. "Surely he told you, didn't he?"

Her silence answered the question.

With a sharp intake of breath, Dorothy nudged her husband. "Look what you did now," she scolded. "I reckon he wanted to surprise her. You best be keeping your lips sealed before you ruin any other surprises Nathanial has for Katie Mae." She leaned forward and whispered into her husband's ear, just loud enough that Katie Mae could hear. "It *is* Christmas. Remember?"

"Nee, nee," Katie Mae said quickly. She didn't want to get the bishop in trouble. Still, she wondered if Nathanial would still pay for the treatment, especially after the pond incident. "I . . . I knew that Daed's treatment was being taken care of."

The bishop clasped his hands together in a melodramatic way. "Oh thank goodness! When Nathanial stopped by on Sunday, he made no mention of not having told you."

Stunned, Katie Mae wasn't certain what to say to the bishop and his wife. Katie Mae felt her heart begin to beat faster. If Nathanial had gone to speak to the bishop on Sunday, that meant one and only one thing: He forgave her! He didn't blame her for the accident! And, if what the bishop was saying was true—and she had no reason to doubt him!—Nathanial had offered to pay for her father's treatment.

Oh joyous day!

Inside, she felt light-headed. The bishop and his wife continued speaking, but Katie Mae was hardly listening. In fact, she could hardly wait for them to leave. There was only one thing on her mind: She needed to go next door, find Nathanial, and thank him for this wonderful Christmas gift.

"Nathanial!"

He looked up when she swooped into the kitchen. Her face glowed and her eyes sparkled as she hurried toward him, her arms outstretched to embrace him.

Taken aback by such an intimate greeting, Nathanial took a second before he embraced her back. "Well, isn't this a different sort of greeting," he said in a teasing tone. "Must be special for Christmas morning."

She pulled back and stared up at him. "The bishop stopped by, Nathanial."

"Oh?"

"And he told me all about your discussion with him."

Nathanial blinked. Why on earth had the bishop told her? "He did?"

She nodded her head, a smile still playing on her lips. "Oh *ja,* he did."

Nathanial scratched at the back of his neck. Her reaction surprised him. "And you're happy about it? Even though you heard from the bishop and not me?"

Again, she nodded emphatically. "Oh, very happy, Nathanial. Why, I don't think I could be happier."

They were interrupted as the children came running down the stairs. Nathanial took a step backward, putting a little distance between him and Katie Mae. But Thomas was too observant.

A devastated expression clouded his face. "Daed! Did you already give Katie Mae her gift?"

Becky shoved a path through her brothers. "He gave her the gift?" She looked at Thomas, Luke, and David before turning to face her father. "You said you'd wait for us."

Katie Mae laughed. "All of the *kinner* knew, too?"

Nathanial could hardly respond. Oh, this had not been the way he had planned it. But her reaction made it all worthwhile. "Seems the bishop let the cat out of the bag," Nathanial admitted.

"But she accepted?"

Katie Mae knelt down and hugged Becky. "Of course I did! Why wouldn't I?"

Becky put her arms around Katie Mae's neck. "What a great Christmas! A new bookshelf and a new *mamm*!"

Nathanial noticed that Katie Mae stiffened. Immediately, she pulled back and stared at Becky. "What did you just say?"

"Daed and my *bruders* gave me a bookshelf for Christmas."

"*Nee,* Becky, the other part."

"About you marrying Daed and being our new *mamm*!"

She stood up and turned to Nathanial. He couldn't help but notice that her cheeks were no longer pink with excitement. "Nathanial?" she asked in a soft voice. "What is this about? Marrying you?"

"Best go get her gift now." He motioned for the boys to go into the first-floor bedroom. Turning to face Katie Mae, he gave her a nervous smile. "I . . . I spoke to the bishop yesterday. I wasn't certain if he'd be willing to

do a January wedding. I know it's not the regular season
and all."

"Wedding?"

"Of course, if you want to wait until spring, I reckon
that's all right. I just figured that you'd be lonely next
door when Abraham goes to that rehab center." He hurried to the bedroom door as Thomas and Luke struggled
with something.

Effortlessly, Nathanial picked up the cloth-covered
gift and carried it to the farm table. He set it down and
stood back.

"Go on then," he said, too aware that he was grinning. "The boys helped me pick it out for you at the auction *haus* on Saturday."

She didn't speak as she moved over to the table. Quietly, she pulled back the cloth and stared at the beautiful
wooden clock. He thought he heard her catch her breath.

"I know it's not new," he said quickly. "But I thought
you'd love how the dark wood matches that table." He
pointed to the wall. "And if you hung it there, you could
see it when cooking or seated at the table."

"A wedding clock." She practically whispered the
words.

Cautiously, Nathanial approached her. She seemed so
thunderstruck and was behaving so oddly. Where was her
exuberance of before? "You do like it, don't you, Katie
Mae?"

Without looking up, she nodded just once.

The boys cheered.

Nathanial placed his hand upon her arm. "I'm awful
sorry that the bishop told you. I had wanted to do it myself." He glanced at the children. "They wanted to be
here, too. But I'm awful glad that you were so happy,
Katie Mae. We're going to have a right *gut* life to-

gether." He let his hand drop down the length of her arm. "All six of us. And your *daed*, too."

Suddenly Katie Mae gasped. "Daed! I left him next door all alone!"

Nathanial took hold of her so that she couldn't dash out of the kitchen. "Boys. Take Becky and fetch Abraham for us."

Without a moment's hesitation, the four children hurried out the door, leaving Nathanial alone with Katie Mae.

"You all right, Katie Mae?" he asked.

She kept her eyes averted. "I'm . . . I'm a little taken aback, Nathanial."

"I can see that." He bent his knees so that he could peer directly into her face. "I know it's soon, Katie Mae. And I know that we didn't exactly get started on the right foot. But I'll make you a *gut* husband and take real *gut* care of you and your *daed*. And I know you'll do the same for the *kinner*." He paused. "And me too."

He put his finger under her chin and tilted her head so that she had no choice but to look at him. His eyes moved back and forth as he studied her face. She looked scared, terrified in fact. And it dawned on him that he might have been mistaken.

"What, exactly, did the bishop say to you?"

She swallowed.

"Katie Mae?"

"He . . . he told me about you paying for Daed's medical bills."

Nathanial felt as if someone had knocked the wind out of him. "He didn't mention anything about marrying me, did he?"

Slowly, and without looking away, she shook her head.

"Oh, Katie Mae, I feel like such a fool!" He stepped backward. He should have realized it right away when she stopped acting so happy. Clearly she had no intention of marrying him. The humiliation was almost too much to bear. "What will I tell the *kinner*? They were so excited." He took a few steps, pacing. "And, Katie Mae, I was excited. I saw you taking such amazing care of Becky on Saturday and it hit me. You already *are* their mother. But I wanted you, too. To be my wife, not just to court!" He stopped pacing and dropped his arms to his sides. "I should've waited, not acted so rashly." He shook his head. What a fool he had been to think that she, too, could care for him as much as he cared for her.

She cleared her throat. "Nathanial."

He sighed and faced her.

"What you are going to tell the *kinner*," she said in a soft voice, "is that it's almost time for Christmas breakfast and their new *mamm* is cooking it . . . here, in *your* kitchen." She paused and looked around, the color returning to her cheeks and her eyes beginning to glow once more. "*Our* kitchen. And then we will spend the day, Nathanial, together and plan our January wedding."

As if on cue, the sound of the children interrupted the moment. When they entered the kitchen and saw their father embracing Katie Mae, Becky's face lit up and she cried out, "Prayers do come true! We've gotten our new *mamm* for Christmas!"

Without hesitation, she ran toward her father and Katie Mae, wrapping her arms around their legs. The boys laughed and, when Katie Mae hugged Becky back, Nathanial saw her motion for his sons to join them.

"Family hug," she said, and to Nathanial's delight, his sons joined them.

He placed his hand on Becky's head and met Katie

Mae's gaze. "Ja, Becky, God does make prayers come true. All it takes is faith in his plan for us."

While still hugging the children, Nathanial leaned down and gently brushed his lips against Katie Mae's forehead. "Merry Christmas, Katie Mae."

Sealed with a Kiss

JENNIFER BECKSTRAND

To Nicole, Jessica, Kate, Haley, Zach, and Tyler.
We don't write letters anymore, but we're sure good
over texts.

Acknowledgments

As always, I want to thank my wonderful agent, Nicole Resciniti, and my terrific editor, John Scognamiglio. They care about my work and make me a better writer. I also want to thank Tonya Robinette. Her prayers pull me through and give me strength to keep writing. My husband, Gary, is everything to me: my biggest fan, my greatest support, and my best friend. And of course, I would be nothing without my Heavenly Father. I acknowledge Him with a humble and grateful heart.

Chapter 1

Dear Cousins,

Clara forwarded me your circle letter, and it got here this morning. I've hardly had a minute to breathe since sunrise, and it is now ten o'clock at night. No matter the time, I wanted to scratch out a few lines to you before I fall into bed. There's no telling when I'll get the chance to write again. I don't wonder that die kinner will drive me straight to the grave.

I can't blame anyone but myself for getting into this pickle. My only excuse is that I've been restless and a little bored in Bonduel. The last real excitement I had was when Anna Helmuth invited me to join her knitting club. In my search for adventure, I've managed to find a place even smaller than Bonduel. The only people who have heard of Greenwood, Wisconsin, are the three dozen or so folks who live here, and Anna and Felty Helmuth, a dear elderly couple who seem to have relations in every Amish town in Wisconsin.

I suppose Anna Helmuth shares some of the blame for my situation. She asked me if I wanted to do something out of the ordinary, and I told her yes. Little did I know that out of the ordinary meant being stuck in frigid Greenwood tending seven—yes, seven—children for Anna's grandson Abraham and his wife, Mary.

So, dear Marybeth, I'm afraid my Christmas this year will be even more dismal than yours. At least Ingrid won't try to lock you inside your room by wedging pennies in the door. I finally had to climb out the window and shimmy down the bare rosebush. For sure and certain, I'm going to have a scar on my ankle.

Please give all the cousins and aunts and uncles my love. I hope you have a wonderful gute Grischtdaag. I will be in Greenwood for another six months unless I decide to run away and find another knitting club to join. I've had my fill of adventure.

With love,
Carolyn

"Freddie! You know better than to spread peanut butter on your sister!"

"She likes it," Freddie said, with that mocking, what-are-you-going-to-do-about-it smile that made Carolyn clench her teeth until they were likely to crack.

For sure and certain, she'd crack every tooth in her mouth before the year was out. "She won't like it when I have to scrub peanut butter out of her hair."

Carolyn Yutzy had always considered herself a sensible, patient girl, someone who was fond of children and capable of handling any situation. But that was before she'd met the oldest Stutzman twins. Those boys would make even Jakob Ammann, the founder of the Amish faith, throw his hat on the ground and stomp on it. Freddie and Felty Jr. were nine-year-old natural disasters, like a pair of tornadoes stampeding over the countryside, grinding rocks and fence posts with their teeth, and leaving devastation in their wake. Carolyn had nieces and nephews. She knew what normal, rambunctious little boys were like, but she'd never seen anything like the Stutzman twins.

Seven-year-old Luke was a dust devil, following the tornadoes wherever they chose to go, with the younger five-year-old twins, Lydia May and Lyle Mark, just trying to keep up. Only Elmer Mervin, who was three, and Rosie, ten months, sat still long enough to eat their supper, and Rosie only sat still because she was confined to a highchair. The two littlest ones were like bystanders caught in the storm with nowhere to go and nothing to do but watch and hope the tempest passed them by.

"You've wasted half the peanut butter," Carolyn said, immediately regretting it. Freddie couldn't have cared one way or the other.

Freddie laughed and stuck his tongue out at her. "Mamm will be wonderful mad at you."

Carolyn closed her lips on a frustrated growl. She really didn't care if Mary Stutzman was mad that Freddie had painted little Rosie with peanut butter, but she was concerned that Freddie and Felty seemed eager to get Carolyn in trouble for it. Carolyn wasn't unkind or inept, she made delicious desserts for *die kinner*, and she'd only been in Greenwood a week. Why did the older twins hate her so much?

Except for Rosie and Elmer, all *die kinner* seemed to hate her. Carolyn wasn't a quitter, but she had half a mind to pack up her things and run back to Bonduel. She could help Mamm and Dat make candy for the Christmas rush, have long talks with Clara, and join as many knitting clubs as she wanted to.

Unfortunately, she'd told both Anna Helmuth and Mary Stutzman that she'd stay for six months. She had thought at the time everything in Greenwood would be pies and cakes. After all, Elsie Stutzman, Abraham's *schwester*, was a dear friend. Elsie was the school-teacher—at least until she married Sam Sensenig next summer—and Carolyn adored her. Half the reason Carolyn had come to Greenwood was because she was excited to get to know more of Elsie's family. Little had she known that Elsie's nephews were the most unlikable children in the world. Still, Carolyn couldn't leave Mary and Abraham high and dry right before Christmas, no matter how many times *die kinner* short-sheeted her bed.

She snatched the peanut butter jar from Freddie. "Freddie, Felty, go muck out the barn like your *dat* asked you almost an hour ago."

Felty lifted his cup to his lips and blew bubbles in his milk. He worked up a *gute* foam, and milk dribbled onto his plate.

Carolyn gritted her teeth harder. Getting angry would only make things worse. It was childish to yell and useless to lose her temper. She'd already tried that, and Felty and Freddie had laughed in her face. "Felty, I said it's time to muck out the barn."

Felty pulled his lips from the cup, his face a foamy, dripping mess. "I'm not done with my sandwich yet." He'd spent fifteen minutes tearing his peanut butter and jam sandwich into small bits, then spacing the pieces apart on his plate and pressing his finger into every piece.

"You've chosen to play with your food instead of eat it," Carolyn said. "You'll have to wait until dinner."

She reached out to clear his plate, but Felty was too fast. He stood, grabbed his plate from the table, and backed up to the wall. With his arm firmly wrapped around the plate, he picked up one of his sandwich bits and threw it at Carolyn. She marched toward Felty, raising her hands to shield her face as he pelted her with sandwich bits. "Felty, shame on you. Stop this minute." She may have raised her voice just a little, but only to make herself heard over Freddie's and Luke's hysterical laughter and Rosie's cries of distress. Carolyn couldn't blame Rosie. She'd cry too if her hair was slathered in peanut butter.

The ruckus must have been why she didn't hear the knock on the door, if there had been a knock. All she knew was that one second he wasn't there and the next second he was. A tall, broad-shouldered man without a beard appeared in the doorway, and Felty stopped throwing bread.

"What is all this?" the man said, with shock and superiority written all over his face.

The children stilled as if they were watching an *Englisch* movie. Carolyn had never been able to capture their attention so completely. The man wasn't old, but there was something about his demeanor that spoke of experience, as if he was used to being right and never spoke until he was sure of himself. He wasn't intimidating in a frightening way, but his presence definitely commanded respect.

Still grasping his plate, Felty slid his free hand behind his back. "I didn't mean to, Onkel Rone. She wouldn't let me finish my sandwich."

Onkel. Elsie Stutzman had three *bruders* living in Greenwood. This must be Elsie's *bruder* and one of Anna and Felty Helmuth's grandsons. He was tall, like Abraham, and had light blue eyes and dark hair like

Elsie. He was handsome, but a *gute* face didn't impress Carolyn as much as a *gute* heart.

Onkel—she hadn't caught the first name—looked around the room in disbelief, his gaze landing on Rosie and her peanut butter headdress. "You're not supposed to feed peanut butter to babies. They'll choke. And Elmer Mervin needs a booster seat. He can't reach his plate sitting on a regular chair like that." Onkel Busybody stormed to the closet and retrieved Elmer's booster seat and an apron. After donning the apron, he scooped Elmer Mervin up in one arm, slid the booster seat onto the chair, and set Elmer into it. Without a peep, Elmer Mervin picked up what was left of his sandwich and stuffed it into his mouth, though not fifteen minutes earlier, he had made the biggest, loudest fuss about being forced to sit in a booster seat. He'd kicked her so hard, Carolyn had finally given up trying.

Onkel What's-His-Name was obviously bent on correcting all of Carolyn's transgressions. He furrowed his dark brow as he stared at the Twinkie on Lydia's plate. Lydia, Lyle, and Luke had finished their sandwiches, including the crust, and eaten all their carrots and apples. The Twinkies were their reward.

Onkel Blue-Eyes studied Carolyn's face as if he were trying to burn a hole through her skull. "You can't feed *die kinner* Twinkies for supper," he said, as if it were the most appalling idea in the whole world. "They need tuna fish sandwiches with whole wheat bread and lettuce."

Carolyn couldn't think of one child she knew who would willingly eat lettuce on his tuna fish sandwich, which was a silly thing to contemplate while the *onkel* eyed her as if she had leprosy. She didn't know whether to feel defensive or hurt, angry or just plain picked on. But Carolyn wasn't the type to allow anyone to pick on her, so she opted for a look of mild annoyance on her face even though she thought she might boil over like a pot of jelly on the stove.

Fully aware that there were probably tiny bits of Felty's sandwich in her hair, Carolyn squared her shoulders, folded her arms, and looked the *onkel* right in the eye. "*Ach*, *vell*, Onkel Macaroni, at least a Twinkie is better than a Ding Dong. They taste like wax."

Whatever the *onkel* had expected from Carolyn, it probably hadn't been impudence. His eyebrows would have flown off his face if they hadn't been attached. "*Cum*, Felty Junior," he said, doing his best to pretend Carolyn hadn't uttered a word. "Put your plate on the table and sit. You too, Freddie. I'll make you a lunch to stick to your ribs. Growing boys need protein and omega-3 fatty acids."

Ach! He was so full of himself. "Don't trouble yourself," she said thinly. "I'm sure peanut butter has plenty of omega whatevers, and I've already—"

The *onkel* had the nerve to give her a patient smile. He wasn't very good at it, and it looked more like a grimace than anything else. He probably would have patted her on the head if she'd been close enough. "I don't wonder that you should stay out of the way. It's plain you don't know the first thing about caring for children or how to feed them properly."

Carolyn was never afraid to give someone a piece of her mind when they deserved it, but it was useless to scold a man who thought he knew everything. He'd probably eat his words someday, but she wasn't going to force-feed him. She took a deep breath, folded her arms across her chest, and leaned against the wall, content to let Onkel Too-Big-for-His-Britches make a fool of himself. She refused to even feel guilty about it. This one was nothing like his sister Elsie.

The *onkel* snatched the three offensive Twinkies off the table and tossed them into the garbage. Lydia gasped. Luke kept his mouth shut, but the disappointment on his face was deep.

"Hey," Freddie said. "I want a Twinkie."

Onkel Omega-3 didn't even glance at his nephew. "A Twinkie is no excuse for a *gute* supper."

"But, Onkel Aaron . . ." Lyle said, his voice trailing off to nothing. He probably didn't want to hurt Onkel Aaron's feelings by telling him that all of them except Felty had already eaten supper. Onkel Aaron busied himself in the kitchen, pulling lettuce and healthy green vegetables from the refrigerator, opening cans of tuna, stacking napkins within easy reach.

Who would want to put a damper on that kind of enthusiasm—or rather, arrogance?

Carolyn tried to hide a smug smile as Onkel Aaron poured each child a glass of milk, not even noticing that each of the glasses had already been drained—except for Felty's, which was overflowing with milk bubbles. Rosie got a small glass of milk, which no doubt would end up on the floor in a matter of seconds.

While Onkel Aaron cheerfully stirred mayonnaise into the tuna fish, Luke must have decided that he didn't want to force down another lunch just to keep his *onkel* happy. "But, Onkel Aaron," he said, fingering the edge of his plate. "We had peanut butter and jelly. Grape jelly."

Onkel Aaron hesitated while buttering the last piece of bread, then barreled on ahead, cutting the sandwiches in half and placing them on the plates at the table. "Jelly has too much sugar." He wiped his hands on his apron and glanced around the table at his motionless nephews and nieces. "Eat up, everyone, and no complaining."

Freddie and Luke glanced at each other and slowly,

reluctantly picked up their sandwiches. Freddie had eaten two sandwiches while he'd painted Rosie with peanut butter. Felty seemed to be the only one with any enthusiasm for a second lunch, probably because he hadn't eaten a bite of the first one.

Lydia scrunched her little face like a prune but did as she was told. She took two big bites, probably thinking it would be less uncomfortable to finish her sandwich off quickly. "I'm done," she said, hopping down from the table without permission.

Onkel Aaron wasn't having any of it. "Sit down, Lydia. You need to finish your sandwich."

Lydia slumped her shoulders, got back in her chair, and took a nibble of bread. "But my stomach is going to 'splode."

"You will not explode." He glanced at Carolyn, reproof flashing in his eyes. "Someone needs to make sure you're well-fed."

A grunt of disapproval escaped Carolyn's lips, but Onkel Full-of-Himself didn't even hear it because at that moment Lydia coughed and gagged and proceeded to throw up both her lunches all over her dress and onto the floor at Onkel Aaron's feet. Onkel Aaron jumped back, but vomit splattered on those nice, clean boots of his. At the same time, Rosie decided that her glass of milk looked like a fun toy. She knocked it over and it tumbled to the floor, sending milk shooting clear to the ceiling. A shower of milk droplets landed in Onkel Aaron's clean white shirt and dripped off the strands of his hair like icicles melting in the heat.

Milk also rained on Freddie and Felty, and they laughed as if it was the funniest thing that had ever happened. Lydia also got wet and started wailing. "I want my Twinkie. I ate four carrots."

Onkel Aaron slid his hands under Lydia's armpits and picked her up, holding her at arm's length, her legs dangling in the air while Aaron paced the kitchen with her. Rosie started to cry again, either sad that her glass had fallen or that she had a whole other sandwich to eat.

In the confusion, Luke abandoned his second lunch, strolled to the garbage can, and retrieved all three Twinkies. He brushed them off, handed one to Freddie and one to Felty, and stuffed the third one into his mouth.

Carolyn considered sliding into a chair next to Elmer Mervin and reading the newspaper while the *onkel* attempted to clean the mess. But she'd be heartless indeed if she let Onkel Got-What-He-Deserved clean it up all by himself.

Carolyn knelt down and took off Lydia's shoes while Lydia hung from Onkel Aaron's grasp. Then she took Lydia from Onkel Aaron and gently lowered her to the floor. "*Cum*, Liddy Bitty. Let's get you in the tub." She took Lydia's slimy hand and led her up the stairs to the bathroom, where she quickly helped Lydia bathe. No matter how badly she wanted to linger in the bathroom, Onkel Aaron was in over his head, and despite everything, she should help him. Lord willing, the boys would behave themselves while their *onkel* had his eye on them.

Once Lydia had a clean dress and some fuzzy stockings to keep her feet warm, Carolyn wrapped her in a blanket and carried her down the stairs. Onkel Aaron was standing on a chair wiping milk drops off the ceiling. He dangled a dishtowel in his other hand over Rosie's head, no doubt in an attempt to keep her entertained so she wouldn't cry. It wasn't working. Rosie, covered in peanut butter, milk, and snot, bawled as if her heart would break.

The four older boys had taken the lettuce out of their

sandwiches and were slapping one another in the face with the leaves, while Elmer Mervin tore his sandwich into pieces and dropped them into his overflowing glass of milk.

And their *onkel* was disinfecting the ceiling.

Carolyn blew a strand of hair out of her face. That was the most urgent task he could think of? She deposited Lydia on the sofa in the great room. "Luke, Freddie, Felty, and Lyle," she said, snapping her voice like a whip. "Put the lettuce down now."

Onkel Aaron looked down, probably noticing for the first time what the boys were up to. He was obviously a very focused person.

Freddie had the courage to stick his tongue out at Carolyn while his *onkel* was watching. "We don't have to do what you say. You're not our *mamm*."

Aaron gasped, teetered, and nearly fell off the chair. Dropping the rag and towel on the table, he hopped down from his perch. "That is no way to talk to your babysitter, Freddie."

Freddie's confidence seemed to wilt slightly. "But, Onkel Aaron, you said she doesn't know how to babysit."

"You need to be respectful of your elders."

Carolyn raised an eyebrow in surprise. She hadn't expected the *onkel* to defend her.

Onkel Aaron folded his arms across his wide chest. "Boys, lettuce is for eating, not fighting. And, Elmer Mervin, it's wasteful to put your sandwich in your milk." He sounded stern and unyielding, but he didn't yell. He'd been rude to Carolyn, but at least he didn't seem to have a bad temper. Since Onkel Aaron was standing at the very center of the chaos, she couldn't help but admire his calm.

Drooping like flowers in the heat, Freddie, Lyle, and Luke set their lettuce on the table. Felty slid his leaf behind his back.

"You too, Felty," Carolyn said. "And help your *onkel* by cleaning up the kitchen."

Felty slapped his lettuce on the table. "Cleaning is women's work."

"Today, it's everybody's job. You all helped make the mess. You can all help clean it up."

Freddie made a face at Carolyn and reached for his coat on the hook by the door. "We have to muck out. Girls aren't smart enough to do man's work."

Onkel Aaron's hand shot out like a flash, and before Carolyn even registered what had happened, Aaron had a hold of Freddie's sleeve and was pulling him across the kitchen. He stopped right in front of Carolyn and nudged Freddie forward. Rosie stopped crying. Elmer quit playing in his milk.

"*Ach,*" Freddie grunted, trying in vain to pull away. "Let go, Onkel Aaron."

"You will apologize to your babysitter immediately," Aaron said, angrier than Carolyn had seen him since he'd entered the room.

"I ain't done nothing wrong," Freddie whined.

"We'll talk about your grammar later, but right now, you need to tell the babysitter you're sorry for saying girls aren't smart."

"But they aren't." Freddie was anything but apologetic. He managed to swagger even with one sleeve firmly in Onkel Aaron's fist. "Brady Simpkins said girls are only *gute* for cooking and having babies."

Aaron's face was a storm cloud. "Who is Brady Simpkins, and why is he talking about such things?"

"My *Englisch* friend. He's ten, and he knows everything about babies."

Aaron raised an eyebrow. "I don't doubt it, but that is no excuse for you. Apologize to . . ." His gaze flicked to Carolyn. "What is your name?"

Her face felt flush all of a sudden, as if she were standing next to a wood-burning stove. He had interesting eyes, light blue rimmed with green and as deep as Lake Michigan. *Ach!* It didn't matter how unsettling she found his gaze, he was still an arrogant know-it-all who couldn't make a *gute* tuna fish sandwich. "Carolyn Yutzy."

"Freddie, apologize to Carolyn." Freddie tried to yank himself away, but Aaron's grip was too strong. "Freddie," he said, his voice low and threatening.

Freddie groaned. "I'm sorry I was disrespectful and said that thing about babies."

Aaron let go of Freddie's sleeve and turned Freddie to face him, gripping him firmly by the shoulders. "It's not only because you were disrespectful. Girls are as smart as boys, and the work they do is just as important—more important, because if the girls didn't have the babies, there would be no people in this world."

"I thought you didn't want to talk about babies," Freddie whined.

Aaron seemed to grip Freddie's shoulders even tighter. "Never, ever, be disrespectful to a girl." Aaron turned his head and spoke to the other nephews at the table. "Do you understand?"

All the boys except Elmer nodded. Elmer was preoccupied with the soggy sandwich in his glass. Aaron's gaze traveled back to Freddie. "*Gotte* does not smile on anyone who mistreats one of his *dochters*."

Freddie didn't look convinced, but he was wise enough to know the lecture would be shorter if he surrendered. "Okay, Onkel Aaron. I'm sorry."

Aaron released Freddie, led him to the table, and handed him the dishrag. Carolyn remembered to breathe before she got light-headed and passed out. Had rude, arrogant, busybody Onkel Aaron really just come to her defense? Not only her defense, but the defense of women everywhere? She half wondered if maybe she'd imagined it.

Aaron Stutzman had been in the house for all of fifteen minutes. He'd been rude and arrogant and insulting, and she couldn't think of one thing she liked about him—except for maybe his fascinating eyes and his steady temperament . . . and maybe the way he cared about *die kinner* . . . and maybe that he'd set his nephew straight about women.

Why did he have to go and make himself likable when she was determined to disapprove of him? She squared her shoulders. She'd seen quite enough of Onkel Aaron's arrogance, and one nice, intelligent, sensitive comment wasn't going to change her mind about him.

Rosie started whimpering again. The poor baby needed a bath something wonderful. Aaron started the boys clearing off the table while Carolyn got Lydia a glass of water and made sure she was comfortable on the sofa. Then Carolyn slowly extricated Rosie from her high chair. Rosie was like a wriggly octopus with her arms and hands always in motion. She grabbed one of Carolyn's *kapp* strings and pulled hard. Even with slippery, peanut buttery fingers, Rosie managed to yank the *kapp* completely off Carolyn's head. Carolyn gasped as the pins holding her *kapp* in place pulled away from her hair. Rosie giggled and clamped Carolyn's *kapp* in her dirty little fingers.

With Rosie firmly in her arms, Carolyn didn't have enough hands to retrieve her *kapp*. She'd just have to figure it out later. In the meantime, playing with the *kapp* kept Rosie happy as Carolyn made yet another trip to the bathroom to give Rosie a bath.

After the bath, Carolyn put a diaper and clean clothes on Rosie, fed her a bottle, and put her down for a nap. On her first day in Greenwood, Mary had instructed Carolyn to fetch her in the bakery after lunch so she could nurse Rosie before her nap. Carolyn didn't even bother to step out to the bakery anymore. Mary and Abraham were up before the children and didn't come back to the house until dinnertime. Sometimes they didn't even make it for dinner.

Six months ago, Abraham and Mary had started a cookie business in a small shop that Abraham had built next to the house. They specialized in white chocolate macadamia nut, snickerdoodles, and whoopee pies. Abraham had partnered with an *Englischer* to help him advertise their cookies, and the shop had become wildly successful. Mary and Abraham's Amish cookies went all over the country, but the largest amount was sold in Green Bay at a specialty Amish shop. Every Thursday, the *Englischer* loaded up his van with Mary and Abraham's cookies and took them to Green Bay. Every day but the Sabbath, Mary and Abraham made cookies and filled mail orders. The Christmas rush was keeping them wonderfully busy.

Carolyn was especially interested in their business because her family had a small candy shop in Bonduel. She and her *bruderen* and *schwesteren* made all sorts of chocolates—peanut butter chocolate drops, coconut haystacks, pecan turtles, and almond bark. They had intentionally kept it small as something for the family to do together to supplement the farm income, but it had been a *wunderbarr* way to grow up—spending time with her family as they laughed and talked and made candy together. Mary and Abraham weren't spending any time with their family. They barely had time to eat.

That left Carolyn with the children from sunup to bedtime. It was taking a toll on her, and she'd only been there a week.

Carolyn resisted the urge to lie down in the bed next to Rosie's crib and take a short nap. The kitchen still needed to be cleaned, and if the *onkel* was determined to wash the ceiling, she'd have to finish the dishes, wipe the table, and mop the floor, all while trying to keep six children from making another mess before the last one was cleaned up. It didn't matter how much Carolyn liked Christmastime, she longed for warm weather so she could send *die kinner* outside and let them have their way with the great outdoors.

She rinsed out her *kapp* as best she could in the bathroom sink, but it would take a *gute* soaking and some elbow grease to get all the peanut butter out. She hung it on the towel rack, then found a baby blue scarf to tie around her hair. From now on, the *kapp* might only be worn on Sundays.

Lydia was in the kitchen with Onkel Aaron and the boys wiping chairs. It looked as if Onkel Aaron had assigned each child a chair, and they were vigorously cleaning, even three-year-old Elmer. Milk still dripped from the table to the floor, and the plates and glasses and pieces of sandwich had not been cleared off. Carolyn clamped her teeth together. At least he was having them clean something, but it seemed that Aaron was one to strain at a gnat and swallow a camel.

"Be sure to get every spindle," Aaron said. "A job worth doing is worth doing well." Lydia nodded as she worked her way slowly around the chair with her own dishrag. Onkel Aaron handed each of *die kinner* a toothpick. "Clean out the cracks too."

Carolyn sighed. At least *die kinner* weren't making mischief while they worked on their chairs. It would have to be her job to clean up the rest of the throw-up and tidy the kitchen before she made dinner, but she'd have to be in the same room with Onkel Too-Big-for-His-Britches, and that wasn't her idea of a pleasant afternoon. She'd rather be locked in a closet with the tornado twins.

It couldn't be helped. She would have to walk right by Onkel Aaron to get to the Pine-Sol. Aaron stopped wiping his chair and held out his rag to her. "You'll need to finish my chair. I can't stay. Be sure *die kinner* use a knife on the bottom of the legs. Kitchen chairs pick up gunk when they slide back and forth across the floor."

Carolyn simply raised an eyebrow. The five-year-olds were not going to be handed knives to scrape dirt off the feet of the chairs. Neither were the nine-year-olds, for that matter.

He showed her a toothpick as if suspecting she didn't know what it was. "Use this to get the cracks around the bottom of the spindles. And use it to clean out the crevices in the table too. It looks like it hasn't been done for a while."

Carolyn could hardly take the blame for that. She'd only been here a week. Besides, a little bit of dirt was nothing to be ashamed of. There were seven children living in this house, for goodness sake.

He paused, and she realized he must have been waiting for her to say something like, "*Ach*, you are the smartest, tidiest man alive. I will be sure to follow your instructions to the letter." Reluctantly taking the toothpick, she kept her mouth shut, just in case something came out he wasn't expecting. She could set the children to work on the real mess once he left. He'd never know how little she cared about his cleaning methods.

He stared at her as if he'd just noticed her *kapp* was gone. "That scarf matches your eyes."

Here's a toothpick and *that scarf matches your eyes*?

Why was he telling her this? She had no idea, but he didn't seem inclined to pull his steady gaze from her face. No doubt he was looking for more flaws in her personality. *Ach, vell,* she had plenty of flaws, but she'd dive into a vat of peanut butter before she let Onkel High-Horse pick at her. She raised an eyebrow. "Don't you have somewhere you need to be?"

He reached out his hand, and she involuntarily gasped as he drew his thumb down the side of her face. He pulled away with one of Felty's sandwich bits on his thumb. Her neck got warm. The piece of bread had been sticking to her face since Aaron had walked in the door. She was mortified. And amused. The more she thought about it, the funnier it became. She clapped her hand over her mouth, but the laughter escaped anyway.

His lips twitched into what might have passed for a smile. "Felty has a *gute* arm. I've seen him play softball."

"I was saving it for a snack later."

His expression didn't change, but she could hear the low chuckle coming from his throat. As quickly as it came, he regained his composure and seemed to remember he seriously disapproved of her. "Neither the color of your eyes nor your interesting smile changes anything. I don't know what you are suited for, but caring for children is not a gift *Gotte* has given you."

Carolyn returned his gaze with an unwavering stare of her own. It was the strangest thing, but she got the feeling that he honestly meant no offense even though he'd just insulted her. He seemed like a person who solved problems, whether it was dirty chairs or disrespectful children. To him, Carolyn was just another problem to be solved, not a person with actual feelings. She almost felt sorry for him. How could someone like that have a meaningful relationship with anybody?

He looked at her as if searching for answers in her face. She didn't even know what the questions were—probably things like, "Do you want me to teach you how to clean mold off the shower?" or "Do you know how to change a diaper?" Maybe he was looking for more of Felty's sandwich. Carolyn tended to become more determined the harder she was pushed. *For sure and certain I can change a diaper, Onkel Lysol. The stinkiest of stinky ones, and I don't even have to hold my breath.*

"I will be talking to my *bruder* about finding a more suitable babysitter," he said. "I'm sure you understand."

She'd never before met anyone quite so blunt. At least she didn't have to guess what he was thinking. Of course, Aaron couldn't have known how badly Carolyn wanted to be fired. She couldn't quit—couldn't leave Mary in a pickle like that—but she certainly wanted to be done with Greenwood, Wisconsin, and the nasty twins who lived to make her life miserable. But her pride was wounded all the same. She was intelligent, capable, and strong. It chafed that Onkel Know-It-All had drawn conclusions about her that weren't true.

She had half a mind to tell him what she thought of him, but the other half of her wanted nothing more than to go home and let the Stutzman children tear the house down board by board.

She opted to try to irritate him. It was a childish reaction, but she couldn't help herself. Hoping it hadn't already been used to scrape gunk off the kitchen chairs, she slid the toothpick into her mouth and let it dangle between her front teeth. "What am I supposed to do with this toothpick?"

He swiped his hand across his mouth as if wiping

away the aggravated reply that was surely on the tip of his tongue. Without another word, he stormed past her and out the back door.

Carolyn smiled to herself.

There was nothing better than the feeling of annoying an annoying person.

Dear Carolyn,

Clara tells me you are having a wunderbarr time in Greenwood. I knew the minute you met our grandson Abraham and his wife Mary and their darling children you would be overjoyed to spend Christmas there. But there is no need to thank me. My reward is knowing that I've made so many people happy just by bringing them together. I don't mean to pry, but have you met the rest of the family yet? He's very handsome.

Love and blessings,

Anna Helmuth

Chapter 2

Dear Aaron,

Thank you for the vegetable peeler. I will make carrot potato cucumber stew tonight in honor of your gift.

Felty says you are thinking of planting soybeans this spring. It's a wonderful-gute idea. Everybody seems to be eating tofu these days. I use it in my squash and raisin stir-fry, and Felty loves it.

We hope things are well for you in Greenwood. There happens to be a girl from Bonduel living there. She is working for Abraham and Mary, tending their children. Have you met her? Her name is Carolyn Yutzy, and she is the most sensible girl you'll ever meet—a gute knitter and not inclined to giggle. The best part is, she's a wunderbarr cook. For sure and certain, someone as lonely as you can appreciate a well-cooked meal. I know how much you love coming to my house to eat. It wonders me that

*you don't find a sensible, pretty fraa to settle
down with. She would cook for you every night.*

    *Please write us back and let us know how
things are coming along. We hate being so far
away when such exciting things are happening in
your life.*

    Love and blessings,
Mammi Anna
P.S. Felty is enclosing a seed catalog.

Aaron reluctantly knocked on Abraham's door. He was
eager for a home-cooked meal, but he wasn't all that
eager to see the babysitter again. No doubt she would
come to the door with a toothpick dangling from her
mouth and strands of shiny chestnut hair escaping from
her light blue scarf. She made him feel grumpy and *ferhoodled* at the same time. How was that possible? He
was never *ferhoodled*. The girl was obviously blind to
her own failings as a babysitter, but she hadn't burst into
tears or even whimpered when he'd told her plainly how
unfit she was. She'd acted as if she didn't believe him or
maybe couldn't care less what he thought. What kind of
person couldn't care less what Aaron thought? He was almost thirty years old, with a farm of his own. Anyone
would be wise to listen to his opinion.

    Aaron frowned. Hardly anyone listened to his opin-
ion. A man wasn't fully respected until he had a *fraa*, as if
a wife made a man smarter somehow. Aaron had made a
few halfhearted attempts to find a wife, but the single
girls he knew were either silly or unappealing or tire-
some. Why would he want to take on a *fraa* when he was
so much happier being by himself? He had complete control of his time and his household. No one made messes
that he had to clean up. No one told him what he should

or should not do. He did exactly what he wanted from
sunup to sundown, and he quite liked just being by himself. A *fraa* would only mess up his well-ordered and
tidy life.

More than one relative or friend had made an attempt
to match him with one girl or another, until he'd insisted
they stop. There was nothing that irritated him more than
someone trying to stick his or her nose into his business.
He would not be pushed, pulled, tricked, or cajoled into
getting a wife. He liked being a bachelor, and that was
that. He'd earn the community's respect with his exem-
plary life, without a wife.

The babysitter—what was her name? Carolyn?—did
indeed answer the door. He was momentarily distracted
by her dancing blue eyes and the fact that she didn't
scowl at him, even though he'd threatened to have her
fired. If she thought looking pretty would make him
change his mind about talking to Abraham, she had another thing coming. Aaron was never distracted by a
pretty face or a nice set of teeth.

Even though he still believed Abraham should get rid
of her, Aaron had been wrong when he'd assumed the
babysitter had given *die kinner* Twinkies for lunch. *Vell*,
he hadn't been wrong—just mistaken, but it wasn't really
his fault because the babysitter could have mentioned that
she had already fed *die kinner*. What was he supposed to
think when he walked in the house only to see Felty
throwing food and Rosie covered in peanut butter?

For some unexplainable reason, his heart stomped
around in his chest like a bull in work boots when he
laid eyes on the babysitter. He should have let himself
in, but he'd done that on Saturday and ended up cleaning milk off the ceiling.

The babysitter wasn't scowling, but it was plain she

wasn't all that happy to see him. "*Cum reu*," she said, opening the door wider. "Make yourself comfortable. I've got to tend to the gravy."

Aaron had no idea what the menu was, but the house smelled like onions, melted butter, and roast beef. His mouth watered. Mary must have spent the whole day cooking.

Freddie, Felty, and Luke sat facing him on the sofa with their arms crossed tightly over their chests and storm clouds looming on their faces. It was obvious they were being punished for something. Freddie bounced off the sofa and threw his arms around Aaron's waist as if Aaron was his favorite relative. Aaron wasn't fooled. He wasn't even Freddie's favorite *onkel*. "Onkel Aaron, I'm wonderful glad to see you."

Carolyn had made it halfway to the kitchen before she turned and propped her hands on her hips. "*Nae*, Freddie. You are not allowed to leave the sofa."

Freddie hung on to Aaron like a leech, but Aaron pried Freddie's hands away. "Do as your babysitter says."

"But, Onkel Aaron," Felty whined, "we've been sitting here for an hour."

Aaron glanced in Carolyn's direction. She had turned her back to stir the gravy. An hour seemed an excessive punishment, but it was *gute* to see she was enforcing some discipline. "Actions have consequences," he finally said. "The next time you think of misbehaving, remember that you can't do wrong and feel right."

Luke stuck out his bottom lip and pointed to Lyle, who sat at the table with Lydia, each with a wooden spoon stirring something in a big metal bowl. "Lyle started it, and she didn't even get mad at him."

Aaron walked farther into the room to get a better look into the kitchen. Chocolate batter ringed Lydia's lips. Lyle's eyes were red and watery, and a nasty purple goose egg protruded from his forehead.

Aaron's mouth fell open, and he turned to the trio of boys sitting innocently on the sofa. "What happened?"

Luke had his finger in his ear, working out some wax. "Lyle started it."

Freddie nodded. "He took one of the cushions off the sofa. We wanted to jump, so we piled all of them in front of the stairs. Lyle climbed too high."

Aaron winced. He went to Lyle and cupped his hand around his chin. "Are you okay, Lyle?"

Lyle sniffed. "We're making brownies."

Elmer Mervin sat in the chair next to Lydia looking at a book, but he wasn't in his booster seat. Rosie was in her high chair playing with some blocks and a furry red stuffed animal. What kind of a toy was that for a baby? Lyle had a serious goose egg, Elmer was going to fall right out of his chair, and there were tiny bits of red fur stuck to Rosie's lips. Carolyn truly was the worst babysitter in the world.

Abraham and Mary were nowhere to be seen. Aaron tried to keep his temper as he stole next to Carolyn at the stove. He was momentarily distracted by the scent of roast beef and carrots that seemed to emanate from the enticing crevice where her throat met her collarbone. Thankfully, Rosie threw a block at his head, drawing his attention back to the matter at hand. "Children should not be allowed to jump off things."

She didn't even look at him, just kept stirring the gravy that smelled like heaven. For sure and certain it was made from the beef drippings, no doubt a thousand calories a spoonful. No matter how *appeditlich* it might taste, he'd be wise to stay away if he didn't want his arteries to clog. "If you're looking for something to do, you can set the table," she said.

He narrowed his eyes. Carolyn didn't seem all that worried about keeping her job. She nudged Aaron out of her way, sprayed a glass dish with nonstick spray, and set it on the table. She took the bowl of chocolate from the twins, and they helped her pour it into the dish and scrape the bowl. She knelt down and smoothed her hand down Lyle's arm. "How is your head?"

Lyle turned up his nose and frowned at Carolyn. "It don't hurt. You didn't have to get Luke and them in trouble."

Carolyn smiled sweetly at Lyle as if she couldn't tell that he didn't like her. "Please help Onkel Aaron set the table. Lydia, you too."

The first thing Aaron did was retrieve Elmer Mervin's booster seat from the closet and set him in it. The babysitter hadn't paid him any heed last time, but he'd said all he had to say on Saturday. She knew he was aware of her negligence. He took the fuzzy animal from Rosie and set it on the counter. She wouldn't be allowed to play with it as long as he was in the house.

Rosie screamed like a catbird and reached out her hands as if Aaron had stolen her best friend. He tried to hand her one of the blocks. Surely she'd be happier playing with a block instead of spitting red fur out of her mouth all night. Rosie screamed louder and swiped every last block off her high chair tray. Reluctantly, Aaron returned the horrifying red bear thing to Rosie. Out of the corner of his eye, he might have seen Carolyn curl her lips smugly.

Something soft and crinkly hit him in the back of the neck. He snapped his head around, but Luke, Freddie, and Felty were sitting on the sofa where he'd left them and the other twins were setting the table. He reached down in the cupboard to get the cups and something hit him in the back. Standing up straight, he eyed Carolyn, who had just put the brownies in the oven. A round ball of paper flew past her head.

The boys crouched behind the sofa, and in unison, Freddie, Felty, and Luke stood and each chucked a ball of paper into the kitchen. Two balls landed on the table. Luke's paper landed right in Carolyn's gravy. The boys giggled and ducked out of sight.

Carolyn quickly spooned the paper out of the gravy. She tossed the dripping gravy ball into the trash and licked a spot of gravy off her finger, even though that couldn't have been very sanitary. She arched an eyebrow in Aaron's direction. "What should a *gute* babysitter do in this situation?"

"How should I know?" Aaron sputtered. "It's your job to discipline *die kinner*." Another paper ball hit him in the ear, this one bigger and wadded more tightly than the others. How he hated that self-satisfied, attractive smile of hers.

Oy, anyhow, who knew getting hit in the head with a paper ball would muddle his usually rational brain.

Carolyn propped her hands on her hips as if waiting for him to do her job for her. "We're about ready to eat. Why don't you change Rosie's diaper, and I'll deal with the boys."

"Change Rosie's diaper?"

That smug smile got wider and wider. "She's stinky."

"I've never changed a diaper in my life, and I'm not about to start now. They're full of disease."

"But *you're* the expert babysitter."

Aaron raised his hands and backed away from Carolyn. "I didn't say that. It doesn't take an expert babysitter to see that you're a very bad one."

She pointed to Rosie, who was sucking on the red raccoon's foot. "Then show me how it's done."

While they'd been disagreeing about whose job it

was to change diapers and care for *die kinner*, pandemonium had broken out in the living room. Freddie was ripping the newspaper to shreds and throwing it at the other two boys, who were in turn throwing paper at each other. Lyle and Lydia abandoned their table-setting duties and ran to the living room to help Freddie tear newspaper. Elmer Mervin, who hated to be left out, tore a page out of his picture book. He nearly toppled over onto his head when he tried to get down from his booster seat. Aaron caught him and saw nothing else to do but put him on his feet and let him run free.

Carolyn gave Aaron the stink eye and pointed at Rosie, but Aaron wasn't about to do Carolyn's job for her. Carolyn turned her back on him and marched into the living room, where she took Freddie firmly by the shoulders and set him back on the sofa. Freddie wasn't happy about it, but he stayed put.

The babysitter might have been a bit more competent than Aaron had first suspected, but she still had a lot to learn—like the fact that she shouldn't try to pass off her diaper-changing responsibilities to someone else.

Aaron was doing his best not to stare at Carolyn when Abraham and Mary came in the back door. Freddie sat quietly on the sofa, but Lydia, Lyle, Luke, Elmer Mervin, and Felty chased one another around the sofa, screaming and tossing shreds of newspaper into the air.

Abraham stopped dead in his tracks, and Mary bumped into him from behind. "What's all this?" he bellowed, gaining *die kinner*'s immediate attention.

They froze in place, even Rosie in her high chair. Their gazes were glued to Abraham's face, except for Freddie, who sat on the sofa with his back to all of them. At the moment, he probably wasn't so mad at Carolyn for insisting he sit on the sofa, because there was nothing for his *fater* to be cross with him about. With her gaze still glued to her *fater*, Lydia reached out and snatched an errant strip of newspaper from Lyle's hair. Luke and Felty Jr. let their paper slip from their hands, no doubt hoping their *fater* wouldn't notice.

Abraham's anger filled the house like the sharp smell of paint thinner. He stomped into the living room and pointed to the floor. "Is that my newspaper?" When no one answered, he raised his voice a little louder. "Is it?"

Felty flinched. "*Jah*, Dat. We're sorry."

Carolyn reached down and picked up some shredded paper. "We were just having a little fun. It's too cold to go outside."

Aaron drew his brows together. Abraham wasn't inclined to yell or carry on like this. Aaron didn't like seeing his *bruder* so out of sorts with *die kinner*.

"I do not want my children behaving like a pack of wolves," Abraham said.

Mary reached out and smoothed her hand down Elmer Mervin's hair. "You never read the paper anyway, Abraham."

"That's no reason for her to let *die kinner* destroy it." Abraham huffed out a breath. "Clean up this mess, and stop behaving like pigs."

Die kinner quickly and silently shoveled ripped newspaper into their arms.

"Freddie," Abraham yelled, "get off the sofa and help your *bruderen* and *schwester*. I'll not have an idler in my household."

"But, Dat," Freddie said, with a smug twitch of his lips, "Miss Carolyn said I wasn't allowed to leave the sofa."

"I don't care what she said," Abraham growled. "Get up."

Freddie slumped his shoulders and grumbled like a porcupine, but he did as he was told under the watchful eye of their *fater*. Carolyn acted as if nothing out of the ordinary had happened, went back to the stove, and stirred her gravy, which by now was surely burned on the bottom. Just as well. Aaron didn't need the temptation.

Mary pulled glasses from the cupboard and set them on the table. Aaron found napkins and salt and pepper and helped her finish. When the table was set, Mary sank into her chair and propped her chin in her hand. Her eyes were ringed with dark circles, and she sighed as if she couldn't catch her breath.

"Dinner's ready," Carolyn said, not seeming the least bit upset by Abraham's bad mood or by the fact that Abraham had plainly seen that she was a bad babysitter, even though he didn't know the truth of what had really happened. Aaron frowned again. Maybe he hadn't seen the truth either.

Aaron gave Mary a reassuring smile. "It smells *appeditlich*. You must have been cooking all day."

Mary's forehead creased like a pulled curtain. "Abraham and I made cookies all day. Carolyn cooked dinner. She always does."

Aaron nodded as if he already knew that, even though he was a little surprised. Carolyn had made roast beef and gravy *and* taken care of *die kinner*? He really had misjudged her.

Nae. Aaron didn't make mistakes like that. Carolyn was simply a much better cook than she was a sitter. And pretty. Even though she shouldn't be allowed to care for his nieces and nephews, Aaron could admit that Carolyn was pretty. It fascinated him the way her eyes sparked into a blazing fire whenever she looked at him.

Carolyn set the gravy on the table. Somehow, she'd managed through the chaos not to burn it. Aaron helped Elmer Mervin into his booster seat and poured water into each of the glasses while Carolyn sliced the roast.

Cheesy carrots, layered Jell-O, corn, and green beans all went on the table. There should have been a green salad. *Die kinner* needed five servings of vegetables a day. Like as not, Carolyn would have made a salad if she hadn't been doing her duty as a babysitter and giving the boys some sorely needed discipline.

Luke threw the last of the paper in the trash and sat down at the table. Still scowling, Abraham took his seat. "What's that smell?"

Which smell was he particularly referring to? The delectable carrots or the roast that still had steam rising from it?

Carolyn placed a dish of mashed potatoes on the table and lifted Rosie from her high chair. "She has a stinky diaper. I'll be right back."

Mary didn't offer to change the baby, just stared glassy-eyed at the tablecloth. Carolyn had gotten dinner on. The least Mary could do was change her own baby's diaper. It certainly wasn't Aaron's responsibility, so he wasn't sure why guilt buzzed in his head like a pesky mosquito when Abraham bowed his head, not even waiting for Carolyn to return before they said silent prayer. It didn't seem right not to wait for the woman who had made them such a fine meal.

Carolyn returned after the prayer and set Rosie in her high chair, then picked up Elmer's plate. "Do you want potatoes, Elmer?"

Abraham and Mary seemed to forget they had children as Mary numbly filled her own plate and Abraham dug into his dinner. Carolyn dished food for Elmer Mervin and Lydia while Rosie fussed.

Feeling more than a little ashamed of his brother and sister-in-law, Aaron nudged Lyle's shoulder. "Would you like me to help you?"

Lyle nodded, and Aaron dished up Lyle's food, giving

him a few extra green beans because he needed more vitamins in his diet. He scooped a spoonful of potatoes and held it out to Carolyn. "Would you like some potatoes?"

She actually smiled at him. "*Denki*, but I need to feed Rosie first. You go ahead and eat."

A little sheepishly, Aaron served himself. Carolyn had spent all day making dinner. She should have been the one to get the first bite, even though Mary and Abraham didn't seem to care.

Die kinner ate, silently keeping a watch on their *dat* while Carolyn mashed two green beans for Rosie. She patiently fed Rosie the beans and a dollop of mashed potatoes and then a bottle of baby food. Aaron felt the warmth of the gravy clear to his toes. Maybe the babysitter wasn't all that bad. She seemed to be unselfish down to her bones.

"Freddie," Abraham barked, "close your mouth. You look like a cow chewing her cud."

Freddie had already been yelled at once, and his *fater*'s disapproval made him wilt like a flower in the heat. "I'm . . . I'm sorry, Dat."

"You are ten years old. Time to stop acting like a baby."

Freddie sank into his chair as if trying to blend in with it. "I'm nine."

Carolyn wiped a bit of bean from Rosie's mouth with her spoon. "You would have been proud of Freddie today. He came home from school and mucked out without being asked; then he entertained *die kinner* while I made dinner."

By "entertained" did she mean Freddie had taken all the cushions off the sofa and put his siblings in mortal danger jumping off the stairs? Knowing how Freddie had behaved earlier, Aaron couldn't be sure Carolyn's praise wasn't an out-and-out lie, but it was nice of Carolyn to try to smooth things over with Abraham.

Felty carefully chewed his mouthful before speaking. "I got the part of the busy farmer in our Christmas program. I have five lines, and I have to stomp my feet and act upset."

Mary sighed and glanced at Carolyn. "*Ach*, we need a treat for the Christmas program."

Carolyn's gaze flicked to Felty before she turned and smiled at Mary. It was a nice, sympathetic smile, not a fake one that hid her true feelings. "We can come up with something. Lydia and Lyle helped me make brownies today. It wonders me if Freddie and Felty would like to help me make cookies for the program." She dished more Jell-O onto Felty's plate. "Felty has a wonderful *gute* speaking voice."

"Teacher says I'm one of the loudest in the class," Felty said.

Mary didn't respond, and Aaron bit his tongue before he said something that wasn't his place to say. Couldn't Mary give her children even the tiniest bit of attention?

Carolyn nodded enthusiastically. "Felty has already started working on his part. He's a very responsible young man."

It was a very nice thing to say considering that Carolyn had been wearing part of Felty's sandwich on her face on Saturday.

"Luke and Freddie have parts too," Carolyn said, glancing back and forth between Rosie and Mary. "And they've been busy at school making decorations."

"There's a big surprise at the end," Luke said, staring at his *mamm*, no doubt hoping for some approval from her side of the table.

"Luke, scoot your cup away from the edge," Abraham said. "It's going to spill."

Aaron couldn't just sit there while his *bruder* ignored his children. Someone besides Carolyn needed to give them some encouragement. "What is your part, Luke?"

Luke skewered one kernel of corn with his fork and popped it into his mouth. "I'm a dumb shepherd. I just have to look scared and say, 'Let's go to Bethlehem.'"

Aaron shook his head. "A shepherd isn't dumb. Shepherds were the first to hear the good news of Jesus's birth. *Gotte* must have thought they were the most important."

"I have to recite a poem," Freddie volunteered. "I don't even get to wear a costume."

"Sounds like a lot to memorize. Your teacher must think you're wonderful smart." Maybe it was wrong to tempt Freddie's pride like that, but someone besides Carolyn needed to give him some support.

One side of Freddie's mouth curled upward. "Memorizing isn't hard for me."

"Don't brag," Felty Jr. said.

Carolyn wiped Rosie's mouth. "It's not bragging to tell the truth, and who better to tell than your own family?"

Aaron dished himself another helping of potatoes and gravy. "Can I come to your school program?"

Felty grinned. "You come every year. You don't have to ask."

"I just wanted to make sure I was invited. It sounds like a special program. Maybe they're only inviting special people."

Carolyn hadn't yet made her own plate of food when Abraham scooted his chair from the table. "I'm going to start filling that Green Bay order, Mary. Come out as soon as you're done."

Mary nodded and gazed at her plate, still half full of food. "I'll be right there."

Abraham closed the door behind him. Neither he nor Mary had even noticed Lyle's goose egg.

Carolyn finished feeding Rosie, wiped up Rosie's hands and mouth, and gave her the red bear animal to play with. Aaron quickly picked up the spoon and scooped some mashed potatoes from the dish. He gave Carolyn an apologetic smile, hoping she knew he felt bad for eating in front of her. "Would you like some dinner now?"

The weary lines around her mouth softened. "*Denki*. I would."

"I hate green beans," Felty said, smashing the three beans still left on his plate with his finger.

Freddie picked up a green bean and pinched it between his thumb and index finger. "Me too," he said, even though Aaron had watched him eat at least a dozen while his *fater* was in the room.

Aaron glanced at Mary. It was her job to correct Freddie for bad manners, but she wasn't paying attention to much of anything.

"Freddie," Carolyn gently scolded, "please do not play with your food."

Freddie ignored Carolyn and swung his bean back and forth until it snapped, flew in the air, and hit Luke on the cheek. "Hey," Luke protested, swiping his hand down the side of his face. "Stop throwing food."

Carolyn spooned some Jell-O onto her plate. "Freddie, you need to apologize to Luke and wipe up your mess from the floor."

With his eyes glued to his *mamm*, Freddie wrapped his arms around his stomach and laughed like he was trying a little too hard. "But it's funny."

Mary still seemed to have nothing to say as she put another spoonful of potatoes in her mouth and chewed slowly, looking at Freddie as if she were watching someone else's child.

Luke picked up a piece of corn and flung it in Freddie's direction. It lodged in Freddie's hair.

"Ew," Freddie said, swiping at his hair and pulling the corn away. He picked up a handful of corn from his plate and aimed it at Luke.

Carolyn stood up so fast her chair clattered to the floor behind her. She grabbed Freddie's wrist before he could throw his corn. "Put it down."

Aaron couldn't remain silent any longer, even at the risk of offending Mary. "Freddie, behave yourself or go to bed right now." He didn't know if he had a right to impose a punishment, but Freddie was obviously bent on defying Carolyn, no matter the cost.

Freddie struggled to pull away, but Carolyn must have squeezed really tight. He opened his fist and let the corn fall to his plate.

Mary finally noticed what was happening at the table. "Freddie, I'm so tired. Can't you be a *gute* boy and obey Carolyn? You're giving me a headache."

Freddie stood and snatched his arm from Carolyn's grasp. "I hate Carolyn."

"We shouldn't hate anyone," Mary said, as if it took all her effort to say even that much.

Freddie growled and squeezed his eyes shut, probably hoping for some tears, which didn't come. "I don't care. I hate Carolyn. I hate everybody." Wailing at the top of his lungs, Freddie ran up the stairs before Aaron had a chance to insist he apologize. He slammed a door upstairs, rattling the windows in the kitchen.

Mary sighed. "He's going through a rough patch at school." She pressed her fingers to her temples. "Felty, be a *gute* boy and fetch me the Motrin from the bathroom cupboard."

Luke jumped from his seat. "I'll get it."

"She asked me," Felty Jr. said. He shoved Luke into the wall as they raced for the bathroom. Luke cried out but didn't slow his steps.

Carolyn frowned after them, a stiff rebuke in her eyes, but she didn't say anything. She was probably tired of scolding *die kinner* when they didn't listen to her anyway.

Aaron pressed his lips together. Maybe the babysitter wasn't the problem.

There was the sound of a plastic bottle hitting the floor in the bathroom and then the hundred tiny pings of pills bouncing off the linoleum. Mary closed her eyes, propped her elbow in the table, and cradled her forehead in her hand. "*Ach, du lieva.*"

Aaron rose to his feet with every intention of marching down the hall and giving his nephews what for. They'd been making trouble ever since Aaron had gotten here, being disobedient and disrespectful to Carolyn and quarrelsome with one another, and they hadn't been the least bit apologetic about it.

Unflustered, Carolyn held her hand up in a gesture to stop him. How did she keep her temper like that? He was beginning to wonder if she wasn't just what *die kinner* needed. They seemed to want a sharp, angry reaction, and she seemed determined not to give them one. "Mary," Carolyn said, "would you like to go upstairs and nurse Rosie before you get back to baking?"

Mary's lips curled slowly into a smile, as if her face had to remember how to relax. "I would love that. Do you think there's time?"

Carolyn nodded, her expression as confident as if Mary were a teenager and Carolyn was the older, more mature sister. "I'm sure there is, and I know you'd like to spend some time with Rosie."

Mary sighed. "I feel like I never see her."

"Why don't you take her up to your room so the two of you can have some time alone?"

Lydia had been fairly silent through dinner, but she whimpered and her little lip quivered like a feather in the wind. "I want to come too."

Mary looked at Carolyn as if getting her approval. "I would like that. You can sit by me while I feed Rosie."

"And tell me stories," Lydia said.

Mary nodded. "I will tell you some stories."

Luke and Felty still hadn't come back with the bottle of Motrin, which meant they were either picking the pills off the floor or throwing them into the toilet to see if they would float. Aaron wasn't especially eager to know either way.

Elmer knew enough to understand that he was being left out of something. "I want stories."

Carolyn glanced at Mary. "I'll tell you what, Elmer Mervin. Let your *mamm* feed Rosie while I give you and Lyle a bath and then she can tell you a story while I give Lydia and Rosie a bath. And then I will put you all to bed."

"I'll do it," Mary said, as if jumping at an opportunity she didn't want to miss. "If you give them baths, I will tuck them all into bed. I haven't done that for days."

Carolyn smiled. "I'm sure you'd enjoy that."

Mary's smile faded. "But Abraham needs my help."

Aaron practically shouted. "What needs to be done? I can help Abraham."

He was rewarded with a smile from Carolyn that made his heart skip a beat. "Aaron could help Abraham while you look after your little ones, Mary."

Mary bit her bottom lip. "The cookies are baked. We're getting boxes ready for the post in the morning."

Gute. He didn't want to back out on his offer, but he

wouldn't have been any help baking cookies. "I can do that."

"Oh, *denki*, Aaron. I'd be so grateful." Mary got a little teary, which was way more gratitude than Aaron deserved for such a little thing. The unexpected pleasure of Carolyn's smile was thanks enough.

Aaron retrieved his coat from the hook by the door and put on his hat. "*Denki* for the *appeditlich* dinner, Carolyn. I'll come help clean up the dishes when all the boxes are packed."

Carolyn shook her head "No need. I'll finish up when *die kinner* are in bed."

Hopefully, she didn't see his hesitation. "I'll come back." Carolyn might be a *gute* cook, but he'd noticed drops of dried milk still on the kitchen chairs from Saturday. Carolyn was no cleaner.

Then again, he'd been wrong about her babysitting skills. There was obviously more going on with *die kinner* than a lack of discipline. It seemed that their behavior was not entirely Carolyn's fault. They didn't behave, and it wasn't because Carolyn wasn't trying.

Maybe he was wrong about her cleanliness habits too—well, not wrong, because he was never wrong, but maybe mistaken. Even Aaron made mistakes occasionally.

He was going to have to rethink Carolyn Yutzy.

Dear Mammi and Dawdi,

1. *It snowed hard yesterday. I shoveled five sidewalks.*
2. *I met your friend Carolyn Yutzy. She has a dimple on her cheek, and I caught her feeding broccoli to my dogs.*
3. *Broccoli is a gute source of dietary fiber.*

4. *Carolyn eats an indecent amount of Twinkies.*
5. *How many Twinkies would you have to eat every day to get diabetes?*
6. *I'm not going to ask Abraham to fire her. Yet.*

    Your grandson,
    Aaron

Chapter 3

Dear Clara,

So Joseph finally took the hint and asked you for a sleigh ride? It's about time he noticed you. I wish I could have been there.

I hope you're not worried about me. Things are not so bad in Greenwood—sometimes. Die kinner are as lively as ever—I do believe Felty Jr. and Freddie want to see me cry. They haven't succeeded yet, but that doesn't keep them from trying. Luke is sneaky. If he's not making noise, he's getting into mischief. Lyle and Lydia are sweet, but Freddie can talk them into anything if he has a mind to. Last night he had them draw a picture of me with fangs instead of teeth. I wouldn't have minded if it hadn't been a four-foot crayon mural on the living room wall.

I told you about Abraham's bruder Aaron. He still thinks he knows more than I do about everything, but I don't mind so much. It's wonderful nice that he comes to the house every day to check on me. He's given me more than one lecture on broccoli, and he showed me the best way *to clean cobwebs off the ceiling. Yesterday he helped me wipe crayon off the wall and washed the breakfast dishes. He's quite good looking and sensible, and he cares deeply about his nieces and nephews.*

He is sure he knows everything about babies, so I finally insisted he change Rosie's diaper. He took off the diaper and washed Rosie's bottom in the sink to save on baby wipes. He never admitted he was wrong, but he was good-natured about scrubbing out the sink.

I'm beginning to think that Anna Helmuth tricked me into coming here, but I can't leave now. Mary needs my help. Abraham barely notices his children, and to be honest, Mary is little better. What will Christmas be like for their little ones when their parents don't seem to care? The problems in this family are bigger than I can ever hope to fix.

Aaron has blue eyes and two big dogs. They like broccoli.

My time in Greenwood has been a blessing if only to help me appreciate Christmas in Bonduel. When it gets difficult, I close my eyes and think of my dear Clara and the rest of the family sitting around the kitchen table telling Christmas stories or singing carols. Of course, I can't close my eyes for too long or Felty will try to duct tape me to the fridge.

All my love,
Carolyn

The smell of smoke punched Carolyn in the nose as she came down the stairs. "Is something burning? Freddie, what is burning?"

Freddie stood with his back to the stove, looking up at the ceiling and whistling as if he had nothing better to do. Carolyn wasn't fooled. Last week, she'd caught Freddie and Felty lighting the garbage on fire in the metal bin behind the house. Two days ago, Freddie had tried to roast a marshmallow by the flames of the gas stove. Thank the *gute* Lord Carolyn had caught him and blown it out before it caught his shirt on fire.

Maybe she hadn't been vigilant enough this morning. Was this the day Freddie would burn the house down around their heads?

A ribbon of smoke trickled from the stove and into the air behind Freddie's head. Carolyn always attempted a calm demeanor, even when one of *die kinner* was purposefully doing something to get a frenzied reaction from her, but a fire required immediate attention. She pushed Freddie aside and opened the oven, which was a very bad idea. Smoke poured from the inside and filled the kitchen before Carolyn could take a breath. She quickly shut the door and turned off the oven. "Freddie," she hissed, unable to keep the irritation out of her voice. "What did you put in there?"

Freddie grinned like a cat with a mouse between his teeth. Why did it always have to be a contest with him? "I was testing some of Rosie's pajamas to see if they'd burn. They're not supposed to catch fire. It says so on the label. You want to make sure they don't burn before she wears them, don't you?"

Carolyn was constantly amazed at how clever the twins were—how clever all *die kinner* were. They thought up tricks and pranks that Carolyn wouldn't have been able to imagine. How *wunderbarr* it would be if they applied all those smarts to doing something productive.

Smoke continued to seep from the oven, filling the kitchen with gray acrid smog, stinging her nose and making her eyes water. Moving quickly, she opened all the windows on the main floor, then grabbed Freddie's wrist and pulled him toward the front door. "Felty, Luke, grab Lydia and Lyle and take them outside. Freddie, you go out too."

"But it's cold out there," Freddie whined, as if he wasn't the reason everyone had to flee.

"I'll bring your coat, but get out now before you suffocate."

Praise the Lord, Felty and Luke did as she asked. No doubt they could see it was no time to disobey the babysitter. Rosie and Elmer sat on the floor playing with Rosie's blocks. Carolyn grabbed Elmer Mervin's hand, scooped Rosie into her arms, and followed the others onto the porch. It was too cold. They'd have to have coats. Freezing was just as likely a way to die as suffocation.

With Rosie still in her arms, Carolyn ducked back into the house and snatched *die kinner's* coats from the hooks on the wall and snagged a blanket from the sofa for Rosie.

Die kinner stood on the porch with their arms wrapped tightly around themselves, stamping their feet to ward off the chill. Carolyn passed out coats and wrapped Rosie in her fuzzy blanket. What was she supposed to do? They couldn't go back into the house. Abraham and Mary would not be happy if she took *die kinner* into the bakery, but they might have no choice. It was too cold to be out for long.

Or . . . they could go to Onkel Aaron's house. He lived just across the street and one house down.

"*Cum*," Carolyn said, holding on to Elmer Mervin's hand and walking him down the stairs. "Let's go for a walk."

Freddie frowned. "A walk? It's too cold."

Carolyn tried to bore a hole through his skull with her gaze. "Whose fault is that?"

His grin made Carolyn's teeth hurt. "I had to test Rosie's pajamas."

"You can't make us stay out here. I'm going back in the house," Felty said. He opened the front door and was met with a cloud of smoke. He coughed and stepped backward.

"Freddie chose to put Rosie's pajamas in the oven. Now we have to wait for the smoke to clear. It's not my fault you're cold, Felty. Maybe you should have a talk with Freddie about being more considerate of his *bruderen* and *schwesteren*."

Felty screwed up his face as if he was going to cry. Carolyn was unmoved by his distress.

She should have taken Rosie's pajamas out of the oven first thing. They'd be smoking for a long time. Carolyn made a decision and marched down the sidewalk with Rosie in her arms. "We're going to visit your Onkel Aaron."

The three older boys glanced at one another before slowly stomping down the steps. It was kind of hard to defy the babysitter when your hands felt like icicles.

Lydia took Elmer's hand and then Lyle's so they made a little chain walking along the side of the road. "Onkel Aaron doesn't like it when we come to his house."

"He doesn't?"

Lyle nodded. "Mamm says it makes him nervous."

Carolyn stifled a smile. She could well believe it. Aaron was a twenty-nine-year-old bachelor who cleaned his ceilings on a regular basis. Even though he was a farmer and regularly dealt with dirt and manure, his life was spick-and-span. Children were messy and unruly and unpredictable, and you couldn't stable children in the barn, not even for the sake of your clean floors.

Even though he'd told her she was an unfit babysitter and he'd questioned her cleaning skills, to her surprise, Carolyn found she liked Aaron. Ever since the night of gravy and roast, he'd come to the house every day—probably because he worried that Carolyn wasn't safe being left with the children, especially Freddie and Felty. He watched out for her, volunteering to wash dishes or play with the baby because he could see that she had her hands full, and Freddie, Luke, and Felty were purposefully trying to make things hard for her.

More than once in the last two weeks, Aaron had lectured his nephews on proper, godly behavior, but nothing seemed to sink in. The boys had a goal and a plan, and not even Onkel Aaron could talk them out of it. How could he? He didn't even know what it was.

It took them five cold minutes to walk to Aaron's house. The little ones could only go so fast. Aaron's sidewalk was immaculately shoveled with not a patch of ice that someone could slip on. Abraham and Mary's sidewalk was shoveled like that too. Aaron did theirs too, every time it snowed.

Aaron's house was a white clapboard with forest green shutters in good repair with no spots of chipped paint. The porch was a simple slab of concrete, but well swept with a black bumpy mat to wipe snow off your feet before you set foot in the house.

Aaron was going to be reluctant to let them in.

She smiled to herself. But he would, all the same. He would do just about anything for his family.

Lydia, Lyle, and Elmer knocked on the screen door all together with their little fists. Aaron opened the inside door and peered through the screen. He hesitated for the briefest of seconds before pushing the screen door open and giving Carolyn a tentative smile. Considering that he wasn't really keen on his house being invaded, it was a very nice smile—the kind that might have taken some other girl's breath away.

"Is everything okay?" he asked.

Carolyn blew a puff of air from her lips. "The house is filled with smoke. Could we sit here until it clears?" She emphasized the word *sit*, though both she and Aaron knew there wouldn't be a lot of sitting going on.

Aaron's brows loomed over his blue eyes. "What happened?" He glanced behind Carolyn to the twins and Luke.

Carolyn didn't want Freddie taking any satisfaction in the retelling of the story. She leaned closer and whispered, "It's a long story about an oven and a pair of pajamas."

Aaron nodded as if he understood exactly what she was talking about. He never wanted anyone to know that he knew less than he did. "*Cum reu.*" He took Lydia's hand, led her to another black mat inside the door, and took off her shoes. One by one he helped Lyle, Elmer, Freddie, Luke, and Felty off with their shoes and lined them up in a neat row on the mat.

Carolyn sat on Aaron's chunky, tan, nicely brushed microfiber sofa with Rosie in her arms. She pulled the blanket more snugly around Rosie. The poor baby's cheeks were ice cold.

Aaron stared at her. Had he turned a darker shade of pink than normal? "Can I help you take off your shoes?"

She glanced at his nice, clean rug. "I'm sorry. I should have thought of that." She slipped her shoes off, and before she had a chance to pick them up, Aaron already had them stacked next to the others.

Aaron put a hand on Felty's shoulder. "Why don't

you take all *die kinner* to the mud room, and you can look at the basket of pinecones I collected."

Lyle and Luke whooped their excitement, and *die kinner* ran down the back hall, Elmer pumping his little legs as fast as he could go.

Carolyn lifted an eyebrow. "That should keep them busy for a minute or so."

"They're wonderful big pinecones. *Die kinner* will like them."

"I hate to tell you, but pinecones are about as exciting as a pile of rocks, less so because you can throw rocks at windows and such. They'll be back before the dust settles."

Aaron folded his arms across his chest. "I don't have dust."

She smiled. "I'm sure you don't."

He knelt down and adjusted the shoes on the mat. "Do I need to put out the fire at Abraham and Mary's house?"

"I've opened all the windows, but I would appreciate it if you would take the pajamas out of the oven. I probably should have done that, but I wanted to get *die kinner* out of the smoke."

Aaron nodded. "That is wise. It's not *gute* for their lungs." He put on his boots and coat. "I'll be back."

Carolyn stood and strolled around the small front room. The wood floor was so shiny she could almost see her reflection in it. The sofa sat against the wall opposite the front door flanked by two sensible blue chairs. A small end table sat next to one of the chairs. There was nothing on the table, and just as Aaron had said, she couldn't see a speck of dust. A small bookshelf stood against one wall, lined with books that looked as if they had never been read, arranged in alphabetical order.

Carolyn started reading the titles on his shelf when she realized that too much time had passed since she'd heard from *die kinner*. Surely they hadn't been quietly gazing at pinecones for five minutes.

With Rosie on her hip, she marched to the end of the hall. From all the noise behind the closed door, it was obvious *die kinner* weren't looking at pinecones. She opened the door, and a pinecone hit her in the face. It appeared that pinecones were just as fun as rocks. An empty basket stood in the middle of the mudroom surrounded by six children with pinecones in their little fists. The floor was covered with pinecones. *Die kinner* had been busy.

Making her voice loud enough to get their attention, but not too loud to make them think she was upset, she said, "Stop this at once. What will your *onkel* Aaron say when he finds out you've ruined his special pile of pinecones?" She wasn't sure it was a particularly special pile of pinecones, but this total disregard for other people's things had to stop.

Lydia, Lyle, and little Elmer looked immediately contrite. Lydia bent over and set her pinecone in the bottom of Aaron's basket. "Sorry. We was having fun."

"Onkel Aaron will be very sad."

"*Nae*, he won't," Felty said. "He lets us throw his pinecones all the time."

Carolyn pinned Felty with a stern, unyielding eye. "That is a lie, Felty Stutzman, and you should be ashamed of yourself. Now please pick up all the pinecones."

Freddie and Felty picked up less than their fair share, but Carolyn wasn't going to press the issue. She had to pick her battles very carefully or lose complete control of the children—even with Aaron's daily help. When the pinecones were back in the basket, she handed Freddie the broom and Felty the dustpan. "Please leave the floor as shiny as you found it."

She led the rest of *die kinner* into Aaron's front room, but she'd have to think of something to occupy them or they'd be throwing Aaron's books next. Aaron had nothing fit for a child to play with. *Die kinner* loved the dogs, but the dogs weren't allowed inside. They had their own little solar-heated house in the barn that wouldn't fit more than two energetic children.

Carolyn glanced into Aaron's clean kitchen. His chairs were metal, and he'd obviously shined the chrome recently. He wasn't going to like it, but *die kinner* needed something to do, and she needed to make some goodies for the school program.

"Luke, what treats should we bring to the program tomorrow night?"

Luke glanced toward the mudroom. "Felty and Freddie like sugar cookies."

"What do you like?"

He scratched his ear. "I like the chocolate chip ones you brought the day you came to our house, but Freddie and Felty said we shouldn't eat them because we don't like you, but I sneaked some anyway."

"I'm glad you liked them. We'll make chocolate chip cookies, and if Freddie and Felty don't like them, that will leave more for us. Would you like to help?"

"I want to help," Lydia said.

Carolyn took Elmer Mervin's hand. "I want you all to help, but you have to sit up to the table." She helped Elmer into a chair just as Aaron came back into the house bringing a dark expression and an overpowering smell of smoke. She didn't have the heart to tell him he stunk when he'd just done her a huge favor and looked so handsome.

"I pulled whatever it was out of the oven," he said, lifting Lyle into one of the chairs, "but there's still a lot of smoke. I opened all the windows upstairs too. Was it one of the boys?"

Carolyn nodded. "Freddie. I won't be able to hide this from Abraham."

Aaron's expression turned even darker. "Why would you want to hide it? I know you're trying to be patient, Carolyn, but Freddie needs to feel the heavy weight of consequences. What if the kitchen had caught fire? Abraham and Mary might have lost their house, and you could have been hurt."

"I know you think I'm a bad babysitter, but you have to trust me that I'm handling it in the way I think best."

Aaron took off his coat and hung it in the closet. Carolyn winced. Everything in that closet was going to smell like smoke. Aaron would be spraying air freshener for days. "I wasn't . . . I don't think I knew the whole story when I called you a bad babysitter."

Carolyn bounced Rosie on her hip and gave Aaron an arch smile. "Are you saying you were wrong?"

"*Nae*, that's not what I'm saying. I simply mean that I don't necessarily think you're a bad babysitter anymore, even if you feed *die kinner* Twinkies."

"It's okay to say it out loud, Aaron."

"Say what?"

She couldn't resist laughing at the look on his face. He knew exactly what, and she wasn't going to let him get away without admitting it. "Come on, Aaron. Say it. Say you were wrong about me."

"It's not that I was wrong, just that I didn't have all the information."

She sidled closer and nudged him with her elbow. "I'll change Rosie's diaper on your kitchen table if you don't say it."

His eyes grew as wide as saucers. "I . . . I was wrong," he stuttered.

She nodded her approval. "*Denki*. It takes a strong man to admit when he's wrong."

"Or maybe just mistaken," he added.

She didn't correct him. Aaron Stutzman had probably never before admitted to being wrong in his life. It was quite an accomplishment.

Any hint of good humor disappeared from his face. "But I'm not wrong about Freddie needing punishment. His behavior has crossed from mischievous to destructive. Abraham should be told."

Carolyn looked around the table. *Die kinner* stared at her in rapt attention. "Do you have some paper and pencils, Aaron?"

Aaron pulled paper and finely sharpened pencils from one of the drawers, and Carolyn passed them out to *die kinner*.

Even at the risk of chaos breaking out in the kitchen, Carolyn motioned for Aaron to follow her into the front room. She pressed her lips together. Aaron wasn't going to like what she had to say. "I don't mean to speak ill of your *bruder*, but Abraham barely notices his own *kinner*."

To her surprise, Aaron nodded. "I have seen as much."

"*Die kinner* don't like me, though I'm a wonderful *gute* babysitter." She smiled weakly. "They don't need me. They need the firm hand of their *fater* and the gentle affection of their *mater*, and they'll do anything to get it. Freddie *would* burn down the house if it meant his parents would notice him."

"Have you told them this?"

She sighed and kissed Rosie's silky hair. "I've tried, but Mary feels guilty enough as it is, and Abraham thinks I'm criticizing him."

He studied her face. "So *die kinner* take their hurt and frustration out on you."

"In hopes I'll either quit or tell their parents. I'm hoping they'll give up if they see I'm not going to do either."

He shook his head. "Freddie won't give up. He'll just do worse and worse things until you have no choice but to bring in his parents." He took a step backward and glanced into the kitchen where *die kinner* were drawing quietly on their papers. Freddie and Felty were still in the mudroom, getting into who knew what kind of trouble. Aaron nudged Carolyn toward the sofa, and they sat down. "This is hardest on you. I appreciate that you're not one to blubber, but you can't be happy about being here. Why did you come?"

Carolyn couldn't tell him that his own *mammi* had tricked her into it. "I was looking for adventure."

He grunted. "*Ach, vell*, you found it. It wonders me why you don't go home."

She wasn't sure why the question pricked her like a pin. "You think I should go home?"

He cleared his throat. "I don't want you to go home."

"You don't?"

He cleared his throat a second time. And a third. "I mean, I'm not telling you that you should go home, but if I were you, I'd go home."

His gaze settled right down to her bones, and she patted Rosie's back to give her an excuse to look away. "I miss my family. This time of year we do our Christmas baking. The house always smells like peppermint and chocolate."

"Now all you can smell is smoke."

"We make Yule logs and Christmas pudding. My *dat* cuts pine boughs from the woods, and my *mamm* ties them up with red ribbon and lights candles all over the house." She flashed a smile so he wouldn't suspect she was miserable, which she was. "I don't think it would be wise to light candles with Freddie in the house."

"Not wise at all."

"There won't be pine boughs or ribbons either. I don't have time to put them up, and *die kinner* would only tear them down and stuff them in the oven."

The corner of his mouth curled upward. "*Ach*, it's just as well. Pine boughs dry out and all those needles make a wonderful mess."

"I miss home, but I couldn't leave Mary. She is at the end of her rope as it is."

She couldn't read the emotion in his eyes, but it made her feel sort of breathless. "You have a kind heart, Carolyn Yutzy."

"You wouldn't think so if you knew what I'd been thinking about Freddie half an hour ago."

He shook his head. "I hate to admit it, but I don't like it when *die kinner* come over to visit. I love them, but I always have to sand the scuff marks out of my floor when they leave. I rather love them at their own house."

"You are still a fine *onkel*. *Die kinner* love you, even when you bring broccoli as a gift."

"But I wouldn't be as unselfish as you. You're helping Mary, a woman who is almost a complete stranger to you."

She tilted her head and gave him a puzzled frown. "But you *have* been. You've come over every day this week and helped me clean up or do the dishes or care for *die kinner*. You don't know me well. I'd say that's a sign of a *gute* heart, even though you criticize the way I scrub the sink."

He got a funny look on his face. "I don't know if that's a sign of a *gute* heart or not."

"Of course it is."

"I'm more selfish than that."

She didn't know what he meant, but the look he gave her made her feel self-conscious. "The question is what to do about Freddie."

Aaron shuddered. "We can't pretend nothing happened. I don't want him to try it again."

"*Nae*. Something has to be done, but I'm not sure what."

"He needs his *fater*." Aaron blew air from between his lips. "Freddie, Felty, and Luke can come here every day after school and help me with the chores. I'll work them hard and bring them home at dinnertime."

Carolyn felt giddy and breathless at the prospect of not having to deal with the older twins and Luke. "Aaron, that is very kind of you, but it's too much to ask. Those boys are terrors."

A smile grew slowly on his lips. "I won't tell Abraham your opinion of his children."

She pasted a look of mock horror on her face. "Please don't. He'd never forgive me." She turned Rosie around to sit on her lap. "But school is out on Wednesday, then almost a whole week until Christmas."

"I'll come get them after breakfast and work them all day. We'll at least get through Christmas and then decide what to do. They might not like hard labor so much. And I'll make them eat broccoli for lunch."

"That's cruel," Carolyn said, tempering her words with a smile. "I hate broccoli."

He narrowed his eyes. "Broccoli is the most nutritious food you can eat. Eating it regularly will add five years to your life."

"I'd rather die young."

His mouth fell open. "You *will* die young if you keep eating three Twinkies a day."

She smacked him lightly on the shoulder. It was as hard as a rock. "You're exaggerating. It can't be more than two."

"It's three and sometimes four."

There was a little commotion in the kitchen, and Carolyn leapt to her feet. *Ach, du lieva*, Aaron had made her forget there were six little whirlwinds in the house who had gone almost five minutes without supervision. "Aaron, you'd better check on Freddie and Felty in the mudroom."

Aaron was down the hall before Carolyn drew another breath. She went into the kitchen, where Lyle was the only child still drawing on his paper. Luke had found a pen and was doodling a charming little picture on Elmer's cheek, and Lydia was etching circles into Aaron's table with her pencil. Carolyn snatched the pencil from Lydia's hand, but it was too late for the table. The marks wouldn't be coming off with a dishrag, no matter how hard Aaron scrubbed. She also confiscated Luke's pen, hoping his artwork would wash off with soap and water.

"Lydia," she said, "it's not nice to draw on Onkel Aaron's table."

"I want to make cookies," she said, as if this excused all bad behavior.

Carolyn handed her a wet rag. "Wipe off as much as you can, but you will have to apologize to Aaron and help him fix your scratches."

Aaron came into the kitchen, his face looking like a thunderstorm. He had a firm hand on each of his oldest nephews' shoulders. Carolyn looked the boys up and down. No singed hair or visible bruises. Maybe they had done as they were told and stuck to sweeping the mudroom.

"The boys are going to sand the mudroom. They

thought it might be fun to scoot around my floor with pinecones as shoes, and the entire floor is scratched."

Carolyn's heart sank to her toes. "Boys," she said, almost losing her composure. "Your *onkel* Aaron welcomed us into his home. How could you do something like that?"

Freddie lifted his chin. "We was ice skating."

"It was fun." Felty laughed a nervous little laugh that didn't fool anybody. He wasn't quite sure about the rightness of what he had done, even if Freddie was.

Carolyn was dumbfounded. Aaron had been right. She couldn't let the boys go on like this. It was almost as if neither of them had a conscience anymore. "Your *onkel* is always so thoughtful with you. He makes you sandwiches and plays softball with you in the backyard and lets you in his nice, warm house because he doesn't want you to be cold." She set Rosie on Luke's lap and took a step toward the twins. "How could you do this to someone you love?"

"We wanted to ice skate," Freddie said, lifting his chin and holding his ground as if he were ready to die on it.

"Shame on you," was all Carolyn could think to say. She was trying to remain calm, to let them see that they hadn't gotten to her, but for some reason, this one had cut her deep. If they wanted to make her life miserable, so be it, but how dare they hurt Aaron when he had been nothing but kind and she had forced her way into his house? "Shame on you." She turned and leaned her hands against Aaron's counter. "I can't even stand to look at you."

Maybe it was because she truly meant it or maybe it was because Felty finally understood the seriousness of his mischief. He started to whimper softly. Carolyn turned around. Tears ran down his cheeks, and his head was bowed in contrition. *Gute*. He should feel deep regret for what he had done. Freddie was another matter. He folded his hands across his chest and gazed out the window as if he wasn't thinking on anything in particular. How would she get through to that one?

It was Aaron's expression that held her attention. The anger was there in his eyes, but there was also another deep emotion that she couldn't define. Was it gratitude? Admiration? *Nae*, it most certainly wasn't admiration. He had never been especially impressed with her. The look gave her goose bumps, all the same.

"I'm sorry, Onkel Aaron," Felty sobbed, swiping his sleeve across his face. "We thought it would be fun. We didn't think about your feelings."

Aaron released the boys' shoulders and pulled his coat from the closet, pausing to sniff it before sliding it on. "Boys, put your coats and shoes on. The sandpaper is in the shed."

Aaron, with Felty and Freddie close behind, went out the front door, leaving Carolyn with only five children to tend to. She rifled through the drawers for an apron, finding a manly one with deep pockets and no ruffles. She pulled two bowls from the beautifully organized cupboards and set them on the table, then handed one spoon to Lyle and one to Luke. She took Rosie from Luke's lap.

"I want a spoon," Lydia said.

"I want a poon," Elmer echoed.

Carolyn grabbed two more wooden spoons. Aaron had a whole drawer of them, as if he were starting a collection. She found butter in the fridge, but look as she might, she couldn't find one grain of sugar in the whole kitchen. Didn't Aaron have sugar with his *kaffee* in the morning? She should have considered that before she'd decided to make cookies at Aaron's house. He probably didn't have refined flour either.

Aaron and the boys marched back into the house each carrying a sanding tool.

"Aaron, do you have chocolate chips?" she said.

"Chocolate is very bad for you."

"Then you're going to have to wait here with *die kinner* while I go back home and fetch chocolate chips."

"Why do you need chocolate chips?"

"I'm making cookies."

He stiffened. "Why?"

She gave him a reassuring smile. "Don't worry. I'll clean up." Without waiting for a reply, she put on her coat and shoes and slipped out the door. She ran all the way to the house and all the way back, bringing chocolate chips, white sugar, brown sugar, vanilla, and flour just in case.

When she returned, Aaron led Felty and Freddie down the hall, and Carolyn suspected she wouldn't see them for the rest of the night. She felt a little guilty for messing up his kitchen, but they needed cookies for the school program, and baking in Abraham and Mary's kitchen was out of the question. Besides, it would give *die kinner* something to do until bedtime, which seemed about as far away as Christmas Day.

Without Freddie and Felty to egg them on, the other children behaved themselves fairly well while they helped Carolyn make cookies. Elmer and Lydia stirred the dry ingredients, and Lyle and Luke creamed the sugar and butter together. It wasn't an easy job. She let Luke crack the egg, and if a little egg white dribbled on the floor, Aaron never had to know about it.

Carolyn searched in the cupboards until she realized with dismay that Aaron didn't have a cookie sheet. He might not believe in sugar, but for goodness sake, he should at least have a cookie sheet. She was left with a bowl of dough and no cookie sheet. She'd have to go put *die kinner* to bed, wait until Mary came home, and come back later to bake the cookies. Aaron would no doubt be annoyed about her lingering in his kitchen, but it couldn't be helped. She'd have to give Mary's oven a *gute* scrubbing before daring to use it again.

Rosie was definitely ready for bed. She rubbed her eyes and fussed in Carolyn's arms. With Rosie on her hip, Carolyn went down the hall and stuck her head in the mudroom, where Freddie, Felty, and Aaron were vigorously scrubbing sandpaper across the floor. The edges and corners of the room were untouched, but the entire center of the four feet by four feet space was covered with sanding dust. It had been almost an hour. Freddie and Felty seemed to be fading a bit, but Aaron was working so hard, sweat dripped from his brow.

"I need to take *die kinner* home for bed," Carolyn said. She pressed her lips together, sorry that she'd brought them over. Would Aaron's floor ever be the same?

Freddie actually looked happy about the prospect of bedtime, but Aaron quashed those dreams immediately. "I'll walk Freddie and Felty home when they're finished."

Carolyn nodded, not even pointing out that it was a school night. If Freddie and Felty were up until midnight, they only got what they deserved—maybe less than they deserved. And they'd be a lot less likely to make mischief if they were sleepy tomorrow. "I'm coming back to bake the cookies," she said, almost as an afterthought.

"What was that?" Aaron said as she shut the door.

Carolyn helped *die kinner* on with their coats and shoes and wrapped Rosie in her blanket, and they walked quickly back to the house. The wind was starting to pick up, and it was icy cold. The house wasn't much warmer than outside. Aaron had opened all the windows. There was still a lingering smell of smoke, but at least they could breathe without coughing their lungs out.

After Carolyn stoked up the pellet stove, she put the five youngest children to bed. There was a minor toothbrush fight before they were finally all tucked in, but Carolyn had been too numb to even scold them.

Mary came slouching into the house at about nine, looking more worn-out than ever. She sighed. "*Ach*. I was hoping *die kinner* would still be up so I had a chance to say good night."

"Bedtime came a little early tonight," Carolyn said. "Luke or the twins might still be awake if you want to go up."

Mary flashed what passed for a smile. "I'd like that." She sniffed the air. "Did you burn something?"

"We had a little accident with the oven. I opened the windows, and we went to Aaron's while the smoke cleared. Freddie and Felty are still at his house helping him with some cleaning."

Mary opened the oven door but didn't comment on the condition inside. "Sometimes I think all Aaron does is clean. I hope he's not working Freddie and Felty too hard. They need their sleep."

Carolyn bit her bottom lip. It was very likely that Aaron *was* working the twins hard, but it was a *gute* lesson. "How did cookie making go today?"

Another forced smile. "*Ach*, we have enough orders to keep us busy until Christmas. We don't have enough time to finish them unless we work late every night from now on."

"Then I hope you'll get a break."

Mary's shoulders sagged lower. "Abraham says Valentine's Day will be even bigger. I'm going to have to quit nursing Rosie. I've all but dried up anyway." Mary slumped into a chair. "She's probably forgotten what I look like."

Carolyn sat next to her and put a gentle arm around her shoulder. "For sure and certain she hasn't. *Die kinner* adore you. They could never forget their *mater*." Carolyn hesitated, then plunged ahead. "Have you thought about hiring a helper in the shop so you can be home with *die kinner*?"

Mary sighed. "Abraham can't see how that will work out. It would be inappropriate for another woman to take my place in the shop and be alone with Abraham all day, and Abraham doesn't think there's a man with the skills to bake cookies."

Carolyn didn't see a solution either, but Abraham and Mary were going to have to make some hard decisions. Mary's children needed her, and Carolyn wasn't going to last much longer, no matter how much Mary needed her.

For some reason, she felt a little twinge of regret when she thought about leaving Greenwood. The regret certainly wasn't because of the children, though the younger ones were growing on her, and it certainly wasn't for tiny Greenwood itself. The truth smacked her in the face like a crisp piece of lettuce, and she felt a smile creep onto her face. The regret was for Aaron, who had somehow wheedled his way into her heart with his unapologetic criticisms and his disdain for Twinkies.

Carolyn put her arms around Mary and gave her a reassuring squeeze. "Why don't you go and wake up Rosie? She hasn't been asleep long. You could nurse her and put her right back to bed."

Mary's brows inched together. "I will. I miss her. I miss all of them."

Carolyn stood and pulled two cookie sheets out of the cupboard. "I'm afraid I need to go back to Aaron's house and bake some cookies. Will you be okay?"

"Now?"

"I don't want to use this oven until I thoroughly clean it tomorrow."

Mary went upstairs. Maybe no one would be asleep yet, and Mary could spend some time with her children.

Carolyn put on her coat just as Aaron, Freddie, and Felty came through the front door. Both boys had lost that twinkle of mischief in their eyes, and Freddie was massaging his knuckles as if they were a bit sore. Aaron smiled, and she could tell he was happy to see her, even if there was a spark of annoyance in his eyes about the boys.

"Is the floor fixed?" she asked, directing her question to Freddie.

Felty eased off his coat and winced. Carolyn did her best not to look smug. His arms must be wonderful sore.

Freddie stumbled to the sofa and fell onto it, sprawling on his stomach as if exhaustion had overtaken him and he could go no farther. "We have to go back tomorrow and varnish it."

Carolyn made her voice extra chipper just so they knew she didn't feel one bit sorry for them. "Sounds like you're making *gute* progress."

Freddie moaned, and Aaron wiped his hand across his mouth, most likely to wipe away any hint of a smile. "They worked hard, but there was a lot of complaining. Tomorrow we'll do it without complaining."

Carolyn zipped up her coat and picked up her cookie sheets. "I am going to Aaron's house to bake cookies."

Aaron cocked an eyebrow. "You are?"

"I can't use this oven, and you didn't have any cookie

sheets, and the school program is tomorrow night." And just in case he needed more convincing, "There's a bowl of cookie dough sitting on your counter."

He smiled with full force now. The charm of it almost knocked her over—maybe because Aaron wasn't one to smile unless he had a very *gute* reason. She had half expected him to be reluctant to let her come because he didn't like the thought of an untidy kitchen and he really didn't like the thought of cookies. "Let's go then."

Carolyn's heart did a little dance, and she picked up her cookie sheets. "Freddie and Felty, go upstairs and get ready for bed. Maybe your *mamm* will read you a story."

Freddie bolted upright. "Mamm's home?"

Carolyn smiled. "*Jah*. She wants to see you."

Felty and Freddie almost tripped over each other to be the first one up the stairs. No matter how hard a nine-year-old's day had been, there was nothing a *mater*'s love couldn't cure.

Aaron opened the door for Carolyn. "Can I scoop the dough onto the cookie sheet?"

Carolyn twisted her lips into a tease. "It's because you don't want me to spill it on your cupboard, isn't it?"

His mouth fell open in mock indignation. "I want to try out my new cookie scoop. My *schwester* Elsie gave it to me, and I've never used it."

"Why would Elsie give you a cookie scoop?"

He smiled and shrugged. "The same reason I gave her a vegetable peeler."

Carolyn was going to make a complete mess of his kitchen *and* bake sweets that were better off in the garbage than in anyone's stomach, but Aaron couldn't have been happier about it. To his shock, he realized he'd rather spend time with Carolyn than have a spotless kitchen. He'd rather spend time with Carolyn than mop his floors or read a book or iron his shirts. What had gotten into him? He'd have to examine his emotions later. Right now, he just wanted to stare into Carolyn's eyes.

It was full dark and the air was colder as they stepped off Abraham's porch, but they took their time to Aaron's house. Aaron wanted to draw out every single minute he could get with her.

Carolyn tucked her coat around her chin. "Did the boys do a *gute* job on your floor, or are you going to have to sand it all over again?"

"I made sure they did a *gute* job. I made them go over their work again if they were careless. It didn't take them long to see that if they did it well the first time, they wouldn't have to be there all night."

Carolyn blew a puff of air from between her lips. It turned into a little cloud in front of her face. "I'm sorry they did that to your floor. If I had known they would destroy something in your house, I never would have brought them over."

Aaron's heart clenched like a fist. No one had ever been indignant on his behalf before. It meant more than Aaron would have thought possible and turned his heart even more firmly in Carolyn's direction. "It wasn't your fault. *Denki* for taking my part."

"I had thought that surely they would have had enough respect for their *onkel* to behave themselves."

"Freddie and Felty have little respect for anyone anymore."

"Except their parents," Carolyn said.

"Not even their parents." He glanced at Carolyn. He

didn't want to say anything against his *bruder*, but surely Carolyn saw the truth as plain as Aaron did. "Abraham and Mary have let them down too many times."

Aaron didn't like that look of disquiet that overtook Carolyn's expression. They were going to his house to bake cookies and none of the *die kinner* would be there, and he wanted to enjoy every minute. He quickened his pace. "If we don't go faster, it will be after midnight when the last of the cookies comes out of the oven." He pretended to be irritated about it. "They're going to stink up the whole house."

Carolyn only laughed. "You know I'm going to make you eat one."

"*Nae*, you won't. They're full of sugar."

"You have to eat one. It's a Christmas tradition to have at least a taste of anything that's been baked in your kitchen."

He narrowed his eyes. "I've never heard of that tradition."

She stuck out her bottom lip, attempting the expression he had seen Lydia give her only this morning. "You don't want to ruin Christmas, do you?"

He tried not to smile. "Anything for Christmas."

Aaron opened the door for Carolyn, and he appreciated the way she stomped the snow off her boots before she took them off and lined them neatly on his special snow mat. After taking off their coats and scarves, which smelled like smoke, Aaron led the way into the kitchen, where he lit the three propane lanterns. They'd need plenty of light to bake.

Carolyn set her cookie sheets next to the bowl of dough on the cupboard and washed her hands at the sink. He appreciated the attempt at cleanliness, even if his kitchen was about to become a wasteland of flour and chocolate chips. "Will you preheat the oven to three hundred and fifty degrees?"

Aaron cheerfully turned on the oven, even though he didn't usually like to be bossed around. He retrieved Elsie's cookie scoop from one of the bottom drawers and handed it to Carolyn. She pulled a soup spoon from another drawer, dug a scoop of dough from the bowl, and lifted it in Aaron's direction. "Have a taste."

He shook his head. "It has raw eggs in it."

She gave him a teasing smile. "The danger of eating it makes it taste that much better."

"What if it makes me sick?"

"I've eaten mounds of cookie dough over the years and never gotten sick." She nudged the spoon closer to his mouth. "Come on, Aaron. It's delicious."

He wasn't prepared for the tightening in his chest as he opened his mouth and she fed him that cookie dough. He couldn't breathe, couldn't speak, couldn't concentrate on anything but the soft curve of her fingers and the even softer curl of her lips. He'd never been so unnerved in his life, and he suspected it didn't have anything to do with the gooey, sweet lump sliding down his throat.

He swallowed, cleared his throat, and tried to gather his wits. "Not bad," was all he could muster.

"Not bad? I'll have you know, I'm famous for my cookie dough." In the lamplight, her eyes sparkled with delight, and try as he might, he couldn't look away.

Maybe it was unwise to have Carolyn here. When he looked at her, the late hour played tricks with his brain, and he never wanted her to leave. He pictured her moving about his kitchen in her quiet way, blessing everything she touched, making his life better just by being in it, no matter how messy or inconvenient her presence would be. He shook his head to clear it. It didn't help.

He couldn't shake the sudden longing that overtook him like a warm summer rain.

The inappropriateness of a single man and a single woman being alone together suddenly hit him. He should tell her he had a headache and make her go home. Surely she could find another oven for her cookies.

"Is everything okay?" she asked, mild and amused concern on her face. "How does your stomach feel?"

"I'm going to get a sugar headache."

"That's the best kind." She scooped some dough with her finger and licked it off.

"That is very unsanitary."

She just laughed. "All the germs get baked out."

He couldn't resist that laugh, and he certainly couldn't ask her to leave. Where would she find an oven this late at night? *Die kinner* were counting on those cookies. "Show me how to use this scoop."

She scooped one ball of cookie dough and dropped it on the cookie sheet, then handed him the scoop and told him to try. It wasn't that hard to scoop, and Aaron was determined to make the balls perfectly uniform and perfectly shaped. If he was going to allow cookies in his house, they should at least look good.

He put the first ball of dough back into the bowl four times until he got an acceptable shape and size. Carolyn quietly watched with that very appealing smile on her face. "You are definitely getting the hang of it."

He glanced at her and then quickly pulled his gaze away, determined not to be distracted by her blue eyes. "You have a spot of toothpaste on your neck." He cleared his throat. He should never look at her neck again. His heart might be doing somersaults for hours.

Carolyn sighed with an exasperated smile on her face. "While I was putting Rosie to bed, *die kinner* brushed their teeth, then painted the walls with toothpaste. Elmer

Mervin brushed the toilet and the floor. You would have been proud of me. I cleaned up the mess and boiled all the toothbrushes."

"*Ach!* Boiling doesn't get rid of all the germs."

"Maybe I should have thrown them away."

"*Jah*. That's what I would have done."

She laughed. "No doubt you would have."

It was after ten when they finished baking the cookies. Aaron poured some nutritious whole milk, and Carolyn ate three cookies and Aaron reluctantly had one. He would never admit that it was the best thing he'd ever tasted and that it only made him like Carolyn more. After they cleaned the kitchen, he walked her home and came back only to notice her greasy handprint on his white fridge.

He didn't wipe it off.

It made him smile every time he opened his fridge.

Dear Mammi and Dawdi,

1. *Chocolate chip cookies are appeditlich, but I won't eat them ever again.*
2. *Carolyn Yutzy likes to smile even though things here are very hard for her.*
3. *Thank you for sending your home remedy for stomachaches, but I think the asparagus bran muffins might have made it worse.*
4. *I found a glob of cookie dough on the underside of my table this morning. I don't blame Carolyn.*

Best regards,
Aaron

Chapter 4

Dear Carolyn,
Your sister Clara happened to mention that maybe you're not having a gute time in Greenwood. My grandson Aaron can be quite stiff, but he's a real treasure when you get to know him. Please give him these three pot holders I knitted for him and tell him you are a wonderful gute girl even if you don't like broccoli.
Love,
Anna Helmuth

The school Christmas program was always the biggest event of the season. Aaron had picked them up in his buggy, and Carolyn and all *die kinner* had stuffed themselves into the front and the back.

Dozens of families—parents and children and grandparents—packed into the one-room schoolhouse where Luke, Freddie, and Felty went to school. Carolyn and Aaron sat on the same bench with Lydia, Lyle, and Elmer Mervin squished between them while Rosie sat on Aaron's lap. Abraham and Mary were meeting them there because they had to fill one more order before they closed the shop for the night. Carolyn kept looking over her shoulder. They'd be able to squeeze Abraham and Mary on their bench if each of them held a child on their lap, but Abraham and Mary weren't there yet and the program was about to start. If they didn't get here soon, they'd have to stand in the back.

Carolyn found herself enjoying the program more than she anticipated. Seeing the scholars eager to do their best with each part, acting out Christmas stories and reciting Christmas poems, took Carolyn right back to Bonduel and filled her with the spirit of Christmas she'd been missing since she had come to Greenwood. It didn't hurt that Aaron kept glancing in her direction with that look of gratitude or admiration or whatever it was in his eyes that made her just a little bit dizzy.

Luke stood to say his part, but he frowned and mumbled his way through it, not at all the way Carolyn had heard him practice it for two weeks. When he sat down, Carolyn turned and scanned the crowd behind her. No wonder Luke had seemed upset. Abraham and Mary hadn't come.

Aaron was a *gute* problem solver, like the time his *mamm* was running out of room in the cellar and he built her those slanted shelves so the cans rolled down to the end of the shelf and she could rotate them easier. Today was no different. Carolyn had a problem, and he'd been determined to solve it for her.

He had to carry the box with both hands, not because it was heavy but because it was so big. He didn't know why he'd spent so much time on a gift for Carolyn except that he liked to see her smile. And he wanted her to be happy. And he thought the sound of her laughter was

about the prettiest thing he'd ever heard. When they had
first met, he hadn't been quite so taken with her, but she
had for sure and certain grown on him until he couldn't
remember what his life had been like before she'd come
to town.

Ach, *vell*. It had been tidier and more predictable. His
house had been much cleaner, and he had no scratches
on his wood floor, and there wouldn't be a handprint on
his fridge. But maybe he didn't mind so much. He'd
take cake batter on the ceiling any day if Carolyn would
just come over and bake something in his kitchen—but
he'd be sure not to stare at her lips or her neck, or let her
feed him cookie dough from a spoon. It was too unsettling.

The snow made down hard last night, and Aaron was
forced to wear his snowshoes to get to Abraham and
Mary's house. He carried his gift carefully folded in a
box from the post office. Hopefully the post office
wouldn't mind that he had used their box in an unautho-
rized way, but the gift had to arrive at Abraham's in *gute*
condition.

Carolyn swung the door open before Aaron even had a
chance to knock. Her face was pale, her eyes and lips
even more pronounced against her porcelain skin. Something was wrong. She wasn't smiling.

She waved a piece of paper in front of his face.
"Look at this."

He set the box on her porch and took the paper. It was
a coupon for a free safety inspection from the gas sta-
tion. Aaron frowned. "What do you want me to see?"

"Look on the back."

He turned the coupon over. A note written in what
looked suspiciously like a nine-year-old's handwriting
filled the back. *"We hate you. We hate this house. We want*

to spend Christmas by ourselves because nobody loves us." Aaron looked up from the note. "Freddie?"

"Or Felty. Or maybe even Luke." Carolyn grabbed his wrist and pulled him into the house. It was plain that she was as mad as a bee with a boil and as worried as the velvet on the driver's seat of a buggy. "They were angels this morning. I should have known they were up to something. I had to go to the bathroom, and when I came out they had disappeared."

"You left them alone?" He sounded harsher than he wanted to.

"I have to go to the bathroom sometime, Aaron. I'm not going to apologize for it."

He shook his head as if to wipe away what he'd just said. "I know. You're right."

He followed her into the kitchen with his snowshoes still on. This was the most worried he'd ever been. He'd never gone into any house wearing his snowshoes. Carolyn snatched her coat off the hook. "When I came out of the bathroom, I found the note and searched the house, but they're not here. You've got to help me find them, Aaron. Rosie's gone too."

With sinking dread, Aaron helped Carolyn on with her coat. "It's new snow. We should be able to follow their tracks."

"They haven't been gone long, and they couldn't have gotten far with the drifts this high."

Aaron took a deep breath and tried in vain to calm his pounding heart and the sick, almost panicked feeling in the pit of his stomach. "I'll have to get my extra pair of snowshoes for you."

"I can make it without."

"You'll be faster with snowshoes. Collect some blankets and get the sled from the shed."

Carolyn nodded. "Okay. Please hurry."

She hadn't needed to say it. Aaron had never moved so fast in those snowshoes in his life. He ran to his house, found the extra snowshoes, and ran back all in about seven minutes. Just as he got to Abraham and Mary's front yard, he groaned. He should have brought his dogs. They could have found the children as easy as pie.

Carolyn was waiting for him on the covered porch, her arms loaded with blankets.

"What about the sled?"

"I think *die kinner* took it. There were footprints and sled tracks coming out of the shed."

He liked that Carolyn was so levelheaded as to put on not only her coat, but her gloves, bonnet, beanie, and snow boots. Mammi had told Aaron that Carolyn was sensible. He liked that quality in a girl. Or . . . he supposed he liked that quality. He'd never stopped to think about what he liked in a girl. He'd never really cared before he met Carolyn.

And he didn't care now. His nieces and nephews were missing. There was no better proof that a girl could mess up his life something wonderful.

He knelt down and helped her put on her snowshoes, which somehow seemed like a very intimate thing to do. If his hand slipped, he'd end up touching her ankle, and that would come to no good. At least he couldn't see her neck from down here.

With his heart beating with the force of a gale against his window, Aaron led the way as they hiked around the house to the shed. Aaron gave Carolyn a quick lesson on how to walk on snowshoes. Snowshoes weren't that hard to use, but he didn't want her to stumble. He took the blankets and tucked them under one arm. It would be easier for her to keep her balance with empty hands.

Sure enough, *die kinner* had been in the shed, and

their tracks led toward the pasture to the north and into the woods beyond. Aaron shook his head. "You should have talked to Abraham days ago. Then they wouldn't have done something so foolish."

"Maybe I should have."

He hadn't meant to make it sound like he blamed her. He was even more to blame than she was. Abraham was his *bruder*. Talking to him had been Aaron's responsibility.

Carolyn was too sensible to wallow, but her hands shook as she turned and followed the tracks the children had left in the snow. It had only been a few minutes. They'd find them before they got too far.

"It wonders me if they wanted to be found," Aaron said. "A blind man could follow these tracks."

"It's like everything else Freddie and Felty have done. They want their parents to notice them. I underestimated how far they would go."

Aaron finally caught up with Carolyn and matched his pace with hers. "But what child hasn't run away from home?"

"*Vell*, I never did. It seemed a rather foolish thing."

She nearly tripped, and Aaron reached out and grabbed her hand to steady her. A bolt of lightning shot up his arm. "I ran away once and was gone for three days."

"Three days?"

"I'd kept a ledger with all my plans in it, including how much money I would need to live off of and things I would eat that wouldn't cost anything. They caught me trying to get on a bus to Milwaukee. I was ten. I'm not sure my *mamm* ever truly forgave me."

Her eyes were wide. "I'm not sure I would have forgiven you either. Knowing how terrified I feel right at this moment, I'm sure you gave her the fright of her life."

He reached out and took her hand again, this time for no reason at all. "They're going to be okay, Carolyn."

The corners of her mouth curled weakly, as if she was grateful for his reassurance but didn't really have any faith in it.

They came to the edge of the pasture and dove into the woods, where the tracks were just as easy to follow. They hadn't needed Aaron's dogs after all. Seven children and a sled couldn't hide their movements in the new snow.

A child's cries echoed up through the bare trees. Carolyn squeezed Aaron's hand, then let go of it and raced in the direction of the sound. She didn't have far to go.

Behind a round outcropping of stone, *die kinner* sat in a circle around a good-sized campfire. Aaron couldn't help but be impressed. Building a fire outdoors was hard enough. Building one in the snow was a feat that even most adults couldn't accomplish. No wonder Freddie had been preoccupied with fire lately. An impressive pile of wood sat on a sheet of plastic next to the fire—probably a garbage bag. Aaron pressed his lips together. Abraham and Mary had a pellet stove. The wood was for sure and certain from Aaron's shed. He added stealing to the list of Freddie and Felty's faults and the things Abraham would have to be told about.

Freddie sat cross-legged on the ground on top of another piece of plastic. They'd probably taken the whole box of garbage bags. Rosie sat on Freddie's lap wrapped in at least three blankets, but it was plain to see she was cold. She squirmed and fussed as Freddie tried to keep her from wriggling off his lap. Elmer and Lydia sat on the sled, which they had pulled close to the fire. Even with such a fine fire, they looked miserable. Elmer was crying softly, and big tears trickled down Lydia's face.

Every head turned as they heard Carolyn and Aaron shuffling through the snow. "Carolyn!" Lydia squealed.

She ran toward Carolyn, sending a mist of snow into the air behind her, and threw her arms around Carolyn's legs.

Carolyn lifted Lydia, gave her a swift hug, and handed her to Aaron. She grabbed one of Aaron's blankets and draped it over Lydia's shoulders. "Hush, Liddy Biddy. Onkel Aaron will get you warm."

Carolyn took another blanket from Aaron and snatched Rosie from Freddie's arms as if she was afraid Freddie was about to throw the baby into the snow. Freddie gave up his *schwester* without resistance. He didn't look like he was up for any sort of fight. Carolyn clutched Rosie to her chest and tightened the extra blanket around her. Rosie cried as if her heart would break.

Elmer didn't move from the plastic sled, but he bawled louder and louder until the bears in hibernation would have been able to hear him. In a show of great coordination and strength, Carolyn bent over and scooped Elmer into her arms without so much as bobbling Rosie. She untucked one side of the blanket from Rosie and wrapped Elmer in with his little *schwester*. Carolyn could very possibly lose hearing in both ears with the racket the two little ones were making.

Carolyn nodded to Aaron, calm and business-like. "We need to get them into the house."

"Do you want to put them on the sled?"

She shook her head. "They need my warmth. Put Lyle and Luke on the sled and maybe Freddie and Felty can pull it."

Lydia sobbed into Aaron's neck. "Freddie said it would be fun."

Freddie, who at this point seemed almost frozen in place, turned and eyed Aaron with a look of absolute despair. He obviously knew that he'd done something very serious this time. Maybe his own feet were freezing, maybe he'd burned himself when building the fire. Maybe he had realized that he had put his *bruderen* and *schwesteren* in danger because of his selfishness. He wouldn't even need a lecture or a punishment. He was punishing himself enough already.

That didn't mean he wasn't going to feel the consequences of what he'd done. He needed a sharp, weighty lesson, and if Abraham was too busy to give it to him, Aaron would do it.

"Felty, Luke," Aaron said. "Throw snow on the fire." He purposefully didn't ask Freddie so Freddie would understand that, right now, Aaron didn't trust him.

With red cheeks and downcast eyes, Felty and Luke got up from the ground and started scooping snow onto the fire. It couldn't have been a pleasant job with ice seeping through their yarn mittens. Freddie jumped from his garbage bag and helped while watching Aaron out of the corner of his eye.

Carolyn was already headed toward the house. Lydia stretched out her arm and called after her. "Don't leave me."

Aaron whispered in her ear. "It's okay. We're going home too."

Lyle sat on the sled, and Aaron slid his last blanket over Lyle's shoulders. Lyle pulled it around himself, but he wouldn't be really warm until he was sitting at home in front of the stove.

Freddie and Felty pulled on the rope attached to the sled, and they trudged out of the woods, Aaron leading the way with his trembling arms wrapped tightly around Lydia. It had been a close call, and Abraham was going to do something about it, whether he thought he had time or not.

* * *

Carolyn sat down and wished the overstuffed sofa could swallow her into its depths. She'd never been so weary, both in body and spirit. If she had been the crying sort, she would have surrendered to tears hours ago, but instead she'd worked herself into a terrible headache that pounded a steady rhythm right between her eyes. Aaron was still in the kitchen talking quietly but sternly to the three oldest boys. Carolyn would have liked to give them a bitter scolding, but she was too tired to do anything but eavesdrop. She could give them "what for" tomorrow and the next day and the day after that if she wanted to. And right now, she wanted to. Badly.

Of course, without a doubt, a good night's sleep would soften her up. The boys, especially Freddie, had been *hesslich*, ugly, to her since she'd arrived in Greenwood. She couldn't condone their actions, but she could certainly understand their pain. Mary had been nothing but apologetic for missing the school Christmas program. They'd been late closing up the shop and had gotten stuck in the snow on the way to the school.

The boys hadn't cared about their excuses. All they knew was their parents had missed their school program, the most important night of the year as far as they were concerned. And it had broken their hearts. When their parents hadn't shown up that night, Freddie had hatched the plan to run away. If his parents didn't care about him, he was going to make them sorry when all their children went missing.

The boys weren't talking all that softly, and Carolyn had no problem hearing their side of the conversation in the kitchen.

Freddie knew he'd made a huge mistake when Rosie's three bottom teeth had started chattering with her four top teeth and her lips had turned blue. In a panic, he'd stopped their little caravan and built a fire. He hadn't understood that there were some temperatures that couldn't be conquered by a fire. He had been more than grateful when Carolyn and Aaron had found them.

Carolyn massaged her fingers, feeling the memory of the cold clear to her bones. She had carried Rosie and Elmer to the house as fast as she could go in those snowshoes and had arrived gasping for air, icy dampness ripping at her throat with every breath she took. She had all but run up the stairs and put Rosie and Elmer into a bath with tepid water, but still Rosie had screamed in pain when Carolyn had lowered her into the tub. The pain hadn't lasted long, and soon Rosie and Elmer had been comfortable, their cheeks losing that harsh red burn of cold and their fingers and toes warm to the touch.

Lydia and Lyle had gone into the tub with Rosie and Elmer as soon as Aaron brought them home, and Carolyn had slowly run warmer and warmer water into the tub until she was sure no one would suffer any frostbite.

Aaron had made tuna fish, tomato, and lettuce sandwiches and creamy tomato soup for dinner while *die kinner* warmed up and changed into dry clothes. Mary and Abraham came in the house just long enough to eat, their urgency evident in the way they left the dinner table without even asking if there was dessert. None of *die kinner*, not even Lydia, had said a word to their parents at dinner, and neither Aaron nor Carolyn were ready to tell them that their children had almost frozen to death that very afternoon.

It was strange that something momentous had occurred in the Stutzman household and Mary and Abraham didn't even know about it. It spoke volumes about what was wrong in their home.

The low, steady rumble of Aaron's voice fell silent,

and Carolyn heard the three boys shuffle up the stairs. Aaron came into the living room and plopped next to her on the sofa. "I think I aged a decade today."

"*Jah*. Me too. I don't think I've ever been so panicked."

He studied her face with those perceptive eyes of his. "You stayed calm. You're not a silly girl who throws up her hands and runs around squealing her head off."

She curled one side of her mouth. "I've never seen anyone actually scream her head off."

"You kept your head. I like that in a girl." He cleared his throat and pulled his gaze from her face. "I . . . I brought you a present."

"A present?"

"It's in the box I left on the porch."

Carolyn drew her brows together. "I don't remember a box."

"*Ach, vell*, we both had more important things to think about." Aaron opened the front door and dragged in a large box. Hopefully whatever was in there wasn't frozen solid. It had been out there for four hours.

He set the box at her feet and cut the double layer of packing tape with his pocketknife. The pungent scent of pine attacked her nose as grayish green tendrils of plastic protruded from the box. Carolyn gave Aaron a doubtful smile and scooped the entire tangle out of the box.

"It's your own pine bough." He didn't smile, but Carolyn could tell he was quite proud of his gift.

"My own . . ." Carolyn sneezed as the sharp smell of artificial pine tickled her nose.

"I sprayed it with pine-scented air freshener," Aaron said. "I wanted it to seem as real as possible." He took the tangle of gray greenery from her and spread it out on the floor so she could get a better look. It was about ten feet long with a bright red Christmas bow attached to ei- ther end. "You told me you missed the pine boughs and ribbons your *mamm* always hangs at Christmastime."

"*Ach*," she said, her face warming at the gesture, even though the strand of plastic greenery was quite *hesslich*. "That is very kind of you."

"I didn't want to bring real pine into Abraham and Mary's house. Dried pine needles are a nightmare to clean up. So I went to the Walmart in Marshfield and found a dozen sturdy plastic greenery sprigs. They look like pine if the light's just right. I wired them together, and now you've got a tidy and inflammable pine bough."

Carolyn gave him a wide smile. Tidy and sturdy, smelly and ugly, but it definitely wouldn't catch on fire. "This is wonderful *gute*, Aaron." It was nothing like the lush, fragrant pine boughs Dat always cut for Mamm in the woods, but Aaron had cared enough about her feelings to try to give her a little piece of Christmas in Greenwood.

She didn't mean for it to happen, but there was sud- denly a hitch in her throat and her eyes stung as if she might cry. It truly had been a long day. She shut her mouth so her voice wouldn't crack if she tried to say anything. Aaron wouldn't understand why this little sliver of kind- ness had touched her.

"Do you want me to hang it above the door?"

Carolyn swallowed the lump in her throat. "That would be *wunderbarr*."

Aaron found a step stool in the kitchen. Facing the door, he climbed up and held the bough of gray green- ery over his head. "What should I hang it with?"

"We could hammer two nails on either corner of the door."

He glanced at her as if she'd just suggested they steal all the forks. "We can't put nails in the wall."

"Packing tape?"

Another look of disbelief. "It will pull the paint off when we take it down."

Carolyn kept giving him wilder and wilder suggestions, just to see his expression register deeper and deeper shock each time.

"Carolyn," he finally said, "I don't think you're taking this seriously."

Carolyn laughed. "I am taking it seriously, but I can't resist that look on your face."

He scrunched his lips together. Carolyn liked to think it was an effort to keep from smiling at her. "You're the expert on pine boughs. Don't you have any other suggestions on how to hang it?"

She shrugged. "We put nails above all our doors."

Aaron finally concluded that they couldn't hang Carolyn's plastic Christmas pine bough at all. He stepped down from the stool, draped the greenery over the back of the sofa, and sat down next to Carolyn. "It looks wonderful nice right here."

Until *die kinner* got up in the morning and tore it to pieces, but for now, he was happy. She'd let it go and figure out a better place for it when he left. "It feels more like Christmas already," Carolyn said. She wasn't lying. It did feel more like Christmas. Christmas was about giving and serving and remembering what Jesus's love had done for the world. Aaron's *gute* heart had brought the Christmas spirit on a very bad day.

A shiver of fear traveled up her spine. "*Ach*, Aaron. Imagine what would have happened if you hadn't made me this gift? Can you imagine me trying to get *die kinner* back to the house all by myself? You saved all of us."

He frowned. "I'm glad I had an extra pair of snowshoes, and I'm glad you are more coordinated than my *schwester* Elsie. She usually ends up facedown in the snow when she wears them."

Carolyn couldn't let him make light of it. She laid a hand on his arm and squeezed his wrist. He stiffened. "*Die kinner* might have gotten frostbite. Rosie could have been seriously hurt. Mary and Abraham should be very grateful. You were the children's guardian angel today."

"*Nae*," he said, his gaze glued to her hand on his arm. "You have spent all this time caring for children who have done everything they could to get rid of you, and you haven't budged. I would have given up on them long ago."

She pulled her hand from his wrist and smoothed her apron. "I don't believe it. It's not your job to babysit, but you come over almost every day to help me. You take the three oldest boys to your house to work."

"I should have taken them today, but I had to go to Walmart."

She smiled. "You have a *gute* heart, Aaron. I don't believe that you would ever give up on these children."

He gazed at her as if he couldn't look away and made her feel sort of tingly and dizzy at the same time. "I suppose you're right, but I already told you I'm not as unselfish as all that. I don't come over to check on *die kinner*."

"You don't?"

"I come over to check on you."

He shouldn't look at her that way if he didn't want to give her the wrong impression. "Of course you come over to check on me. You're afraid *die kinner* will tie me up and lock me in the closet."

"I come over because . . . because I feel like smiling when I see you."

It wasn't a declaration of undying love or anything, but the tone of his voice and the look in his eye made her heart go around and around as if someone had taken a whisk to it. "You're not really a smiler."

"But you make me feel like smiling, all the same. Isn't that strange?"

"I like it when you come over," she said, her voice a barely audible wisp of breath.

He slid his arm around her shoulders and knocked the pine bough to the floor behind them. "Can I kiss you?" he said. "To see what it might feel like? On the lips, I mean."

"Okay," she said, loudly enough so he could hear her over the noise of her heartbeat.

He leaned in and gave her a brief and gentle kiss. She barely had time to kiss him back before he pulled away. "That was nice."

Nice, but who wanted *nice* when it came to kissing? Carolyn refused to let that be her only experience. "Can we try that again?"

He raised an eyebrow. "I think I would like a second chance."

This time, he slid his finger under her chin and nudged her face upward. He traced his thumb down the contours of her throat as he brought his lips down on hers and kissed her with an intensity that Carolyn had not thought possible. She slipped her hands around his neck and pulled him closer. This was more than nice. This was peanut butter chocolate drops, s'mores, and German chocolate cake all rolled into one. The wonder of it made her dizzy.

He pulled away, and she could tell he was just as shaken and stunned as she was. "That was better than broccoli. Salted and buttered."

Carolyn laughed. Like as not, it was a compliment. Obviously, tuna fish for dinner hadn't satisfied either of them.

"I can't believe I'm so happy," Aaron said. "I think it was *Gotte* who brought you to Greenwood."

Carolyn grinned. "*Gotte* or your *mammi*."

"My *mammi*?"

"She's the one who asked me to come to work for Abraham and Mary. She said it would be a great adventure." Carolyn rubbed the spot on her arm where Felty had poked her with a pencil earlier today. "I suppose snowshoeing into the woods in search of runaway children is an adventure, but I'd rather do without that kind of excitement in my life."

Aaron's face took on the color of a looming storm. "I didn't know my *mammi* got this job for you."

"I thought she had tricked me into taking a job nobody wanted. But now it wonders me if matching you and me wasn't her goal all along. She's a famous matchmaker, you know." Carolyn could forgive Anna for that. She might not like babysitting very much, but for sure and certain she liked Aaron something wonderful.

Aaron paused for a few seconds, then shot off the sofa as if he had somewhere very important to go. He didn't actually go anywhere. He stood there, still as a post, staring at Carolyn as if she might have a case of chicken pox. "I should have known."

"Is everything okay?"

"I should have known." His expression grew darker. "Ever since I turned twenty, Mammi has tried to match me with one girl after another. I have told her time and time again that I want to make my own choices and run my own life, and yet she persists in sticking her nose into my business."

His sudden change of mood was more than puzzling. "What are you so upset about? Her meddling has worked out well so far."

"That's just it. I don't want my *mammi* meddling in

my life. Mammi is more persistent than a hound dog, and she's clever too. You're the last person in the world I would have suspected to be one of her schemes."

Carolyn was usually willing to give people the benefit of the doubt, but it seemed as if he was purposefully trying to offend her. "The last person?"

"How could Mammi have imagined that I'd be interested in a girl like you? You don't like my nieces and nephews, you leave globs of cookie dough under the table and handprints on my fridge, and you eat sugar like a cockroach. You caught me off guard. I didn't even suspect."

Carolyn narrowed her eyes. "Let me understand correctly. You think Anna sent me out here to trick you into being my boyfriend?"

"Mammi and Dawdi sent you, all right. That's why you've put up with *die kinner* for so long. You were hoping I'd propose."

This wasn't quite what Carolyn had hoped she'd feel like after kissing a boy. She didn't know whether to be deeply hurt or ferociously angry. Neither emotion was all that attractive on her. Her cousin Treva had a fondness for throwing dishes. Her *aendi* Edna sobbed into her *kaffee* at regular intervals. Carolyn liked to think things through before doing something she would regret, and right at this moment, she feared she was inches from embarrassing herself.

For sure and certain, this had been one of the worst days of her life. She wouldn't make it worse, no matter how badly she longed to show Aaron the sharp edge of her disdain.

She stood and headed toward the stairs, as if she couldn't care less that Aaron was standing in the living room. She was too tired to even pretend. "*Gute nacht*, Aaron. Don't forget your snowshoes."

"I don't want a wife," Aaron said, unwilling or unable to grasp that she was finished with the conversation. "They're messy and complicated and bothersome. I'm happy the way I am, with a clean fridge and a shiny wood floor. And if I ever decide to get a wife, she will be of my choosing. Not Mammi's and certainly not yours." He took a deep breath as if to calm himself, picked up the plastic pine bough, and arranged it carefully on the back of the sofa.

Carolyn took a little bit of perverse satisfaction in the fact that his thoughtful gift would be shredded beyond recognition by morning. Freddie would probably try to burn it. She just might give him the matches.

> *Dear Anna,*
> *I love that you are always trying to make your grandchildren happy, but I would advise against sending any more girls to Greenwood. Aaron chews them up and spits them out.*
> *Love,*
> *Carolyn*

Chapter 5

Dear Aaron,
I am not sure what is happening in
Greenwood, but it sounds like you might need a
lesson in table manners. No matter what Carolyn
cooks for dinner, you have to eat it. Spitting out
your food is no way to win a girl's heart.
Love,
Mammi Anna

It was the day before Christmas Eve and Aaron had hardly slept a wink for three nights. The night after he'd kissed Carolyn, his head had barely hit the pillow when his frustration at Mammi and Carolyn and conniving girls in general bubbled up like a pot of gravy on the stove and kept him awake, stewing in his own resentment. The next day, he'd steered clear of Carolyn and *die kinner* at *gmay*, and Carolyn had ignored him completely, which was *gute* because he didn't want her throwing herself at him to get a marriage proposal—not that he had ever noticed Carolyn throwing herself at him before, but she and Mammi were smart like that. For sure and certain, they had made a plan to be sneaky about it so he wouldn't notice.

The second night was little better. All he could think about was Carolyn and her smooth, creamy skin. That was a girl who hadn't ever had a pimple in her life. But because of Carolyn, there was a chip on his smooth white oven door. He'd found a spot of chocolate on his cupboard, six chocolate chips under his fridge, and five cookie crumbs on his rug. And that floor in his mudroom would never be the same. Even though it had only taken seconds to wipe her handprint off his fridge, it would take weeks to get his things and his life back into perfect order. Carolyn was not much of a cleaner, and she was going to give herself diabetes with all the Twinkies she ate. What man needed that in his life?

On the third night, for the first time in his life, he had gone to bed feeling lonely. Why would he feel lonely? Carolyn had eyes that he couldn't look away from and lips that tasted like chocolate chip cookies, but he'd never been a fool for a pretty face. He'd avoided her ever since he'd kissed her, and he never would have imagined the hole in his heart in the space she used to fill. Abraham and Mary's three oldest boys came to his house for chores every day, but Aaron had avoided going to their house so he wouldn't have to see Carolyn. Was it because he was on his guard, or because he felt guilty for the way he'd treated her?

At about two o'clock this morning, Aaron had finally considered the very real possibility that he had been wrong. Wrong about Mammi, wrong about himself, and totally wrong about Carolyn. The thought of being wrong gave him a stomachache, so he took some Pepto-Bismol and did his best to put Carolyn out of his mind. He hadn't been very successful.

Freddie, Felty, and Luke had been doing chores—hard, exhausting chores for him for three days as punishment for running away. They had been behaving themselves, like as not because they all realized they had gone too far. But the improvement didn't mean Aaron wasn't going to talk to Abraham. *Die kinner* were lost, as sure as if they had run away, and Abraham needed to know about it.

Aaron had put off talking to Abraham because he didn't want to accidentally run into Carolyn, but he knew he couldn't avoid it any longer. Something had to be done, and Aaron was the one to do it.

Abraham and Mary's bakery stood right next to the house. Abraham had built it two years ago with grand plans for a cookie business. It was literally five steps from the kitchen door of the main house. The four long tables were stacked three feet high with white cardboard boxes and plastic trays. It was two days before Christmas. Mary and Abraham were trying to get the last of the orders out today so they could be shipped overnight and arrive in time for Christmas morning.

The smell of chocolate and peanut butter and caramel filled the air, and Aaron took shallow breaths. Could you gain weight just by breathing in an aroma?

Abraham and Mary were standing at one of the tables, packing a new batch of cookies into their plastic containers. Dark circles curved under Mary's eyes, and her face held none of its youthful fullness. Abraham looked worse. He was tall, like Aaron, but stooped like a tired old man. He had lost weight, and his pallid complexion told Aaron that Abraham wasn't eating enough vegetables.

Even so, Abraham glanced up and gave Aaron a smile as he came in. Maybe he hadn't completely lost the Christmas spirit. Aaron didn't smile back, mostly because he wasn't prone to smiling, but also because he had something very serious to discuss. "Abraham, Mary, I need to talk to you."

Abraham picked up another cookie from the sheet. "We have to get this order out by three o'clock. Can it wait?"

Aaron squared his shoulders. "I've waited too long already."

Both Abraham and Mary stopped what they were doing and eyed him doubtfully. "What is the matter?" Mary said, knitting her brow and peeling off her gloves.

Aaron slid three stools to the center of the room. "*Cum*, sit."

Abraham packed five more cookies, as if a slight bit annoyed at the interruption, then shuffled to the stool and sat next to his wife. "What is this about?"

Aaron folded his arms across his chest. "It's about Carolyn." Well, it wasn't exactly about Carolyn, but she was as *gute* a place as any to start. It didn't help that his pulse surged through his veins when he thought of her. He needed to stay focused on the problem at hand.

Mary frowned. "What about Carolyn?"

"I told you she wasn't working out," Abraham said. "She can't keep control of *die kinner*."

"There was no one else, Abraham. Few girls are willing to tend seven children for what we can pay. And I think she has done a fine job. *Die kinner* are clean and well-fed."

Well-fed if you thought Twinkies were part of a balanced diet.

Aaron sighed. "They are fed well enough, and I don't really want to talk about Carolyn."

Abraham's brows inched closer together. "Then why did you say you did?"

Ach, why did Abraham have to ask such questions?

Maybe Aaron would rather not mention that Carolyn filled his thoughts so completely that there wasn't much room for anything else. "Carolyn has done her best to care for *die kinner*, but they have tried everything to get rid of her."

Concern and sadness overtook Mary's expression. "Don't they like her?"

"*Die kinner* don't like having a babysitter." Aaron didn't want to hurt Mary's feelings, but she needed to know what was going on with her own children. "They want their *mater*, Mary. They need their *mater*, and you ignore them, just like Abraham does."

Mary lowered her eyes. "I see."

Abraham grunted. "Nothing to feel bad about, Mary. Business has been *gute*. We've been busy. We might not be at home as often as we would like, but that doesn't mean we ignore them. I'm surprised at you, Aaron. You're not one to exaggerate."

"Lydia lost a tooth last week," Aaron said. "Did you see the gap? Lyle had a goose egg on his forehead for three days. Did you notice? Or what about the time Freddie tried to set the house on fire?"

Mary pursed her lips. "When did that happen?"

"You missed their school program."

"I told you, Aaron, we got stuck in the snow. *Die kinner* understood," Mary said, the uncertainty evident in her voice.

Aaron leaned forward. "*Die kinner* understood that their parents didn't care enough to come to the program. The next day, Freddie and Felty took *die kinner* and ran away. They loaded Elmer and Rosie onto the sled and hiked into the woods."

The lines deepened around Abraham's eyes. "Why didn't Carolyn stop them?"

"She had to go to the bathroom. Freddie had it well

planned. They were out of the house and away in less than five minutes."

Mary clapped her hand over her mouth. "*Ach, du lieva.*"

"Carolyn and I found them, shivering and cold, trying to keep warm by a small fire. It could have turned out very badly for them."

"Carolyn knows better than to leave them alone," Abraham said.

Aaron shook his head. "Their bad behavior is not Carolyn's fault. Felty throws food at her, Luke spills his milk on purpose, and Freddie puts spiders in her bed."

"You make them sound like monsters," Abraham said, his voice rising with his agitation. "My children would not do such things if the babysitter knew how to exercise discipline."

"They've done worse, but not because Carolyn can't control them. They've been trying to get your attention, and Carolyn has taken the brunt of their abuse."

Mary lowered her head and looked at her hands. "Carolyn has been nothing but kind, Abraham. It's plain to see *die kinner* have been struggling. I can't take the time to help them, so I've turned my face from them and ignored it." She took a deep, shuddering breath. "I'm ashamed of myself."

"We haven't done anything wrong, Mary. Carolyn has let *die kinner* run wild."

That's what Aaron used to think, until he had actually gotten to know her. "You're wrong, Abraham. Carolyn does her best for *die kinner*, but she cannot be their *mamm* or their *dat*. They ran away because they think you don't love them anymore, and you've done nothing to show them that you do. It wouldn't matter who you hired to babysit. *Die kinner* want their parents."

Abraham still wasn't convinced. "Don't they know

that we work hard at the cookie business to put food on the table and shoes on their feet?"

"*Nae*, Abraham," Mary said. "We've made plenty more than what we need this year."

"Well, then, when the Christmas orders are filled, we will be able to spend more time with *die kinner*. After our shipment goes out today, that's all until New Year's."

Mary placed a hand on Abraham's arm. "Then it is only six weeks to Valentine's. We will always be making more cookies."

"My children are not wicked," Abraham said.

Mary shook her head. "They need us, Abraham."

Abraham wasn't convinced. "You have no *kinner* of your own, Aaron. I don't expect you to understand. *Die kinner* are not getting the firm hand they need. That is all."

"They need *your* firm hand and your love."

"They will always have my love. They should know that."

Aaron couldn't be cross with his *bruder*. It was easier to blame Carolyn for Abraham's own failings, and Aaron had made the same mistake a few weeks ago. A lump settled in his throat when he thought about the way he'd treated her.

Abraham might be stubborn, but Aaron had been blinded by his own pride. For sure and certain, Carolyn was the best and brightest thing that had ever come into his life—better than his new thresher, better than his microfiber cleaning cloth, better than the cow he'd bought at auction two years ago. He might as well face the truth. When a new pair of boots was the biggest thrill he'd had all year, his life was decidedly boring.

Aaron had been content with his comfortable, predictable world, but now he realized he hadn't known any better. What was a clean floor to a night of cookie baking with Carolyn? What was a strict weekly schedule compared to a toe-curling kiss?

Carolyn had brought more excitement to his life in the last month than he'd had in the last nine years combined. Maybe a little bit of chaos in his life was better than a whole lot of loneliness.

What did it matter if she was one of Mammi's schemes? What did it matter if she liked chocolate chip cookies and hated broccoli? She filled his life with wonder. He loved her, and he wanted to spend the rest of his life with her.

That was what really mattered.

Aaron wanted to run into the house and shout his love at the top of his lungs. What would Carolyn think of that? Maybe he should wait until *die kinner* were in bed. He should bring her another gift too, because he'd said some *dumm* things and she might not be so willing to forgive him yet another time.

Abraham and Mary had already put their stools back against the wall. Aaron sat in the middle of the room all by himself, thinking that Carolyn might not be so eager to kiss him again.

"*Cum*, Aaron," Abraham said. "Help us finish the rest of these orders."

Mary was already putting plastic cookie containers in boxes. "Unless you have somewhere you need to be."

Abraham laughed. "Aaron doesn't have anywhere to go. He's a bachelor. He has nothing better to do."

Aaron couldn't argue with that. He couldn't very well tell Abraham and Mary that he needed to go into the house and check to see if Carolyn would even talk to him. He put on some gloves and started packing boxes.

He spent the rest of the afternoon getting orders ready, then helping Abraham and Mary clean up the shop for the Christmas break. As much as he wanted to talk to

Carolyn, he wanted to do it right, with some sort of gift in hand so she knew he was sorry for being . . . wrong. And he wanted to be able to say the word "wrong" out loud when he spoke to her. She'd doubt his sincerity if he choked on his own apology.

Aaron stumbled home well after ten, determined to declare his undying love to Carolyn first thing in the morning.

Not even a glass of warm milk and an hour of Bible study could put him to sleep.

Chapter 6

Dear Cousins,

Frehlicher Grischtdaag!

My Christmas cake is in the oven so I have a few minutes to send you my Christmas wishes, even though this letter won't reach you until after the holiday.

I have bad news and good news. The bad news is that I have been dismissed from my babysitting job in Greenwood. That is also the good news. I no longer have to fear pinecones or smoke inhalation. Abraham Stutzman fired me this morning and there was a car waiting to return me to Bonduel before I put breakfast on the table. I don't regret missing breakfast even though I made my special buttermilk pancakes.

I don't want you to feel bad for me. My pride is wounded, but I get to spend Christmas at home with the family. There is no one, absolutely no one, I regret leaving in Greenwood. I hope he's happy in his dull life.

Please write soon. I'm curious to know how

*everyone spent their holiday. Marybeth, I do
hope you and Ingrid had a wonderful gute time
together. I can only hope that Ingrid did not
make a batch of her fruitcake.*

> *Blessings,*
> *Carolyn*

Carolyn was not one to wallow in self-pity, but for sure
and certain, the temptation was great. Who ever heard
of firing someone on Christmas Eve? At least Abraham
Stutzman had the foresight to have a car waiting for her.
As soon as he had fired her, she had run upstairs, packed
her things, and slipped out the front door before *die kinner* had a chance to say goodbye—not that they would
have wanted to say goodbye, but Carolyn hoped that
maybe some of them would miss her a little.

It really couldn't have worked out any better, even if
she felt like crying every time she looked at the basket
of pinecones on Mamm's table. Carolyn was home for
Christmas, she could go to the bathroom whenever she
wanted, and she would never see Aaron Stutzman again.

It was a happy day.

But it smarted just a little that she had been fired because of Aaron. He'd told Abraham all the bad things
that had happened and then blamed Carolyn for them.
Abraham had pulled out a list of all of Carolyn's failings
this morning, telling her that Aaron had said she was a
terrible babysitter and that Abraham needed to get rid of
her.

Vell. If that didn't take the cake.

Aaron had blamed her all along.

She used to like Aaron. She even thought she maybe
loved him four days ago, but it seemed that nobody in
Greenwood cared for her at all. Aaron thought she was
one of Anna Helmuth's tricks, another desperate girl

who wanted a husband, the last person in the world he would ever dream of marrying. And he also thought she was a bad babysitter.

She didn't care about the bad babysitter part. If the Stutzmans refused to see what was really happening with their family, then Carolyn refused to care more than they did. But all those other things Aaron had said stung like a mud wasp. He had the nerve to kiss her and then accused her of trying to trick him.

At least she was home with people who loved her. With Christmas tomorrow and family gatherings and then New Year's and Groundhog Day, as well as being a bridesmaid at her cousin Marybeth's wedding in February, she'd forget about Aaron Stutzman soon enough. She'd forget how thoughtful he had been and how much he cared for his nieces and nephews. She'd forget about the time he washed off her ceiling or helped her rescue *die kinner* in the woods. She'd even forget about that kiss, because Aaron had obviously not been thinking clearly when he'd done it.

The timer rang like a fire alarm, and Carolyn turned it off before it vibrated off the counter. Mamm and Clara were in the candy shop, making last-minute candy for the Amish and *Englisch* who frequented their shop. There had been a line of cars and buggies all morning. Like Mary and Abraham's cookies, chocolates made *gute* Christmas gifts.

Carolyn had agreed to make the cake while Mamm and Clara worked the shop. She'd also thrown together a batch of chocolate chip cookies, just because Aaron Stutzman was so opposed to them. It was like sticking her tongue out at him from a hundred miles away— though Carolyn was too mature to stick out her tongue at anybody. She took the cake out and slid a sheet of cookies into the oven. She was nothing if not efficient.

Someone knocked on the kitchen door, which customers sometimes did when they weren't sure how to get into the candy shop. Carolyn took the oven mitts from her hands, but before she could get to the door, Aaron opened it and marched into the kitchen as if he was on some sort of mission.

"Aaron," Carolyn said, more than a little *ferhoodled* that Aaron was standing in her kitchen looking so handsome and yet so stiff, as if his neck would crack if he turned his head too far to the side. With nothing to say to him, she closed her mouth. All the sharp speeches she had imagined giving him flew out of her head, partly because he really was very good looking, but mostly because his appearance was so unexpected, she wasn't prepared to upbraid him. She hadn't thought she'd ever see him again to deliver the very impressive lecture she'd been composing in her head.

He neglected to shut the door, and he glanced behind him as if fearing what was outside. He lifted a hand toward her. "I asked them not to come. *Begged* them not to come. I only stopped by their house because I needed directions to your house. Before they get here, I want to tell you . . ."

Anna and Felty Helmuth shuffled into the house bundled like two *buplies*. Felty had the *gute* sense to shut the door before all the warm air fled the kitchen. Under his straw hat, Felty wore a lime-green scarf tied over his ears and a Christmas red scarf tucked around his neck. Anna had a pink scarf draped over her black bonnet and a darker pink shawl wrapped around her shoulders over her coat. No doubt, Anna had knitted all the scarves and shawls the pair was wearing. Her knitting skills were legendary.

"Carolyn!" Anna squealed, pulling off layer after layer of knitted outerwear. "What a thrill it is to see you fresh from your adventure in Greenwood." She laid her scarf on the counter dusted with flour and leaned toward Carolyn as if sharing a secret. "I'm sure it was everything we hoped it would be."

Aaron cleared his throat. "Mammi, I need to talk to Carolyn alone. I love you very much, but please would you go to the candy shop and wait for me there?"

"Stuff and nonsense. Carolyn used to be in my knitting club. We're very close. Anything you can say to her, you can say to us."

Aaron's shoulders sagged for a second, but he wasn't one to be discouraged when he wanted something. He eyed Carolyn with determination and pasted a serious look on his face. What he didn't know was that Carolyn wasn't one to be deterred either. Anna and Felty's arrival had given her enough time to gather her wits, and she wasn't about to squander the opportunity to give Aaron a piece of her mind.

Aaron turned so that his back was to his grandparents. "Abraham fired you."

Carolyn pursed her lips and arched an eyebrow in his direction. "You didn't have to come all this way to tell me that. I already know."

"Oh, dear," Anna said. "What happened? Abraham can be wonderful cheap. Don't tell me he decided he didn't want to pay you."

Carolyn pointed at Aaron. "Aaron got me fired."

Anna's mouth fell open. "Aaron, that's a terrible thing to do. I sent you pot holders. Doesn't that mean anything to you?"

Aaron all but growled, in frustration or irritation Carolyn couldn't tell. "I didn't get Carolyn fired."

"Oh, really?" Carolyn said, letting the sarcasm drip from her mouth. "It wasn't you who told Abraham everything *die kinner* had done? It wasn't you who told him I am a terrible babysitter?"

"Of course not. I mean, I told him what *die kinner* did, but I never . . ."

Anna propped her hand on her hip. "What in the world were you thinking, Aaron? There's no one more patient with children than Carolyn. She's not afraid to play Kick the Can and Annie I Over, and she can change a diaper with a single baby wipe. It's a gift."

"I didn't . . ."

Carolyn wasn't about to let Aaron get a word in edgewise, not until she'd said everything she wanted to say. "And another thing. Anna asked me if I wanted to go to Greenwood to tend Abraham and Mary's kids. She did not mention that Abraham had a *bruder* or that she wanted to match us. I stayed because I wanted to help Mary, not because I was hoping you'd propose." Aaron opened his mouth to say something, and she shushed him. "I have never been desperate for a husband, and now that I've met you, I realize I don't want a husband. I don't need the headache."

Anna sighed as if she was barely putting up with both of them. "Of course you want a husband. That's why I sent you to Greenwood. I knew you and Aaron would be perfect for each other. Don't worry about headaches. Walmart sells a big bottle of generic ibuprofen. It's cheap, and it works, doesn't it, Felty?"

"Works wonders."

Carolyn shook a dishtowel in Aaron's direction. "I might be the last person in the world you'd consider as a suitable girlfriend, but I don't care what you think. I might not be up to your standards, but I like myself just the way I am."

"I love Twinkies," Felty said. "And broccoli."

"I don't know why you're mad that your *mammi* tricked you," Carolyn said. "You didn't fall for her trick, so what does it matter now? No one will ever make a fool of you."

Some of Carolyn's indignation seemed to rub off on Anna. "I'm not sorry I tricked you, Aaron. I don't mean to hurt your feelings, but bachelors are a nuisance. They're persnickety and fussy and set in their ways, and if you can't see that Carolyn would be the greatest blessing of your life, then you deserve to sit in that house and grow mold on your shoes."

Yes, he did. Carolyn couldn't have said it better herself. *Good for you, Anna.* "You can go back to Greenwood now, Aaron. I've said all I want to say."

Aaron frowned in frustration. Or exasperation. Or maybe it was dejection. Carolyn couldn't tell. "But I haven't said what I want to say."

Carolyn furrowed her brow. She'd been so eager to say what she had to say that she hadn't even stopped to consider that Aaron probably hadn't come all this way to tell her that Abraham had fired her. She already knew that.

Anna's lips curled into an expectant smile. "What do you want to say, Aaron?"

Aaron stiffened his spine and folded his arms as if he were going to deliver a sermon. "Carolyn, I want you to know that I pride myself on remaining calm and levelheaded." He paused, scrubbed his hand down the side of his face, and growled. "Oh, forget it."

He tromped around the butcher block island like a bear chasing a hiker, grabbed Carolyn's hands, and pulled her toward him. Without warning of any kind, he tugged her into his arms and devoured her lips like a hungry man attacks a Twinkie, or in his case, a starving man with a plate of broccoli. She couldn't begin to want to resist, not after all the trouble he'd gone to getting all the way around the island. She threw her arms around his neck and kissed him back. It was the most glorious feeling in all the world.

Behind her, Anna squeaked in delight. Felty was silent, so Carolyn had no idea of his opinion on the subject.

He pulled away and whispered in her ear. A shiver traveled up her spine. "When I found out you'd been fired, I had a very long, very loud talk with Abraham. I finally convinced him none of this was your fault and he was foolish to fire you. He feels wonderful bad for all the things he said, and he and Mary want you to come back."

"To be perfectly honest," Carolyn whispered, "I'd rather not go back."

He squeezed her tighter. "Would you come back for Christmas next year as my wife?"

Carolyn's heart was trying to pound its way out of her chest. She'd never known such happiness. "I want live pine boughs and candles all over the house."

"Anything."

"And a box of Twinkies every week."

He cringed and dusted his thumb across her cheek, no doubt to remove a spot of flour. "I adore Twinkies. And diabetes." He brushed his lips across hers. "And you."

She thought she might burst. "It could get messy."

He gave her one of his rare smiles. "I wouldn't have it any other way. I love you with all my heart, Carolyn. I need you desperately. My life is too tidy without you."

She tugged him closer to her heart. "Merry Christmas, Aaron."

"Merry Christmas, my dearest Carolyn. Could I have a cookie?"

P.S. Dear cousins, Mary was upset with Abraham for firing me. He wants me to come back, but I'm not going to fall for that one again. Abraham is going to hire two of his sisters-in-law to help in the shop, and Mary is going to be with the children. Aaron didn't tell Abraham I am a bad babysitter, which is a gute thing since I let him kiss me before I found out. I hope you all have a lovely Christmas. I hear Christmas in Greenwood is wonderful nice. You're all invited next year. Bring Ingrid. Aaron would really enjoy one of her special fruitcakes.

Amish Circle Letters: What are they?

As I was growing up and my siblings and I were moving apart, our mother became the Keeper of the News. We all called Mom, but my brothers and I were poor about calling or writing to each other. Mom simply passed on all the news when we called her, or she called us. So how do Amish siblings keep in touch without telephones? The answer is a unique sort of communication called a circle letter.

Circle letters consist of a group of people with similar interests or connections, such as siblings, cousins, people who were friends at school, or family members operating the same kinds of business. I'll use my family as an example to show you how they work. There are five of us.

My oldest brother Greg sends a letter to me telling about his new grandchild.

I read Greg's letter, then write about the news in my family: I wrecked the car. I send both letters to our brother Bob.

Bob learns Greg has a new grandchild and I need a new car. He adds a letter of his own about his new horse and sends the packet of letters on to Mark.

Mark learns Greg is a grandpa again, I wrecked my car, and Bob has a new horse. Mark writes his fly fishing business is booming and sends all the letters to sibling number five, Gary.

Gary reads the same news that everyone else got. Greg is a grandpa again, I need a new car, Bob has a new horse and Mark's fly fishing business is booming. Gary writes to say someone dumped a puppy at his farm. Does anyone want a free dog? He sends the packet of letters to Greg.

Greg then takes out his old letter and writes a new one, sends the packet to me and the cycle continues. Every person in the circle replaces their old letter with a new one when the packet comes back to them. Everyone gets exactly the same news in the same order.

Cool idea, right? You don't have to be Amish to enjoy the circle letter experience. All that's required is a group of people who want to participate and who enjoy writing letters or sending cards rather than shooting off an e-mail or a text.

To begin, write everyone's names and addresses on a piece of paper and indicate who they should send the packet to next when it arrives. Be sure to include your name and address at the end. Write your note in a letter or card and send it off to participant number two. Sending funny or inspirational cards is another way to enjoy a circle letter experience. What's more fun than shopping for a funny card to share with an entire group of friends? Getting a packet of funny cards in the mail time and time again.

The internet has made communication instantaneous, but many of us enjoy finding a good old-fashioned letter or card in our mailbox. If you are one of those people, maybe starting a circle is right for you.

Look for new Amish romance from Sarah Price and
Jennifer Beckstrand!

AN AMISH COOKIE CLUB CHRISTMAS

Sarah Price

Baking cookies every other Friday for their respective church districts gives Edna Esh and three of her closest friends a chance to give to the Plain community and strengthen their bond with each other. Now, with the blessings of Christmas in the air, they may even whip up a recipe for love . . .

With the holidays around the corner, Edna is busier
than ever juggling baking with her business serving
meals to Englische tourists. Thank goodness for
Mary Ropp's help—until she breaks her leg. Mary's
daughter, Bethany, is available to fill in, but Edna isn't
so certain. She knows Bethany is so painfully shy that
she's never even courted, never mind interacting with
Englische tourists! But the remedy may be closer than
they think . . .

When Bethany gets into a scrape with her bicycle, a
personable, talkative young man comes to her rescue,
and even accompanies her home. And he's none other
than John Esh—Edna's oldest son. When he stops by
again the next day, Mary gets an idea. Soon, with the
encouragement of the Cookie Club, Bethany is indeed
helping Edna, and spending more time around the Esh
household—and John. As Bethany slowly comes out of
her shell, it seems she and John have much in
common—maybe enough to inspire a winter
wedding—and the club's sweetest creation yet . . .

Includes Cookie Recipes!

ABRAHAM

Jennifer Beckstrand

Known as "The Peanut Butter Brothers" for their Wisconsin family business, hardworking Andrew, Abraham, and Austin Petersheim have their plates too full for romance—until their little siblings decide to play matchmaker . . .

With their house full to bursting since *Mammi* and *Dawdi* moved back in, the Petersheim twins know the only way to get their bedroom back is to get their older brothers married off. But Abraham is so shy, he'll barely speak to girls. Still, they've noticed how he looks at Emma Wengerd at church. Emma is so talkative, Abraham's quiet ways wouldn't matter a bit. Soon, the boys have hatched a scheme that sends Abraham right to Emma's door—and her chicken coop . . .

Abraham doubts that pretty, popular Emma would be interested in him. Yet when he finds himself by her side, having to straighten out the twins' mischief—more than once—he can't help imagining a future with her. And the more time they spend together, the more Abraham realizes that perhaps no matter how many boys buzz around Emma, with faith, it's only the right one that counts . . .

Connect with

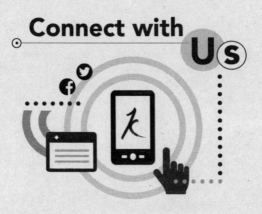

Visit us online at
KensingtonBooks.com
to read more from your favorite authors, see books
by series, view reading group guides, and more.

Join us on social media

for sneak peeks, chances to win books and prize packs,
and to share your thoughts with other readers.

facebook.com/kensingtonpublishing
twitter.com/kensingtonbooks

Tell us what you think!

To share your thoughts, submit a review,
or sign up for our eNewsletters, please visit:
KensingtonBooks.com/TellUs.